Georgie Long was born in London in 1961. After moving around a lot during her childhood, she has been settled in North Wales for the last 35 years. She has a lifelong love of nature and animals and spent over 20 years working as a zookeeper. Georgie has been writing poetry for most of her life and has had many poems published in various anthologies.

Georgie Long

COOPER'S LAW

AUSTIN MACAULEY PUBLISHERS™

LONDON * CAMBRIDGE * NEW YORK * SHARJAH

A CIP catalogue record for this title is available from the British Library.

ISBN 9781398462311 (Paperback)
ISBN 9781398462328 (ePub e-book)

www.austinmacauley.com

First Published 2023
Austin Macauley Publishers Ltd®
1 Canada Square
Canary Wharf
London
E14 5AA

Introduction

The crematorium chapel was full, she had a lot of friends and colleagues who wanted to say goodbye. On the front row, a father and his teenage son sat staring at the coffin, the man with tears streaming down his face, the boy unblinking and biting his lip so hard, that a small trickle of blood ran down his chin. Then, with her favourite song playing quietly in the background, the curtains started to close across the coffin.

As soon as they were shut and the song had finished, the boy turned to his father. 'Why did she have to be burnt?' He demanded, before getting up and running from the chapel. His father watched him go, then looked at the mass of faces and wondered what they must be thinking. He suddenly felt a hand on his arm, and looked round to see her best friend. 'He'll be alright,' she said through her own tears.

He closed the front door on the world a few hours later, and sat in the hall wondering how he was going to manage. He shut his eyes and saw her smiling at him, she was everywhere; her laughter filled the silence. He opened them again and looked around almost in despair, then made his way up to his son's room.

After hesitating for a second, he took a deep breath and knocked gently on the door. 'Come on son, you can't stay in there forever,' he called, there was no reply. He tried the door, it was locked. He knocked again a fraction harder.

'Go away,' a choked voice ordered.

'Come on, let's talk,' he begged, his own voice shaking with emotion.

'I don't want to talk to you, leave me alone,' his son demanded.

The unthinkable suddenly crossed his mind. 'What are you doing in there?' He called, trying to keep the panic from his voice, but his son stayed silent. 'Open this door,' he ordered, but there was still no reply.

He stood on the landing debating with himself as to whether or not his son was distraught enough to do something stupid, then without really thinking, he put his foot against the door, a couple of hefty kicks later, the wood splintered and the door flew open. His son was standing in the middle of the room with his fists clenched and a look of grief etched on his face. 'What the hell did you do that for? This is my room and I don't want you in here,' he yelled.

He tried to run to the door, but his father grabbed him and pulled him into a hug. 'Talk to me,' he said as he desperately held on to the wriggling boy. His son looked up at him and scowled, then bit his lip and looked away as tears filled his eyes. 'It's alright to cry, it shows that you care,' his father told him gently.

'You cry enough for both of us,' he said bitterly, and then weary with grief, he gave up the struggle. 'Why did you burn her?' He asked again with his lip trembling. 'There's no grave to visit, there's nothing left to remember her by.'

His father loosened the grip on his arm. 'Your mum wanted to be cremated, she didn't want us to be slaves to the grave, because we'll have our memories, and you can carry memories anywhere,' he explained.

The distraught boy gave him a disbelieving look, then suddenly relaxed; he put his arms around his father and finally gave in to the tears. Then they sat down on the bed, and father and son cried together.

Case One
The Girl with Red Hair

Chapter 1
Seventeen Years Later

Steven swore as the car slipped on the wet uneven surface. He changed gear noisily, and told himself that his next big purchase would be a car that was more suited to the unpredictable country roads, although the narrow track that he was crawling up could hardly be called a road, more like a sheep track. However, since moving back to the area after an absence of nearly thirteen years, work had kept him so busy that he'd barely time to unpack and settle in, let alone go shopping for cars.

He swore again as he swerved to avoid another pothole. A few minutes later, the robotic voice of the satellite navigation system announced that he had reached his destination; the destination being the disused quarry on the edge of Burney, a small town thirty minutes' drive from his house.

The track suddenly ended. Steven skidded to a halt in a small car park, where two police cars, the mountain rescue jeep and a shogun, were parked alongside the quickly recognisable mortuary van. He got out of the car, acknowledged the nod from the two attendants who were waiting in the van, and then looked around the bleak landscape.

There was a mist hanging over the cliffs, which had he been there under different circumstances would have looked slightly romantic, but he wasn't there under different circumstances, and even if he had been, then romance was the furthest thing from his mind.

He shivered as the cold and damp seeped into every joint. He zipped his coat up and shivered again, then glanced at his watch, it was nearly ten past eight in the morning, but only just light. 'I must be bloody mad,' he muttered.

'It's not always like this; the sun does shine sometimes,' a voice behind him declared. Steven turned around to find a thin faced wiry looking man standing behind him. He was huddled into a duffle coat and spoke with a broad London accent, he put his hand out.

'Ds Jack Taylor, and with a face like that you've got to be Steven,' he said amusedly. Steven chuckled as they shook hands, and nodded towards the shogun.

'Dad's here already then?' He commented.

'Waiting up top,' Jack confirmed. 'Do you cycle?' He asked as he noticed the mountain bike attached to the back of Steven's car. Steven glanced over and nodded. He'd taken up cycling when he was nineteen, after being advised by one of his tutors to "get a hobby and channel the energy away from your foul temper before you get into real trouble".

This being after an incident in college, which had left himself and his then best friend in hospital. He had taken the tutor's advice albeit reluctantly, and quickly discovered that a good couple of hours out riding gave him time to think and work off any anger he was harbouring, as an added bonus it made him calmer, more relaxed, and able to cope better with pressure. 'As often as possible,' he told Jack wryly as he retrieved his case from the back seat of the car.

As a pathologist, Steven's work consisted mainly of accidents or deaths within the hospital, but he was also the police's first port of call if there was a suspicious death, and this being the first incident he had been called to that involved not only the police but also his father, he was feeling slightly apprehensive. He gave a smile of resignation. 'Shall we go then?' He suggested.

Jack led the way, and the two men set off through the mist. 'Who found the body?' Steven enquired as they walked.

Jack looked back. 'A dog walker about ninety minutes ago, the local constable got here first, he called the mountain rescue unit and they called us.' Steven looked around and wondered what he was going to find. 'We're nearly there, it's just beyond that group of rocks; she's on a ledge about fifteen feet down,' Jack called over his shoulder.

They rounded the rocks a minute later, and Steven saw his father's familiar figure. He was standing with another policeman, and even though he was hunched into his donkey jacket with his hands pushed deep into the pockets, at six-feet-one tall, he seemed to tower over the other men. At five-feet-eleven, Steven was slightly shorter than his father, and like his late mother of a stockier build.

His mop of straight sandy coloured hair was a contrast to his father's tight curls, which now turning grey, had been brown in colour. But as Jack Taylor had just observed, one look into their faces confirmed that they have to be father and son, both sharing the same deep set blue grey eyes, slightly upturned nose and mouth, and each with a small dimple in one cheek, which is only obvious when they smile, although interestingly, they are on opposite sides.

The group turned as the two men approached, his father's face was grim. 'Morning, son,' he said quietly. He pointed to the edge of the cliff. 'She's down there, there's a dog too. It looks like she may have gone over after it, maybe to rescue it, or maybe she threw it over first and then threw herself over.'

Steven peered over the edge of the cliff, through the mist, he could see the woman lying on a ledge, a member of the rescue team was standing next to her. A little further down, he could just make out the body of a large black dog. A group of men from the mountain rescue team were waiting with ropes and a stretcher. 'Do you want us to bring her up?' one of the men asked.

Steven looked over the edge again and shook his head. 'I think I'd better look her in situ.' He took a protective suit out of the case and let them harness him up, and a few minutes later, he was clambering down the cliff to the ledge. The man waiting there introduced himself as Mack, and unharnessed him.

Steven crouched down and looked at the body. It was as he already knew, a woman. At first glance, he saw that she was wearing good walking boots, jeans and a waterproof coat, but oddly only one glove, the bitter cold leaving her slender fingers a deep purple colour. 'She's wearing the right clothes for the time of year, so it looks like she was a regular walker,' he commented,

then noticed the bitten nails on her bare hand, and wondered if she had bitten them out of nervousness, or like him, out of habit, but quickly told himself that it didn't really matter because she wouldn't be biting them again.

The woman was lying face down; there was a large wound on the top of her head leaving her blond hair matted with blood. Steven looked around, and was puzzled to see a distinct lack of blood in the immediate area. He gently turned her head so that she was facing him, and was surprised to find that although icy cold and damp to the touch, it moved easily.

He looked up and could see his father peering down at him. 'She can't have been here for long there's no rigour,' he called, then returned his attention to the woman.

Her eyes were closed; there was a blue tinge around her lips making them stand out against her grey pallor. Her heart shaped face was cut and bruised, but beneath the wounds, he could see that she was only young, mid-twenties he guessed, and with a button nose and full lips she had been a good-looking woman. 'Christ! What a waste,' he muttered. 'What happened to you then?' He asked quietly.

He continued to stare at her for a good minute or two, was he imagining things, or did her eyelid twitch? The mist was getting heavier. He pushed his soaked hair off his face, then blinked to refocus and stared harder. 'What is it?' Mack asked apprehensively.

'I'm not sure,' Steven muttered, he put his fingers against her neck, pushed hard into the carotid artery, then closed his own eyes and held his breath. 'Jesus! She's alive,' he whispered, as a few seconds later, he felt the fluttering of a pulse. 'Get the air ambulance here and send some oxygen down,' he yelled.

He felt down the woman's neck and back but found no sign of any breaks, so he carefully turned her over and put his ear next to her face, he could just make out her shallow breathing. 'You hang in there,' he said under his breath as he continued to examine her.

One of her legs was broken, the unnatural angle obvious through her jeans. He unzipped her coat and ran his hands gently over her body checking for other broken bones, after checking her chest he guessed at several broken ribs, but was relieved find normal movement when he rocked her pelvis. The wound on her head puzzled him though, he could see that it was deep, but the angle was such, that falling down the cliff could not have caused it.

Her clothes seemed undisturbed so it probably wasn't a sexual assault, he thought thankfully. When he had finished examining her, he checked her pockets and found house keys, a small torch, tissues and the missing glove. 'Choppers on the way, Steven,' his father shouted over the edge. Steven put his hand up to acknowledge him without looking up.

The rescue team sent the stretcher down along with survival blankets and an oxygen cylinder. 'Christ! I just stood there,' a shocked looking Mack said as they gently manoeuvred her onto the stretcher.

'Don't worry, her pulse is so weak it was easy to miss,' Steven assured him. He slipped the oxygen mask over her face, covered her with the thin but insulated blanket and then put his fingers back on her neck; he could feel her pulse beating weakly. 'Do we know who she is?'

Mack nodded. 'The bloke who found her said she's called Heather. She lives down in the village, and the dog's called Harry, or was,' he added as an afterthought.

'Where is the man who found her now?' Steven enquired.

'Apparently, he had to go to work so he went home,' Mack said dryly.

Steven looked at Heather's pale face and wondered if anyone was missing her. He cursed as he felt a few spots of rain. 'I hope that helicopter hurries up,' he muttered, and then stood aside as another member of the mountain rescue team arrived on the ledge. He watched as they hoisted Heather slowly up to the waiting policemen, and then scrambled up after them.

When he got to the top, he checked her pulse again. It was still there but very weak. 'Hang on Heather,' he whispered.

The air ambulance arrived ten minutes later, and despite the mist the pilot managed to land nearby. Steven gave the doctor an update on the injuries as he checked Heather's vital signs, then he attached an intravenous line and they loaded her into the helicopter.

'The position of wound on her head isn't consistent with falling down the cliff, unless she landed head first of course, in which case the other injuries wouldn't fit,' Steven told his father as it sped away. 'And there's not enough blood on the ledge for a wound like that either,' he added.

They watched the rescue team bring the body of the dog up. 'This chap's not so lucky,' Jack commented as they reached the top. The dog was stiff and had obviously been dead for some time. There was a large bloody wound on the side of his head and congealed blood around his mouth and nose.

'There's no collar,' Steven observed as he examined the body. 'I'd keep hold of him if I were you,' he advised as he inspected the wound. 'This looks a similar shape to the wound on Heather.' His father nodded his agreement.

'I'll give the veterinary investigation centre a call and ask them to take a look,' Jack volunteered. Steven gave his father the bag containing the contents of Heather's pocket; he looked at it and frowned.

'There's no dog lead. Spread out and search the area,' he told the waiting policemen. Steven picked his case up. 'I'd better get back to the hospital, I'll catch you later Dad.' He nodded to the rest of the group, and made his way back to the car park where the mortuary van was still waiting. 'False alarm,' he told the attendants, then got into his car wondering if Heather would survive the journey.

He reached the hospital forty minutes later and went straight to the accident and emergency unit. A doctor took him into a side room where Heather lay surrounded by machines and medical staff. 'We're warming her up and getting some fluids into her, she's going to theatre as soon as she's stable.'

Steven stared at her for a minute. 'Can you take some swabs from the head wound, and send them and her clothes over to forensics?' He asked, the doctor nodded.

'Well done by the way,' he called as Steven turned to go. Steven glanced back and raised his eyebrows. 'Spotting her pulse,' the doctor reminded him.

'Well, I just hope she makes it,' Steven said quietly, he took one last look at her battered swollen face, and made his way over to the mortuary.

It took him less than five minutes to get to the mortuary, an unimposing two-story building standing in the same grounds as the hospital. Steven's small but efficient team consists of Charlie Malkin his mortuary technician, who has worked in the unit for four years since graduating from York University. At twenty-seven, he is the youngest member of the team, but at times appears much older.

Matthew and Bill, the mortuary assistants are both in their fifties and have been there for years. They never say much, and go about their business in a meticulous and methodical way. Upstairs is the Chief forensic technician, Sue's domain. A matronly woman in her mid-forties, she is married to Fred who stays at home to look after their two children.

Sue takes on the role of mother figure of the team; she will listen patiently to any problems, before dishing out advice where appropriate, or just provide a shoulder to cry on if needed. Three other technicians work with her, she calls them her girls, even though one of them is a man called Raymond, but not wanting to embarrass himself or Raymond, Steven had never asked why.

Judy is the final member of the team and deals with the day to day running of the office. Thirty-five years old and a bit of a hippy, she favours long floaty skirts coupled with multi coloured tops, strings of bright beads, and usually sandals whatever the weather. Judy sees the best in everybody and never seems to lose her temper; she is also a trained bereavement councillor, and so much to Steven's relief, able to help with distraught relatives, something that he had always found extremely difficult to deal with.

Judy was the first member of the team he met when he arrived, and had impressed him with her greeting of a cheery "hello". She in turn was overjoyed when he introduced himself. 'It's a young one,' she shouted excitedly up the stairs, and then quickly apologised for her fervour, explaining that as they were a small mortuary, it seemed to be a dumping ground for all the oldies who were due for retirement but didn't want to go.

Steven had settled in very quickly. He had been told by Sue soon after arriving, that Charlie and Judy were a couple. 'But the last pathologist, who had been made a dame years earlier, and made us call her Dame Meadowcroft, was one of the oldest oldies. She was very strict about dating colleagues, and so they kept their relationship a secret, but it doesn't seem fair on them, so I think you should know from the start,' she explained.

Steven agreed that honesty was the best policy; however, having been through the dating colleague's scenario and finding out the hard way that it didn't work, he was dubious. But he told himself that what they did in their own time was none of his business, and so he agreed to turn a blind eye.

'Where have you been boss?' Charlie asked when he arrived back. Steven brought him up to date with the morning's drama.

'The doctor is sending her clothes and some swabs over when they get her into surgery; can you let me know as soon as they arrive?' He went into his office and started to write a report on the morning's events; when he got to the wound on Heathers head, he stopped writing and stared into space. I hope she survives; it would be a shame if I had to post-mortem her, especially given how attractive she is, he thought.

Charlie appeared in the doorway a minute later. 'Penny for them,' he chuckled. Steven looked up. 'I was just thinking that I hope she makes it,' he confessed.

'Well, she's still with us at the moment and the swabs are on their way over,' Charlie informed him. Steven got up and followed him into the lab.

'Let's see what we've got then,' he said brightly.

Chapter 2

Across town, Detective Chief Inspector Edward Cooper was looking out of his office window. It was another wet day in early October and the rain was bouncing off the pavement. He sighed despondently; he hated the winter and couldn't wait for the summer, when he could shed the heavy jumpers and woolly socks that weighed him down.

A softly spoken mild tempered man; he had been based at the police station in Kimberwick for the best part of twenty-five years. His patch covered a fifty-mile radius, and he was kept busy most of the time, usually with minor offences. But any offence brought the mountain of paperwork that he hated. He sighed again, then returned to his desk and started to write.

Twenty minutes later, there was a knock on the door and Jack Taylor came in. Edward gave a sigh of relief; it was a good excuse to stop writing. Jack had been born and bred in London. He had requested a transfer three years previously so that his wife, who was originally from York, could be near to her mother after she had been widowed. He was a gritty thirty-nine-year-old, who after twenty years of coping with the manic pace of life in London, had found the rather slow pace of life in Kimberwick hard to adjust to.

Edward quickly found out that he had a short fuse, with a tendency to fly off the handle, but he was a good solid officer, and apart from terrifying him with his somewhat erratic driving, and his habit of calling him guv, Edward liked, and more importantly, trusted him. He put his pen down and sat back. 'What have you got?' He asked expectantly.

Jack sat down and opened his note book. 'She's called Heather Brooks, aged twenty-nine. She lives at 2 green lane, Burney. I spoke to her neighbour, and she's been there for about three years. She lives alone except for the dog, and works part time at the local post office.' He shut his notebook with a snap. 'And that's all anyone appears to know about her.'

Edward handed him the evidence bag. 'Her house keys are in there; you'd better take a uniform and see if you can find anything useful.' Jack nodded and stood up.

'Have you spoken to the post master?' Edward enquired; Jack shook his head.

'He's on holiday, but I did speak to Vicky Morris, the woman that she works with. Heather has been there for eighteen months; she gets on with everyone but keeps to herself. She was working yesterday afternoon and was her normal self.'

Edward looked at his watch. 'She's still in surgery at the moment, but I want a uniform there, and as soon as the doctors give the ok, we need to talk to her.'

'Assuming she survives,' Jack mused, he opened his notebook again. 'I've spoken to John Simmons, the man who found her. He took his dog, went on his usual early morning walk before work, the dog went mad barking and whining, that's what made him look over the edge.

'He said Heather is usually up there in the early evening but not normally on that side of the cliff. Apparently, there's a path that starts at the quarry cottages, it passes across the top and then back down to the village green.'

'Where does he work?' Edward enquired.

Jack glanced at the notebook. 'He drives for a delivery firm in York; he's offered to show us the route she generally walks tomorrow.' Edward nodded appreciatively.

'Have scene of crime come up with anything?'

Jack shook his head. 'Nothing on the ledge or surrounding area, and there's no sign of the dog's lead or collar, but it's still pretty misty up there. Don't you think it was an accident then, guv?'

'I'm not sure yet. The pathologist thinks she may have been attacked; the angle of the head wound in relation to the other injuries, and the lack of blood at the scene is raising questions. I'll go over after lunch and see if he's found anything,' Edward said thoughtfully.

Jack opened the door. 'I'll let you know if there's any news from the hospital guv.' Edward nodded his thanks.

'Can you get onto the VI centre as well and find out if they have anything on the dog?' He called. 'Oh, and let's try and keep her name out of the papers, at least until we know what we are dealing with.' Jack nodded and went out leaving him to continue with the paperwork.

17

Edward could see Steven working in the lab when he arrived later that afternoon. He watched him for a while before tapping on the door. His son looked up and smiled. 'Put a coat on and come on in Dad,' he invited, then resumed looking through a microscope at something decidedly bloody.

Edward shuddered inwardly as he went in and glanced around the lab. He had often wondered how his son could bear to deal with death every day, and not just natural death, sometimes it was unnatural and violent.

Still, it was his choice, and although Edward had never told him as much, he was incredibly proud of the way that he had pulled himself back from being a somewhat troubled teenager, who with a tendency explode with anger at the slightest provocation could well have ended up in real trouble, into a fairly patient man running his own department.

There was concentration etched on his son's face as he peered at the image that he had now transferred to the monitor. Edward smiled inwardly as he remembered Steven confessing that didn't want to follow in his footsteps and join the police force, but wanted to be a chef. 'People will always have to eat,' his son had said by way of an explanation.

But three years into catering college, and after an incident with his then girlfriend, he had changed his mind. What a change of direction Edward thought as he watched, mind you the lab looked like a kitchen of sorts, with its array of knives, sinks and containers, and cutting up meat and cutting up bodies are maybe not that different. Steven suddenly broke into his thoughts.

'Look at this dad, this swab was taken from the wound on Heather Brooks head; can you see this hair caught in the blood?' Edward moved around to look and nodded. 'It's dog hair,' Steven explained. 'I think she was hit with the same rock that killed the dog.

'I've asked the veterinary investigation centre to send samples of the dog's hair and blood over for comparison. I'll get forensics to check this swab and see if there's any of the dog's blood mixed with Heather's. I am sure its dog hair. Heather is blond, the dog is black and this swab was taken from deep inside the wound on her head.

'There's no other way it could have got there. I think that whoever attacked Heather killed the dog first, and then used the same lump of rock on her.' He plucked the hair from the bloody swab with a pair of tweezers and the two men inspected it.

'Are you sure it was a rock?' Edward checked.

'Definitely,' Steven said confidently. 'There were traces of the local lime stone in the wound, and the VI centre thinks the dog was also hit with a rock, they are checking his wound for fragments.'

'Did you find anything on Heather's clothes?' Edward asked hopefully. Steven shook his head.

'They are still with forensics; I'll let you know if we get anything,' he promised. 'There were no blooded rocks near to where she was found, and given the lack of blood, I can only assume that she was attacked elsewhere, then taken to the edge and thrown over,' Edward said thoughtfully. He looked at the time.

'She came out of surgery an hour ago, so I'm going over to see her.' Steven took his gloves off. 'Give me a minute to get changed and I'll come with you.'

They stood at the end of Heather's bed twenty minutes later. With a ventilator covering most of her swollen face, and bandages hiding the wound on her head, she was barely recognisable as a woman. 'Christ,' Edward said quietly. 'How on earth did you know that she was alive?'

Steven shrugged. 'I didn't know, it was just a feeling. I've looked into dozens of dead faces over the years, but when I looked into hers it was different, there was character there,' he said thoughtfully. 'What are her chances?' He asked the doctor.

The doctor sounded positive as he gave them an update. 'The fact she's made it through the operation is a big plus,' he said brightly. 'But she has lost a lot of blood, and there is pressure on her brain from the fragments of bone and rock that were imbedded in her skull. I think we got it all out but there could be brain damage. We'll try taking her off the ventilator when she's stable.

'She's one tough lady though, because if she was lying out in the quarry all night, it's a miracle that she survived the weather never mind the wounds.' He gave her a concerned look. 'I'm afraid it's just going to be a case of wait and see for now.'

'Is there any sign of a sexual assault?' Edward enquired. The doctor shook his head.

'Thankfully no, but she is menstruating, so if that was the plan then it may have put whoever it was off, but there are some odd shaped bruises on the outside of both thighs; it looks like she may have been kicked.' He lifted the sheet up and they leant down to look. The bruises were about four inches long and almost oval in shape.

'Can I send someone to take a picture of these?' Steven asked. The doctor nodded his consent, then pulled the sheet down and opened Heather's gown, which revealed the mass of bruising around her ribs. He pointed to a scar low down on her abdomen.

'I would say that's a caesarean section scar, and given its position probably an emergency one, so there may be a child somewhere,' he said to both men's dismay.

Steven suddenly felt embarrassed for her and covered her up again. 'What about the broken bones?'

'There's a bad break to the lower left leg which we've pinned, her left wrist is fractured and she has three broken ribs which thankfully hadn't punctured her lungs,' the doctor reported.

'Jesus,' Edward muttered silently. 'How long before we can talk to her?'

The doctor shrugged. 'I can't say; we're keeping her sedated to give her body time to recover. We'll bring her out of it when she's stable, it could be hours or days, and that's assuming that she can talk or remember anything when she does come round, short term memory loss is common with traumatic head injuries,' he explained.

They looked at her for a few more minutes, the only noise coming from the array monitors around her. 'All the broken bones are on the left-hand side, there's no way that she could have got the wound on her head by falling down the cliff because the angle is all wrong. I think you can rule out attempted suicide, I would say you're looking at attempted murder,' Steven said to his father.

Edward's phone rang as they made their way out. 'The dog was killed by a single but very violent blow to the side of the head. It was probably a lime stone rock but they're still testing it. They've estimated that he was killed between six thirty and ten p.m. last night.

'Two of his legs were broken post-mortem, indicating that he was thrown over the cliff after death,' Jack reported.

'She must have lain there for eight hours or more. It's lucky that John Simmons took his dog out when he did, another hour or two and she wouldn't have survived,' Edward told Steven.

'Well, she's not out of danger yet,' his son reminded him wryly. They walked back to the mortuary in silence, knowing that the next few hours would be critical. And although neither of them was particularly religious, they were both praying that she would make it.

Later that day Jack Taylor went into the incident room which had been set up in the local library. 'Any joy with the door to door?' He asked the constable behind the desk.

The PC shook his head. 'No Sir not yet, the men are still doing the rounds. So far no one has seen any strangers about, the bed and breakfasts are both closed for the winter. There was a man enquiring about a room at the Merrifield but that was ten days ago.

'The owner told him to ask at the pub, but the landlord says no one has enquired about rooms since the end of the summer. We have got a description,' he added before Jack could ask.

'Also, a Mrs Richardson came in; she lives next door to Ms Brooks. Ms Brooks baby sits for her grandchildren occasionally, she thinks there is a sister but doesn't know where. Ms Brooks doesn't seem go out very much apart from going to work or walking the dog.

'She normally takes him around the quarry, or sometimes up on the moors. Mrs Richardson thinks she goes bird watching because she usually has a pair of binoculars with her.' Jack took the offered reports and skimmed through them.

'Who's available to come to her house with me?' The constable looked at the rota.

'WPC Blackwell is due in at four.'

Christ! Not her Jack groaned inwardly. 'I'll just go and get a bite to eat, ask her to wait here for me, will you?' He ordered. At four fifteen, he and WPC Blackwell stood outside Heather's house, situated at the end of Green Lane. It was the last one in a small row of terraces that backed on to one side of the quarry. A footpath ran up the side of the house, which in turn led onto the village green.

As Jack put the key in the door, a middle-aged woman came out of the house next door and looked at them suspiciously. 'Mrs Pat Richardson?' Jack asked. She nodded as he showed her his identity card.

'I was just going to go over to the hospital to see if she needs anything.'

'She's still unconscious, you'd be better off waiting until she's a bit more stable,' Jack advised. Pat nodded.

'I'll leave it for now then. I can't say that I was looking forward to seeing her all battered, but I thought someone should go and support her,' she said sadly, and then went back inside.

Jack opened Heather's front door and stooped down to pick up the mail from that morning. 'Bills and junk,' he commented as they stepped into the hall. Ahead of them, a narrow staircase led up to the first floor. He sent WPC Blackwell to look upstairs and went into the lounge.

The place was neat and tidy; there were no ornaments to speak of, no photographs, and only one picture hanging on the wall. A settee and armchair sat together on one side of the room, a television and video stood opposite, and next to them a sideboard containing paperwork, all neatly in order. Jack picked the telephone up and pressed redial, it rang a couple of times before a woman's voice answered.

'Burney post office.'

'Sorry wrong number,' he said and replaced the receiver. He picked it up again and dialled one four seven one, there had been a call two days earlier but the number had been withheld. He took a recent phone bill from the sideboard and put it into an evidence bag, then went through the arch into the kitchen diner.

A small dining table and two chairs stood in the corner, there were dishes on the draining board and a pan on the stove. Jack lifted the lid; it contained macaroni cheese, her tea from last night he guessed. He looked with sadness at the dog bowl next to the back door, and noted that the hooks on the door were bare; he unlocked it and went out into a tiny yard, which apart from a washing line was empty.

WPC Blackwell came into the kitchen and handed him a photograph in a frame. 'It was by her bed, Sir,' she reported. Jack looked at the picture of a pretty blond woman, who was smiling happily and holding a tiny baby.

'So that's what she looks like normally,' he commented. He turned the frame over and unclipped the back. "Me and Malcolm aged two months" was written in one corner of the picture. 'Nip next door and ask Mrs Richardson if she would come in for a minute,' he told WPC Blackwell.

He continued to look at the picture until the policewoman returned with Pat. 'Do you know anything about the baby?' He asked. Pat shook her head.

'She's never mentioned a baby and I've not seen that picture before,' she said in surprise.

'Has she ever mentioned a husband or a boyfriend?' Jack asked. She shook her head again.

'No never. She's never talked about any family, except once when she referred to a sister, but she didn't want to talk about her.'

22

Jack put the picture in the bag and pointed to the empty hooks on the back door. 'Do you happen to know what would usually hang here?'

Pat thought for a minute. 'Harry's lead, Heathers coat and her binoculars I think,' she said uncertainly.

'Do you know what sort of binoculars they are?'

Pat thought again for a while. 'They're green rubber things, but I don't know what make they are,' she said apologetically.

When she had gone, they searched the house for the binoculars, but there was no sign of them. 'They must be up on the quarry somewhere, unless whoever attacked her has got them,' Jack surmised. As they turned to leave, he spotted a handbag under the hall table.

Inside there was a purse, a driving license, a few unpaid bills and an address book. 'We may find a relative in here,' he muttered as he flicked through it. 'Get on to the D.V.L.A tomorrow and see if they can give us anything,' he told WPC Blackwell, then took a last look around and closed the door firmly behind them.

They called next door to let Pat know they were taking the picture bill and bag. 'Has Heather got a car?' Jack enquired. Pat shook her head.

'She said she didn't need one, but she did hire one a few months back when she went away for a few days,' she remembered.

'Do you happen know where she went?' Jack asked hopefully.

'I'm sorry I didn't ask,' Pat admitted.

'Can you remember how long she was away for?' Pat nodded.

'Just two days.' Jack thanked her again, then dropped the WPC off at the incident room before driving back to the station.

Chapter 3

Steven pulled into his yard and yawned, it had been a long and eventful day. He listened to the silence of the surrounding countryside and suddenly felt very small and insignificant. He could see the lights of Burney flickering dimly in the distance as he looked across the moors, he looked the other way, but all he could see was pitch blackness.

It was a stark contrast to the flat he had owned previously, where at night the streetlights shone through the windows, and noise had been a constant source of annoyance. He had declined his father's offer to move back to the family home, because although it would have been cheaper and very convenient, he knew it would be a disaster, So he looked for somewhere to buy instead, and the estate agents description of Gorse Farm had sounded perfect.

A traditional stone-built farm house with three bedrooms, a range of outbuildings, and a large garden. Steven had brought it on impulse after just one viewing. Situated between York and Burney, it was ideally positioned for his work at the hospital and his father's house on the outskirts of Kimberwick. Lying a quarter of a mile back from the moor's road, it was reached via an unmade track, and with the nearest house being over a mile away, there were no close neighbours.

Although, the house was structurally sound, the inside was a different story. The previous owner had lived there for over sixty years and had neglected the décor. It looked like it hadn't been touched for the entire sixty years, and needed stripping right down to the bare walls.

So, with peeling paint, old lead water pipes, and no mains gas, it needed a lot of work. Having first arranged for the water pipes to be renewed, and as he hated cooking on electric, propane gas to be installed. The workmen had finished fitting the heating system along with a new kitchen and bathroom just before Steven moved in, and although most of his furniture was now in place, it still looked fairly unlived in.

Not being a great handyman, Steven had for a fleeting moment when he first arrived, wished that he was back in the noisy but modern flat in Oxford, then he remembered the reason that he had left and put the thought out of his head. Now, after living there for several months, he found that he loved the tranquillity it afforded.

Monty, a tortoise shell cat of enormous proportions, greeted him at the door. Steven crouched down and rubbed his ears. 'Do you want some tea old boy?' He asked affectionately. Monty purred loudly and twitched his tail.

'I'll take that as a yes,' Steven chuckled as he went into the kitchen with the cat hot on his heels. The three years that he spent at catering college before he changed his mind had not been wasted. He loved cooking, had designed the kitchen to his own specification, and still possessed a wide range of utensils, so unlike a lot of single men, he could prepare himself a decent meal without too much trouble. He left his dinner cooking and went upstairs for a shower.

He thought about Amy as he stood under the warm water, he had tried to block her out, but found it increasingly difficult. They had met in his final year at university. He was studying hard but finding the work difficult, and was trying to steer clear of any distractions.

It was a further six months and after his final exams before he had given in to her and her friends pestering, and gone out with her. They were an established couple for nearly five years and had talked casually about marriage on a few of occasions, but ultimately it was she who had proposed to him, although, when he thought about it later, a breathless "Are we getting married or not?" whilst they were having what she called an "early morning setting me up for the day quickie", was hardly a proposal,

but given the position he was in, and under the illusion that he had found his soul mate, Steven had agreed.

But as he waited nervously at the alter a few months later, she left it to her brother to tell him that she wasn't coming, and had run off with Martin, the best man. Not content with simply running off with him, she had then taken him on what should have been their honeymoon.

Upset and humiliation had turned to anger when Steven later found out that she had been sleeping with him for over a year, and to make matters worse as they all worked in the same building; everyone seemed to know about it. Then, on their return from the "honeymoon", they cruelly proceeded to rub salt into the wound by brazenly going about their business, as though Steven had never existed. And that had been the last straw.

Desperate to get away and struggling to stop himself from punching Martin, whilst enduring the constant whispering and pitying looks; he had applied for the position in Kimberwick. But only being fully qualified for five years and not holding out much hope of getting it, he had already decided that he would pack it in and go back to catering.

However, much to his surprise he was offered the post, and even though he was running the department which was a great step up for him, as it was a small rural practice and away from the affluent areas of the country, it had meant a cut in salary and relocation. 'Bitch,' he muttered angrily as he washed the shampoo out of his hair, then he remembered that he'd had a lucky escape and told himself to snap out of it.

Twenty minutes later, he was sitting in front of the television with his dinner on a tray. Monty sat next to him washing himself. Steven watched as he cleaned between every toe before settling down to sleep. How uncomplicated cat's lives are, he thought, then his mind wandered back to Heather. 'She's stable,' Edward informed him when he rang.

'Did the collar and lead turn up?' Steven asked.

'No, but we're resuming the search tomorrow. John Simmons is going to show us the route that she usually takes. We're meeting at her house at eleven if you want to come along,' his father invited.

'I'll see what I've got on in the morning,' Steven yawned. He hung up and looked at the sleeping cat, time for bed he thought.

Chapter 4

There was quite a crowd outside Heather's house the next day. The rain had stopped, and in its place a cold wind that blew leaves around the feet of the men who were waiting to start the search. John Simmons, a short stocky middle-aged man, with a mop of ginger hair and a broad Scottish accent, waited nervously by the footpath next to her house.

His dog, a wire-haired Jack Russell terrier called Chester, sat patiently at his feet, whilst Edward and Jack organised the constables 'Are you ready Mr Simmons?' Edward asked. John nodded, and they set off along the footpath towards the village green.

John Simmons and Chester walked in front with Edward and Jack, half a dozen policemen followed behind, all looking closely at the ground on either side of the path. When they reached the green, the policemen fanned out to check in the hedgerows that ran across the back of the gardens. 'Can we stop here for a minute, Sir, so the men can have a good look?' Edward asked.

'Do you know Heather well?' Jack enquired as they waited. John shook his head.

'Only through the dogs. We sometimes meet up halfway round, the dogs like to socialise,' he added as an afterthought.

'And you live where in relation to her?' Jack checked.

'Nine Rosemary Lane, two streets over,' John said curtly, and pointed in the general direction of Heather's house.

A few minutes later, the policemen regrouped having found nothing. They continued across the green and passed through a gate, then joined a narrow track to start the accent up the side of the quarry. There was a fence on one side of the path to protect walkers from a steep drop.

'She goes up to the top of this track and then usually cuts left across the middle of the cliff, or sometimes she goes right and back past the yard. I've never seen her on the other side. Harry was quite old and she was worried that he may

27

go over the edge,' John explained. 'It's such a shame, she adored that dog, and he was loyal as they come. He never left her side,' he added sadly.

They carried on walking, halfway up they found themselves overlooking the old quarry yard. There were three cottages, half a dozen storage sheds and a large barn, all surrounded by a high wire fence and big double gates. 'Does anyone live there?' Jack enquired. John shook his head.

'They've been empty ever since the quarry closed. A few people have tried to rent them, but the company that owns the site, don't want to know.'

Edward turned to Jack. 'Get someone to call the company and get permission to go down and search. Get a warrant if you have too,' he added as Jack got his radio out.

The policemen finished looking in the immediate area and moved on to the top of the path. It was fairly steep but the path was well used, and although it was wet, it wasn't a bad climb. They reached the top, and as John Simmons had said, the path split three ways. He pointed to the path heading left. 'That's the path she usually takes.'

'Where do the other two lead to?' Edward asked.

'The right hand one goes back down and skirts around the back of the yard, it comes out by the entrance gate. The middle path goes over to the other side of the cliffs where she fell, it goes past the car park and comes out on the other side of the green,' he said somewhat impatiently.

'And you're sure that Heather never goes that way?' Edward checked.

'Well I've never seen her over there, but I'm not up here all the time am I?' John snapped. Edward looked at him sharply.

'I'm sorry I have to keep asking you these things Sir, but if we are going to find out what happened, then we have to be clear about her habits.' John nodded.

'No, I'm sorry,' he started to say, but he was interrupted by a shout from one of the policemen.

They went over to where the PC was waiting, he pointed to a patch of gorse. 'In there Sir. I think it's a pair of binoculars.' Edward put a glove on and plucked the green rubber binoculars from the middle of the bush.

'Do you know if these belong to Heather?' He asked John.

'They look like hers,' he said thoughtfully. Edward looked at them closely; there were what appeared to be small spots of blood on one of the lenses. He put them into a bag and handed them to one of the constables. 'Get these over to forensics straight away,' he ordered.

They continued along the path to the top of the quarry, with no mist left to speak of the views were breath-taking. The moors stretched for miles ahead, uninterrupted by anything remotely man made. Edward looked down the quarry face, where heaps of stones lay, remnants left behind when the quarry closed, and now mostly covered with a coarse grass.

'It's lucky she didn't fall all the way down; she'd never have survived that drop,' he commented.

'Is this going to take much longer? I've got to get to work,' John sighed, as Edward turned away from the view.

'We will be as quick as we can, Mr Simmons. I'm sorry to put you out,' he stared at him for a few seconds before moving on.

They made their way around the rest of the route without finding anything else, and arrived back at the green half an hour later. 'Well, thank you Mr Simmons, you've been most helpful,' Edward said dryly. He watched John hurry down the road, he knew he was hiding something but he couldn't put his finger on it. John looked back at the policemen several times before turning the corner out of sight.

A few minutes later the other three constables arrived from the quarry entrance with nothing to report. Jack saw the frustration in Edward's face. 'Well at least we've got the binoculars, so we know that she was in that area at some point unconscious or otherwise.' Edward gave a big sigh and nodded despondently.

'I wonder why she was attacked; it must have been someone who knew her habits,' he mused. 'I'm going over to the hospital after lunch, you get back to the station and chase up the phone company, see if they can give us the numbers for Heather's incoming and outgoing calls, someone must know her beyond the last three years.' Jack nodded.

'I'll get onto the D.V.L.A as well; they should have a former address.' Edward took his arm as he turned to go. 'Check if John Simmons has got form,' he said quietly. Jack nodded again. Like Edward, he too had felt that John Simmons wasn't all he was cracked up to be.

Jack left Edward and made his way over to the incident room to check progress. A few people had been in to find out how Heather was, but no one had any relevant information to help with the investigation. The house to house had proved fairly fruitless as well, of all the addresses that had been visited so far, no one had seen anyone suspicious or any strangers. Most of the people who had been interviewed knew Heather from the post office, but frustratingly no one seemed to actually know anything about her.

Progress remained slow over the weekend. Heather remained unconscious but stable, and the doctors informed Edward that if she continued to improve, they would take her off the ventilator on Monday and bring her round. Edward was on call, but apart from a couple of drunken assaults in the early hours of Sunday morning, he wasn't really required, and so spent his time pondering on Heather's case.

Why someone would try to kill her? Was there something in her past? Did she see something that she shouldn't have seen?

The kitchen was where he did his pondering, in fact he did most things in the kitchen except sleep, and he had been known to do that on the odd occasion. The house was big, he had lived in it for the past twenty-five years, and he suddenly felt very alone. He'd been feeling it a lot lately. Sometimes he thought he should take Steven's advice and move somewhere smaller,

then he remembered all the good memories the house held; they far outweighed the bad ones. In fact, the only really bad memory was Elizabeth telling him that she was dying, and then the two of them having to tell a fourteen-year-old Steven, that the mother he adored had a brain tumour and probably wouldn't last another year. Biting his lip so hard that it bled in a bid to stop himself from crying, Steven had stood numbly in the middle of the kitchen and stared at them in disbelief, before finally breaking down.

God! What a year that was. Edward looked at the picture of their wedding day and smiled to himself. They had been teenage sweethearts, and even though her parents were against the relationship, their love had never wavered. They eventually warmed to him, and when Steven came along, they were ecstatic.

He was so deep in thought that he jumped as the doorbell rang; he got up to find his neighbour Sheila Parkinson on the step. An unflappable homely woman who had lived in a bungalow two doors down for longer than he could remember. Sheila had been good friends with Elizabeth, who as a nurse had helped with her elderly parents until their death just three weeks apart, and two years before Elizabeth herself had died.

Ever since then she had been keeping an eye on Edward. In truth it was more than an eye, she had been a tower of strength when he was struggling with a stroppy teenager, who although old enough to understand why his mother had died, was at an age when her calming influence would have kept his behaviour in check. Edward had found coping with Steven and trying to do his job whilst grieving for Elizabeth very tough, and he had been grateful for Sheila's company and advice on more than one occasion.

At fifty-six, she was a year older than him, but looked a good ten years younger, and she was very attractive, especially her eyes, Edward had always thought privately, he found it odd though that she had never married, or as far as he knew even had a serious boyfriend. She smiled at him as he opened the door. 'Do you want to come over for lunch?' She asked brightly.

Edward hesitated but didn't really know why, because apart from being hungry and not relishing the thought of yet another frozen microwave meal, he would welcome her company. 'I've got a lot on at the moment, and I'm on call,' he offered as an excuse. 'I should really stay here, maybe next week.'

Sheila half smiled at him. 'You've got your mobile phone haven't you?' Edward nodded. 'And you still have to eat, don't you?' She asked.

'Yes, I suppose so,' he conceded.

'So come; I've got roast lamb in the oven,' she said temptingly. 'They'll ring if they need you.' He looked at her smiling invitingly, and noticed her nice eyes again.

'Roast lamb you say?' Sheila nodded enthusiastically.

'With all the trimmings. It'll be ready in half an hour, so come over when you like,' she chuckled.

Chapter 5

With the weekend over, Monday morning found Steven in the mortuary working on the body of an old man who had apparently fallen down the stairs; No one had noticed him missing, and he had lain decomposing in the hallway for over a month. The heating had been on in the house which escalated the decomposition process.

A policeman doing the house to house had noticed the smell and broken in. Charlie came in and stood at the end of the post-mortem bench. 'Very smelly,' he commented through the face mask. Steven felt around the old man's head and neck until he found what he was looking for.

'Come and feel here.' Charlie put his hands on the back of his neck.

'Broken?'

'Yep,' Steven confirmed. 'He must have fallen from the top, but according to his neighbours, he's eighty-two years old, so his bones are probably quite brittle. I'll just have a look at his organs assuming they are not too far gone; he may have had a heart attack or a stroke at the top of the stairs.' The two men worked in silence until the phone rang.

'Steven it's your father,' Judy called from reception,

'Tell him I'll ring back when I've finished,' he called back. Judy spoke into the phone and then came to the cutting room door,

'He says it's urgent,' she said quietly.

'I'll finish off here boss,' Charlie offered. Steven took his gloves off and picked the phone up.

'What's up Dad?' He asked anxiously.

'I'm at the hospital with Heather, she's conscious,' Edward informed him. Steven's heart leapt.

'Has she spoken?' He asked hopefully.

'She's asking who Steven is, and as you're the only Steven who was up on the quarry, we are assuming that she means you. I think it may be a good idea if you came over,' his father suggested.

'I'll be there as soon as I can,' Steven promised.

'How does Heather know your name?' Judy asked when he told her.

'Well, it's commonly thought that hearing is the last thing to go before you die, so she may have heard someone speaking to me, or maybe she's lost her memory and she genuinely knows the name but can't remember who Steven is,' he explained. 'Can you manage here?' He called. Charlie looked up from the old man's chest and nodded.

There was a policeman sitting outside Heather's room. Steven showed him his identification and went in; his father was standing next to the window talking to the doctor. Steven glanced towards the bed; there was a cage protecting Heathers broken leg, and her head was still covered in bandages, but with the ventilator gone, he could see her face properly, and beneath the bruising her colour was much better.

He bent down for a closer look at the picture of her and the baby that Edward had placed on the bedside cabinet; she looked so happy. 'How's she doing?' He asked concernedly.

'Surprisingly well; we took her off the ventilator first thing and she came round a couple of hours ago. She's booked in for a brain scan later, but the first signs are good,' the doctor said brightly. He looked at his watch. 'Don't stay too long,' he ordered, and then left the room.

'Heather,' Edward said quietly, she half opened her eyes.

'Who are you?' She asked, her voice barley a whisper. Edward reminded her who he was, and put his hand on his son's arm. 'This is Steven.' Heather turned her head slightly and looked at him. 'Do you remember asking who Steven was?' Edward checked, she closed her eyes and a tear ran down the side of her face.

'Harry,' she said quietly.

'I'm sorry, he didn't make it,' Steven told her gently, he took a tissue from the box on the cabinet and wiped the tear away. 'Can you remember what happened?' Heather opened her eyes again and stared at him through her lashes.

'Choppers on the way Steven,' she whispered. 'You told me to hang on, are you Steven?' He smiled at her.

'Yes, I am,' he confirmed.

'Did you find me?'

Steven shook his head. 'John Simmons found you.'

She frowned slightly. 'Who are you then?'

Steven smiled again. 'I'll explain when you're stronger, you should rest now. Is there anyone you want us to call?' She shook her head slowly and closed her eyes again. 'I think we should leave her now,' Steven whispered. Edward nodded his agreement, and they went out closing the door quietly behind them.

'Make sure that this door is never left unattended, if whoever did this knows that she survived, then they may have another go,' Edward told the PC.

Steven was horrified. 'Do you really think so?' Edward gave a small shrug.

'It's happened before.' They looked through the window again, and then walked down the corridor in silence, each deep in thought.

Back at the station, Jack had news from the D.V.L.A. 'Her name used to be Heather Mason; she changed her name and moved here from Chipping Norton just under three years ago. I've contacted the local force to see if they can come up with anything.' He looked up from his notes.

'Is there anything from the phone company yet?' Edward checked.

'We're still waiting, guv, and there's nothing in the address book, only local numbers, tradesmen, work etc.,' he reported.

'Keep on at the phone company, she must have rung someone sometime' Edward ordered. He went into his office and sat down. It was three forty-five and there was still a stack of paperwork to get through.

He was interrupted an hour later by a knock on the door and Jack came in. 'The phone company have been on; they're sending an itemised list over, it should be here first thing, and someone from the company who owns the quarry is coming over at lunchtime tomorrow to let us into the site.' Edward nodded appreciatively.

'Are you nearly done for the day?'

'I'm just sorting out the list for tomorrow,' Jack confirmed, then went out leaving the door ajar. Edward leaned back in the chair and listened to the chatter coming from the squad room. Most of the team including Jack would be going home to families. Edward disliked the solitude of an empty house, and avoided going home too early most nights.

His mind wandered back to Steven, alone in his cottage. He was so like his mother; she had never minded being on her own. She said it gave her time to be herself without having to worry about other people. He closed his eyes and could still see her smiling at him; he sat there reminiscing, until the phone brought him back from his musings.

'I've just had the results from the swab, and there were traces of blood other than Heather's in the wound. Sue has just finished looking at the samples from the VI centre; it was the dog's blood and his hair, so I think we were right about the order of attack,' Steven told him.

Edward tried to stifle a yawn. 'Thanks son. Are you off home now?' He asked.

'I'm just finishing today's reports and then I'm gone,' Steven confirmed, and then sensing that his father was feeling low asked. 'Do you want to come over for dinner tonight?'

Edward smiled to himself. 'I'll come about eight,' he accepted without hesitation.

Father and son at the table that evening, Monty sat on a chair watching them closely. Edward eyed him suspiciously. 'That cat hates me.' Steven shook his head.

'No, he's a big softy really.' He got up and stroked the cat who responded by purring loudly. 'Have you had enough to eat?' Edward nodded and started to clear the table. 'Leave that dad, I'll see to it later,' Steven ordered.

'You cooked so I will clear,' Edward insisted.

'You used to say that to mum,' Steven remembered. Edward smiled fondly at the memory.

'I did, and she used to say that she'd rather clear than cook, but as I couldn't cook that wasn't an option,' he chuckled. They were still chuckling as they went into the lounge with their coffee.

Steven glanced at his father. 'Have you ever thought of remarrying?'

Edward frowned at him. 'No never.' Steven looked into his father's still sad face.

'Don't you think it's about time you stopped grieving,' he said before he could stop himself, and then waited for the backlash.

'No! Don't you think it's about time that you stopped blaming yourself for what happened to Sally?' His father snapped. They stared at each other, both lost in unhappy memories, and both regretting the comments. Edward gave a big sigh and forced a smile. 'I'm too busy to think about remarrying, not to mention too old,' he said resignedly.

'You're only fifty-five! That's hardly scrap heap material. I mean look at Hugh Hefner,' Steven exclaimed.

Edward screwed his nose up. 'I'd rather not if you don't mind, anyway you've got no room to talk, you were twelve by the time I was your age.'

Steven gave an ironic snort. 'It's hardly a comparison Dad; you and mum were married for sixteen years. I only got as far the church.' He bit his lip as he felt the anger rising again.

'Have you heard from Amy?' His father enquired.

'No. And I don't want to, thank you. I don't want anything to do with women ever again,' he said curtly. Edward could see the pain in his son's eyes and knew that it was still hurting, so he changed the subject.

'Still no curtains then?' He commented as he looked at the bare windows.

'I don't think they are top priority, after all I'm not exactly overlooked,' Steven said, hoping that he wasn't going to get a lecture.

'No, I suppose not,' Edward conceded; he looked at the bare floorboards. 'No carpet either? Only I was just thinking I've got one in the attic going spare,' he said hurriedly as Steven scowled at him.

'Right thanks,' his son muttered. They sat in silence both realising that the current topic was over. It was Steven who spoke first. 'Do you want me to speak to Heather tomorrow as I'm right on the doorstep?'

Edward nodded thoughtfully. 'You may as well, but make sure that Constable Higgins is there to take notes.' He got up and yawned. 'I'd better be off, thanks for dinner.' Steven walked him to the door. 'You should unpack some of this stuff,' Edward said as he navigated the boxes that were still piled up in the hall.

'Yes Dad; right Dad; bye Dad,' Steven laughed.

He watched his father drive away. It had been seventeen years since his mother died, his father had been on his own ever since and it worried him. Steven was fifteen when she died, he had only been at home for a couple of years before going first to catering college and then university, to his regret, he spent those couple of years rebelling against the system and habitually arguing with his father, who by immersing himself in work had coped with her death.

He still seemed lost without her though, especially rattling around alone in the old house, but he steadfastly refused to move somewhere smaller. 'Too many good memories to leave behind,' he always said when the subject was broached.

Steven sighed loudly and closed the door, then went into the kitchen and groaned at the pile of washing up.

There was a report from forensics on Edward's desk when he arrived the next morning. 'The blood on the binoculars is Heather's, and there were fibres from what they think is a carpet on her clothes. They're going to get samples from her house and compare them,' he told Jack as he came in. The sergeant sat down to give his own update.

'The phone company has sent a list of incoming and outgoing call from the last year; we're checking them now, and Chipping Norton has sent a file over, you're not going to like this guv.' Edward looked up expectantly. 'Mason was Heather's married name. Barry Mason, her ex-husband, is in a high security mental hospital.' Edward raised his eyebrows in surprise.

'He was convicted of killing their baby son nearly four years ago,' Jack continued. 'He pleaded guilty to manslaughter whilst the balance of his mind was disturbed and the jury believed him.'

'So, Heather reverted to her maiden name and moved here,' Edward finished for him.

'It would appear so,' Jack agreed.

'I assume that the husband is still in the hospital,' Edward checked.

'Yes, I got off the phone a few minutes ago. Chipping are sending someone to see his family,' Jack confirmed.

'What about Heather's family?' Edward enquired.

'Just her parents; we're still trying to trace them. Apparently, they moved a couple of years ago but no one knows where.'

Edward took the file from him. 'Leave it with me, I'll see if anything jumps out. Oh! And Steven is going to talk to Heather today if the doc gives the ok,' he added quietly.

When Jack had gone, Edward opened the file, a picture of an unshaven gaunt looking man stared blankly at the camera. 'So that's Barry Mason, is it?' he muttered. He turned the page and found details of the injuries sustained by the baby after he had been thrown from a railway bridge. 'Good God! What on earth could have possessed him to do something like that?' He said to himself.

As he read through the transcript, he discovered that for the four years that they were married, Barry Mason had mentally and physically abused Heather. The physical abuse included marital rape, which Heather had testified happened on a regular basis throughout their marriage, the baby's conception being the result of one such attack. Convinced that Heather was being unfaithful and that Malcolm was not his son, Mason had kept her a virtual prisoner, even when a DNA test confirmed that the baby was his, he accused her of sleeping with the person doing the test.

Heather eventually found the strength to leave him, taking Malcolm aged four months with her. Mason found them a week later in a local hotel, and after breaking down the door, he dragged her, still carrying the baby over to the railway station and up the bridge steps. Edward stopped reading and took a deep breath before reading on.

He then pried the baby from her arms and threw him off the bridge killing him instantly. He would have pushed Heather over too if a passer-by hadn't intervened. Edward closed the file and sat back in his chair, then picked up the phone and rang Steven to tell him what had happened.

'So that was her. I remember reading about the case,' he said in surprise. 'Anyway, the doctor says she's much better today and the brain scan was clear, so I'm going to see her after lunch,' he reported.

Jack drove up to the quarry gates an hour later; there was a jeep parked by the fence. A man got out as he pulled up. Jack showed him his warrant card. 'I'm Tim Atkinson. I used to be the foreman here,' the man said somewhat suspiciously. He got a bunch of keys out and selected one, then went to open the padlock.

'Wrong one,' he muttered, then frowned as he tried several others with the same result. 'This isn't our padlock,' he exclaimed as he turned it over and looked at the back.

'How long is it since you were last here?' Jack asked.

'It must be about three weeks. I come up once a month just to check around,' Tim explained, he put the keys away and pulled a pair of bolt cutters and a new padlock out of the back of the jeep. The gate swung open as he cut the lock off, and the two men went in.

The ground was muddy and wet; Jack crouched down to get a better look at what looked like fresh tyre tracks. 'Do you drive in when you come?' Tim shook his head.

'I just park out the front, check the gate is locked and then walk around the perimeter fence.' They walked over to the centre of the compound, Jack looked in the window of the first building which was the end cottage in a row of three, and along with the rest of the buildings was falling into disrepair. He gave the door a push, it opened with a groan, disturbing a mass of cobwebs, there was a thick layer of dust everywhere, including the floor.

'Well, it doesn't look like anyone has been in here for years,' he commented, as they moved onto the other cottages, none of which looked like they had been entered

They followed the tyre tracks around the back of the cottages until they reached several large sheds and a stone-built outhouse. 'What was kept in those?' Jack asked.

'Tools and trucks in the sheds, and the men's locker room showers and toilets were in that building,' Tim pointed to the outhouse. Jack studied the concentration of tyre tracks; they suggested that a vehicle or vehicles had been turned in front of the outhouse.

'Has anyone from your firm been up here?' Tim shook his head.

'No one is authorised to come here.'

Jack got his phone out to call the station. 'Can you leave me the key? We need to go over this area thoroughly.' Tim took several keys from his bunch and handed them over, then they walked back to the gate and shook hands before Tim drove away.

Jack got into the car and dialled Edward's number. 'We need to get forensics up here guv, there's been unauthorised activity,' he reported, and then sat back to wait.

Steven went into Heather's room later that afternoon. PC Higgins followed him in and stood by the window. Steven pulled up a chair and sat down next to the bed. The swelling on Heather's face had gone down, she some colour to her cheeks, and as he had observed on the quarry ledge, she was very pretty; something started to stir inside him as he watched her sleeping.

'I'll leave it until she wakes up,' he whispered.

'Doctor Cooper,' Higgins said quietly as Steven turned to leave, he nodded towards Heather. Steven turned back to see her watching them. His stomach did a little flip as he saw her eyes that were wide open for the first time, and were almost emerald green in colour.

'Sorry, I thought you were sleeping,' he said as he tried not to stare at her.

She gave him a small smile. 'My throat is sore; can I have a drink?' She whispered hoarsely.

'I'll ask the nurse,' Higgins volunteered, and left the room.

Steven sat down again. 'Do you remember me?'

'Steven?' Heather whispered. He smiled at her and nodded. 'You found me,' she said gratefully.

Steven shook his head. 'John Simmons found you, I came along later.' Heather frowned as the PC returned with a nurse; she sponged some water onto Heathers lips.

'Better?' The nurse asked. Heather licked the water from her lips and gave a small nod. 'The doctor says you may be able to take some fluids properly tomorrow,' the nurse said brightly. 'Have you got any pain?' She enquired.

'No,' Heather said quietly.

'Well, ring if you do and I'll give you something,' the nurse tidied the bed and smiled at Steven as she left the room.

Heather stared at Steven.

'Are you a policeman?'

He shook his head 'No, but I work with the police sometimes.'

She continued to stare at him; he stared back and saw her confusion as they locked eyes. 'So, what are you then?' She asked after a minute.

'I'm a sort of doctor,' he answered truthfully.

'A sort of doctor,' she repeated, and frowned again 'A psychiatrist or something? I don't need a psychiatrist,' she said firmly.

'It's ok. I'm not a psychiatrist,' he assured her. She gave him a disbelieving look and turned her head towards Higgins.

The PC nodded encouragingly. 'It's the truth,' he said earnestly.

Heather looked Steven again. 'Ok, I believe you.'

Steven smiled at her. 'Thanks. Can you remember what happened on Wednesday last week?'

'What day is it?' She interrupted.

'Tuesday, do you remember going out last Wednesday evening to take Harry for a walk?' Her eyes filled with tears, she blinked and they ran down her cheeks. Steven gently wiped them away. 'It's ok; I'll not ask anything else until you're feeling better.'

Heather swallowed nervously. 'Red hair,' she whispered. 'I remember red hair.'

Steven looked at Higgins. 'The man who attacked you had red hair, is that what you mean?' He checked.

'I don't know, I just remember red hair, and then my phone rang,' she started crying again.

'We'll leave it for now,' Steven said quietly. 'This could be a full-time job for me,' he chuckled as he wiped her eyes again. 'I'm sorry to upset you, but the more the police know the sooner they can get whoever did this.' She nodded miserably. 'If you want to talk to me, then just ask the nurses, they know where I am. Ok?' Steven checked.

'Ok,' she said quietly and closed her eyes again.

When Steven got outside, he called Edward to update him, and then made his way back to the mortuary and turned his attention to the paperwork from the day before, but he was unable to concentrate. His mind kept wandering back to Heather and how upset she was about the dog. They knew that he had died first; the evidence from the wound on her head had confirmed that, but why kill the dog? He couldn't identify anyone.

John Simmons said that Harry was devoted to her, and the more Steven thought about it, the more he knew that he had to look at his body. He pushed the paperwork to one side and called the VI centre. 'Sorry, they've all knocked off and the dogs in the freezer,' a voice told him.

He sighed in frustration and replaced the receiver, then picked it up again and called his father. 'I really think we need to examine the dog; can you authorise him to be brought over here? Meet me for a drink after work and I'll explain,' he added as an afterthought.

It was late afternoon before Edward arrived at the quarry. Jack was waiting for him along with half a dozen white suited members of the forensic team. Edward updated him what Heather had remembered. 'So, we need to look for her phone and men with red hair, assuming that she meant a man,' Jack deduced.

Edward nodded and looked around the yard. 'Is there anything interesting here?'

'Oh yes,' Jack said almost gleefully as he took him out to the perimeter fence; they walked around it until they were standing between the fence and the side of the quarry. Lumps of rock were scattered around, lying where they had fallen over the years. One of the white suits was scrapping mud into specimen pots.

'Blood and quite a lot of it, someone has tried to cover it up with the soil,' she said as they approached.

Edward looked up at the quarry. 'Where are we in relation to the path that Heather uses?' He asked.

'It's right above us,' Jack confirmed. Edward looked into the compound, from their position by the fence, there was a clear view of the sheds.

'I think that she saw something whilst she was up on the path, so she came down for a closer look and that's when they saw or heard her. She said that her phone rang and then the dog growled, but beyond that she can't remember,' he said a touch frustratedly.

The white suit had finished filling the pot. 'We'll get this sample back to the lab and test it against Ms Brooks and the dog,' she told them.

They looked up as a constable came over to the fence. 'Can you come to the outhouse?' He requested. They made their way back to the compound, a constable handed them a protective suit each and they went into the building, which apart from several pallets and a broken bench was empty. The policeman handed him a specimen bag. 'Fresh ciggie ends, Sir.'

Edward sniffed them and turned his nose up in disgust. 'Are they foreign?'

'Yes Sir,' the PC confirmed.

'We may get some DNA off them,' Jack said hopefully. 'And we've taken casts from the tyre tracks outside, so we should be able to get the make of vehicle from them.'

Edward thought for a minute 'check them against John Simmons van,' he said quietly.

'Hello! What have we got here?' one of the forensic team suddenly exclaimed. They went over to the area that had presumably been the showers; all that remained was the drainage channel. The technician was pulling something from between the planks of the broken bench. 'Ginger hair,' he said as he handed it over.

Chapter 6

Edward was already in the bar when Steven arrived. He ordered two pints and sat down next to him, then looked around the room. There were a couple of farming types wearing wellies and overalls and playing darts, and a group of girls sitting by the fire smoking, every few minutes high pitched giggling emerged from the smoky huddle. 'They don't look old enough to be in here or to be smoking,' Edward commented.

'They're probably not but you're off duty,' Steven pointed out.

'Pints here,' the barman shouted.

Edward collected them and took a long drink. 'That's better,' he sighed. 'So, what's on your mind son?'

'Heather is devastated about Harry, and John Simmons says that he was devoted to her,' Steven started. 'We know he was killed before Heather was attacked.'

'So you say,' Edward interrupted.

'So the evidence says,' Steven corrected, he sat forward. 'If Heather was being threatened, he might have gone to protect her, and that may be why he was killed.'

'That's very possible,' Edward conceded. He looked round as the pub door opened and a large crowd of youths came in. They both grimaced as the pitch of giggling coming from the girls increased tenfold, so they quickly finished their drinks and headed outside.

'Harry might have bitten whoever attacked her, and if he did there may be blood in his mouth, in which case we should be able to get a DNA profile from him, and we'll get the results faster if you get him over to me,' Steven explained.

'I'll call them first thing,' Edward promised. 'Is that it?' Steven nodded. 'You could have asked me that over the phone,' Edward pointed out.

Steven shrugged. 'I fancied a pint with my dad,' he chuckled as they parted company.

The next morning as promised, Edward rang the veterinary investigation centre and arranged for the dog's body to be taken over to the mortuary. Jack came in as he put the phone down. 'Well, I hope he's right, because at the moment we've drawn blank on everything,' Jack muttered when he told him Steven's thoughts 'Oh! No record for John Simmons by the way guv,' he said as he got up to leave.

'Well, it was just a thought, but he has got ginger hair,' Edward said thoughtfully.

'And he did seem very nervous, didn't he?' Jack added.

'He did,' Edward agreed. 'We'll ask him for a sample, if he doesn't make a fuss, then he's probably clean, we'd better get samples from all the ginger haired men in the area,' he mused.

'Just the men,' Jack checked. Edward nodded.

'Get Steven to go with you if he's got time,' he called as Jack went out.

Jack was back within minutes. 'The Chief Super wants to see you guv, and he said now.' Edward groaned inwardly and wondered what he had done to warrant being summoned to the inner sanctum. Chief Superintendent Whittle didn't often call him in, in fact beyond the weekly report meetings, he hardly saw him.

Not that he was bothered, because Whittle, a forty-three-year-old rather odd-looking man, with big ears that he tried to hide under his hair, and bulbous eyes that he tried to hide behind tinted glasses, was not well liked. Having risen to the rank of Chief Superintendent very quickly and without appearing to do any real police work to speak of; "Friends in high places" had been mentioned on more than one occasion.

Arrogant and egotistical were just a couple of the descriptions that Edward had heard in reference to him, and Edward could think of at least half a dozen more, but was far too polite to say them out loud. 'I'd better go then, hadn't I?' He said despondently. Jack grinned at him as he pretended to tremble.

'Come in Edward,' Whittle called when he knocked on his door a few minutes later. Edward went into the large bright office which looked out onto the neatly tended gardens at the front of the building; it was dominated by a huge ornate mahogany desk that made Whittle look like a dwarf when he sat behind it. 'Sit down, would you like some coffee?' He offered.

Edward shook his head as he sank into one of the large soft chairs. Whittle sat back and pushed his glasses onto the bridge of his thin pointed nose. 'So,

44

how's the Brook's case going, are there any new leads?' Edward watched the glasses slowly sliding back down his nose as brought him up to date.

'We are trying to find out what happened from Ms Brooks, but she's still very weak and obviously very scared.' Whittle nodded gravely, increasing the speed that the glasses slid.

'We need to clear this up quickly, the public are frightened,' he said authoritatively, by now the glasses had reached the end of his nose, he pushed them up again and continued. 'There's a maniac on the loose and we need to reassure them that they are safe.'

Edward let out a long sigh. 'I do realise that, and we are doing our best, but until we can speak to Ms Brooks at length, we really haven't got a lot to go on,' he reminded him dourly.

'Just a minute, Edward,' Whittle barked as got up to leave. Edward sat down again. Whittle looked at him over the top of the glasses, which had started to slip again. 'I hear that your son has been interviewing Ms Brooks, since when did the forensic department start talking to witnesses?' He asked semi-sarcastically.

Edward swore inwardly. 'Steven is just trying to keep her at ease; she seemed to take to him, so I thought that it would be nicer for her to chat to him informally, rather than having a load of policemen firing questions at her. There is a PC there when he talks to her; Sir,' he added as an afterthought.

Whittle gave him a despairing look. 'Well make sure that he knows the boundaries,' he ordered.

'Yes Sir, he does. Will that be all?' Edward asked hopefully, and started to get up again.

'Just one more thing,' Whittle said sharply. Edward sat down again.

'Yes, Sir,' he said impatiently.

Whittle glared at him and took a sheet of paper from the pile on his desk. 'Have you heard of a man called James Montgomery?'

Edward shook his head. 'No, should I have?'

Whittle looked stunned that he didn't know who he was. 'He owns a large number of shopping malls across Scotland,' he explained as if it would jog Edward's memory, and then frowned at his blank look. 'Last Wednesday he received a ransom demand for his wife, Rowena, along with what appeared to be most of the hair from her head.'

Edward looked at the fax that Whittle had handed to him. 'How does this affect us?'

Whittle ignored the question and continued. 'The ransom was for two million pounds, but the fact is, that when James Montgomery opened the package, Rowena Montgomery was sitting right next to him, with a full head of hair I should add,' he finished; then sat back and waited for Edward to comment.

Edward looked at the fax again. 'They got the wrong woman?' Whittle nodded. 'So why have they contacted us?'

Whittle got up and looked out of the window. 'No one fitting the description of Mrs Montgomery has been reported missing locally, so they have contacted all the other forces,' he explained.

'I'll get onto missing persons and see if anyone has been reported missing in the last ten days, what does this Rowena Montgomery look like?' Edward enquired.

Whittle looked over his shoulder at him. 'Strathclyde are e-mailing pictures over. I've given them your e-mail address, you will give them your full cooperation, won't you?' He raised his eyebrows.

'Of course I will,' Edward said scathingly. 'I just hope that whoever has got this woman, doesn't realise that she isn't Mrs Montgomery, or God knows what they will do.'

Whittle nodded. 'The Montgomery's have been placed in a safe house until it's over. They're waiting to be contacted again so the local force can try and set up an exchange.'

Edward rubbed his chin. 'If it's a week since they got the note, I would have thought they'd have been contacted by now, so it's possible that they realised they'd got the wrong woman soon after they snatched her,' he said thoughtfully.

'I agree,' Whittle said to Edward's complete amazement.

'So why did Strathclyde leave it so long?' Edward asked.

'Because they were checking for missing women in the local area first, and then across Scotland,' Whittle explained somewhat impatiently.

Edward got up again. 'Will that be all?' he enquired, and then gave a sigh of relief as Whittle dismissed him with his usual hand gesture.

After leaving Whittle's office he went to brief the rest of the team. 'Check my e-mails will you please Jack, see if the pictures have arrived yet.'

Jack leant over the computer. 'Nothing yet guv, do you want me to show you how to check them yourself?' He offered mischievously.

Edward ignored him and returned to the current case. 'So, how's it going tracing ginger haired men?'

Jack got his notebook out. 'There are only seven in Burney. I'm seeing four of them tomorrow morning and the other three, including John Simmons, in the evening when they get back from work. I'm meeting Steve in the incident room at ten for the first four, and six thirty for the rest,' he added anticipating the next question.

Edward nodded his thanks and went back to his office. He sat at his desk and stared into space until the phone rang. 'None of the carpets in Heather Brook's house are a match the fibres on her clothes,' the forensic department reported.

Jack stuck his head round the door a few minutes later. Edward beckoned him in and brought him up to date, then rang Steven to ask if the dog had arrived. 'He's on his way, but I'll have to wait for him to defrost before I can do anything,' his son informed him.

Edward put the phone down and redialled the hospital for an update on Heather. 'Sleeping but improving all the time,' the doctor reported to his relief.

WPC Blackwell was sitting behind the desk in the incident room. She looked up as a tall rugged looking man with sandy coloured hair came in. He gave her a smile and started reading the posters that were dotted about the walls. He was wearing khaki chinos coupled with a heavy corduroy jacket, and doc martin boots.

She eyed him up as he browsed, and immediately decided that he was just her type, after checking that he wasn't wearing a wedding ring, she flashed him her most alluring smile. 'Can I help you?' She asked, in what she hoped was her sexiest voice.

Steven showed her his identification. 'I'm waiting for Sergeant Taylor.' She smiled at him again as he sat down, he smiled back, then stretched his legs out and stared at the ceiling, seemingly deep in thought. The WPC continued to watch him, and wondered how she could incite conversation. A few minutes later, and conscious that she was staring at him, Steven glanced over.

'Would you like a coffee or something?' She looked him straight in the eye, a trick that usually worked, but apparently not today. She sighed disappointedly as he shook his head, then he got up as Jack came in. She watched closely as they shook hands.

'It's good to see you again,' Jack said genuinely. 'Shall we go?'

Steven nodded and glanced at her again as they went out. He got into the car and looked at the list of ginger haired men. 'We'll do Jim Davis in priory road first, shall we?' He suggested.

'A word of warning,' Jack said as they pulled away. Steven looked at him expecting it to be something to do with the case. 'Watch out for Tracey Blackwell,' Jack warned.

'Who's she?' Steven asked.

'The WPC in the incident room. I saw her eyeing you up, and if she's set her sights on you, then you'd better beware,' Jack said dryly, they looked back to see her watching them through the window. 'If she invites you to a party then don't go,' Jack advised. 'Her parties are legendary.'

'Really,' Steven said disinterestedly, he glanced back again as Jack nodded.

'She invites all the unattached men, boasts that she can have any of them she chooses, which she usually does, but not very discreetly, and then she gives them marks out of ten. Her nickname is trampoline Tracy, and the boss's son would be quite a conquest,' he said amusedly.

'Well, she won't be having me because I'm not interested,' Steven muttered.

'I'm glad to hear it,' Jack chuckled quietly.

It only took them a few minutes to get to the Davis's house. Jack showed the small grey-haired woman answered the door his identification. She invited them in and they went through to the dining room, where they were greeted by a man in his late fifties sitting in a wheelchair.

There's not much chance of him scrambling about in the quarry in the dark, Steven thought to himself. Nevertheless, he took a swab from his mouth and thanked him before moving on to the next one. Richard Hughes didn't seem to be the "bashing women on the head", type either, barely seventeen and just out of school, He was more interested in texting his girlfriend to tell her he was a suspect than opening his mouth for Steven.

'Those two can't be high on the list of suspects,' he commented as they drove away.

Jack shook his head despondently. 'No, but it's always worth checking.' Number three, a man called Mick Jarvis had forgotten.

'I'm so sorry, he's just nipped down the town for some washers. Do you want to come in and wait?' She asked nervously.

'No thank you,' Jack said curtly. 'I rang and checked that they all would be in this morning. We'll do Bob Lattimer and then come back,' he muttered angrily as they went down the drive. Bob Lattimer hadn't forgotten, and was more than willing to give a sample. He opened his mouth as wide as he could and tried to talk whilst Steven took the swab.

48

'I'm sorry Mr Lattimer, what did you say?' He asked.

'I said you can have a blood sample as well if you want.' He started to roll his sleeve up.

'That won't be necessary thank you,' Steven assured him. He put the sample in his case and got up to go.

'It was a terrible thing to happen,' Bob said insincerely.

'Yes, terrible,' Jack agreed. He looked at him suspiciously. 'Is there something you want to tell us Mr Lattimer?'

Lattimer thought for a minute and then shook his head. 'No, nothing at all,' he said slowly, and then smiled knowingly.

'What a prick' Jack commented as they made their way back to the Jarvis house.

Once he had dropped the samples off at the lab, Steven went over to the hospital to see Heather. 'Shall we see if she's up to talking?' He asked the policeman on guard. The PC nodded and followed him in. Heather was propped up sleeping.

Steven stood and looked at her for a few minutes. Her head was still heavily bandaged, but the drip was no longer attached and the bruising was fading. How the hell could anyone do that? He thought about both Barry Mason and whoever it was that had attacked her.

'It's rude to stare,' she said suddenly, she half opened her eyes and smiled at him.

'Sorry, I thought you were asleep,' he apologised. 'How do you feel today? Are you up to talking?'

She nodded slowly. 'I feel much better thank you.'

Steven sat down next to the bed and smiled at her concernedly. 'You said the other day that you remembered red hair, can you remember anything else about the person with the red hair?'

She shook her head. 'It's all very muddled, my phone rang and then Harry growled,' she stopped talking and wiped a tear away. 'Where is Harry?'

'He's with us,' Steven told her gently. 'Do you know if he bit whoever did this to you?' She stared at him, her face set in concentration. He looked into her tear-filled eyes, and could see that she was struggling to remember.

'It's ok, it will all come back,' he assured her. 'You said that your phone rang, do you know what happened to it? We haven't found it.'

'It was in my pocket with Harry's lead. I took it out when it rang,' she remembered.

'We haven't found his lead either, and he didn't have a collar on, did he always wear a collar?'

She looked puzzled. 'Yes, he did, his name and my phone number are engraved on a plate next to the buckle. What are you going to do with him?' She asked miserably.

'Well, if he did bite whoever did this to you, then we may be able to get a sample from his mouth, so he will stay in the lab until I've finished testing him.'

Heather raised her eyebrows. 'The lab?'

Steven nodded lightly. 'The forensics lab.' She looked at him enquiringly, but he didn't feel brave enough to tell her what he did for a living, and so didn't elaborate.

'Keep him until I'm better will you?' She begged. 'So that I can bury him.'

He nodded again. 'Is there any one I can call for you?'

'No thank you,' she said unconvincingly.

'Are you sure?' He checked. 'Any family or a friend perhaps?' He tried.

'Yes, I'm sure,' she answered firmly. 'Pat's been in, thanks anyway.'

Steven got up, convinced that she was holding something back. 'I'll leave you to rest, but if you do remember anything else, there will be a PC outside the door, just tell him, ok?'

'Ok,' she said quietly. 'Can I ask you something now?' She asked as he turned to go. Steven looked back. 'You and the other policeman, you're related, aren't you?'

Steven nodded. 'He's my dad,' he chuckled.

Heather smiled at him. 'I thought so, you look very alike.'

Steven rolled his eyes in mock horror. 'Yes, we do,' he opened the door as a nurse came in with a tray.

'Lunchtime,' she said cheerfully. Heather looked at the plate of mush and turned her nose up. The nurse smiled at Steven. 'Is your saviour going to help you with your lunch?' She asked.

'What do you mean? I thought John found me,' Heather said in surprise.

The nurse bit her lip. 'I'd better get on; you eat up now,' she ordered, and bustled out blushing slightly.

'What did she mean?' Heather demanded.

'I'll tell you when you are stronger,' Steven promised. 'But it was John Simmons who found you,' he smiled at her and then looked at his watch. 'I'd better get going, can I bring you anything?'

Heather eyed the plate of food suspiciously. 'Something decent to eat,' she said hopefully. 'And maybe something to listen too.' Steven laughed at the look of disgust on her face.

'What do you fancy?' He waited as she thought for a minute.

'Do you know what I would really like?' He shook his head. 'Macaroni cheese,' she said longingly.

'Well as it happens, I'm a dab hand at macaroni cheese,' he said not untruthfully. 'I'll knock a pot up tonight and drop some in tomorrow?' He opened the door again. 'Oh! And music?' He looked back enquiringly.

'Anything with a bit of oomph, there's a serious lack of oomph on hospital radio,' she said ruefully.

'I'll see what I can do,' he promised, then left her contemplating the mush and went back to the mortuary.

Chapter 7

Unable to stall the press any longer, Edward had issued a short statement; he didn't give too many details; merely that a woman had been found badly injured at the quarry and was recovering in Kimberwick hospital. He had just put the phone down when Jack stuck his head round the door. 'Pat Richardson's been on the phone, guv, she says that there has been a man sitting in a car outside Heather's house for most of the day and she's scared to go out.'

Edward got up. 'Well let's go and see who the mystery man is then, unmarked car though we don't want to scare him off.' They turned into green lane half an hour later; there was a maroon escort parked opposite Heather's house. After noting the registration number, they knocked on Pat's door.

'That's him; he's been there for hours. He rang the bell and looked through the windows, then he just sat there,' she told them nervously.

'You go in and lock the door,' Jack ordered. They waited until they heard the chain going on, and then went over to the car. Edward tapped on the driver's window; he displayed his warrant card as it was opened.

'Can you tell me what you are doing here Sir?' Edward asked the middle-aged man who looked out at them.

'Waiting for someone, is there a law against it?' the man counter asked.

'Not at all,' Edward assured him. 'Can you tell me your name please Sir?'

The man glanced around anxiously. 'Have I done something wrong?'

Jack was starting to get cross. 'Can you tell us your name please Sir? And then tell us who you are waiting for and why?' He said forcefully.

'My name is Malcolm Brooks and I am waiting for my daughter, Heather,' he snapped.

They sat in an interview room an hour later. Malcolm's face crumpled as Edward gently told him what had happened. 'She said she was safe here, she said that no one knew her. I knew they would find her,' he whispered, and started to sob.

'Are you talking about her ex-husband's family?' Jack asked.

Malcolm nodded and clenched his fists. 'Do you know about him? Is that bastard out?' He demanded.

'No Mr Brooks. Barry Mason is still in the psychiatric hospital,' Edward assured him.

Malcolm's face relaxed slightly. 'Can I go and see her now?'

Edward motioned to the constable by the door. 'Arrange a lift for Mr Brooks to the hospital,' he said quietly. He studied the Malcolm's distraught face; he looked older than his fifty-two years, and very tired. 'What can you tell me about Heather?'

Malcolm smiled sadly. 'She used to be so alive, so happy. She loved to go dancing with her friends; she had a lot of friends, but he turned her into a recluse,' he said bitterly. 'She hardly ever left the house, not even to see us, and she had such a bad time when Baby Malcolm was born, then he went and,' he stopped talking as a tear ran down his face.

'How did Heather cope after the baby died?' Edward asked.

Malcolm looked up sharply. 'She watched that monster kill her child, how the hell do you think she coped, Inspector?' He snapped sarcastically; then almost immediately his expression softened. 'I'm sorry,' he muttered.

'It's alright,' Edward reassured him. 'What I meant was did Heather receive counselling?'

Malcolm shook his head. 'She wouldn't talk about the actual, well you know,' he nodded, unable to bring himself to say it. 'She said that she didn't need some shrink telling her how to grieve.'

Edward backtracked slightly. 'What did you mean about her having a bad time when Baby Malcolm was born?'

Malcolm started crying again. 'She had to have an emergency caesarean section. She was in intensive care for nearly a week, all that and now this happens,' he sobbed.

By now, Edward was feeling desperately sorry for the distraught man sitting in front of him; he tried to imagine what he had been through. 'After she moved away did you speak to or see her often?'

Malcolm wiped his eyes. 'She rang us every other evening at six thirty from her mobile phone, she brought one of those pay and go ones, she said the landline could be traced so she rang us when she was out with Harry,' he said tearfully.

'Did she always ring from the quarry?' Edward checked.

Malcolm nodded. 'She said it was the best place for a signal.'

'What if you needed to contact her?' Jack asked.

'We would send her a text message and she rang us back as soon as she could, sometimes we would meet up in Kimberwick for lunch. We live in Bishops Glen.'

Edward raised his eyebrows. 'You said we?'

'My wife, Patricia,' Malcolm explained.

'And where is she?' Jack asked.

Malcolm started to cry again. 'She died of cancer seven months ago. Heather came to the funeral. I didn't think she would, but she wanted to say goodbye.' Edward remembered the report about her hiring a car and nodded.

'When did you last speak to her?'

'Last Monday week, she rang at six thirty as usual, but when she hadn't rung by ten to seven on the Wednesday, I tried to ring her, but after a couple of rings it went dead, and I've not heard from her since. I've been trying to ring her all week but it just goes dead.'

So now we know approximately what time she was attacked Edward thought, but decided not tell Malcolm that it may have been his call that caused her attacker to strike. 'Thank you Mr Brooks. Can you write Heather's mobile phone number down before you go, and then there's a car waiting out the front to take you over to the hospital.' Malcolm scribbled a number on the offered notebook, and followed the PC out to the car.

'Is the dog defrosted?' Steven asked Charlie. 'Bring him in then, let's see if he can help,' he said as Charlie nodded confirmation. Judy appeared at the door as he started putting his overalls on. 'I'm going now. It's my afternoon off,' she reminded them,

'So you'll have to answer the phone yourselves,' Charlie winked at her. 'Part timer,' he teased. Steven suddenly remembered macaroni cheese.

'Hang on a minute, can you do me a favour?' He called as she started to leave. Judy turned back.

'What?' She asked suspiciously.

'If you're in town, can you pick me up a couple of those fat flasks, the ones with the wide tops that you can put food in?'

'Fat food flasks?' She said amusedly.

Steven nodded. 'There's some money in the wallet on my desk.'

'I'll have a look around,' she promised, and went off, chuckling to herself.

'Did I say something funny?' Steven enquired.

Charlie shook his head. 'Not a thing boss! Now shall we see what the dog has to say?' He asked brightly.

Steven felt a twinge of sadness as they stood over Harry. He died trying to protect her he thought as he inspected the wound. Charlie held the dog's mouth open whilst he took swabs from his teeth and tongue. 'Look at the size of those canines. If he did bite the attacker then I bet it hurt,' Steven commented.

'Are you done boss?' Charlie asked.

Steven took a small torch from the trolley. 'I'll just have a look down his throat.' He shone the light into the dog's mouth; as he moved his tongue from side to side, he caught sight of something hooked on the molars, he delved right to the back with a pair of long tweezers and pulled a strand of thread.

'It's cotton of some sort,' he said as he inspected it. Charlie gathered up all the samples and took them to a waiting technician. 'Hang on a minute,' Steven called, as having parted the hair on Harry's back he found some fibres.

'They could be carpet fibres, like the ones we found on Heather's coat.' He plucked them out and handed them over. 'Quick as you can please,' he requested.

'Shall I take the dog to the incinerator now?' Charlie enquired.

Steven shook his head. 'Put him back in the freezer for now.'

Charlie looked surprised. 'Do you think we may need him again?'

Steven shook his head again, and told him what Heather had requested. 'There's no need to tell anyone, just put him in number ten and forget about him,' he instructed.

Jack stamped his feet as he waited outside the incident room, the ground was already frozen and it promised to be a cold night. 'Shall we do Jim Cookson first?' he suggested when Steven arrived. Mr Cookson gave the sample and they moved on to John Simmons house; where they were greeted by Chester who jumped up at Steven wagging his stumpy tail furiously.

'Come on in,' John's wife invited. 'You'll have to excuse the mess we're having hardwood flooring put down,' she explained as they picked their way over the panelling and tools. They followed her into the kitchen where John was eating his tea.

'How is Heather?' He asked.

'Much better but still poorly,' Jack told him as Steven took the swab. 'Richard Green and then home for tea,' he said as they made their way down the path. Richard Green lived right at the other end of the town in one of the bigger houses; they were greeted by four rowdy children, all boys, and all with ginger hair and freckles.

'You've got your hands full,' Steven commented to Mrs Green, as she tried to grab the smallest boy.

'you're telling me,' she panted. Steven caught the child as he ran past and handed him to her. 'Thanks,' she said gratefully. 'I just hope the next one is a girl.'

'When's the next one due?' Jack asked, as Mr Green watched his wife disappear up the stairs with the wriggling boy under her arm.

'Three months,' he looked heavenwards. 'I've told her four is enough, but she's determined to keep going until she has a girl,' he said ruefully.

As Steven drove home, his mind wandered back to John Simmons. There was something amiss there, he didn't trust him or his wife for that matter, but he couldn't put his finger on why. He glanced at the clock; it was nearly eight o clock. He yawned loudly and then remembered that he still had macaroni cheese to make.

There was a parcel on the doorstep when he got home, he opened the bag and found two flasks "Happy cooking Gordon Ramsey! Hope they are fat enough", it said on the note. 'Good old Judy,' he chuckled as he went inside.

Heather's father was sitting by her bed when Edward arrived at the hospital the next day. 'How you do feel?' he asked her.

'Much better thanks,' she squeezed her father's hand.

'I need to ask you a few questions about Barry Mason's family; do you think you can manage that?' Edward asked, she glanced at her father and bit her lip. 'We need to find out if they had anything to do with what happened to you,' he explained gently.

'What do you need to know?' She asked nervously.

Edward got his notebook out. 'Everything you can remember.'

Heather continued to hold her father's hand tightly as she recalled that Barry had a brother and a sister. She hadn't been particularly close to either of them, but when she was pregnant with Malcolm, his sister Diane, had come to the house nearly every day. She still came round occasionally after he was born, but she seemed indifferent to her and the baby, and more interested in chatting to Barry.

Charlie, his brother, was away a lot working, or so he said, but he never seemed to have any money, and when he did come round, it was to ask for a loan or to stay over for a few days. 'What does he do for a living?' Edward interrupted.

'I don't really know,' she admitted. 'I think he has a mate who he helps out.'

Edward raised his eyebrows. 'Do you know the name of this mate?'

She shook her head. 'I was never introduced; he used to wait outside in the van,' she glanced at her father again.

'You're doing really well,' Edward told her and encouraged her to continue.

'After we got married, we moved in with Barry's mother, Alice, she had arthritis and I used to help her get washed and dressed. She was lovely; we used to chat for hours,' she smiled as she remembered. 'She was so excited about the baby,' she said sadly.

'Is she still alive?' Edward asked.

'I don't know; they put her in a home two months after I came out of hospital and I didn't see her again.' Her eyes filled with tears.

'What about their father?'

Heather gave a light shrug. 'Apparently he disappeared when the three of them were small, they never talked about him.'

Edward sighed inwardly. 'Have you seen or heard from any of them since the trial?' He asked tentatively.

She tightened the grip on her father's hand. 'No, the last I saw or heard from any of them was on the day of the verdict. Barry yelled that he was going to make me pay, that's why I moved here so no one would know me. Dad and mum moved as well just to be sure,' she stopped talking as Steven came into the room.

'Sorry is this a bad time? I'll come back later,' he said quietly.

'No, it's ok,' Edward assured him as he introduced Heather's father.

'I hear from Chief Inspector Cooper that I have you to thank for saving my daughter's life,' Malcolm said as they shook hands. Steven went red and glanced at Heather; she was staring at him in bewilderment.

'What are you talking about?' She demanded, directing the question at Steven.

'I'll let your dad tell you. I've just come to drop off macaroni cheese and music as promised.' He put the flask on the cabinet along with his CD Walkman and a selection of discs. 'I hope they've got enough oomph for you,' he said quietly.

'And I'm glad that you're feeling better. I'll look in this evening and you can give me your verdict.' Edward followed him as he turned to go. 'I'll come with you; I need a word. Oh! One last thing,' he said to Heather. 'Does John Simmons always walk his dog on the quarry in the mornings?'

She nodded. 'Yes, most mornings. He goes up the path next to my house.'

Edward smiled at her. 'Thanks. If you remember anything else just tell the PC on the door.

'How did it go with the dog?' He asked Steven once they got outside.

'I got swabs from all of his teeth and a piece of cotton out of his mouth. I also found some fibres in his coat which could have come from a carpet. We should have some results on Monday,' his son reported.

Later that afternoon, one of the Detective Constables knocked on Edward's door. 'I'm sorry to disturb you, Sir, but Vicky Morris has been on the phone, she works with Heather Brooks,' the constable reminded him. 'She says she's sorry but she gave Heather's name to a reporter, he was in the post office yesterday morning asking questions about the injured woman.'

'Oh well, I suppose she would have been identified eventually,' Edward sighed. 'Is there something else?' he asked as the constable hovered by the door.

'Yes Sir, the photograph of Rowena Montgomery has come through at last.'

He put the photograph on the desk and went out. Edward picked it up and stared at the picture of a woman who was smiling into the camera. She was good looking and smartly dressed, but the thing that stood out dramatically was her full head of long red hair. He went into the squad room. 'Where's Jack?' He asked no one in particular.

'Over at the incident room; apparently a woman said there was a strange man in the butchers last week and I think he went to follow it up,' someone answered.

'Ask him to see me as soon as he gets in please,' he ordered. He went back to his office and looked at the picture again. 'Red hair,' he muttered to himself. 'Heather said "I remember red hair". Red hair in the picture and red hair at the quarry,' he put his hands over his face and yawned.

Jack appeared in the doorway a few minutes later. 'Late night guv.' Edward shook his head and handed him the picture. 'Red hair,' Jack exclaimed. 'We need to get in touch with Strathclyde and get a sample of the hair that came with the ransom note that was sent to James Montgomery,' he said before Edward could speak.

Edward nodded confirmation. 'I'll get onto them,' Jack offered and started to leave.

'Hang on Jack,' Edward called. 'Can you check if Charlie Mason has got form?' Jack nodded and went out. 'Oh! And Jack,' Edward called. Jack stuck his head around the door. 'Did you find the strange man in the butchers?'

'New delivery man,' the sergeant said dryly.

A couple of hours later, they discovered that Charlie Mason did indeed have a record. 'G.B.H and aggravated burglary; he looks a bit of a thug, but there's been no arrests for six years, so maybe he's a reformed character,' Jack mused.

'Or maybe he just hasn't been caught again,' Edward said wryly. He looked at the time and yawned loudly. 'I'm off home; do you fancy a quick pint?'

Jack nodded. 'Just one though or the wife will be after me,' he said despondently.

'Edward!' A voice called as they made their way across the car park. They looked round and saw Whittle approaching at top speed.

'Christ! What does he want?' Edward muttered under his breath. 'Yes Sir,' he said, trying to look pleased to see him.

Whittle smiled at them. 'Off home?'

'Yes Sir,' Edward confirmed.

'How's the case going?' The Chief Superintendent asked. Edward groaned inwardly and brought him up to date. 'Good. Well, we need to get this cleared up pronto,' Whittle said pompously. 'I've got the press clamouring for information and people are scared, they need to feel safe.'

'Yes Sir. We know,' Edward interrupted.

Whittle looked at them expectantly for a minute. 'I'll let you get home then,' he said generously; then turned on his heel and strutted off across the car park.

'All he needs is a few feathers and a wattle,' Jack observed amusedly.

'So, what's the verdict?' Steven asked Heather that evening. 'That all depends on whether you mean the macaroni cheese, your rather eclectic taste in music, or the fact that you saved my life,' she gave him a grateful smile, the tears in her eyes making them shine.

'The macaroni cheese of course,' he said brightly. 'It was the doctors who saved your life.'

Heather shook her head. 'Dad told me, you're a pathologist and you were there because they thought I was dead.' She stared at his hands as he sat down. 'But you found my pulse,' she looked up and gave a resigned smile. 'If I had been dead, would you have had to cut me up?'

Steven gave a light nod. 'So you would have touched parts of me that no one else had ever touched.'

Steven had never thought about it like that before. He looked into her serious face and nodded again. 'But you weren't dead, so how was the macaroni cheese?'

'You're changing the subject,' she accused.

'Yes, I am,' he confirmed.

'It was delicious, the best I've ever had,' she said quietly.

'Good. Then it was worth the effort, and as for my eclectic taste in music,' he smiled at her and gave a light shrug. 'I don't like to be pigeon holed.'

She smiled back at him. 'No, me neither, but you don't look like a Westlife kind of guy.' She raised her eyebrows in amusement and held up a CD.

'It belonged to a,' he was going to say Amy but stopped himself. 'A friend,' he gave her a wry smile.

'doesn't your friend want it back?' She asked.

'Actually, were not friends anymore and I thought you may be a fan,' he looked away as he felt a sudden urge to lean over and kiss her, and saw a pile of cards on the cabinet. 'Do you want me to help you open them? It must be difficult with one hand.' He opened the first one and handed it to her as she nodded her thanks.

'It's from Pat and Jim next door,' she exclaimed, and then smiled at him as he passed her the next one. He opened another one as she read it; then quickly put it back in the envelope and slipped it into his pocket. Heather was still reading the previous card.

'Who's that one from?' He asked.

'It's from Vicky at work, and a lot of the customers have signed it too.' He opened the next one and quickly checked the front before handing it over.

'It's from John and Lottie Simmons. I must thank him for finding me,' she said quietly. Steven passed her the last two cards and then looked at the time.

'I've got to get going,' he got up and arranged the cards on the windowsill.

'Will you come back tomorrow?' She asked. He nodded enthusiastically, just try and stop me, he thought as she gave him a smile that made his pulse quicken. 'Bring more macaroni cheese with you please.'

He gave a small salute and picked the empty flask up. 'Bye then,' he said quietly. He looked back as he shut the door; she had closed her eyes. As he watched, a tear ran down her cheek. He fought the temptation to go back and comfort her and instead turned away and took the card out of his pocket.

Lilies entwined around a cross adorned the front. "With sympathy", was picked out in silver, and on the inside, someone had written, "With regret that you didn't get to be with your bastard son, better luck next time". He sat down and showed it to the PC. 'Who on earth would send something like that?' The constable asked in shock.

Steven shook his head. 'I don't know, but thank God she didn't see it.' He looked up as Edward appeared next to him.

'Didn't see what?' Steven gave him the card. 'Bloody hell,' he exclaimed. 'Is the post mark legible?'

Steven looked at the smudged stamp. 'I'll take it over to the lab and get it under the scope.'

Edward looked through the window at Heather sleeping. 'I'll come with you. I was going to talk to her, but I think I'll come back tomorrow,' he said thoughtfully.

Twenty minutes later, they had the envelope under the microscope. Steven looked up from the magnifier. 'Chipping Norton,' he transferred the image to the monitor and enhanced it, which revealed that it had been posted first class the previous afternoon.

'The day the story was printed,' Edward observed. 'I'll get onto the boys at Chipping and ask them to check out Barry Mason and the rest of his family. His brother Charlie has a record so they'll probably start with him.'

When Edward had gone, Steven called Charlie into the lab. 'Can you take this up to Sue and ask her if she can get anything from the stamp or the envelope.' But before Charlie could leave Sue came in, Steven handed her the envelope.

'I came to tell you that I've finished looking at the hair from the quarry,' she gave him the print out of results.

'Dyed red?' He said in surprise.

'The natural colour is dark blond and it's definitely female, the blood they found by the quarry fence was from Heather Brooks and the dog, and as it's gone seven, I'm going home.'

'Anything on the cigarette ends?' He asked as she started to leave.

'Not yet we're still working on them.' She hovered in the doorway as he thought for a minute.

'Has the hair sample from Strathclyde arrived?' She shook her head, and then left before he could ask anything else. Steven called Edward who had only got as far as the car park; he updated him and then decided to take Sue's lead and went home himself.

Later, as he lay in the bath, his thoughts turned back to Heather, he couldn't seem to get her out of his head; leaving her crying was a cruel thing to do. He sighed heavily as he recalled her tears, and then glanced at the clock. 'Half eight; what do you think Mont, is it too late to go over?' He asked the cat, who was sitting on the toilet seat watching him.

The cat ignored him, then stuck his leg in the air and proceeded to wash himself. 'Fat lot of good you are,' Steven muttered. He lay there for a few minutes longer and argued with himself that it probably was too late, but then decided to go anyway. The cat followed him as he ran down the stairs. He gave Steven a disdainful look as he put his jacket on, then settled down on the couch and went to sleep.

The PC outside Heathers door stood up as Steven approached. 'Good evening Dr Cooper, do you need me in there?'

Steven shook his head. 'It's just a quick social visit I'll not be long.' The policeman sat down again as he opened the door and went in. Heather was lying down; the small night light over the bed was on, casting a shadow.

'Who is it?' She asked nervously as he approached the bed.

'It's only me, I've just come to see if you're alright,' he whispered. He put the head rest up and arranged the pillows, then helped her to sit up. 'Sorry if I disturbed you, I thought you might need some company.'

She looked at the clock. 'It's nine fifteen are you still at work?' Then she noticed his wet hair. 'Is it raining?'

He shook his head. 'No on both counts. I've been home and had a bath; I thought I'd pop back and see if you needed anything.' She stared at him thoughtfully. 'You're not going to say macaroni cheese are you,' he laughed.

'No, but a bath sounds great,' she said longingly. 'Which is out of the question until I get this off,' she pointed to the plaster. 'So I'd like a mirror instead.'

'A mirror?' He queried.

She nodded seriously. 'They haven't let me look at myself, do I look that bad?' He studied her face and smiled, the bruising had almost disappeared and the cuts were healing. 'Not too bad, but you did have some nasty wounds.'

'They're going to take the bandages off on Monday, and I want to see before they come off,' she insisted.

Steven went and spoke to the nurse at the desk, who produced a hand mirror from a drawer. 'Are you sure you want to look?' He checked when he went back in. Heather took a deep breath and nodded. He held the mirror up in front of her and watched her looking at herself. She put her hand up to her head and felt the hair that was sticking out from the sides of the bandage.

'Did they shave my hair off?'

Steven nodded. 'They had to take some off to get at the wound, but don't worry it will grow back in no time once the bandages are off.' He put the mirror down. 'You see, you don't look that bad do you?' He said brightly.

'I suppose not,' she conceded. They locked eyes for a second and then Steven glanced at the clock.

'I suppose I'd better go,' he said unenthusiastically.

'Is there someone waiting for you at home?' Heather asked.

'Just Monty and he's asleep on the couch,' he chuckled.

'Monty! Oh sorry, I didn't realise,' she muttered.

'Realise what?' He asked.

Heather turned away. 'Nothing,' she mumbled embarrassedly.

It suddenly dawned on him what she was thinking. 'Monty is a cat,' he laughed as she went red.

'Sorry, I thought with the Westlife CD. Sorry,' she said again.

He gave her an affectionate look. 'Don't apologise, and there's no one human waiting at home, the CD belonged to my ex-fiancé.' He found himself telling her about Amy and Martin.

'So, you ran away too like me,' she said when he had finished.

'I suppose I did,' he said resignedly, and then realised that he had talked about them without getting angry. They carried on chatting for a while; Heather glanced constantly at the photograph of her and the baby as they talked.

'Barry was really nice before we got married, but afterwards he changed. I couldn't even look at someone without him accusing me of being unfaithful. I thought it would be different when I got pregnant but he got worse,' she looked at the photograph again and suddenly burst into tears. 'That's the only one I've got left; he destroyed them all.'

Steven took her hand and found it was shaking. 'You have your memories and they can't be destroyed,' he said gently.

She nodded miserably. 'I know, but I can't bear the thought that he died like that. I should have protected him, that's what mothers are supposed to do, isn't it?' She sobbed. She looked at him in despair with tears streaming down her face.

He moved from the chair to the edge of the bed and put his arms around her. Her voice came in convulsive gasps as she buried her face in his chest and clung to him. 'I wish I had died, then at least I'd be with him.'

Steven felt tears pricking his own eyes; he blinked them away and rubbed her back. 'It wasn't your fault,' he whispered.

'Of course it was my fault. I married him, didn't I?' She sobbed. He sighed quietly, and unable to think of anything to say that might comfort her. He continued holding her tightly as she shook with grief.

It was several minutes before she stopped crying. 'I'm sorry; you don't want to know all this.' She looked up at him through swollen red eyes and tried to smile.

'Don't apologise,' he said gently. 'It must have been terrible. I can't imagine what you've been through,' he pulled a tissue from the box on the side and gave it to her.

'I think about him every day,' she said as she wiped her eyes. 'Harry was a kind of substitute, and now he's gone too.' She looked so vulnerable that his heart pounded with the sorrow that he was feeling for her.

'You don't have to cope with all this on your own, do you want me to arrange for someone to come and talk to you?' He asked, thinking that maybe Judy could help.

'No,' she said firmly. 'Thanks anyway,' she looked at his chest and gave a tearful laugh. 'I've wet your shirt.'

He looked down. 'Well, I've had worse things than tears down my shirt,' he chuckled. They stared at each other for a minute; then he glanced at the clock again. 'It's nearly midnight; I'd really better go before I get thrown out; will you be alright?'

She gave a light nod. 'Thanks for coming, it's been nice to talk normally without having questions fired at me.'

'You're welcome. It was nice to have a captive audience,' he joked.

'Go on, go home to your cat,' she ordered amusedly. 'But come back soon, won't you.'

Steven nodded enthusiastically 'As soon as I can,' he promised.

The PC gave him a half smile as he closed the door. 'Goodnight Dr Cooper,' he said quietly.

Chapter 8

The weekend was quickly upon them, and Steven arrived at his father's house on Saturday morning having arranged collect the carpet, he let himself in to find the house silent. 'Dad,' he called as he went into the kitchen, but there was no answer. There was a box on the table, the packaging had been ripped off and was scattered around. Steven smiled to himself and went through the integral door to the garage.

As suspected, his father was on his back underneath the car, a classic Morgan that he had been restoring for the last three years, and waiting for a certain part for nearly as long. 'The part came then?' He said brightly. Edward pulled himself out, his satisfied grin telling Steven that he was right in the assumption. 'It's about time, how much longer before you can take it for a spin?' He asked.

'Not it! Her,' Edward corrected.

Steven looked into the half-built engine. 'Not for a while then,' he surmised.

'Parts are expensive, I get what I can when I can,' Edward said disdainfully. They gave the car one last look and went back into the house. 'Do you fancy a quick pint before carpet laying and lunch?' Edward suggested hopefully. As it was, they stayed well beyond lunch time, and it was mid-afternoon before they finally managed to get the carpet out of the attic and over to the farm, having come from a large room it had to be cut to size before being laid.

Steven looked at it and frowned. 'I think you'd better cut it. I'm no good at angles,' Edward gave him a despairing look and got the Stanley knife out.

They inspected their handiwork two hours later. 'Not bad for a couple of amateurs,' Steven congratulated.

'You speak for yourself,' Edward scolded, and then looked at the time. 'I'd better get going.' Steven leant on the porch door and watched him drive away, then before he could stop himself his mind wandered back to Heather.

It pelted down for most of the day on Sunday, despite the weather, Steven spent a good hour or two exploring the moors on his bike. He called out of courtesy on his closest neighbour, Bob Jackson as he passed, and found him drinking heavily. 'She's gone,' Bob said miserably, referring to his wife.

Steven declined his offer of a drink, and realised that if he had married Amy, he could have ended up the same way, so he kept the visit brief and continued his ride. He stopped at the top of a rise to catch his breath a while later, he had been riding for a good forty-five minutes, and although the rain was almost horizontal, his cottage was still visible in the distance.

As he looked, he spotted something moving across the dead bracken; he pulled a pair of binoculars from the rucksack on his back, and almost immediately focused on Monty, who was slowly picking his way towards him, shaking the water from each of his feet as he lifted them. 'What the hell is he doing out in this?' Steven muttered as he freewheeled back down the slope.

An hour later they were both back in the dry. They sat in front of the fire wrapped in towels, and Steven's thoughts turned to the case, and in particular what Heather had been through. 'You'd like her,' he said absentmindedly as he stroked Monty. 'Maybe I'll introduce her to you when she's better.' He suddenly realised what he was thinking and shook his head. 'Don't even think about going there,' he told himself firmly.

'Who's first?' He asked Charlie the next morning, and then yawned loudly.

'Busy weekend boss?' Charlie enquired, he looked at the day's list. 'There's an old boy who was found at the back of Kimberwick cinema. He came in last night, and the family of an overdose victim have requested a second opinion, she's been sent through from York,' he looked up, and grinned at him. 'Apart from that, there's only the paperwork on your desk, so you might have time for a kip later,' he added cheekily.

'Maybe, but we'll get the old boy sorted out first,' Steven chuckled.

Whenever an unidentified body arrived at the mortuary, Steven always picked a working name to give them a bit of dignity. Bearded and dirty, the old man looked like he'd been living on the streets for years. 'Shall we call him Sid?' Steven suggested.

It didn't take them long to discover that Sid had died from liver failure. 'Hardly surprising,' Steven muttered as he examined the spongy mass that used to be his liver. 'I wonder if anyone cares?' He said sombrely.

'Probably not boss,' Charlie conceded. What a sad way to end up, Steven thought as they returned him to the chiller.

The woman who had apparently overdosed was called Karen Sharp, and she turned out to be a bit more complicated than they first thought. There was no doubt that the cause of death was a heroin overdose, but the toxicology showed a small amount cocaine was also present. There was bruising on her wrists, a large oval shaped bruise in the middle of her chest, and finger bruising on either side of her face.

'It looks like she was held down,' Steven observed. He lowered the table and leant over Karen's body, then he held her arms above her head and brought his knee up over the bruise on her chest. Charlie placed his hands either side of her face with his fingers covering the bruises.

'Well, the bruise is the right sort of shape,' Charlie observed. Steven checked Karen thoroughly for needle marks, and was surprised to find only one puncture wound on her entire body. After comparing the colouring of the bruises to the date that she had been found, he concluded that the bruising had been made before the heroin had been injected, and the heroin had been injected not long before death.

There was a roughly sewn up wound where her heart had been examined, but other than that she was scar free. 'So, it was a selective post-mortem,' he said thoughtfully. 'I wonder why none of her other organs have been looked at? What did the first pathologist say?'

Charlie scanned down the report. Cause of death, heroin overdose.'

'No mention of the bruises?' Steven asked in surprise.

Charlie shook his head. 'Nothing significant, he's put them down to over enthusiastic sex, which she apparently had just before she died.'

Steven sighed in exasperation. 'Who was the pathologist?'

Charlie looked at the signature and raised his eyebrows. 'Professor Murdoch no less,' he said dryly.

'Jesus Christ! Not Bernard Murdoch over in York,' Steven muttered.

Charlie nodded. 'Do you know him?'

Unfortunately, Steven did know him. So, he's a professor now is he? I wonder how he managed to wangle that, he thought. 'Yes, I know him,' he said dryly. 'Did he take vaginal swabs, stomach contents or urine samples?'

Charlie shook his head. Steven took the report and read through it. 'Right, we will do a full post-mortem. Swabs, toxicology, stomach contents and urine, the whole damn lot,' he said through gritted teeth. An hour later the samples were on their way up to the forensics lab. Apart from her heart, all of Karen's other organs were normal.

'So much for being an addict,' Charlie muttered.

'Shit! She was pregnant,' Steven said quietly as he checked her womb. 'Christ almighty! What a bloody waste,' he took a deep breath as he removed the foetus. 'Get this up to Sue please, age, sex and toxicology,' he started to close her up as Charlie disappeared upstairs.

When he reappeared a few minutes later, Steven left him to finish off, and went to write the report for the coroner. He hated paperwork, it was the worst part of the job, apart from having to ask people to identify the bodies of loved ones, and then having to tell them how they had died. Maybe the paperwork's not so bad after all, he thought as he typed.

Sue stuck her head round the door a couple of hours later. 'I've got results on a three of the cigarette ends from the quarry, they are a French brand, there is unknown female DNA on one of them, and a DNA match to John Simmons on two of them,' she handed him a report. 'There were also two sets of tyre tracks, one of them is from John Simmons work van, and the other is from an as yet unidentified long wheel base.'

Steven picked the phone up. 'I'll give DCI Cooper a call and let him know.'

'Why don't you just say dad? We all know who you mean,' Sue chuckled.

'Ok, I'll ring dad,' he laughed as he pushed the number.

'I had a feeling he was up to no good,' Edward exclaimed. 'I'll go over first thing and see what he's got to say for himself.' but when they called at the Simmons house the next morning, Edward and Jack were told that they had just missed him. His wife Lottie, was very evasive, and couldn't or wouldn't give them a time when he would be home.

'It depends on where his deliveries take him,' she said sharply and started to close the door.

Jack put his foot in the way. 'Tell him that we would like a word as soon as he gets back please.' Lottie nodded curtly and then slammed the door shut as he moved his foot.

'Not quite as helpful today is she guv, she's got guilt written all over her face. Maybe we should speak to her too,' he suggested.

Edward nodded his agreement. 'We'll wait and see what he has to say first; we can always bring her in later.' He pulled his phone out of his pocket as it rang and frowned as he listened intently to what was being said.

'They've had the hair sample from Strathclyde, it's the same hair that we got from the shed at the quarry, and can you believe they hadn't realised that it was dyed. They've been looking for missing red heads instead of dark blondes,' he said in disbelief. He glanced back at the Simmons house as they pulled away.

Lottie was watching them through an upstairs window, she darted back out of sight when she saw him looking. 'There's definitely something going on there,' he muttered.

It was late afternoon before John Simmons rang to say he was home. Edward was at the hospital when he got the call and went straight over. Steven went with him to get a swab from Mrs Simmons. 'Let's see if hers is the female DNA on the cigarettes,' Edward said hopefully.

John was sitting in the kitchen smoking; Edward fished the half-smoked cigarette from the ashtray. 'Do you mind if I take that?' He stubbed it out and handed it to Steven. 'It's the same make as the ones that we found at the quarry,' he commented as he put it into a pot.

'I got them from a mate in the pub, I expect most people around here smoke them,' John said defensively.

Edward gave him a disbelieving look, and then glanced at Lottie who was sitting at the table looking pale. 'We would like to take a mouth swab from you Mrs Simmons, if we may.'

Lottie stood up defiantly. 'Why? I've not done anything wrong,' she snapped as Steven took a swab kit from his bag.

'Just to eliminate you from our enquiries, as you've just heard, we found some cigarette ends at the quarry and they are the same brand that your husband is smoking.'

'I got them from a friend, he's just come back from holiday,' John interrupted.

'Was the friend in the pub?' Edward asked quizzically.

John nodded, then suddenly realised what he had said and backtracked. 'Yes. A friend in the pub who has just come back from holiday,' he said slightly nervously.

'That may be so, but two of the cigarettes ends that we found at the quarry had your DNA on them, can you explain how they got there?' Edward asked benignly.

John went white but didn't answer. Lottie sat down again and folded her arms. 'What does that have to do with me then?' She asked sarcastically. Edward looked at her sternly. 'We also found unknown female DNA on one of the cigarette ends, and as I said we need to eliminate you from our enquiries, so if you don't mind Mrs Simmons.'

Lottie's mouth fell open in anger. Steven took the opportunity to take a sample. 'Thank you. You can close your mouth now,' he told her.

Lottie glared at her husband. 'You bastard, you've been up there with another woman,' John went from white to red. 'Of course I haven't, you stupid woman.'

Edward intervened before it got nasty. 'Are you saying you have never been to the quarry Mrs Simmons?' He checked.

'No! I have not, and for your information, I don't smoke.' She gave John a look of disgust, then got up and flounced out of the room.

'You're going to have to come down to the station and answer a few questions,' Edward told John.

'Anything to get out of this house, especially with her in that mood, it'll be a pleasure,' he muttered.

An hour later, he was sitting in an interview room. 'Do you want a solicitor?' Jack asked. John shook his head. 'Can you say it for the tape please?' Jack requested.

'No solicitor,' he said unconvincingly.

Jack sat back and stared at him. 'The problem we have, is that you are directly linked to an area where we believe Heather Brooks was attacked, so you need to start telling us the truth,' he said firmly. John shifted in the chair and looked at his hands. 'Mr Simmons?' Jack said sharply.

John looked up. 'I didn't attack her, why would I have called the police if it was me?'

'Guilt maybe,' Edward suggested as he entered the room.

'I took Chester for a walk and he started barking at the edge. I shone my torch over and I saw her lying there so I called you lot. End of story,' John snapped.

'So how do you account for your DNA being in a shed at the quarry complex, and tyre tracks from your van in the mud outside the shed?' Edward queried.

John put his hands over his face and groaned. 'Alright; I've got a mate who gets cheap fags and booze. I store it there for him,' he looked up. 'It's the truth,' he insisted.

'Cheap fags and booze meaning illegally imported goods?' Jack checked.

'Yes,' he sighed resignedly. 'I meet him on the motorway in the works van once or twice a month, he gives me the stuff to bring back here, then he collects it a bit at a time as and when he needs it,' he explained.

'Are you expecting a delivery anytime soon?' Edward asked.

John shook his head. 'I had one about ten days ago,' he said quietly.

'So where is the stuff now?' Jack asked.

'I knew that you lot would look at the compound so I moved it,' he admitted.

'When exactly did you move it?' Edward enquired.

'On the morning I found Heather,' John mumbled.

'And that's why you rushed off to work was it?' Edward checked. He nodded guiltily.

'For the tape please,' Jack instructed.

'Yes,' he said quietly.

'You didn't go and move it before you called the police, did you?' Edward asked suddenly. John looked at his hands again.

'Yes,' he said almost inaudibly. Edward stared at him in disgust and fought the urge to call him a callous bastard. 'So, what did you do with the stuff?' He asked.

'I kept it in the works van for a couple of days and then I put it in the garden shed.'

'Is that why your wife was so nervous?' Jack asked.

'Yes, she found it the other day,' he glanced up nervously as Edward went into interrogation mode.

'What do you get out of this arrangement?'

John stared back at him. 'A hundred and fifty quid for each load, plus a couple of packs of fags and couple bottles of booze,' he mumbled.

'And how long have you been using the quarry for storing this stuff?'

'About nine months.'

Edward raised his eyebrows. 'The place is checked regularly, so how did you get in?'

John gave a small shrug. 'I used to have a key for the original lock but I lost it.'

'So you cut the padlock of the quarry gates and replaced it with a new one?' Jack butted in.

'Yes,' he admitted.

'How did you get the original key?' Edward asked.

'A friend of mine used to work there. I told him that the dog had taken to going under the fence after rabbits, and asked him if I could have a key in case I couldn't get him back.'

'What's your friend's name?' Edward checked.

'Tim Atkinson.'

'Did Mr Atkinson know what was going on?'

John shook his head. 'No.'

'And this mate who you store the goods for, did you give him a key to the new padlock?'

'Yes.'

'Is there a woman involved?'

'No. I've never seen one. We never meet at the quarry, only on the motorway and he's always alone, maybe he takes a woman with him when he collects it,' John suggested helpfully.

'So it's just your friend?' Jack checked.

'Yes,' he confirmed firmly.

'We need his name,' Edward told him.

'I think I'll have that solicitor now,' John said, then he folded his arms and refused to say anything else.

'Put him in the cells until his solicitor gets here,' Edward told the PC on duty. 'And get someone to check out the key story with Tim Atkinson, will you?' He asked Jack, as John Simmons was led away protesting loudly. Jack took a couple of uniformed officers and went over to the Simmons house. As John had said, the shed was full of boxes of cigarettes and alcohol.

'Blimey! There must be a few thousand quid's worth here,' one of the constables commented.

'Get a van over here to collect it, and make sure it's all listed,' Jack ordered, he turned to Lottie who was watching nervously. 'You could be in big trouble for handling illegally imported goods,' he told her sternly, 'So it would be in your best interest to co-operate. Do you know who this friend is?' He asked.

'No, I don't,' she said unconvincingly.

'Are you sure?' he checked.

'Yes I'm sure, are you going to arrest me now?' She asked scathingly.

'No, I'm not, but you may have to come in for questioning at a later date Mrs Simmons,' he said seriously. 'She knows more than she's letting on,' he told Edward when he got back to the station.

Chapter 9

As Edward sat pondering the next morning, his thoughts turned to his son, he smiled to himself, then rang the mortuary. 'I was just going to call you,' Steven exclaimed when he answered the phone.

'Go on then,' Edward encouraged.

'There was female DNA on the envelope that the sympathy card came in, and also on the stamp, so even if she didn't write it then a woman licked it.'

'I'll get onto Chipping Norton and see if they've come up with anything,' Edward said. He promptly put the phone down, then suddenly remembered that it was he who had rang Steven intending to invite him out to dinner. He chuckled at his senior moment and picked it up again, but before he had time to dial out Jack came in looking grim. 'What's the matter?' He asked apprehensively.

'A couple of kids have found a body on Stan Fairclough's land,' the sergeant reported.

Edward's heart sank as he redialled Steven's number. 'You'd better get over there,' he told him with all thoughts of dinner forgotten.

Richard Hughes was sitting in the back of a police car, there was a young girl sitting next to him. Edward recognised her from the pub, and noted that she was wearing a school uniform. He got into the front of the car and turned to face them. 'Are you alright?' Richard nodded; the girl was crying quietly.

'Can you tell me what happened?' Edward asked gently.

'Kelly and I are seeing each other, we come up here to be alone, you know a bit of privacy?' Richard started. Edward nodded his understanding and urged him to go on. 'We go in the old sheep shelter in the corner because no one goes in there anymore.'

Edward looked at the girl. 'How old are you Kelly?'

She looked up with a tear-stained face. 'Fifteen,' she sniffed.

'You should be at school then?' He checked. She nodded nervously.

'We wanted to see each other,' Richard stated firmly. 'But her dad won't let us, so we have to do it on the quiet,' he said bitterly.

'Do what on the quiet Richard?' Edward enquired.

'See each other of course,' he said exasperatedly.

Edward sighed inwardly. 'Ok, so you were up here seeing each other and then what?'

'We saw the rug thing in the corner all tied up with a dog lead, so we untied it, and that's when we saw the body.' Richard put a protective arm around Kelly as she started crying again. 'So I rang the police on my mobile and we waited by the gate.'

Edward handed Kelly a tissue. 'When were you last in the shelter?' He asked.

'Not for about three weeks, my dad's been away so we saw each other at my house,' Kelly explained.

Edward got out of the car. 'Take them home and make sure they both have officers with them until we can get full statements,' he told the driver.

Steven arrived as the police car pulled away. 'What have we got?' He asked as he suited up and collected his case from the boot.

'I don't know, we were waiting for you,' Edward said wryly. They climbed over the gate and made their way across the field. The ground was sodden from the rain, destroying any hope of identifying footprints.

Edward shoved his hands in his pockets as they reached sheep shed, which was an old half fronted corrugated iron affair. 'You go first son; I'll wait here for a minute.' Steven went in and looked around, as his eyes adjusted to the dim light, he saw a couple of straw bales against the back wall, and in the far corner, a partially rolled up rug with a dog lead lying nearby.

He called the photographer in to record it, then bagged it up and handed it to the constable outside before turning his attention to the rug.

There was a leg sticking out from one end; the toenails were painted red so he concluded it must be a woman. He stuck his head out of the shed whilst the photographer took a shot. 'If anyone touched the carpet, we'll need to get samples from them,' he told his father.

'The kids who found it took the dog lead off, one of them was Richard Hughes and you've already got a sample from him,' Edward reminded him.

Steven went back in and slowly unrolled the rug, with the photographer recording every stage. As more of the body was exposed, he saw that it was definitely a woman. He unfolded the last corner and stood up. 'You'd better suit up and come in Dad,' he called. Edward struggled into the suit and went in.

'Bloody hell,' he exclaimed, as he was confronted by the woman's battered body.

Steven turned her over. 'Jesus,' he muttered. 'Get some shots will you?' He said to the photographer.

'What is it?' Edward enquired tentatively. Steven untied her hands and held up a brown leather dog collar, the name Harry and a phone number were clearly visible. He bagged it up and continued with the examination. There was a large plastic bag covering the woman's head;

As Steven lifted the edge, they could see that her red hair had been crudely cut short, her eyes were open, as was her mouth, and her lips were almost black. The photographer leant in close to get a shot, then spotted something in her mouth and pointed it out to Steven. He took a pair of tweezers from his case and started to remove the object; then he realised what it was and stopped.

'We'd better get her back to the lab,' he said angrily.

'What is it?' The photographer asked.

'Her underwear is in her mouth,' he said through gritted teeth.

Charlie unzipped the body bag ninety minutes later, and with the help of the mortuary attendants, they manoeuvred the woman's body onto the table. Edward waited in the observation room as Steven suited up. He pulled on a pair of gloves and a mask and psyched himself up to deal with her. 'Name boss?' Charlie asked when he went into the cutting room.

Steven thought for a minute as he studied her. 'Rose I think,' he decided.

Rose looked to be in her mid-twenties. A combination of the cold weather and being wrapped in the rug had slowed the decomposition process, but with skin discolouration and bloating, the signs were still there. There were abrasions on her hands and feet.

Her face was scratched and dirty, but with an oval shaped face and high sharp cheekbones, she was a striking woman. She was barefoot, but was dressed in a leather coat, which when removed revealed a mid-length skirt and tight white jumper, which again when removed revealed no underwear. 'Well we know where her pants are,' Steven muttered as he extracted them from her mouth.

One heart shaped earring hung from Rose's left ear, the right one was missing. He passed the clothes and earring to Sue who was waiting. 'The rugs on the way,' he told her, then looked across to the observation room; he knew that his father hated post-mortems. 'Are you going to be ok Dad?'

Edward nodded, and watched as Steven scraped under her nails and took a hair sample. 'We'll test her hair but it looks the same shade of red as the other two samples.' On further inspection, he found that Rose also had bruises around both of her wrists and one on her outer thigh. Steven looked closely at the bruise. 'I've seen a bruise similar to this recently,' he said thoughtfully.

He continued talking his way through the procedure with Charlie taking pictures when requested. 'She has what looks like a ligature mark around her neck.' He stopped talking as he suddenly remembered where he had seen the bruise before. 'Can you get the photographs of Ms Brook's legs?' he asked the technician.

Charlie held them next to Rose's leg for comparison. 'They look the same shape, boss.' Steven nodded his agreement and continued with the examination.

I wonder what goes through his head when he's doing this, Edward thought, as he watched his son taking vaginal swabs. 'Dad,' Steven was looking at him. 'Are you sure that you're, ok?' Edward nodded confirmation.

'There's bruising and scratches on her inner thighs. I would say she had sex not long before death, but it probably wasn't consensual,' Steven reported. Edward turned away as he picked a scalpel and started to open her up.

Unable to stomach anymore, Edward had retreated to Steven's office to wait. 'Sorry son, I don't think I'll ever get used to those things,' he admitted.

Steven sat down and sighed despondently. 'No, me neither.'

Edward gave him a puzzled look. 'So why do you do it then?' He asked incredulously.

'To find the truth,' his son said without hesitation. They looked each other in the eye for a second, and then Steven took a deep breath. 'Rose was approximately thirty years old, given the time of year and the location of the body, I would say she has been dead for at least seven days. Her pants were stuffed into her mouth and she was suffocated with a plastic sheet, which was probably tied around her neck with the dog lead.'

'Not strangled with it?' Edward interrupted.

Steven shook his head. 'The bruising on her neck is consistent with the dog lead being tied around it, but not tight enough to do any real damage, and as you know her hands were tied behind her back with the dog collar so she couldn't get the bag off. There is an odd shaped bruise on her left shoulder, it looks like she was gripped very hard with something, but not with a hand as there are no finger marks, and we're trying to enhance the shape to see what made it.

'She has bruising and scratches to her inner thighs, some of the bruises were inflicted several days before she died, but there were also some fresh ones. I think she was raped just prior to death, but there was no semen inside her so whoever it was used protection, which was very sensible of them as she appears to have an std and quite a bad dose of thrush. I've sent swabs up to the lab and we should get the results back within forty-eight hours.

'The scratches on her face and arms are superficial. I would say she was dragged along the ground after death as there are cuts on her feet and her toenails are chipped.' He stopped talking and looked at his father.

'Are there any clues to her identity?' Edward asked hopefully.

'Well looking at her teeth, I don't think she's British, because the dental work is very basic, and there are mercury fillings in there which we don't use in this country anymore, so Polish or Rumanian something like that.' Edward sighed despondently. 'But she's given birth within the last four months or so which might narrow the search, so let's hope there isn't a baby somewhere too,' Steven said wryly.

'Can you tell if it was a hospital birth?' Edward asked.

Steven nodded firmly. 'Definitely; she had stitches.'

Edward grimaced inwardly. 'What about her clothes?'

'They're up in the lab, Sue will let us know as soon as she has anything. There was one thing that I found a bit odd though,' he said thoughtfully. 'Her skirt and top were cheap market type things; they had no labels and were very poor quality, but she had an expensive leather jacket on. Sue is checking the label out, and that's all I've got for now,' he finished.

Edward got up. 'Thanks son. I'll get onto Strathclyde and ask them to check out the hospitals for anyone giving birth in the last five months.'

Steven watched him as he put his coat on, he looked tired. 'Come over for dinner tonight if you want,' he invited. Edward nodded appreciatively and headed out into the rain.

It was still raining when he arrived that evening. 'I'm in the kitchen,' Steven called.

Edward shook his coat in the porch then went through and sniffed. 'What is it?' He asked.

'Beef bourguignon al a Cooper,' Steven replied with a flourish. 'Cooked slowly all day, the meat should be really tender so it shouldn't give your old teeth any trouble,' he added seriously.

Edward gave him a look of mock distain. 'You're not too big for a thick ear you know,' he threatened. Steven grinned at him as he dished it out. Edward looked at the steaming plate, thinking how proud his mother would have been of him.

Steven broke into his thoughts. 'Do you want a beer?'

Edward nodded and tasted the meal, Steven was right, the meat melted in his mouth. 'You'll make someone a lovely wife one day son,' he said brightly.

They chatted happily over dinner, not just about the cases they were each working on, but father and son remembering things from the past, things that made them laugh or made them sad. It's nice to be able to talk openly about things Edward thought, as remembered his own father, who he hardly ever saw, and who never discussed anything with him, no memories to chuckle over or advice to pass on he thought sadly.

'Dad!' He looked up. 'You were miles away, are you ok?' Steven checked.

'I was just thinking how nice it is that we can talk,' he admitted.

'Yes, it is,' Steven agreed 'Do you want another beer?'

Edward looked out at the rain as it ricocheted of the windows. 'I'd better not; I've got to drive home. In fact, I'd better go now before it gets too bad to drive.' He got up reluctantly and yawned loudly 'God I'm tired,' he admitted.

'Why don't you stay?' Steven suggested. 'I'll make the spare bed up.' Edward looked at the rain again and sighed, he felt totally worn out and it was bucketing down. 'Is there a carpet on the floor?'

'Why, do you sleep on the floor?' Steven counter asked disdainfully.

'No,' he chuckled. 'Ok I'll stay, but I'll have to let the station know where I am.'

Steven grinned at him. 'I'll get you that beer then, shall I?'

'Did you know that they took Heather's bandages off yesterday?' Edward asked a little later, they were sitting in front of the fire whilst the rain lashed down.

Steven nodded. 'How did it go?' he asked, trying not to sound too interested.

Edward smiled at him. 'Fine, the doctors say she's healing well. She was a bit upset about having her head shaved, but I told her it would grow back again.' They sat in silence for a while both deep in thought. 'I thought I might ask Sheila to nip in and see if she could do anything with it for her, she's good at hair; she used to do your mum's,' Edward said thoughtfully. 'What do you think?'

Steven nodded. 'I think it's a great idea, how is Sheila? I've not seen her for ages.'

Edward smiled fondly. 'She's fine. She often asks after you, you'll have to come over for lunch one Sunday she usually pops in.'

'You don't cook, do you?' Steven asked in mock horror.

Edward shook his head. 'I gave up trying to entertain after I gave you and your mum salmonella, do you remember?'

'No,' Steven lied, even though he remembered the sickness and diarrhoea vividly.

'It's ready meals and tins for me unless someone else is cooking,' Edward assured him. They fell silent until Edward yawned loudly again. 'I'm off to bed,' he said wearily.

Steven watched him go up the stairs, and recalled how he used to sling him over his shoulder and carry him up to bed when he was a child. I wonder if he remembers he thought. 'Night night, popsicles,' he called.

Edward stuck his head over the banisters. 'Night night sausage dog,' he called back.

Steven was filling one of the flasks with left over beef bourguignon when Edward came down the next morning. 'For Heather,' he explained to his father's raised eyebrow.

'Oh I see! Going into catering, are we?' Edward chided.

'Well the hospital food doesn't look great and she enjoyed the macaroni cheese,' he screwed the lid on. 'Anyway, Monty won't eat it and it'll be a shame to waste it.'

Edward put his hands up. 'I was just wondering,' he chuckled knowingly.

Steven frowned and handed him a mug of tea. 'I'd better be off; have some breakfast,' he ordered.

He left Edward making toast and drove over to the hospital; it was too early to visit Heather, so he went straight to the mortuary to find Judy already in the office. 'There's someone here to see you,' she said quietly. Steven looked through to the waiting room where a woman was sitting with her head bowed, she sensed him watching and looked up.

'Who is she?' He enquired.

'Karen sharp's mother. She wants to know what you found.'

Steven groaned inwardly, what a horrible thing to have to do first thing in the morning. 'Get her a coffee and tell her I'll see her in a minute.' He went up to the lab taking the stairs two at a time. 'Have you got anything on Karen Sharp?' He asked.

Sue brought the case up on the computer screen. 'The foetus was approximately fifteen weeks old. There was no sign of drug abuse in Karen's organs, but there was enough heroin in her blood to kill an elephant, so she must have died very quickly. We also got two semen samples from the swabs; we're still waiting for DNA from them.' She stopped talking and looked at Steven's furious face.

'Check the semen against the baby, and see if either of them was the father,' he ordered angrily 'What sex was the baby?'

Sue glanced at the screen again 'Male.' Steven waited for the printout, then psyched himself up and went back downstairs.

Mrs Sharp sat nervously in front of him. 'Did you find anything?' She asked with her voice shaking.

'Before I answer that, can you tell me if Karen took drugs?'

She blew her nose and shook her head. 'Not anymore, but she used to take cocaine. She got in with the wrong crowd a few years ago and we caught her sniffing it in the bathroom, my husband was so cross he threw her out,' she said quietly.

'You said used to take it, had she stopped taking it?' Steven checked.

Mrs Sharp nodded. 'She'd been home for six weeks, she said wanted to make a fresh start. It was hard for her at first, but I know she hadn't taken anything for weeks. I'm her mother I would have known,' she started to cry.

'That's why I wanted a second opinion. I saw the way that other man looked at us as if we were to blame, and the way he spoke about Karen, as though she deserved to die,' she sobbed.

'You weren't happy with the first post-mortem?' Steven asked.

'No!' She said firmly, 'he said she was an addict, he said that she had overdosed on heroin, but I told him she never took that. She never injected anything, she only sniffed it, and she hadn't taken anything for six weeks. She was clean,' she said firmly.

Steven's heart went out to the small fragile looking woman who looked like she had the troubles of the world on her shoulders. He was just wondering how to tell her that her pregnant daughter had probably been murdered when she broke into his thoughts.

'She seemed so happy; we were going to go out for dinner that evening; she said she had something to tell us.'

Christ! They didn't know she was pregnant he thought. 'Did she give any indication as to what the news was?' He asked.

She shook her head. 'Just that it was good, and it was going to make a huge difference to her life,' she smiled at him through her tears. 'We thought she may have decided to go back to university.' he listened patiently as she continued reminiscing. 'She was studying to be a solicitor before, well you know, the drugs and that,' she stopped talking.

'I'm sorry Dr Cooper, I'm taking up too much of your time,' she looked at him expectantly. 'So, did you find anything?' Steven took a deep breath and told her as much as he knew. She seemed to get smaller with each detail that he disclosed; when he got to the baby, the chair nearly swallowed her up.

'I am so sorry; we are still waiting for some of the test results and I will have to pass these details to the police,' he told her gently.

'Are you sure about all of this?' Her voice was barley a whisper and her eyes were wide with grief.

'Yes, I'm afraid so, the evidence is consistent with your daughter being forcibly injected with the heroin that killed her.'

'And the baby?' She choked.

'There are indications that she had intercourse with two men just before she died, we have tested to see if either of them was the baby's father and the results will be back in a couple of days.'

Mrs Sharp's face crumpled again. 'Two men, she wasn't raped, was she?' She asked in horror.

'I'm sorry I can't say for sure that she was raped. There was bruising that would suggest it was against her will, but being able to prove it will be tough.'

Mrs Sharp stood up with tears streaming down her face. 'Thank you, Dr Cooper, I'll go and tell my husband.' Then almost as if she could read his mind she added, 'He's outside in the car, he couldn't bear to come in.'

Steven walked her to the door. 'I really am very sorry Mrs Sharp,' he said as they shook hands. 'I hate this job,' he said to Judy when she had gone. Judy handed him a cup of coffee.

'Well at least they know what happened, it's better to know the truth even if it's not good news.'

Steven nodded knowingly. 'I just wish it wasn't me who had to tell them.' They sat in silence until the phone rang. Judy answered it and gave a small smile before handing him the receiver.

'It's Tracy for you,' she said amusedly.

'Tracy who?' He enquired. Judy shrugged; he was about to speak when he remembered Jack's warning. 'Tell her I'm busy,' he whispered and gave her the phone back; she gave him a puzzled look and returned to the call.

'I'm sorry but Dr Cooper is tied up; can I take a message?' Steven watched her expression as she listened, then she wrote something down. 'I'll make sure I tell him,' she said brightly, then hung up and went back to her coffee.

Steven looked at her expectantly. 'Well?' He asked impatiently.

'Well what?' She teased.

'What did she want?' He asked.

'Oh I'm sorry,' she said innocently. 'I thought if you didn't want to speak to her then you wouldn't be interested in what she had to say,' she handed him the note. 'Tracey says she's having a party tomorrow night, and that's her address if you would like to go.' She gave him a knowing smile.

'It looks like you're in there boss.' Steven screwed the note up and threw it in the bin without bothering to look at it. 'Perhaps not then,' Judy muttered.

'If she calls again tell her I'm busy,' he ordered.

Edward and Jack had been over to interview Richard Hughes and Kelly Shelton. Richard couldn't tell him any more than he had the previous day, and although Kelly was still very upset, her account of events tallied with Richards.

Her father, a "smug self-opinionated Pratt", as Jack was to call him later, seemed more concerned with the fact that she had been seeing "that boy", and informed them that finding a body was a life lesson. 'She'll be stronger for the experience,' he told them pompously as they were leaving.

'Just a minute,' a voice called as they walked down the path. They turned back to see Kelly running after them.

'Is there something you want to tell us?' Edward asked.

She glanced nervously at her father who was watching from the door. 'I just wanted to ask if Rich is going to be in trouble,' she said quietly.

Jack raised his eyebrows. 'Your call guv,' he said brightly.

'Well Kelly, underage sex is a criminal offence even if it's consensual, but unless a complaint is made against him, then we won't be pursuing the matter,' Edward smiled at her. 'You've had enough to cope with so don't worry about it.'

Kelly looked confused. 'We haven't had sex, we're waiting until our wedding night,' she said proudly.

'Oh, I see, so why would Richard be in trouble then?' Edward said in surprise.

'For doing me a note to bunk off school of course,' Kelly said exasperatedly.

'Kids with morals, guv, whatever next,' Jack chuckled as they made their way back to the car.

There was an e-mail from Strathclyde waiting when they got back to the station; Jack read it out. 'There were two hundred and thirty-seven babies born in the Strathclyde area between two and five months ago. All the mothers except eleven have been traced, nine of the babies were, or are going to be adopted, they're still trying to trace the other two.

'One of the eight who is waiting to be adopted was born to a foreign woman who walked into Edinburgh Royal infirmary four months ago in the final stages of labour. She gave birth to a baby girl but wouldn't even look at her. She disappeared two hours later and they haven't traced her. Strathclyde are sending the hospitals CCTV tape over,' he looked up.

'What about the babies?' Edward asked.

'They're with adoptive or foster parents. I'll let Steve know, shall I, guv?' He picked the phone up as Edward nodded thoughtfully.

Steven was on his way to see Heather when Jack rang. 'Can you ask Strathclyde to get blood samples from all the babies whose mothers haven't been traced, one of them may be Rose's,' Steven requested; he ran up the hospital stairs deep in thought, then jumped as he bumped into to Heather's father who was on his way down.

Mr Brooks put his hand out. 'I didn't get a chance to thank you properly the other day, Dr Cooper.'

Steven shook the offered hand. 'I was just doing my job,' he objected. 'And please call me Steven.'

Her father gave him a knowing smile. 'That may be so, but I know that she would have been dead now if you hadn't felt for her pulse.' Steven started to object again. 'Don't argue,' her father butted in, sounding almost paternal.

'I've spoken to the doctors and they told me that another hour or two and she wouldn't have made it,' he smiled warmly. 'So, thank you, and if you're Steven then I'm Malcolm, ok.'

Steven nodded. 'Ok.' He watched Malcolm make his way down the stairs, and remembered the feelings he'd experienced when he found Heather's pulse. Relief, that she was alive and fear that he had found it too late. He stared into space for a minute as he relived the moment.

'Hello Steven,' he jumped again and turned around to find Sheila standing behind him. 'Are you alright?' she checked. He nodded and told her what Malcolm had said. 'He's right, you should be proud of yourself,' she said genuinely.

Steven felt himself blushing and changed the subject. 'How are you? I've not seen you for ages.' They chatted as they walked along to Heather's room, when they reached the door, they looked through the window. Heather was sitting in a wheelchair eating lunch from a bed table.

Her newly washed blond hair hung loosely down to her shoulders; on top just off centre there was a fairly large shaved patch. She looked up and smiled as Steven tapped on the door. 'Are you ok?' He mouthed; she gave a brief nod and smiled again as he waved the flask at her. 'I've brought beef bourguignon.'

'Thanks,' she said gratefully. 'I don't know what that was but it was pretty yucky.' Steven moved the table for her and introduced Sheila. 'It's good to meet you, although I don't know what you can do with this.' She put her hand up to the wound and felt along the scar. 'They took the staples out this morning; how's it looking?' She asked anxiously.

Steven inspected the area, the scar was big, but her hair had already started to grow around it. 'It looks good, a couple of months and you won't be able to see it at all,' he assured her. 'Anyway, I'll leave you too it,' he said quickly as Sheila smiled knowingly. 'I'll call back for the flask later,' he left them to discuss hair styles and went back to the mortuary.

Sue came down with the results from Harry's teeth as soon as he got back. 'You were right; there was alien male blood on a couple of the swabs. We're searching the national data base for a match, and the thread of cotton you found was from jeans material.

'I would say whoever he bit must have had a substantial wound, and the fibres that you found in Harry's coat were the same as the ones we got from

Heather's clothes. We're still running tests but I think they are from the carpet that Rose was wrapped in.'

Steven took the offered printout. 'Can you check the blood against the samples we took from the locals as well, you never know it could be one of them.' Sue nodded and left Steven to ring the results through to Jack.

Judy stuck her head round the door an hour later. 'There's someone here to see you.'

Steven looked up as Sheila came in. 'Is Heather alright?' he asked anxiously.

'Don't worry she's fine,' she assured him. 'But she remembered something whilst I was cutting her hair, so I thought I should come and tell you straight away.'

'Did you tell the PC?' he checked, she nodded again and explained what had happened.

'As I was cutting her hair, I commented on the lovely colour and she started shaking; she said that she remembered someone shouting. "You idiots it's not her, the hairs not even the same colour". She was very upset, so I stayed with her until her father came back, and then I came straight over to tell you whilst it was fresh in my mind.'

Steven picked the phone up. 'I think you should tell dad.' Sheila wound the phone cord around her fingers as she spoke to Edward. Steven noticed that she had a slight pink tinge to her cheeks.

He smiled as he remembered how good she had been when his mother had died, helping with the washing, showing his father how to work the oven, reminding him about appointments, doing the shopping. Even now after all this time she was still there in the background, quietly keeping an eye on him. What a great mum she would have made he thought, and wondered why she had never married.

She said goodbye to Edward and passed him the phone. 'He wants to speak to you.' He watched her watching him as he spoke, and it suddenly dawned on him. My God! She's in love with him.

'Are you even listening to me Steven?' His father enquired.

'Yes,' he lied. 'Sorry Dad, what did you say?' He smiled at Sheila as Edward sighed loudly.

'I said Strathclyde are going to have to get court orders to take blood samples from the babies so it may take a few days, and do you want to come out to dinner on Friday? I've asked Sheila too as a thank you for helping with Heather.'

'Yes, thanks, that'll be nice,' Steven accepted.

'Eight p.m. at the moorhen inn, it's on the old Kimberwick road.'

'I know it,' Steven interrupted and rang off.

'Dinner on Friday then?' He said brightly.

Sheila smiled at him. 'Yes, are you coming?'

'Of course I am,' he said with no intention of going at all. 'You don't think I would pass up a free meal, do you?' He chuckled.

Sue had some good news an hour later. 'I've got a match for both of the semen samples from Karen Sharp, and one of them is the father of the baby.'

Steven sighed with relief 'Can you inform the investigating officer, and let's hope they get the bastards,' he added under his breath. He popped over to see Heather before going home. She was sitting in bed reading; her face lit up as he went in.

'You've just missed Dad,' she held the book up with a grimace. 'Mills and Boon; you'd think he would know by now that I don't do happy endings,' she put it down and smiled up at him. Sheila had done a good job with her hair, cutting it into a bob and styling it so that it almost hid the scar.

'It looks nice,' he complemented.

'Do you think so?' He nodded enthusiastically and sat down. 'It's a bit shorter than I usually have it but at least it covers the scar.' He studied her face as she spoke, the bruising had practically gone, and looking at her sitting there it was hard to believe that two weeks ago she had nearly died.

'You're staring again,' she scolded impishly.

Steven grinned at her. 'Sorry, I was just thinking that it suits you short.'

She beamed back at him, the smile lighting her face up. 'Sheila's nice. Is she your dad's girlfriend?'

He shook his head. 'No, she just a friend.'

Heather looked surprised. 'Well, she spent nearly the whole time talking about him, so I thought they were an item.'

'I think she would like to be,' Steven said thoughtfully; he told her about his mother dying and how Sheila had helped his father over the years. When he had finished, she gave him a knowing look. 'What? Did she say something about me?' He asked suspiciously.

Heather pursed her lips together and tried not to smile, but her eyes were twinkling mischievously. 'Tell me,' he demanded. She shook her head firmly.

'No more home cooking for you then,' he threatened; she stared at him and then sighed in defeat.

'She told me about the time that you were sent home from school because you were ill, your dad was at work so you went to her house, except you weren't ill, you were drunk!' She stopped talking and gave him a stern look 'And then you threw up all over her kitchen.'

Steven put his hands over his face. 'My God, I'd forgotten all about that, not one of my finest hours,' he said ruefully. 'And she never did tell dad.'

Heather laughed at the look on his face as he remembered. 'Well, we've all done it,' she giggled.

'Yes, but not at sixteen years old and ten o clock in the morning,' he confessed. They sat silently for a minute, each deep in thought.

'I think you should give your dad a push,' she said suddenly. 'Seventeen years is a long time to wait.'

Steven let out a long sigh. 'He probably hasn't noticed; he's always so wrapped up with work. I only realised a couple of hours ago,' he admitted.

'Men,' she groaned. 'They've either got a roving eye or they walk around with blinkers on.'

Steven nodded his agreement. 'Well, I know which one I am. I didn't even notice what was going on with Amy and Martin did I?' He yawned loudly. 'Anyway, dad's taking us both out to dinner tomorrow night, but I'm not going to go.' He told her about his plan to forget or be busy.

'Playing cupid, eh? Well, I hope it works,' she chuckled.

Steven nodded his agreement then yawned again and got up. 'I'm going home, if you've finished with the flask, I'll take it with me.' Their hands brushed as she gave it to him. He felt a slight tingle at her touch and fought the urge to give her a hug.

'Thanks, it was very nice,' she complemented.

'You're welcome, let me know if there's anything else you fancy. just make sure I can fit it in the flask,' he added. He glanced back at her as he went out. She had picked her book up again, but rather than reading it she was watching him over the top, their eyes locked for a couple of seconds. 'Bye,' he mouthed before shutting the door quietly.

Chapter 10

The following morning, Edward was forced to release John Simmons. 'Pending further inquiries so don't leave the area,' he told him sternly. He watched as he walked to the car. Lottie got out as he approached; they both looked back and glared at him.

'Do you still think he's hiding something guv?' Jack asked.

'Yes, I do, but I'm not sure what,' he muttered.

Whilst Edward was releasing John Simmons, Steven was working in the lab. He looked up as Judy stuck her head around door. 'Bernard Murdoch's been on the phone. He said he wants to see you and he didn't sound very happy.'

Steven turned his nose up. 'He did the first post-mortem on Karen Sharp,' he said dryly.

'What shall I tell him if he rings again?' She asked.

'Tell him to make an appointment,' he ordered. He went into his office and sat staring into space until Charlie came in.

'We've got a customer boss.' Steven got up and followed him into the cutting room where the body of a youth lay. Charlie looked at the admission sheet. 'Robert Havers, aged sixteen, he crashed a stolen car into the front of a shop at sixty miles an hour.'

Steven sighed sadly. 'Sixteen you say?' Charlie nodded. 'Let's get started then,' he said despairingly. It wasn't difficult to find out how Robert had died, he hadn't been wearing a seatbelt and had gone straight through the windscreen. He hit the shop counter head on sustaining massive brain injuries which would have killed him almost instantly.

After checking the contents of his stomach and taking blood samples, it was obvious that he had been drinking as well. 'What were you doing when you were sixteen?' Steven asked Charlie.

'You don't want to know, but I certainly wasn't drinking and joy riding,' he said dryly.

'What about you?' Steven looked at the broken body lying on the table. 'My mother had just died of a brain tumour and I went off the rails.'

He frowned as he remembered his father's dismay when he had been brought home in a police car for the third time. 'Breaking into cars this time Sir,' the PC told him.

Unsurprisingly, Edward had lost his temper. 'For Christ sake, use your head son, and think what you're doing,' he shouted.

'I was thinking, I'm not drunk this time,' Steven shouted back.

'Well, your mother would have had something to be thankful for then, wouldn't she? And behaving like a bloody imbecile won't bring her back,' his father snapped.

The stinging comment had brought him to his senses just in time. When he realised that not only was he letting himself and his parents down, but the fact that his father was a well-respected policeman was the only reason that he hadn't ended up in a young offender's institution. 'That could have been me a few years ago,' he said thoughtfully.

Charlie rolled his eyes at him. 'Blimey boss, don't get all religious on me and start confessing.'

Steven gave a wry smile. 'Ok, you close him up and I'll write it up,' he ordered.

He was just finishing the report for the coroner when Judy burst in; she was closely followed by a thick set man with white hair and a beard that covered most of his very angry looking face. 'I'm sorry Dr Cooper, I couldn't stop him,' she apologised.

Steven nodded at her. 'It's alright Judy.' He turned to the man. 'Have a seat,' he waited until the man was seated. 'What can I do for you, Mr Murdoch?' He enquired.

'It's Professor Murdoch to you, and I think you know perfectly well why I am here,' the man snapped.

Steven shook his head. 'I'm sorry I have no idea.'

Murdoch gave him a disbelieving look, his small black eyes glinting menacingly. 'Don't insult me any more than you have already by pretending you don't know what this is about.' He waited for a response but it was unforthcoming. 'Did you or did you not send a report to the coroner regarding Karen Sharp?'

Steven nodded. 'A request for a second post-mortem was made which I carried out.'

'Yes! And in your report, you question my competence,' Murdoch interrupted. 'And you've passed it on to the police,' he glared at him. 'Do you know how long I've been doing this job?' He enquired sarcastically.

Steven pulled the report out, he scanned through it then shook his head. 'I merely stated that certain aspects of the girl's condition had been overlooked,' he looked up. 'If you want to interpret that as questioning your competence then that's your prerogative, and no, I have no idea how long you've been doing the job,' he said benignly.

'A lot bloody longer than you,' Murdoch spat superiorly. The two men sat in silence watching each other, each waiting for the other to react.

'If there's nothing else then I really should get on,' Steven said eventually.

Murdoch got up. 'You haven't heard the last of this, Mr Cooper.'

By now, Steven was having trouble keeping his temper in check. 'It's Dr Cooper to you,' he corrected angrily. 'And I'm very glad to hear it.'

'What the hell do you mean by that?' Murdock demanded.

Steven was now on the verge of completely losing it. 'Well, if you really want me to spell it out for you; there have been far too many people who can't defend themselves Branded addicts or prostitutes and not given the dignity they deserve, because a narrow minded lazy old pathologist, who probably should have retired years ago, didn't think they were worth the effort, is that clear enough for you?' he enquired sarcastically, then got up and opened the door. 'Now if you don't mind, I really am very busy.'

Bernard Murdoch had gone red in the face. 'You had better ask Judy for a glass of water on the way out. I'd hate you to expire on the premises, you may not be very happy with the service you get here,' Steven said benignly. Murdock glared at him and started to say something; then he changed his mind and turned on his heel.

Steven slammed the door as soon as the older man had gone through. He took a few deep breaths to calm himself down then looked up to a knock on the door.

'Do you mind if we come in?' Judy asked tentatively.

He sat down and forced a smile. 'No, what's up?'

She came in closely followed by Charlie. 'We were going to ask you the same thing. We've never seen you lose your rag like that before,' Charlie said concernedly. Steven shrugged dismissively. 'You do know that Murdock's got a lot of clout, don't you?' Charlie asked.

Sue appeared at the door. 'What's going on?'

'Steven just lost his rag with Bernard Murdoch; he practically threw him out,' Charlie told her.

Sue raised her eyebrows. 'The Bernard Murdoch from York?'

Steven glared at them. 'Yes! The Bernard Murdoch from York, and I didn't throw him out, not physically anyway,' he muttered angrily.

'You don't want to make an enemy of him,' Sue said seriously. 'He's got...'

'Yes, I know, he's got a lot of clout,' Steven interrupted sarcastically.

'He's been practicing for years,' Sue continued.

'Then he should be able to do his bloody job properly then. Now if you don't mind, I don't want to talk about him,' Steven interrupted again. Charlie and Judy glanced at each other, then took the hint and went out. 'Did you want something Sue?' Steven enquired.

'The female DNA on the cigarette end was Rose's, the fibres that were on Heather's clothes and in Harry's coat were from the same rug that Rose was wrapped in. I also found hairs from a second dog in the rug, and the DNA found in the dog's mouth hasn't matched anyone on the data base, or any of the men sampled locally,' Sue informed him.

She put the report on his desk and went out closing the door quietly behind her. 'Hang on,' Steven called, he got up as she opened the door again. 'Check the DNA against Lottie Simmons, will you?'

'It was male,' she reminded him.

'Yes, I know but check it anyway, Dad said she was very cagy and there may be a link.' Sue gave him a concerned look and then made her way back up to the lab.

Steven sat down and put his head in his hands. 'Christ. Bernard bloody Murdoch,' he scowled as he remembered listening to him years ago. 'He's still spouting crap,' he muttered. In fact, it had been Bernard Murdoch's crap spouting that had inspired him to leave catering college and study pathology.

Something he had never even thought about, never mind considered taking up as a profession. He looked at Judy sitting in the reception and suddenly felt guilty. He got up and stood in the doorway, then gave her an apologetic smile as she eyed him over a mug of coffee. 'I was going to make you one but I thought you wanted to be left alone,' she said dryly.

'Can you get Charlie and Sue and come in for a minute please?' He asked. 'I want to apologise for my behaviour before,' he said when they were all assembled. 'I suppose I should explain why I lost my rag, as you so eloquently put it,' he looked at Charlie with a remorseful smile.

'We know why boss,' Charlie butted in. 'The man is incompetent; I saw Karen Sharp's body and his report.'

Steven nodded. 'Yes, I know that.' He looked at them waiting expectantly and took a deep breath. 'Thirteen years ago, a friend of mine died, she died after taking an ecstasy tablet. It was the first one that she had ever taken in her life, and she took it because everyone else was taking them,' he paused and bit his lip.

'Everyone; including me.' He watched their reaction as he continued. 'Bernard Murdoch did the post-mortem on her, and at her inquest he tore her reputation to pieces. He called her an addict, which she wasn't, and that broke her parent's hearts all over again.' He shook his head as he recalled the event. 'Jesus! She didn't even smoke.'

He stopped talking and looked at their now shocked faces. 'Her parents could have asked for a second opinion but they didn't. They just accepted his word that their daughter was a drug addict and they disowned her.' He could feel tears welling up as he remembered; he blinked to try and stop them.

'They didn't come to her funeral and they have never visited her grave,' he said in a choked voice. The blinking didn't work; he wiped his eyes on his hand and stood up. 'That's why I lost my temper, and I know I shouldn't let personal feelings interfere with work, so I'm sorry, and that's all I wanted to say,' he finished.

They stared at him in disbelief, and then unable to think of a suitable response, got up and went silently back to the reception. He was just contemplating how he could get out of dinner when Judy knocked on the door. 'Your fathers on line two,' she said quietly.

He lifted the receiver still racking his brains for an excuse. 'Dad, what's up?' he asked.

'Nothing,' Edward assured him. 'I'm just running a bit late, can you pick Sheila up on your way to the moorhen, and I'll come straight from the station and meet you there.'

Steven sighed inwardly. 'Ok,' he agreed, then put the phone down and stared into space until Charlie came in.

'Robert Haver's father is here; he wants to see him. I've laid him out ready.'
Steven went out to the reception where a devastated looking man was waiting. I
hate this job, he thought, as he led him through to the chapel of rest.

He stuck his head around Heather's door on his way home. 'Do you want
anything?' He went all the way in as she smiled at him.

'I'll have a think,' she smiled again as her father came in behind him.

'Think about what?' He enquired. 'So that's why she's making such a good
recovery,' he chuckled when she told him about the flasks of food.

Steven glanced at the time. 'I'd better go I've got a dinner date,' he said
despondently.

'I thought you were going to back out,' Heather said in surprise.

'Dad asked me to pick Sheila up, so I can't really say I'm too busy, can I?'
he sighed. 'Never mind, I suppose there will be other times.'

Heather smiled at him knowingly. 'Yes, I suppose there will,' she agreed.
'Well have a good time,' she said brightly.

'Thanks,' he muttered unenthusiastically; and reluctantly made his way
home to change.

'You look nice,' he complemented to Sheila as they waited in the moorhen
for Edward. He looked round as a familiar voice floated across the restaurant.
'Christ,' he muttered as he spotted Bernard Murdoch holding court at a corner
table.

'I'm really sorry about what happened with Amy,' Sheila suddenly blurted
out. 'But it's nice to have you back and your dad missed you.'

Steven tried to ignore Murdoch and smiled at her. 'It's nice being back near
to dad, although I do worry about him all alone in that house.'

Sheila nodded in agreement. 'I've asked him why he doesn't sell up and get
something smaller, but he said there are too many happy memories to leave
behind,' she said wistfully. They fell silent until Edward appeared.

'Sorry, I got held up,' he apologised breathlessly. 'Have you ordered? Oh!
You look nice, Sheila,' he exclaimed. She went red, reminding Steven of a
schoolgirl who had been caught ogling the school hunk. 'And it's nice to see you
out of your overalls son,' he teased.

Steven's phone rang as they were perusing the menu; he looked at the display
and frowned. 'It's the hospital.' Edward looked at him enquiringly as he
answered the call.

'I'm sorry to disturb you Dr Cooper,' the ward sister apologised. 'But Ms Brooks says she has remembered something and needs to speak to you urgently, she's asking if you can come over?'

He frowned again. 'What now?' He checked.

'Yes please, she says if you're not too busy.'

Steven looked at his father's expectant face. 'Ok, tell her I'll be there within the hour.' Edward raised his eyebrows as he rang off. 'Heather's remembered something and she wants to speak to me,' he explained. A small smile played on Sheila's lips as he glanced at her. 'Do you mind Sheila? Maybe we can do this another time,' he suggested.

'It's fine, you go,' she said generously.

'Do you want me to come with you?' Edward asked.

'No, there's no point us all going, you two stay here and enjoy yourselves,' Steven insisted.

'Make sure the PC is there to take notes,' Edward called as he made his way out. He lifted his hand in acknowledgement, and then scowled at Bernard Murdoch, who having spotted him, was pointing him out to his companions and telling them in a very loud voice what a disgrace he was to the profession.

He arrived at the hospital forty minutes later and went straight up to Heather's room. 'You'd better come in too,' he told PC Higgins. Heather was sitting up in bed listening to the Walkman. 'Westlife?' He mouthed.

She took the headphones off. 'No meatloaf actually,' she chuckled.

'Good choice,' he commended. 'Right, what have you remembered?' He asked expectantly.

She smiled at him mischievously. 'What?' He glanced at Higgins; the PC shrugged in bewilderment. 'I've remembered what I would like to eat,' she said brightly.

Steven rolled his eyes at her. 'You've brought me all the way over here at nine o clock at night to tell me that?'

She nodded enthusiastically. 'Did you leave your father and Sheila at dinner?'

Steven suddenly realised what she was up to. 'Ok, miss matchmaker, what do you fancy to eat then?' He chuckled. 'You don't need to write this down,' he told Higgins.

'Yes, do write it down,' Heather ordered. 'I'll have a number forty-two and a number seven please.' She passed Steven a menu from the local takeaway and gave the two men a satisfied smile.

Steven was the main topic of conversation over dinner. 'I'm glad he's back but it's a shame it didn't work out with Amy, I quite liked her,' Edward said thoughtfully.

'How can you say that after what she did to him, you said yourself that he was gutted,' Sheila said incredulously.

'He was,' Edward agreed ruefully.

Sheila picked at a roll. 'You know I don't understand some women, they flit from one man to another, and then they find a good decent one and blow it,' she said almost bitterly.

Edward smiled at her affectionately. 'Get off your soap box woman, most men are the same you know.'

Sheila nodded. 'I know they are, present company excepted of course,' she added quietly. Edward watched her as she carried on picking and felt a sudden pang of guilt; she felt his gaze and looked up at him. 'What's the matter?'

He shook his head. 'Nothing; I was just thinking how lucky I am to have had your friendship for all these years. I don't know if I would have managed without you, and I think that maybe I've taken you for granted.'

'Don't be daft, I love your company,' she exclaimed.

It was Edward's turn to be embarrassed; he quickly changed the subject. 'I wonder what Heather's remembered.'

I dare say Steven will ring you if it's anything significant,' Sheila said sensibly. 'She's taken quite a shine to him,' she added knowingly.

'Well, he saved her life, so I'm not surprised,' Edward commented.

Sheila nodded her agreement. 'But I think it's more than that, she hasn't said as much but I think she quite fancies him.'

Edward shook his head sadly. 'Well, I think she'll be out of luck because he's off women, or so he says,' he added.

'I might be wrong,' Sheila continued 'But she said that she likes to make him smile so that she can see his dimple.'

Edward laughed raucously. 'I've got a dimple too, has she taken a shine to me as well?'

Sheila stared at him longingly. 'She didn't say so, but I wouldn't blame her if she had.' Edward gave her a puzzled look. 'Anyway, she was singing his praises whilst I was doing her hair,' she continued quickly.

'Really,' he enquired interestedly. Sheila put her spoon down.

'She said that if she had died then she couldn't think of anyone nicer to cut her up.'

Edwards jaw dropped. 'She really said that?'

Sheila nodded enthusiastically. 'She said that she trusts his hands, whatever that means.'

Edward grimaced. 'How morbid.'

'Do you think so?' Sheila asked in surprise.

'Yes, I do,' he said firmly.

'Well, I think it's very practical,' she chuckled.

'Practical in what way?' He asked disbelievingly.

'Well, if you know and trust the person who is cutting you up, then you know that they're going take care of you and not just hack away,' she explained.

Edward stared at her in wonder. 'I've never thought about it like that.' They suddenly felt themselves being watched and turned around. Edward smiled at the couple on the next table who were looking at them in disgust.

'Do you mind, we're eating,' the man snapped.

'Sorry,' Edward apologised whilst trying to hold back a smirk. 'We'd better go,' he whispered.

After a pleasant hour chatting to Heather and managing to drop half his dinner down his shirt, the nurses told Steven that the ward smelt like a chip shop, and suggested in no uncertain terms that he should leave immediately. He collected the empty food wrappers and thanked Heather for a lovely evening. 'Much more diverting than dining with dad,' he chuckled.

'Thanks for coming, and I hope your dad is having a good time with Sheila, he won't be mad with you for leaving him, will he?' She checked.

'No; and even if he is, then he'll get over it,' he assured her. 'Anyway, I'd better go,' he said quickly as a nurse appeared at the window and glared at him. When he got home, he turned his attention to the washing, something he realised he should have done before going out. He loaded the machine, then took his shirt off as an afterthought and smiled at the sweet and sour sauce stain.

Although it had been a bit unconventional, he'd had a nice evening. God knows what dad will say when he finds out he thought as he stuffed his shirt into in the machine. Bribing Higgins with chicken chow mien was a good idea of Heather's though.

'Only if it works though,' he said to Monty who had just appeared. The cat rubbed his face on his leg and purred loudly. Steven bent down to stroke him and sighed at the hairs that came away with each stroke. 'I thought animals only moult in the summer,' he muttered.

As he rinsed his hands and watched the hairs gathering in the plug strainer, a thought suddenly struck him. He dragged the clothes out of the machine onto the floor, and searched through them until he found the pair of trousers that he was looking for, then he laid them on the kitchen table and looked down each leg from top to bottom, three quarters of the way down the left leg he found several white hairs.

He collected a specimen tube and tweezers from his case and plucked them off. He was just congratulating himself when he heard the front door open and his father appeared in the kitchen doorway. 'Your phone's switched off,' he scolded, and then wondered why his son was standing in the kitchen bare chested and surrounded by dirty washing. 'Should I ask?' He enquired amusedly.

Steven waved the specimen tube at him. 'Possibly hairs from John Simmons' dog.'

Edward took the tube and looked at the hair. 'Go on,' he encouraged.

'We found dog hair imbedded deep in the rug that Rose was wrapped in, the same rug that had Heather's and Harry's blood on it,' he explained.

'Right,' Edward exclaimed. 'So, if the dog hairs belong to the Simmons' dog, the rug must have come from their house?'

Steven nodded. 'They're having hardwood flooring put down.'

Edward looked at the specimen tube again. 'Is this hair definitely from their dog?'

Steven nodded. 'I think so, he was jumping up at me, and I haven't been near any other dogs as far as I can remember.'

Edward looked at his watch. 'It's a bit late to do anything now, do you fancy meeting up tomorrow about twelve? We can have lunch and you can tell me what Heather remembered.' Steven grimaced and started to try and explain, but his father put his hand up. 'It's ok, Sheila told me all about it,' he said semi-seriously.

'What did Sheila tell you?' Steven asked suspiciously.

'About Heather taking a shine to you. Apparently, she likes your dimple, although I don't know what your dimples got that mine hasn't,' he laughed at the look on his son's face. 'Don't worry son, it happens a lot.'

Steven was bemused. 'What does?'

'Patient doctor crushes, she probably just wanted to see you,' Edward explained.

'I'm not her doctor,' Steven reminded him dryly.

Edward patted him on the back. 'But you did save her life son,' he glanced at the clock. 'I've got to go, Sheila's waiting in the car,' and with that he was gone.

Although the mortuary was officially closed at the weekend, there was always someone on call for emergencies. Steven rang Sue first thing and arranged to meet her there at ten thirty. 'I hope this is important,' she grumbled when she arrived. Steven showed her the dog hairs.

'Can you match them to the hairs from the rug.' She put both specimens under the microscope and transferred the image to the monitor. 'Well, they look like they're from the same sort of dog. I'll DNA them first thing on Monday to be certain,' she started to leave, when she reached the door, she turned back.

'I'm really sorry about your friend who died Steven, and I quite understand why you reacted the way you did,' she smiled at him. 'We all do, anyway I'd better go. I promised the kids they could go swimming.' Steven watched through the window as her husband opened the car door for her, the children were bouncing around excitedly in the back.

'Happy family,' he sighed, and then went to his office to wait for his father. 'Pub lunch then?' He said hopefully when Edward finally arrived. Twenty minutes later they were sitting in a corner of the black bull, eating a ploughman's and drinking beer.

'So how did you get on with Sheila?' Steven ventured.

Edward frowned at him. 'How do you mean?'

Steven gave him a knowing look. 'You know? Alone with her, a nice romantic meal for two,' he said suggestively.

'We've been alone lots of times,' Edward snorted. 'And it was hardly romantic. We spent most of the evening either talking about you or trying to phone you; we're just good friends, there's no romance you know that,' he insisted.

'She's been looking after you for seventeen years Dad, don't you think that's a bit odd for a just friend's scenario?' He said exasperatedly.

'What do you mean?' His father queried innocently.

'Well why do you think she's never married? I mean she is a good-looking woman.'

Edward nodded his agreement. 'She is good looking; but I don't know why she's never married, maybe she's not found the right man,' he suggested.

'You think?' Steven groaned. He resisted the temptation to enlighten him on her feelings and changed the subject. 'It looks like the dog hairs will match, but we'll know for sure when Sue has done a DNA test.'

'So, if they do match, we will have another connection to Rose, Heather and Simmons?' Edward said thoughtfully.

Steven nodded. 'Is there anything new from Strathclyde?'

Edward shook his head 'I'll give them a ring on Monday morning and gee them up, but Chipping Norton called and it was Barry Mason's sister, Diane, who sent the card. She said that Barry told her to do it,' he added.

'What will they do about it?' Steven asked.

Edward shrugged. 'Not a lot, they'll probably just caution her for sending offensive mail,' he said despondently. They sat in silence for a minute, and then looked up as someone approached the table.

'Shit,' Steven muttered quietly as he recognised Tracy Blackwell, who out of uniform and with her face heavily made up looked like a painted doll.

She smiled at them. 'Hello Sir,' she said to Edward. He nodded his greeting, and then watched with interest as she turned to Steven. 'You didn't fancy the party then?' She asked with a disappointed air in her voice.

'Sorry I already had plans,' he lied. 'Maybe the next time.' Tracy looked at the empty chair next to him, he gave his father a desperate glance, please don't ask her to join us, he thought. There was an awkward silence for several seconds.

'Well, I'll leave you to it,' she said eventually and started walking away. Steven gave a sigh of relief, and then groaned inwardly as she turned back. 'Do you fancy going to see a film next Saturday?' She asked hopefully.

Steven hesitated for a second, and then decided to be honest. 'No, but thanks anyway,' he said kindly. She nodded resignedly and went back to the bar.

'So that's how it's done these days is it?' Edward commented amusedly.

'She called me at work,' Steven confessed with a grimace.

'She's not that bad, is she?' Edward asked quietly.

Steven glanced across to the bar to see her watching him. 'She's not my type. I prefer a more natural look.'

The confession surprised Edward as he recalled how much makeup Amy used to wear. 'Well it's about time you started courting again,' he said concernedly.

Steven glared at him. 'I told you I'm finished with women, especially pushy ones,' he snapped.

'You don't mean that, son,' Edward started to say, then he saw the anger appearing on his son's face and put his hands up in defeat. 'Ok, I'll drop it,' he said quickly.

Chapter 11

Two days later, Edward was looking at a report that he had just received from forensics. 'Get a warrant and bring John Simmons back in,' he ordered. Jack raised his eyebrows. 'It's definitely hair from his dog in the rug,' Edward explained.

'A break at last,' Jack exclaimed, and went off whistling happily. He returned an hour later with John Simmons in tow, and after waiting for his solicitor to arrive, he was taken to the interview room.

Edward put a photograph in front of him. 'Do you recognise this rug?'

John glanced at it. 'It looks like one we used to have in the lounge,' he said disinterestedly.

'You said used to have in your lounge, what happened to it?' Edward enquired.

John pushed the photo back across the table. 'We got rid; we're having hardwood floors put down,' he said innocently.

'How did you get rid of it?' Jack asked suspiciously. John shrugged. 'I don't know! The blokes that were putting the floor down took all the carpets so you'll have to ask them.' he shifted in his seat and looked at his hands.

Edward stared at him thoughtfully. 'We have your DNA on the cigarette ends and the DNA from a murder victim at the scene of a serious assault. We also have blood from that assault victim, blood from the assault victim's dead dog, and the body of the murder victim all wrapped up in a rug from your house.'

John went white 'There must be hundreds of rugs like that,' he said defensively.

'You're right! But they wouldn't all have hairs from your dog embedded in them, would they?' Edward asked forcefully.

Jack put a picture of Rowena Montgomery in front of him. 'Do you know this woman?'

John shook his head. 'No I don't,' he said quietly.

'Look very closely and think hard,' Edward suggested. A few seconds later, there was a tap on the door and a PC entered the room.

'I'm sorry to disturb you Sir, but Dr Cooper is on the phone and he says it's urgent.'

Edward nodded and got up. 'Interview suspended eleven forty-five,' he said for the tape.

'What do you think guv?' Jack asked as he followed him out.

'I think he's still not telling us everything, but I'm not sure that he did it' Edward sighed. Jack watched him as he listened to what Steven had to say, but as usual his face never gave much away. 'Are you sure son?' Edward checked, and then put the receiver down.

'Get a warrant for Lottie Simmons and bring her in too,' he ordered. Whilst Jack went to arrange a warrant, Edward went back to the interview room. John was still staring at the picture.

'Who is this? I have no idea who she is,' he said firmly.

Edward picked the photo up and put it back in the folder. 'Her name is Rowena Montgomery.'

'Montgomery,' Simmons repeated.

'Yes, do you know her now?' Edward asked dryly.

John nodded. 'I know the name, and if it's who I think it is, then my mate and his wife work for her husband.'

Edward sat down and turned the tape on again. 'What is her husband's name?' He asked.

'James Montgomery,' John said confidently.

'And your friend's name?' Edward checked. 'Craig MacDonald, he's the area manager for Montgomery's in Glasgow, his wife Helen, is Montgomery's PA,' John said sullenly.

'So how do you know Mr MacDonald?' Edward enquired.

John took a deep breath. 'I went to school with him. His sister Barbara, was married to Lottie's brother.'

Edward sat back in his chair. 'How long have you been married Mr Simmons?'

'What's that got to do with anything?' He counter asked.

'Just answer the question please,' Edward said dryly.

'Fifteen years,' John snapped. Edward looked him straight in the eye. 'And this brother-in-law of yours; is he the man who you store the illegal goods for?'

John gave a sigh of resignation and nodded again. 'Yes,' he confirmed.

'And that's why you didn't want to tell us who he was,' Edward surmised.

'Yes,' he said quietly.

'There's no other reason?' Edward checked.

'No,' John insisted, he shifted in his chair as Edward stared at him thoughtfully.

'So, you've known your brother-in-law for fifteen years?' he asked after a minute.

'I knew him before I got married, he married Craig's sister and I met Lottie at their wedding,' he explained.

'Has your brother-in-law had access to your house over the last three weeks?' Edward asked.

'He and his mate Chas were doing the flooring for us,' John glanced at the clock. 'Can I go now?' he asked impatiently.

Edward ignored him. 'You said they were doing the floor?' he questioned.

'The buggers went off and left it half done. I've not heard from him for a couple of weeks,' John said bitterly.

'Does your brother-in-law own a van?' Edward enquired.

'Yes, it's a dark blue Ford Transit, and no; I don't know the registration number,' he snapped before Edward could ask.

Edward got up and went into the corridor. 'Put him in a cell for now,' he told the PC who was waiting outside. 'We'll see what his wife has to say.' He watched as John was led away and then went to ring Strathclyde about Craig MacDonald. 'They're going to pick him up' he told Jack when he got back.

They watched Lottie Simmons sitting nervously in an interview room. 'Has her solicitor arrived yet?' Edward asked Jack. 'I didn't have to arrive because I was already here,' a voice behind them announced.

They turned around to see John Simmons solicitor Bill Hardy standing there. 'Let's get on with it,' he demanded.

Lottie jumped as they opened the door. 'What can you tell me about your brother?' Edward asked when they were seated.

'Warren?' She enquired.

'Is Warren your brother?' Lottie nodded. 'Can you speak for the tape please?' Jack directed.

'Yes, Warren is my brother,' she said quietly.

'Is he your only brother?' Edward checked.

'Yes,' she confirmed.

'Then tell us about Warren.'

Lottie swallowed nervously. 'What about him?'

'What's his last name?' Jack asked.

'Walker; so, what else do you want to know?' She asked.

'Maybe you could start by telling us where he is,' Edward suggested.

She gave a small shrug. 'I don't know, I've not seen him for weeks.'

Edward looked at her disbelievingly. 'Where does he live?'

'Stirling.'

'Why does he live there?' Jack butted in.

'Because he married a Scottish woman and she wouldn't move,' she said sullenly.

'Are they still married?'

'No, she left him seven years ago,' she said almost inaudibly.

'Why did she leave him?' Edward asked. Lottie bit her lip nervously. 'Why did she leave him?' Edward repeated.

'She said he was beating her, but he wasn't, he would never do something like that,' she snapped defensively.

Jack gave her a sheet of paper. 'Write his address down please.' Lottie scribbled an address down. Jack gave it to the PC by the door. 'Check it out,' he instructed.

'What does Warren do for a living?' Edward continued.

'Why?' Lottie asked.

'Just answer the question please,' Edward requested.

'He's a carpenter; he was doing the floor for us,' she said impatiently. Edward glanced at Jack. 'Was he in Burney on the night that Heather Brooks was attacked?' Lottie nodded curtly.

'Can you say it for the tape please?' Jack reminded her.

'Yes, he was,' she mumbled.

'And when was the last time you saw him?'

'The morning that John found Heather. He stayed over for the night, and then they went to move the stuff from the quarry.'

'Did he often stay for the night?' Edward asked.

She shook her head and then remembered to speak. 'No.'

'So why did he stay that night?' Edward enquired.

'He said that Chas had borrowed the van, so he slept on the couch, and I've not seen or heard from him since,' she started to cry. 'Warren wouldn't have attacked Heather, I told you, he's not like that.' She sobbed.

Edward waited until she had composed herself, and then showed her the picture of the rug. Like her husband, she recognised it, and gave the same account of where it had gone. 'Warren probably put the carpets in a skip, anyone could have taken the rug out,' she said defensively.

'I agree,' Edward conceded. 'But how would you account for your brother's DNA, being present in blood that was found in the mouth of Heather Brooks' dead dog?' Lottie stared at him in disbelief. 'Did your brother appear to have any wounds the last time you saw him?'

Lottie looked at Bill Hardy. 'If you know anything you'd be better off telling them,' he advised.

'He was limping and his jeans were torn; he said he'd slipped with the stanley knife and gashed his thigh,' she said quietly.

'Did you see the wound?' Edward checked. 'No, I told him to go to casualty, but he said it would be ok.'

'Did he change his jeans?' Jack asked.

'Yes, I gave him a pair of John's' she confirmed.

'Did you keep the torn jeans?'

By now, she was white with fear. 'I think that I should speak to my client in private,' Bill Hardy interrupted.

'Of course,' Edward agreed, he got up and went out closely followed by Jack. 'Let's get a coffee,' he suggested. They waited in the office for half an hour until the PC told them that Mrs Simmons was ready to continue. Jack turned the tape recorder on. 'Did you keep your brothers ripped jeans Mrs Simmons?'

'Yes, I did, they're in the rag bag in the shed. I cut them up to use as dusters.'

Edward stared her in the eye. 'Did you wash them?'

She returned his stare. 'I just cut them up and put them in the rag bag in the shed,' she repeated.

Now you're telling the truth Edward thought. 'Ok Mrs Simmons, you are free to go, but we will need to see you again, so don't leave the area,' he ordered. Lottie gave a sigh of relief and stood up. 'Sergeant Taylor will drive you home, and whilst he's there, perhaps you would be good enough to give him the rag bag from the shed and a recent photograph of your brother?'

105

Lottie nodded her agreement and rushed out as fast as she could. Edward took Jack's arm. 'Go with her to the shed and make sure she doesn't take anything out of the bag,' he instructed.

'Rose's skirt and top are cheap market type things; they could have come from anywhere, and the pants had been contaminated by the decomposition of the soft tissues in her mouth so we couldn't get anything from them. The jacket on the other hand is a different kettle of fish,' Sue reported later that day, she picked it up and handed it to Steven. 'It's hand made in a place called Doune, that's in Scotland by the way, and it costs over a grand to buy.'

'A thousand quid for a jacket,' he exclaimed. 'She must have nicked it,' he studied the label. 'I wonder if Rowena Montgomery is missing a leather jacket with DLW on the label.'

The phone rang as he turned to go. 'Strathclyde are biking down the blood samples from the babies whose mothers haven't been traced. They should be here in a few hours,' she informed him when she hung up.

Steven went over to see Heather whilst he was waiting for the samples to arrive. 'How is she doing?' He asked the doctor who had just finished examining her. 'Very well, her ribs and wrist have more or less healed so we can start physiotherapy and get her up on crutches,' he said brightly.

They watched her through the window for a minute. 'What about her memory?' Steven asked.

'She appears to have blocked the attack out; she may never remember what happened, or something may trigger it and it will come back suddenly which could be a very traumatic.' The doctor stopped talking mid-sentence and rushed off as his pager bleeped. Steven watched her for a while longer before knocking on the door. 'Do you want some company?'

Her eyes lit up. 'Yes please. Dad's gone home for a few days to sort out some crises or another at work,' she looked at him seriously. 'One of the nurses said that a woman's body has been found.' He nodded lightly. 'Did you have to deal with her?' She asked.

'Yes I did, but I can't discuss it with you.' They sat in silence for a few minutes, Steven spoke first. 'The doctor says you're doing well and should be up on crutches now your wrist has healed.' She nodded enthusiastically.

'I can't wait. It'll be so good to be able to go to the loo, without having someone standing over me asking if I've finished, what I've done and is it normal.'

He looked at her serious face. 'No, that can't be very nice,' he agreed.

'Not for them anyway,' she said ruefully.

'There's a phone call for you Dr Cooper,' a nurse called from the passageway.

Steven sighed silently and got up. 'I'd better go, that may be some samples I've been waiting for.' Heather nodded her understanding as he went to the desk. It was as he suspected, Sue calling to tell him that not only had the blood samples arrived, but there was also a security tape from Edinburgh royal infirmary with them, and Sergeant Taylor had brought in a bag of rags.

Steven stuck his head around Heathers door. 'I'll call back later,' he promised and then made his way back to the lab.

Sue had already started on the blood samples when he got there. He took the security tape into his office, then called his father to tell him he had the footage before pushing it into the video player. Charlie stuck his head in a few minutes later. 'Come on in and watch this,' Steven invited.

The black and white image was grainy, but they could still make out a woman being helped into a wheelchair in the casualty area. The angle of the camera gave a side view which made it obvious that she was pregnant, but her head was covered with a scarf, making it impossible to see if it was in fact Rose.

They watched as she was wheeled away; the time in the corner read seven forty-four am. The scene then moved to the corridor in the delivery suite. They watched the wheelchair being pushed into a side room; the time read seven fifty-two. It then jumped to nine thirty-six. The corridor was busy with nurses moving from room to room.

Steven pointed to the doorway where the wheelchair had been taken. 'Look at that,' he said to Charlie. There was a woman peeping out; she looked both ways and then ducked back in as a doctor approached. She waited until he had gone into another room, and then unnoticed by a porter who pushed another patient past her, she slipped out, pulling a coat on over the hospital gown.

With the scarf now gone they could see that she had long hair, but her face was still obscured as she walked towards the camera with her head down; suddenly something made her jump. She spun around and looked behind her, the two men leant in closer. Charlie pushed the pause button as she turned back. Her features weren't very clear, but they could see the fear in her partially visible face.

'It could be her,' Charlie muttered.

Steven rewound the tape to the point where she spun around, as she moved her head her hair flew back. He pushed pause again and knelt in front of the television. 'We need to get this enhanced, but I'm pretty sure that the earrings this woman is wearing are the same as the one in Rose's ear.'

Charlie knelt down next to him, and they peered at the heart shaped object which was just visible through the blur of hair. 'I think you're right boss,' he agreed.

Judy appeared at the door a few seconds later. 'Wow! Two men on their knees; every woman's dream,' she chuckled, and then went bright red as she realised what she had said. Steven tried to give her a stern look.

'Are you speaking from experience? Is that where she makes you spend all your time Charlie?' He asked innocently, and then lost the battle to keep a straight face; they glanced at each other guiltily, and then looked at Steven who was grinning at them. 'Secrets out chaps,' he said amusedly.

'Well, I'm glad to see that you all enjoy your work so much.' They looked up to see Bernard Murdoch, who had come into the reception and was watching them.

Steven got up. 'What can I do for you?' he asked.

'Oh, nothing much, I just thought I would come and tell you in person that I have made an official compliant about your conduct towards me,' Murdoch said pompously.

Steven narrowed his eyes. 'Have you really?' He said dryly.

Murdoch smirked at him. 'Yes, I have. I will of course withdraw the complaint, if you apologise publicly for the way that you spoke to me,' he looked at him triumphantly. 'Well?' He snapped.

Although he could feel the anger welling up inside him, Steven managed to keep his expression calm as he stared at the older man. Charlie and Judy looked on, wondering what he was going to do; when he eventually spoke, it was calm and deliberate.

'So, you want me to apologise to a man, who over the last thirteen years has destroyed the reputation of at least one person, and put the families of God knows how many more through hell, with his outdated narrow-minded assumptions, which are based on his inability to accept that dead people, even drug users, are still people and deserve respect?' He checked benignly.

The bits of Murdoch's face that were visible through his beard went purple with rage. 'Drug users don't deserve anything,' he spat vehemently.

'So you admit that you fit the description of the man I have just described?' Steven said calmly. Murdoch's beard bristled as he tried to think of a response. Steven shook his head sadly, and making a point of not calling him professor, stated dryly. 'An apology Mr Murdoch, I think not.'

He turned to Charlie. 'Would you escort Mr Murdoch off the premises please, and tell him to make an appointment the next time he wants to see me.'

'This way Sir,' Charlie said, and starting walking towards the door. 'I know the way out; I don't need some lackey technician leading me about,' Murdock sniffed sarcastically.

Steven's patience was now stretched to breaking point; he took a step towards him. 'Mr Malkin is my technician, and I have more faith in his abilities than I do in yours Mr Murdoch, now you claim to know where the door is so use it,' he snapped the last words out as a direct order.

Murdoch glared at them. 'Bunch of bloody misfits,' he muttered, before stamping out and slamming the door behind him.

Steven took a deep breath. 'Right, where were we?' He said calmly. 'Oh yes, we need to get this tape enhanced.' he took it out of the machine and headed to the forensics lab, leaving Charlie and Judy speechless.

Sue was sifting through the bag of rags; she had collected the bits of jeans material and was busy reconstructing them; she looked up as he came in. 'Look at this,' she pointed at a ragged tear in the top of one of the legs, there was dried blood around it.

'Can you type it and check it against the stuff you got from the dog's mouth,' Steven asked.

Sue nodded. 'I may even get some of the dog's saliva from the material. It'll take a day or two though, and the babies' blood is in the system. It'll be tomorrow or the day after at the earliest,' she added before he could ask.

Steven gave her the tape. 'Can you get it enhanced as soon as possible,' he asked and then went back downstairs.

'Thanks for that boss,' Charlie said when he joined him in the cutting room.

Steven raised his eyebrows. 'Thanks for what?'

Charlie gave a little shrug. 'For what you said about me to Murdoch,' he muttered self-consciously.

Steven pulled a pair of surgical gloves on with a snap and smiled at him. 'I meant every word.' Charlie looked surprised and embarrassed. 'So how about proving me right, and dissecting this rather nasty looking pair of lungs?' Steven suggested.

Charlie turned his nose up. 'Do I have a choice?' He asked hopefully.

'Of course, you can do the even nastier looking bowel if you'd rather,' Steven said brightly; after examining the bowl of guts and deciding on the lesser of two evils, Charlie started on the lungs.

Once again John Simmons had been released. 'I think the most we'll get either of them for is handling illegally imported goods, but we'll keep an eye on them just in case the brother gets in touch,' Edward said despondently.

'Do you want twenty-four-hour surveillance guv?' Jack checked.

Edward nodded. 'You'd better clear it with Whittle,' he added thoughtfully. He was twenty minutes into the pile of paperwork on his desk when he was interrupted by the phone. An officer from Strathclyde informed him that they had been to Walkers house at the address given by Lottie Simmons, but the place was deserted, so they had put surveillance on it.

Craig MacDonald wasn't at home either. His wife told them he had gone away on business, but his office said that he had taken a fortnight's holiday, which basically meant that no one knew where he was, so they had issued a warrant for his arrest. They had also spoken to Rowena Montgomery about the jacket, and hers had been stolen from a nail salon in Glasgow two days before they received the ransom note.

'She did report it, and we've got the incident logged,' the officer confirmed. Edward thanked him and hung up as Jack reappeared.

'The Chief super's not happy guv, but he's given the go ahead for the surveillance.' Edward gave a sigh of relief and brought him up to date. 'So Rose took the jacket whilst Mrs Montgomery was having her nails done,' he surmised.

Edward nodded. 'She dyed her hair and stole the jacket, and in doing so she signed her own death warrant,' he said quietly.

Chapter 12

Edward sat in an armchair later that evening and thought about Heather. The hospital had reported that she was making good progress, and once she had mastered the crutches, she would be discharged. He sat back and wondered how she would manage when she went home.

'She's going to need protection if we haven't caught Warren Walker,' he told Whittle earlier, and whoever else is in on it he thought to himself. He yawned loudly, and then jumped as someone tapped on the window. He got up and pulled the curtain back to see Sheila standing there.

'Are you ok?' She asked when he let her in. 'I've been ringing the bell for ages.'

He gave her a rueful smile. 'Sorry, I didn't hear you, I must have been miles away.'

Sheila handed him a dish wrapped in a tea towel. 'I'm assuming that you haven't eaten, so I've made some hot pot, it's only just out of the oven so it will still be very hot,' she warned.

'Aren't you having any?' he enquired as she turned to go.

'Mine's at home cooling down,' she smiled at him and continued on her way. Edward suddenly felt incredibly lonely.

'Why don't you bring yours round, I think I've got a bottle of wine,' he called.

She turned back and smiled again. Illuminated by the porch light, she was looking very attractive. 'Well if you're sure, it would be nice to have some company. I'll be back in a minute.'

He smiled to himself as she disappeared into the night, then went into the kitchen and retrieved the bottle of wine from the back of the cupboard. He quickly wiped the dust off and started searching for a corkscrew, but before he found one the bell went again. 'It's about time you had a key,' he observed as he let her in.

'Here,' she said, and produced a corkscrew from her pocket.

'How did you know that I couldn't find one?' He enquired.

'Just a hunch,' she said knowingly, as he took it from her and opened the bottle.

'Hot pot and wine, what a combination,' he commented a few minutes later. 'I don't know what Steven would think of it.'

Sheila shook her head 'There's probably some weirdly named drink brewed especially for having with hot pot,' she chuckled.

Edward started to relax as they ate. Sheila's face lit up as she laughed at his anecdotes from the force, and it suddenly struck him that she had never been far away. Always waiting quietly in the background, and always willing to give help whenever he needed it. He also knew that he could confide in her, and had often done so over the years; and that was the moment the realisation that he had strong feelings for her hit him.

Had they always been there he wondered, or had he been so wrapped up in his work that he had either missed, or maybe feeling guilty, ignored the signs that he was actually in love with her. 'Are you alright, Edward?' Her voice made him start.

'Very alright, thank you,' he assured her.

They finished the meal, and Sheila started to gather the dishes. Edward put his hand over hers to stop her. 'You cooked so I'll clear,' he said firmly.

She gazed at him lovingly as he squeezed her hand. 'You used to say that to Elizabeth.'

He gave a light nod. 'Did she tell you that?'

Sheila gave a little laugh. 'Yes, she did, she told me a lot of things about you.'

'Not everything I hope,' he muttered.

Sheila moved her hand and got up. 'She told me all I needed to know.' Edward looked up at her and remembered Steven's words, "She's been looking after you for seventeen years". He had butterflies as he pulled her onto his knee.

'And what was it that you needed to know exactly?'

Sheila blushed slightly, then wrapped her arms around his neck and gently kissed him. 'I needed to know what it would feel like to do that, and do you know how long I've waited to find out?' She ran her fingers through his curls as he gazed at her.

'I would guess about seventeen years,' he whispered. They stared into each other's eyes for a while until Sheila broke the gaze.

'I'd better go.' She tried to get up, but he kept a firm grip on her waist and reciprocated the kiss.

'Do you really want to go?' He asked when he pulled away; she shook her head. 'Well stay then,' he whispered.

She stared at him intently, her eyes shining with hope. 'Do you want me to stay?' She asked quietly.

'More than anything,' he confessed.

'In that case, I will,' she said shyly. Later, as he watched her sleeping beside him, he felt a pang of guilt. He leant on one elbow and stared into the darkness. Seventeen years is a long time.

A tear ran down his face as Elizabeth's words came back to him, "I'm dying, don't be alone". He looked down to find Sheila watching him. She pulled him back down and kissed his eyes. 'Don't feel guilty,' she whispered. How does she know me so well? He thought as she moved from his eyes to his lips.

'Blimey guv, you're chirpy this morning,' Jack commented the next day.

Edward smiled knowingly. 'Am I?' Jack nodded. 'Well you'd better make the most of it then,' he chuckled. Having reluctantly left Sheila sleeping, he was for the first time in years, looking forward to going home.

'So, what's first?' Jack asked, wondering what could have happened to put him in such a good mood. Edward jolted back to the current situation.

'We need to take the photograph of Warren Walker over to the hospital and see if Heather can identify him.' They looked at the snap of Lottie's brother; a rough looking man with a shock of blond hair, and several day's worth of stubble on his chin. He was standing in the kitchen of the Simmons house with a smug sort of smile on his face.

Using the cabinets as a guide, Edward estimated that he was nearly six feet tall. They could see part of a tattoo sticking out of his sleeve, but even with a magnifying glass, it was to obscured by his shirt to see what it was. 'Get onto Lottie Simmons and ask her what it is,' Edward told one of the Detective Constables.

'Evil looking eyes,' Jack muttered as they set off for the hospital.

Heather was sitting looking out of the window; she looked round as they entered with the doctor. 'This looks ominous,' she said nervously.

'We need to ask you a few more questions, and we would also like you to look at a picture, and tell us if you recognise the person,' Edward told her. 'Will you do that for us?' Heather nodded.

'But only if you feel up to it. If she starts to get upset then you'll have to stop,' the doctor insisted.

Edward sat down on the bed. 'Do you know a man called Warren Walker?'

'No,' she said confidently.

'Have you ever met Lottie Simmons brother?' He tried. She shook her head. 'You told Sheila that you remembered someone shouting,' Edward reminded her.

'Yes,' she confirmed.

'Can you still remember what was said?'

Heather shifted nervously in the chair. 'He said, you idiots it's not her, the hairs not even the same colour,' she said quietly.

'And you're sure that it was a male voice?' Jack checked.

She frowned as she struggled to remember. 'I think it was a man,' she said uncertainly.

'Did you notice if he had an accent?' Edward asked hopefully.

'He may have been local; I don't know,' she said anxiously.

'You're doing really well; can you remember what happened after you heard the shouting?' Edward asked.

Her eyes filled with tears. 'I could see lights in the quarry yard, so I went down to the fence. There was a van inside the compound.'

'Can you remember the colour of the van?' Jack butted in.

'I think it was dark blue, or black maybe, it was facing one of the sheds with the headlights on. The back door was open and the little light was on inside,' she stopped talking and wiped her eyes. 'There was someone lying in the back of the van, so I got my binoculars out to see if I could get a better look.' She stopped talking again, and stared at a ginger haired nurse who had just entered the room.

'Red hair, the person in the back of the van had red hair,' she whispered as the tears ran down her cheeks.

'Can you remember what happened then?' Edward asked gently.

She stared at him with concentration etched on her face. 'My phone rang so I switched it off, then Harry growled and I turned around,' she put her hands over her face.

'I think that's enough,' the doctor said worriedly.

'No, it's ok, I want to help,' she insisted.

'Will you look at a picture,' Edward asked. She swallowed hard and nodded. Jack gave her the picture of Warren Walker; her hand shook as she stared at it. 'Do you recognise that man?' She nodded slowly and started to sob. 'Is that the man who attacked you?' Edward asked.

'I really think you should stop now,' the doctor said firmly.

Edward reached to take the picture from her. 'I'm sorry that we've upset you, but you are the only witness,' he said quietly. She tightened her grip on the picture and continued to stare at it.

'We need it back, it's the only copy we have,' Jack told her gently. She let go, and looked up at them with terror in her eyes.

'It's Charlie's friend.'

Edward looked at the picture and frowned. 'Are you saying that the man in the picture, is the man that Charlie Mason works with?' He checked.

'Yes,' she managed to choke, and started to cry again.

'You really should leave it now,' the doctor insisted, the nurse put her arm around her as she continued to sob.

'Don't worry, there's a policeman outside the door at all times,' Edward reassured her.

'Christ! Is that a coincidence or what?' Jack commented when they got outside.

'I don't know, but I do know that we need to get onto Chipping and find out where Charlie Mason is,' Edward muttered.

They went over to the mortuary to let Steven know what Heather had remembered. 'He's out on a call, apparently there's a body in a burnt-out car,' Judy told them.

'Where is it?' Jack enquired; Judy looked at the log.

'Nubbin, five miles the other side York, the pathologist over at York was unavailable,' she explained to Edward's look of surprise.

'Can you ask him to give me a call when he gets back?' He asked.

Sue appeared with a handful of results as they were preparing to leave. 'The thread that Steven got from the dog's mouth, matched the jeans that came from the Simmons house, and there were traces of the dog's saliva on the material. We've also enlarged and enhanced a frame from the hospital CCTV,' she handed him the enlarged photograph.

The woman's face was partially covered by her hair, but the heart shaped earring was obvious. Sue gave him a picture of Rose taken during post-mortem to compare it with. 'We're pretty sure that it is Rose, the earring is definitely the same, but that's the best we can do without losing anymore clarity,' she summed up.

'We'd better go and talk to the Simmons again,' Edward said a little less than enthusiastically as they made their way back to the car, and then to Jack's surprise he got into the passenger seat.

'Wrong seat guv.'

Edward looked up at him. 'You can drive,' he said to the sergeant's quizzical look. 'But slowly please,' he ordered, and then called Chipping Norton, and asked them to pick Charlie Mason up.

'Come on then,' Jack said when he'd rung off.

Edward glanced at him. 'Come on what?' he asked suspiciously.

'What's happened to put you in such a good mood that you let me drive?'

Edward frowned, and tried unsuccessfully to stifle a yawn. 'I don't know what you mean, I'm always in a good mood,' he said disdainfully. Jack glanced at him again. 'Just keep your eyes on the road and your mind on the job,' Edward instructed semi-sternly.

John and Lottie Simmons were far from pleased to see them. 'we've told you everything we know,' Lottie said curtly when she opened the door.

'Not quite everything,' Jack accused. 'What is the tattoo on your brother's arm?' Lottie stared at him guiltily. 'Mrs Simmons?' Jack said sharply.

'It's a snake, it starts at his shoulder and finishes at his wrist. I've already told the other policeman,' she said sullenly.

'But you didn't tell us that your brother knows Charlie Mason,' Edward said dryly.

The Simmons's looked puzzled. 'We don't know him, who is he?' John asked.

'Chas, the man who was helping your brother to put your floor down,' Jack reminded them.

'We don't know him! He just came with Warren, did the job and left,' Lottie said firmly.

'Except he didn't finish the job,' John muttered angrily.

Edward looked at the half-laid flooring and got up. 'I would like you to come to the station to look at some pictures, will you do that please?' He asked them.

'Yea ok, when?' John asked impatiently.

'Tomorrow, and I don't have to remind you to contact us if you hear from Mr Walker, do I?' Edward checked.

'We haven't seen or heard from him for weeks, and we don't need to contact you because there's a policeman sitting in a car watching us, isn't there?' Lottie snapped.

Edward gave her a stern look. 'Do you realise the severity of the situation Mrs Simmons?' Lottie scowled at him, then shrugged dismissively and turned away. 'You and your husband may well be accessories to murder, and you would be as well to co-operate as much as you can.'

Lottie went pale, whilst John paced around the kitchen. 'Murder? What are you talking about? We didn't murder anyone.'

Edward was starting to get angry. 'Perhaps not, but we believe that Warren Walker has, and if you withhold evidence or lie, then you will be classed as an accessory, do you understand Mr Simmons?'

John nodded curtly and sat down. 'Yes,' he snapped.

'Do you think they'll come?' Jack asked as they drove away.

'Yes I do, I think they will cooperate fully,' Edward said confidently.

They arrived with their solicitor at eleven the next morning. Jack sat them in an interview room and gave them an album to look at. 'Just go through it and let me know if you see anyone that you recognise,' he instructed. They opened it and looked at the first photo; they shook their heads as they turned page after page until they got halfway through.

'That's him,' Lottie exclaimed, she pointed to the picture of Charlie Mason that Jack had slipped in as they arrived.

'Do you know that man?' Jack enquired.

'That's Chas who was doing our floor,' she confirmed.

'Ok, carry on looking,' Jack encouraged. They reached the end of the album and John shook his head.

'Only Chas, we haven't seen any of the other men before,' he closed the album with a snap. 'Can we go now?' he asked curtly.

Chapter 13

Steven put a bouquet on the reception desk. 'Nice flowers boss, who's the lucky lady?' Charlie asked and sniffed the bouquet. 'Very nice, they wouldn't be for a certain lucky lady not too far away, would they?' he said knowingly.

Steven shook his head. 'She's neither lucky nor nearby.' He picked the flowers up and looked at the clock. 'I'll be a couple of hours.' Charlie watched intrigued as he headed out to the car, then looked round as Sue ran down the stairs.

'Where's he going? I've got some results for him.'

'I don't know and he didn't say, but somewhere with flowers,' Charlie said mysteriously.

Steven stood in the graveyard an hour later, and looked at the remains of last year's bouquet. 'Happy birthday Sal,' he whispered. He replaced the dead flowers with fresh ones, and looked at the simple engraving for a few seconds. Then he closed his eyes, and contemplated how things may have turned out until he felt the usual tears pricking his eyes. 'Bye Sal, see you next year,' he said quietly.

He was still thinking about her that afternoon when his father arrived at the mortuary. 'I hear you had a burnt-out car.'

Steven nodded. 'Yes, burnt car and burnt body, it was in the woods just outside Nubbin. It looks like it's been there for a while,' he added before his father could ask.

'Was it an accident?'

Steven shook his head. 'Not with a screwdriver through his neck, that's assuming it is a he, we're still working on the body.'

Edward sat down. 'Who's on the case?'

Steven looked at the notes. 'DCI Paul Finch over at York.'

Edward raised his eyebrows. 'Why didn't the local pathologist take it?'

'Unavailable,' Steven said curtly.

'He's not unavailable because of you, is he?' Edward asked semi-amusedly.

Steven frowned at him. 'What do you mean?'

'Just some gossip I heard on the grapevine,' Edward chuckled.

'Since when do you listen to gossip?' Steven enquired dryly.

'Since it involves my son,' he said seriously.

'You're not going to lecture me on the art of diplomacy, are you?' Steven asked impatiently.

'I wouldn't dare, but your Mr Murdoch is making sure that anyone who will listen knows exactly what you said to him.'

Steven sniffed indifferently. 'A, he's not my Mr Murdoch and B, I don't really care what he says, the man is totally incompetent.'

'That's exactly what I told him when he told me what you'd said,' Edward said brightly.

'You told him he was incompetent?' Steven asked incredulously.

'No, I told him that you wouldn't care what he said,' Edward said wryly and changed the subject. 'So, what about the burnt body?'

'It's a tough one,' Steven admitted. 'The whole thing is totally charred; we may get some DNA but I doubt it. I've x-rayed it and taken dental impressions, so we'll see if any of the local dentists can help, and the York boys are checking the car out,' he added anticipating his father's next question.

'Any prints on the screwdriver?'

Steven shook his head. 'No chance, the handle had completely melted.'

Edward suddenly remembered why he had come to see him, and told him about his visit to Heather the day before. 'She was very upset, have you seen her?'

'Not since Tuesday,' Steven said a touch disappointedly.

'Well, I think she would like to see you,' Edward said knowingly.

Steven squinted at him suspiciously. 'You're not trying to set me up are you?'

Edward exhaled loudly. 'I wouldn't do that to you son,' he said innocently. 'Well, no more than you would do it to me anyway,' he muttered under his breath.

Steven sat by Heather's bed a little later. 'Dad said you had a bad day.'

She gave him a nervous smile and nodded. 'It was a shock seeing the picture,' she looked towards the door. 'I'm glad the policeman's outside, but I can't believe that Charlie's mixed up in all this. I didn't have much to do with him but he always seemed ok,' she sighed despondently. 'Anyway, that's enough about me. How's it going with your dad and Sheila?'

Steven shrugged. 'I don't know, but Jack said he was in a very chirpy mood this morning,' he said thoughtfully.

'That sounds promising,' Heather said brightly; they both looked up to a knock on the door, and Sheila popped her head in. 'We were just talking about you,' Heather told her.

'Oh! All good things I hope,' she said suspiciously.

'All bad I'm afraid,' Steven chuckled.

Sheila came right in and sat down. 'I just came to see if you wanted some company, but I see you already have some.' Heather went red as she gave her a knowing look.

Steven got up. 'It's ok; I've got to go now anyway. I just popped in to see if everything was alright,' he glanced at Sheila. 'Have you seen dad recently?' He asked casually.

It was Sheila's turn to blush. 'I saw him last night, and the night before,' she confessed. 'I made him some hot pot.'

Steven raised his eyebrows. 'Oh, I see, Hot pot eh,' he looked at Heather and smiled. 'Let me know what you fancy to eat or you'll have to take pot luck.' He glanced back as he went out; they were watching him go. Heather smiled at him, he smiled back and lifted his hand in a mock salute.

As he sat at home that evening, he thought about the burnt body. It was a particularly nasty case. The whole of the inside of the car, including the body, had been doused in petrol before being set alight. The fire must have been intense, and it was going to be virtually impossible to get any forensics from it, but he had confirmed that it was male.

'At least he was dead before he was burnt, I suppose that's some comfort,' he told Monty. He lay back on the couch and looked into the fire, making pictures in the flames. Monty seized the opportunity and climbed onto his stomach. 'Christ! You're heavy,' he groaned.

The cat purred loudly as he stroked him and then settled down to sleep. They were both woken an hour later by the phone. Steven rubbed his eyes and looked at the time. It was eleven fifteen. 'Steven Cooper speaking.' He yawned, hoping that it wasn't a call out.

'Sorry to wake you son,' his father's voice said.

Steven sat up, tipping the cat onto the floor. 'What's up Dad?' He asked anxiously.

'Don't panic, I just want to ask if you've had any luck with the body in the car.'

Steven yawned again. 'Not much, why do you ask, isn't it York's case?'

'They've just handed it to me; they think it may be linked to Heather's case,' Edward informed him.

'Why?' He asked, with his interest ignited.

'Because they've traced the registered owner of the car.'

'And who is it?' Steven interrupted.

'Charlie Mason,' his father said to his dismay. 'So, as you can imagine, we need to try and get a positive identification,' he added.

'Can you contact all the dentists in Chipping Norton,' Steven asked Charlie the next morning. 'You never know he may have looked after his teeth,' he peered into what was left of the man's mouth. 'They don't look too bad; I think I can see a couple of fillings in there.'

Charlie went into the office to start ringing around; he was back within minutes. Steven looked up in surprise. 'That was quick.'

'There are only two dental surgeries in Chipping, and the first one I rang has a Charles Mason on the books, they are going to send some X-rays over, and the second one has no Mason,' Charlie told him brightly.

Edward appeared as they took the body back to the chiller. 'Any luck?' He asked hopefully.

'We will have to wait for the dental X-rays, but I don't think we're going to get anything else from the body,' Steven told him. 'I hear you had hot pot for dinner the other night,' he commented as he made his father a cup of coffee.

Edward smiled broadly. 'And where did you hear that?'

'Sheila told me,' Steven said mischievously and then nudged him. 'So?'

Edward frowned at him. 'So what?'

'Hot pot, and?' Steven enquired.

'And what?' He asked innocently, and then remembered. 'We had some wine too.' He smiled at his son's expectant face and refused to elaborate.

'Sergeant Taylor is on the phone,' Judy called from the reception. Steven gestured to her to put it through to the office, and watched his father's expression change as he listened to what Jack had to say.

'Get it back to base,' he ordered. 'I'll get forensics over there. We may have found Warren Walker's van,' he announced when he hung up.

Steven and Sue went over to the police garage. Having been found in scrap yard in York, the dark blue Ford Transit van now stood surrounded by plastic curtains. Jack appeared through the plastic. 'It's been wiped clean but it is registered to Walker.'

They suited up and started to inspect the back of the van. 'There are a few strands of red hair in here, and a few fibres that could have come from a carpet,' Sue observed.

'There's quite a few of pieces of polished wood as well, it looks like ends from the hardwood flooring that the Simmons were having laid, you may get prints from this,' Steven called. Jack sent the fingerprint boys over to the Simmons' house to dust the unlaid floor panels for prints, and Steven started to take the pieces of wood out.

As he handed them to Sue, he noticed something wedged under the seat belt fixing by the driver's seat. 'Eureka,' he exclaimed, then backed out of the van and held up a heart shaped earring.

'It's definitely the same as the other one,' Sue confirmed as she inspected it. 'I'll see if there's any of Rose's DNA or prints on it, but I think we can safely say that they belong together,' she concluded.

As soon as they got back to the mortuary Steven called Edward to update him. Judy came in with a package as he put the phone down. Steven opened it and found the dental X-rays for Charles Mason; he went through to the lab and put them up on the light board alongside the ones he had taken earlier.

'What do you think?' he asked Charlie as they compared the images.

'I think they are the same,' the younger man observed.

Steven nodded. 'I agree,' he said, and went to call his father again.

'Thank God for dental records,' Edward said thankfully. 'I'll get onto Chipping Norton so they can inform the family.'

'What about Heather? She needs to be told,' Steven interrupted. 'Do you want me to do it?' He offered, as he heard his father sigh heavily.

'No, it's ok I'll go over later,' Edward said despondently.

Heather was in the physiotherapy unit trying out crutches when Edward arrived. Having never been very good at breaking bad news, he'd asked Sheila to go with him for some moral support. They walked slowly back to Heather's room, stopping every so often to let her rest.

'My legs don't feel like my own,' she commented as she hobbled into her room and sat down. Once the door was closed, Edward gently told her what had happened to Charlie. 'Do you think that this Warren Walker killed him?' She asked nervously.

Edward nodded. 'We are making that assumption; at least until we find him and he tells us otherwise.'

Heather stared at him; her eyes wide with fear. 'Will he try and get me?' Sheila put her arm around her.

'There's a PC outside your door twenty-four hours a day; he won't get to you,' Edward assured her.

'But you think he will try, don't you? And no bullshit, tell me the truth,' Heather demanded.

'Well, we think he has killed twice already, so if he thinks you can identify him, then he may try,' Edward conceded.

Heather went white. 'Killed twice?' She whispered, and then unable to hold back any longer, she burst into tears. Edward waited outside with the doctor whilst Sheila calmed her down.

'Your wife is very good,' he commented.

Edward shook his head. 'She's not my wife.' He smiled at her as she glanced up and wondered if she could be.

'Heather's having a brain scan next week, so all being well, she should be able to go home,' the doctor said brightly. 'We will arrange for a nurse to check on her each day of course, but she shouldn't be alone.'

'She won't be alone, she's going to stay with her father, and I've already arranged for her to have police protection,' Edward added before the doctor could ask.

He was still wondering about Sheila two days later, when the results from the babies' blood samples arrived. He called Jack in. 'Baby number four is Rose's.' He picked the phone up and called Strathclyde to inform them, and then listened as they informed him, that they still hadn't been able to find anything out about her.

'Nobody has reported her missing, we can't find out where she came from or where she's been living, it's a complete blank,' the Scottish DCI reported to Edward's dismay.

It was nearly a week later when they reported that they had located Walker's ex-wife, Barbara, and were bringing her in for questioning. Edward decided that he needed to talk to her in person, and so set off to Glasgow with Jack. 'She's not what you would call delicate, is she?' He commented, as they looked at the bleached blond overweight woman, who was sitting in the interview room with her arms folded over a huge bosom.

'I can't see anyone pushing her around,' Jack said quietly.

'Well let's find out shall we?' Edward suggested.

After talking to Barbara for several hours, they realised that she wasn't as tough as she looked, and had no idea where her ex-husband or her brother were. 'I haven't seen either of them for months and I don't want to, the pair of them are nothing but trouble,' she said curtly.

'Can you explain that comment?' Edward asked.

Barbara sighed impatiently, and then went on to tell them that Warren was a nasty piece of work, and was into black market goods. A fact that they already knew, she also told them that her brother, Craig, had in her words 'lost his marbles,' when he thought his wife was having an affair with their boss. 'He went completely berserk; it was like he was possessed,' she said in her strong Scottish accent. Everything suddenly fell into place.

'Where is Craig's wife now?' Jack asked.

'How should I know?' She counter asked.

'Can you tell us why you left your husband?' Edward asked. A faint red tinge started to appear on her neck. 'Why did you leave him Barbara?' He asked gently.

She stared at them with fear in her eyes, and then looked at the table. 'We think he may be responsible for the deaths of two people, and we need to get as much background on him as possible,' Edward explained. 'Do you think that he is capable of murder?'

Barbara looked up at him and nodded slowly. 'Yes, yes I do,' she said quietly.

'This makes some reading,' Jack muttered. He was leafing through the statement that Barbara had given as they drove back to Kimberwick. 'Can you believe what he did to her?' he said incredulously. 'Why the hell didn't she report him? She may have saved a few lives.'

They sat in silence for a few miles. 'We should to get Steven to look at Rose's body again, now that we know Warren Walker's habits, he may find the final bit of evidence to convict him,' Edward said thoughtfully.

'That's assuming we ever find him,' Jack muttered.

They had only just got back to Kimberwick when Strathclyde were on the phone again. 'They've found Craig MacDonald; they dragged him out of the Clyde in Glasgow this morning, his throat had been cut.' Jack sighed with frustration.

'Are they sure that it's him?' He checked.

'One hundred percent, his wife has just identified him.'

Edward sat back and stared into space. 'It looks like Walker is killing anyone who knew what he was up to.'

'And that only leaves Heather,' Jack finished for him.

Edward rubbed his head. 'I think we should move the Simmons to a safe house. Walker may think of them as witnesses,' he said thoughtfully.

'Heather is safe whilst she is in the hospital, but I really think that the Simmons should have protection,' he told Whittle.

'Do you think he will harm his own sister?' Whittle asked seriously.

'Yes, I do,' he said firmly. The Chief Superintendent gave him a hard stare. Edward returned the look and hoped that he wasn't going to have to argue about it.

'Ok, get them out, but keep the surveillance on their house,' Whittle agreed after a minute.

John and Lottie Simmons were not very happy; they sat in the back of an unmarked police car whilst Jack explained why it was necessary to move them. 'I've already told you that Warren wouldn't hurt anyone,' Lottie snapped.

'That's not what his ex-wife is saying,' Jack snapped back.

Lottie turned her lip up. 'Well she would say anything to get him into trouble. She's nothing but a common tart.'

'For Christ's sake, shut up; you know as well as I do that he's a nasty piece of work,' John snapped.

Jack intervened before the row escalated. 'If your brother is innocent then he can prove it when we find him, until then, you will remain under our protection,' he said firmly. He put the dog on John's knee and shut the door, then watched as they sped off with Lottie glaring at him out of the rear window.

Steven was in the middle of a post-mortem when Edward arrived. Judy made him a coffee and they sat chatting in the reception. 'Have you heard anything about Bernard Murdock. Is Steven going to be in trouble?' She asked apprehensively.

Edward shook his head. 'I don't think so, the last I heard, Mr Murdoch was considering suing him for defamation of character, but since Steven stood up to him, there have been others who are saying the same. They were just too scared to speak out. My guess is that he will be asked to retire quietly before he is totally discredited.'

Judy gave a sigh of relief. 'I was worried that we would lose him when he's only just arrived.' Edward smiled at her, pleased that his son had made such a good impression. The phone rang a few minutes later and interrupted their chat.

'Christ!' Judy muttered when she answered it. 'Hold on a minute,' she said to the caller; she put her hand over the mouthpiece. 'It's that Tracy again, this is the third time she's called. Can't you tell her to leave him alone?' She whispered.

Edward gestured for her to give him the phone. 'Hello, Tracy,' he said, but before he could say anything else she interrupted him. 'Steven! At last,' she said breathlessly. 'I've been trying to speak to you for days but that receptionist keeps telling me you're busy.'

Edward smiled at Judy and decided to play along. 'Oh, does she now?' He said, trying to sound like his son. 'What can I do for you?' He enquired.

'I just wanted to say, that I know you only blew me out the other day because your dad was there, but I think we could have a lot of fun together.'

Edward raised his eyebrows. 'What did you have in mind?'

'Well, a romantic meal to start with and maybe something sweet for dessert. I can do wonderful things with cream,' she added suggestively. Edward stared at Judy suddenly lost for words. 'So what do you think?' Tracy asked.

'Well, WPC Blackwell, I think that you should stop harassing my son or you will be in serious trouble, do you understand?' The line went silent for a few seconds. 'Well?' He asked sharply.

'Yes Sir,' she spluttered and quickly hung up. He handed the phone back to Judy. 'She'll not bother him again.' She gave him a quizzical look. 'Don't ask, but apparently it involved cream,' he chuckled.

'Steven told us about his friend who died,' she said a few minutes later. Edward was surprised. 'Yes, Sally; she was his first real love. He was only nineteen, and she died in his arms.'

Judy stared at him in horror. 'He never told us that, he just said a friend.'

'I'm surprised he told you anything because he never talks about it,' Edward said wryly. He went silent as he remembered his son's grief, and the constant nightmares that he had suffered for months afterwards. 'He was devastated;

126

Sally's brother, Mick, was his best friend, they had the most terrible fight over it and both ended up in hospital.

'Her whole family blamed Steven for her death; it's taken him years to get over it. In fact, I'm not sure that he has,' he said thoughtfully. 'He still puts flowers on her grave each year on her birthday, and even when he was in oxford, he came back every year without fail,' he sighed sadly. 'I told him that she was a grown woman and responsible for her own actions but,' he stopped talking as Steven appeared at the door.

'I hope you're not drinking all my coffee,' he said with a grin. 'So is this a social call?' He enquired. Edward handed him the statement that Barbara Walker had given.

'Will you have another look at the bruise on Rose's shoulder?' Steven read through the report and then led Edward through to the cold storage room; he retrieved Rose from the chiller and Charlie helped him to turn her over. Edward looked at the bruise closely. 'What do you think?'

'I think if you get a cast of Warren Walker's mouth then we can compare it to the shape of the bruise,' Steven said thoughtfully.

Charlie peered at the bruise. 'It's the right shape for a bite but there are no teeth marks.'

Edward shook his head. 'Warren Walker is toothless; he lost all his teeth when he was in his twenties. It's some sort of inherited genetic condition, apparently his father and grandfather both lost theirs after puberty as well. Walker wears a full set of dentures; his ex-wife told us that he used to take them out and bite her shoulder whilst he raped her.'

Charlie stared at Rose's body. 'So he was recreating what he did to his wife, with Rose.'

'Except he went one step further and killed her,' Steven said quietly.

'Will Walker's ex-wife testify?' Whittle asked when Edward got back.

He nodded confirmation. 'Strathclyde have got a guard on her until we get him, and Craig MacDonald's wife is in hospital, apparently she collapsed after identifying his body and they are still waiting to interview her.' Edward sat down and went through all the evidence that they had on Walker.

'We've got a nationwide alert out for him, but he's obviously gone to ground so all we can do is wait and hope that he shows himself.'

Whittle rubbed his chin. 'I'll speak to the press office and see if we can get it on the news, you never know he may just give himself up,' he said optimistically. 'How is Heather Brooks?' he asked as he picked the phone up.

'She's being discharged next week. I've arranged for her to have protection when she goes home,' Edward reported. Whittle nodded his approval and went back to his call.

Twenty-four hours later, Warren Walker's face was all over the news. There were sightings of him almost immediately in every county, and as far afield as the Isle of Man. 'The local forces are going to love us,' Jack muttered as the reports started flooding in. By Friday afternoon there had been over four hundred sightings, all were followed up, and all were cases of mistaken identity.

Edward rubbed his eyes. 'I'm going home.'

Jack nodded his agreement. 'I've had enough this week, I'm knackered.' The phone suddenly rang disturbing their fatigue.

Edward tried to stop a yawn and picked it up. 'Ok bring them up,' he said to the caller. 'Richard Hughes and Kelly Shelton are downstairs, and they won't see anyone but me or you,' he told Jack. He sat down again, and failing to stop it yawned loudly. Jack pulled two chairs up as a PC brought Kelly and Richard in.

As they looked nervously around Edward noticed they were holding hands tightly. 'So, what can we do for you?'

Richard put his hand in his pocket and pulled out a silver mobile phone. 'We got this from that bloke on the telly.' He put it on Edward's desk.

'How did you get it?' Edward asked suspiciously.

Jack went into the main office and came back with an evidence bag. 'Are you the only two who have touched it?' He checked. Richard nodded.

'So how did you get it?' Edward asked again.

'He left it on the bus,' Kelly said quietly.

'He was already on the bus when we got on. We sat behind him and it fell out of his pocket when he got up to get off,' Richard explained.

Edward sat back and stared at them thoughtfully. 'Which bus?'

Kelly and Richard glanced at each other nervously. 'The number seventy-four, we were coming back from York.'

'Can you remember where the man got off?' Edward checked.

'In York town centre,' Richard said confidently.

'Why didn't you hand the phone in?'

Kelly went red. 'Kell's dad took her phone off her, so we kept that one and I got a new sim card for it,' Richard confessed.

'What did you do with the old sim card?' Richard looked at his feet.

'I burnt it,' he mumbled.

'And when was this,' Edward asked.

'About four weeks ago, in the morning, on the day we found the body.'

Edward put the picture of Warren Walker on the table. 'Are you absolutely sure that it was this man?'

They both looked at the picture and nodded. 'We think he realised he'd lost the phone as soon as he got off the bus, because he started walking back to the door, but the driver had closed it and the bus was moving. He looked straight at us as we passed him, it was almost as if he knew that we'd picked it up,' Kelly started to cry. 'Will he come and kill us too?' She sobbed. Richard put his arm around her.

'No, Kelly, you're safe here,' Edward assured her. 'But we are going to have to call your father.'

The expression on Kelly's face, told Edward that she was more afraid of her father than of Warren Walker, nevertheless, her father and Richard's mother were called and duly arrived, both were obviously concerned but surprisingly understanding. 'I assume that you will be protecting her,' Kelly's father said to Edward.

'I've arranged a patrol to keep an eye on your house and also Richard's,' he reassured him, and then excused himself as Jack appeared at the door. 'I've spoken to the bus company, and the seventy-four goes through Nubbin,' he reported.

Edward raised his eyebrows. 'So our Mr Walker could have been on the way back from disposing of Charlie Mason' he mused.

Whilst Richard and Kelly were giving statements, Edward took the phone over to the hospital. 'What make and colour is your mobile phone?' He asked Heather.

'It's a silver Nokia. Have you found it?' She asked expectantly.

'Maybe. Are there any identifying marks on it?' He checked.

'The number seven is almost worn away, it's the speed dial number I've got dad on, and there's a scratch on the display where I dropped it,' she remembered.

Edward took the evidence bag out of his pocket and looked at the numbers, the seven was barely visible and there were several scratches on the display. He handed it to her. 'Is this your phone?' He watched as she inspected it.

'Yes, I'm sure it is. Where did you find it?' He told her briefly how it had arrived on his desk and then went over to the pathology unit.

'He's out on a call,' Judy informed him; she smiled as Charlie came into the reception. Edward handed him the phone.

'You should already have Richard and Kelly's prints,' he reminded him. 'I don't suppose there will be any of Walker's prints left on it because they've had the phone for a month but it's worth looking.'

Charlie took the phone up to Sue who was just leaving for the weekend. 'Is it urgent?' She asked and then took her coat off as he explained where it had come from. 'I'll do basic print testing now but it maybe Monday before any results come through,' she told him as she set to work.

Steven arrived back as Edward was leaving; he followed his son into the locker room and put him in the picture. 'If Walker put a new sim card in the phone, he might not have thought to wipe the inside so there might be some prints,' Steven suggested.

'I've already checked,' Sue confirmed when he called up. 'I've got two sets of prints from the outside and partials from inside. They're in the system and I'll check for DNA on Monday,' she promised.

Steven thanked her then put the phone down and yawned. 'Do you fancy a quick drink?'

Edward looked at the time and shook his head. 'I told Sheila I'd be back at six and I'm already late.'

Steven gave him a knowing look. 'Hot pot and wine again,' he said suggestively.

Edward ignored the comment. 'Come over for lunch on Sunday if you like. Don't worry Sheila will be cooking,' he added hastily. Steven nodded his acceptance and watched him hurry off. Then he sat down at his desk and started to write the day's reports.

'Goodnight,' Sue called on her way out. Steven stopped typing and looked at the deserted reception area.

'Bugger this,' he said silently; then turned the computer off and made his way over to the hospital.

'They've said I can go home next week,' Heather told him. They were sitting in the WRVS tea bar with the PC from the door sitting close by, a few people stared at her as they went past. 'I wish people wouldn't stare,' she whispered worriedly.

'Just ignore them, they're only curious,' he whispered back. She frowned as a woman who was looking at her nudged her companion.

'That's the woman who got thrown down the quarry,' she said loudly.

Steven glared at her and changed the subject. 'Dad says you're going to stay with your father when you get out.'

Heather nodded. 'Just until the plaster comes off, and with a policeman for protection,' her eyes filled with tears. 'I'm sorry I'm always crying, but I've seen the news, I know what he's done and I'm scared that he will find me and dad.'

Steven put his arm around her and gave her a squeeze. 'He won't know where you are and you'll have protection.' He felt all warm inside as she leant into him, so he left his arm where it was and pulled her a little closer. As he looked around the café, he realised just how self-conscious she must feel.

Most people were just curious to see what this woman who had been on the brink of death looked like, and contented themselves with a quick glance, but a few were just downright rude. He scowled at a man who was staring at them, the man quickly picked a newspaper up and started to casually flick through the pages. Prick! Steven thought and then had an idea.

'How about I come and get you tomorrow, you can come home for a couple of hours. I'll make you some lunch and you can meet Monty.'

Heather perked up and smiled at him. 'Really?'

He nodded enthusiastically. 'Absolutely, come on let's go and find the doc.' He helped her up and glared at the man who was still watching them over the top of the newspaper.

'As long as she doesn't exert herself too much,' the doctor said when they eventually found him.

Steven suddenly felt like a teenager on a first date. 'Don't worry, it'll just be for a couple of hours. I'll make lunch and bring her straight back,' he promised. 'I suppose I should ask dad as well,' he mused.

'Take Higgins with you,' his father told him when he rang. 'It's a date then, permission all round,' he said happily.

Getting Heather into the car in the pouring rain with a plaster cast on her leg was a feat in itself. After a lot of rearranging, she eventually ended up sitting lengthways across the back seat. 'Are you ready?' PC Higgins checked; she nodded enthusiastically.

'It's so good to be out. I hate being stuck inside,' she glanced at Steven, who was watching her at her in the mirror and smiled as he caught her eye. They turned into the lane twenty minutes later. 'What a lovely place to live,' she exclaimed as they drew up at the cottage.

They got her out of the car which proved a lot easier than getting her in; Higgins retrieved the crutches from the boot and they went inside. Monty greeted them purring loudly and climbed onto Heather's lap as soon as she sat down. 'He's gorgeous,' she said as she stroked him.

Steven stuck his head out of the kitchen. 'You've a friend for life there; he doesn't sit on just anyone.' They spent a good hour over lunch.

'That was lovely,' she complemented. 'Shall I do the dishes?'

Steven shook his head. 'Absolutely not, you're a guest, and anyway the doctor said not too much exertion,' he reminded her. She sat in the kitchen whilst the two men washed up.

'How long have you lived here?' She enquired.

'A few months,' he said without turning around.

'That long! It looks like you've only just moved in,' she said in surprise. Steven glanced over his shoulder and raised his eyebrows. 'No curtains. No wallpaper,' she questioned.

'No time,' he offered up as an excuse and went back to the washing up.

'There should always be time for decorating,' she muttered.

'I expect I'll get round to it eventually,' he said unconvincingly.

'Can I ask you a big favour?' She said a few minutes later. Steven turned around and leant on the sink.

'Of course you can, as long as it doesn't cost me money or cause me pain,' he smiled at her and then saw the serious look on her face. 'What is it?' He asked anxiously.

'Can I bury Harry in your garden? It's so peaceful here and I've only got a yard,' she said quietly. She was blinking back the tears as she spoke.

Steven resisted the urge to give her a hug and nodded. 'Of course you can, pick a spot wherever you like, and you can plant a bush or something over him if you want too.' She wiped her eyes and gave him a grateful smile.

'We'd better get back,' Higgins suggested.

'I suppose so; we don't want the doctors telling us off, do we?' Steven agreed half-heartedly.

'No, I suppose not,' Heather conceded. She gave the cat one last stroke then they helped her back into the car. 'Thanks for lunch,' she said when they got back to the hospital.

'Yes, thanks,' Higgins echoed. 'It beats the sandwiches my wife gave me,' he chuckled.

After seeing Heather back to the ward, Steven went over to the mortuary. There was a print out on Sue's workbench confirming that fingerprints on the phone matched both Richard and Kelly, but there was also a partial print on the inside of the phone which matched samples taken from the boards from Warren Walkers van. He picked the reports up and found a note underneath.

"Hi, sad one! I knew that you wouldn't be able to stay away so here are the results". He chuckled to himself as he read it. I've got a really good crew here, he thought contentedly.

He sat at the dinner table the next day and watched his father and Sheila; his father looked happier than he had for a long time. They really suit each other. I can't believe that dad didn't realise how she felt. Mind you, I didn't notice either he mused, but there again I've not been here much, he argued with himself in self-defence.

'Steven?' Edward said loudly, he jumped and looked at them. 'What's on your mind, son?' His father enquired. 'You were miles away.'

He shook his head. 'Nothing. I was just contemplating life.' Edward rolled his eyes at him.

'You don't want to be doing that, it's depressing.' Sheila handed him a dish. 'Contemplate some dessert instead,' she suggested.

Chapter 14

Jack stuck his head around Edward's door two days later. 'Whittle wants to see you, guv.'

Edward grimaced. 'What have I done now?' He got up and made his way despondently down to Whittle's office.

'There may have been a sighting of Walker in York; traffic think they spotted him in a stolen Nissan. They followed him but he dumped the car and they lost him by the Minster,' Whittle informed him when he went in.

'When was this?' Edward enquired.

'In the early hours of this morning. I think you'd better post another couple of uniforms at the hospital,' Whittle said seriously.

'Heather is being discharged this afternoon,' Edward interrupted. 'Steven's taking her to her father's house in Bishops Glen.'

Whittle looked surprised. 'Your son is taking a keen interest in her.'

'Meaning what?' Edward demanded, but Whittle was busy cleaning his glasses and didn't bother to answer. 'Meaning what?' He asked again.

'Nothing, it's just an observation,' Whittle said dryly.

'I hope that you're not suggesting that my son is being anything but professional,' Edward said angrily.

Whittle shook his head. 'I wouldn't dream of it,' he said semi-sarcastically.

'You do know that young woman has been through hell over the last few years, don't you?' Edward reminded him.

Whittle put the glasses back on and stared at him. 'I know exactly what she has been through,' he answered curtly.

'Well she seems to trust Steven, and if he can help her to get through this then I think we should let him,' Edward said firmly.

Whittle glared at him. 'Make sure that the local force has a man inside the house and a car outside around the clock,' he instructed.

'It's already been done,' Edward said curtly; then left the room as Whittle dismissed him with the usual wave.

It was late afternoon when Steven helped Heather into his car again. 'Can I say goodbye to Monty?' She asked.

'Of course you can, we'll call in at home and then I'll take you over to your dad's,' Steven said brightly. PC Higgins was on duty again; he got in the front seat and they moved off with another police car following behind. Heather looked back as they drove away. Steven glanced at her in the mirror and saw that she was trying not to cry.

As promised, they stopped at his cottage en-route. Steven made them a quick cup of tea; whilst Heather made a fuss of Monty, then they headed over to Bishops Glen. Higgins ushered her inside where she was met by her father and a plain clothed detective. 'There are two policemen outside in an unmarked car; they will be there around the clock, and I or one of my colleagues will be here in the house,' he told them.

'Thank you for bringing her home,' her father said nervously as Steven reluctantly prepared to go.

'Try not to worry, Malcolm. I'm sure that Walker will be caught soon,' Steven said brightly; he was trying to sound positive but in reality feeling far from it. Heather dominated his thoughts as he drove Higgins back to Kimberwick. Although, he had tried to ignore the feelings which had been growing inside him from almost the first time he saw her, he couldn't get her out of his head.

He sighed inwardly and hoped that she was feeling the same way, and that he would see her again, and sooner rather than later. Higgins broke into his thoughts. 'Don't worry, she'll be fine,' he reassured him.

After dropping the PC off, he called into the squad room to see his father. 'He's in with Whittle,' Jack told him. 'Come in and wait if you like.' They went over to the evidence board and looked at the pictures which were all set out in neat columns. Heather's wounds, Harry's body, Rose in the sheep shed, the burnt remains of Charlie Mason, and Craig MacDonald's name, all under the heading victims.

'Has this bloke got a record?' Steven asked as he looked at them. Jack shook his head. Steven looked at the picture of Walker standing in the Simmons' kitchen. 'He looks familiar,' he muttered.

Jack joined him by the board. 'He's Lottie Simmons' brother; it's probably a family resemblance.'

Steven peered closer. 'No, I've definitely seen this man recently.' He sat down and stared at the picture. 'He had black hair and he had a tattoo on his arm.' He closed his eyes and tried to picture him.

Edward came into the squad room a minute later. 'Don't fall asleep there, son,' he chuckled.

Steven opened his eyes as an image flashed through his mind. 'His sleeve was open; there was a tattoo of a snakes head on his wrist,' he exclaimed.

'Are you sure?' Jack checked. 'Absolutely, he was in the café last Friday, he kept staring at Heather. I thought it was just curiosity because everyone was looking at her, but when he saw me looking at him, he pretended to read a newspaper, and that's when I saw the tattoo.'

Edward stared at the picture. 'Are you sure it was him?'

Steven looked at the picture again. 'Absolutely sure,' he said firmly. Edward called Bishops Glen. 'They're going to put some extra men on the house,' he said when he rang off, then he took Steven to tell Whittle about the new developments whilst Jack went to inform the team about the change of hair colour.

Karen Sharp's parents were sitting in the reception when Steven got back. 'They've been here for ages,' Judy whispered.

Steven took them into his office. 'What can I do for you?' He asked when they had sat down.

'We've come to thank you,' Mrs Sharp said quietly.

'Thank me for what?' He asked in surprise.

'For finding out what happened to our daughter; thanks to you, the two men who were responsible for her death have been caught,' she said tearfully.

'I just did the post-mortem,' he objected.

Mr Sharp stood up. 'You did a thorough job, that bloody idiot in York would have had everyone believing that our Karen was a drug addict. We wouldn't have even known about the baby if you hadn't done your job properly, so thank you,' he said humbly.

Steven shook his outstretched hand. 'I'm sorry it had to end the way it did,' he told them as he showed them out. 'It's people like that who make my job worthwhile,' he said to Judy when they had gone. 'Because even though they know that their daughter was murdered, and they know how she was murdered. Knowing the truth has given them closure so they can move on.'

Judy stared at him thoughtfully. 'Is that what you want for Sally?'

The question surprised him. 'What do you mean?' She blushed slightly as she told him what his father had divulged. 'Yes, I suppose I do,' he sighed. The phone interrupted their conversation.

Judy picked it up and handed it to him 'Sergeant Taylor,' she mouthed. Jack was calling to find out if they had managed to get anything from the phone.

'I'll call you back,' Steven said and then ran up to the forensics lab. 'I got DNA from Richard and Kelly which we knew we would, but there were also traces of wood dust between the keys, and the dust was consistent with the wood that we got from Walker's van,' Sue told him.

'So it's probable that the phone was in Walker's van at some point,' Steven told Jack when he rang back. There was a letter from the home office on Steven's desk the next morning; he smiled as he read it. 'Good news, boss?' Charlie enquired. Steven handed him the letter. 'Due to the retirement of Professor Bernard Murdoch on the grounds of ill health, there is a vacancy for senior pathologist at the university hospital in York,' he stopped reading.

'You're not going to take it, are you? You've only just got here,' he asked in dismay.

'Take what?' Judy asked as she came in with coffee cups.

'Murdoch's job in York,' Charlie told her; she put the cups down with a bang.

'You're not leaving, are you?' She exclaimed.

'They've only asked if I would be interested in applying for it,' Steven said exasperatedly; he took a sip of coffee and grimaced. 'I wonder if they have decent coffee in York,' he muttered, and then keen to know what his father thought he rang and invited him and Sheila over for dinner that evening.

'Only you can decide, son,' Edward told him later. 'Do you want to work in York?'

Steven shrugged. 'I don't know, but they will have sent the letter to all the pathologists, so I doubt I would get it anyway.'

'I think you would have as good a chance as anyone,' Sheila said generously; she gestured towards Monty who was crying at the back door.

'Haven't you put the cat flap in yet?' Edward enquired semi sternly.

137

Steven gave him a sour look and got up to let the cat out. 'Anyway, I've only just got here and the team is really great,' he continued thoughtfully. As they ate, Steven noticed that his father and Sheila seemed preoccupied.

'That was delicious, Steven,' Sheila complemented when they had finished. 'You must tell me what was in it so that I can make it for your dad,' she looked at Edward and smiled shyly.

'I'll write it down for you,' Steven offered, he leaned back in the chair and looked at them suspiciously. They looked almost guilty about something. 'Are you two ok? Has something happened?'

Edward took a deep breath. 'Well, yes on both counts actually. Yes, we are ok and yes something has happened.'

Steven leant forward and raised his eyebrows enquiringly. 'What?'

Edward took Sheila's hand and smiled at her. 'I've asked Sheila to marry me,' he looked at his son with trepidation.

'And,' Steven enquired impatiently.

'And she has said yes,' Edward said tentatively.

Steven smiled broadly. 'About bloody time.' He shook his father's hand, then leant over and kissed Sheila. 'Congratulations; do you think you can cope with him?' He asked wickedly. 'This calls for a celebration; I think I've got some champagne left over from my not wedding.'

'Not for me, I'm driving,' Edward called as he got up and went out of the room. 'Anyway, I bet he doesn't know which box it's in,' he whispered to Sheila.

'I heard that, Dad,' Steven shouted from the hall.

He smiled to himself as he waved goodbye to them a little later, then went into the kitchen and looked at the pile of washing up. He was very tempted to leave it until the morning, but decided against it and started filling the sink. He thought about his father and Sheila as he watched the bubbles form and pop.

He knew that his mother would have approved one hundred percent. 'It is about time,' he muttered to himself. He glanced up as Monty appeared at the window, and gasped as he saw the reflection of someone lunging towards him across the kitchen.

He felt a sharp pain in his neck as he spun around. He grabbed the first thing that came to hand and lashed out; the copper-bottomed pan connected with the side of the attacker's head, sending him crashing down, and a bloodied knife clattering to the floor. Steven dropped the pan and grabbed a tea towel to try and stem the blood that was gushing from the wound in his neck. He managed to dial 999 and gasp 'ambulance,' before sinking to the floor leaving the phone hanging.

He leant against the wall and pushed hard on the wound, not daring to move and not taking his eyes off the body that was sprawled face down on the floor, the snakes head obvious on his still hand. The tea towel was quickly saturated in blood; it dripped down forming a pool on the floor. He could hear the operator's voice on the phone urging him to stay on the line.

He closed his eyes as he started to feel light headed and prayed that the ambulance wouldn't be long. After what seemed like hours, but was in fact less than five minutes, he heard the front door opening and his father's voice in the hall. 'It's only me, Sheila forgot her bag,' Edward called.

'Kitchen,' Steven managed to gasp.

'Jesus! Steven,' he heard his father say before passing out.

Steven could hear talking in the dark; very distant but getting closer. He opened his eyes and tried to move his head towards the sound. His neck was stiff and hurt as he moved. He blinked hard and focused on his father who was standing at the end of the bed with a doctor beside him.

'Welcome back, Dr Cooper, try not to move too much,' the doctor ordered.

Edward sat down next to him and squeezed his hand. 'I thought I'd lost you son,' he whispered tearfully. Two days later, Edward sat by his bed again. 'I need a statement if you feel up to it.' Steven closed his eyes and could still see the knife lying on his kitchen floor. 'Can you remember what happened?' Edward asked anxiously. Steven gave a small nod and gave a full account of the attack.

'Was it Warren Walker?' He asked hoarsely.

'Yes,' Edward confirmed. 'He had been watching the hospital, he saw you and Heather when you went out last Saturday, then he followed you on the day she was discharged. You went to your house before taking her to Bishops Glen, didn't you?'

'She wanted to say goodbye to Monty,' Steven whispered.

'Well Walker assumed that she was living with you, but he was in a stolen car and the police escort was waiting at the gate, so he decided to come back when they had gone,' Edward explained. They went silent for a moment.

'Where is Heather, is she alright?' Steven asked worriedly.

'Don't worry, she's very safe with Sheila,' Edward reassured him.

'And where's Walker? How did he get into my house?' He asked.

'He came in through the back door whilst you were seeing me and Sheila off. He's under armed guard down the corridor with a broken jaw. You must have really whacked him he was out cold. We found part of his denture under your fridge, and his leg doesn't look to good either, infected dog bite,' he explained.

Steven gave a sigh and closed his eyes. 'You'd better let him rest now,' the doctor advised, he looked at the chart on the end of the bed. 'A few more days and he'll be up and about.'

Steven opened his eyes again. 'How long have I been here?'

'Six days,' the doctor said brightly.

Steven was horrified. 'Six days,' he exclaimed, and tried to sit up.

'Take it easy; you lost a lot of blood and we had to restart your heart during surgery; but you'll have a nice scar so it should attract the women,' the doctor joked.

Steven lay back again. 'Is someone looking after Monty?' He asked anxiously.

'Sheila and Heather have got him at home; stop worrying will you,' Edward ordered.

Steven gave a sigh of relief, then closed his eyes and drifted back to sleep. Three days later, he was up and sitting looking out of the window. He turned stiffly as the door opened and his heart leapt as Heather hobbled in on her crutches. 'Hi,' he said his spirits lifting.

'How are you feeling?' She asked concernedly.

'A bit sore but much better, thanks.'

She smiled as she sat down opposite him. 'This makes a change, me visiting you; I would have come sooner of course but they said family only,' she said despondently.

'Well, it's good to see you. So are you ok? Glad to be home?' He asked.

She stared him in the eye making his pulse race. 'Yes, except I'm not at home,' she said to his surprise. 'I'm staying in Sheila's bungalow until I get this plaster off. I had trouble with the stairs at dad's house, so Sheila said I could stay at her house,' she explained.

They sat in silence for a while still staring at each other until she suddenly leant across to him. 'I never really thanked you for saving my life, did I?'

He shook his head. 'There's no need to.'

She looked at him seriously. 'Well, I think there is, you were told that I was dead but you checked anyway,' she touched his neck gently. 'And you took a knife because of me.'

Steven took her hand. 'What happened to me wasn't your fault. I'm just glad it was the pan I grabbed because I doubt the colander would have had the same effect,' he said wryly.

She smiled at him; then lifted his hand to her lips and kissed it. 'Well, thank you,' she said quietly. 'I suppose I'd better go; they only let me in if I promised not to stay for too long,' she said a few minutes later. Steven reluctantly let go of her. 'Let me know if you want anything,' she ordered.

He watched as she opened the door and wished that she didn't have to go. 'Actually, there is something I would like,' he called; she turned around and smiled.

'Anything you want, just as long as it fits in the flask,' she quoted.

'Oh right! Never mind then,' he said, feigning disappointment.

She closed the door and hopped back over to him. 'What is it?' She asked anxiously. Steven stood up and supported himself on the window sill, then bent down and kissed her cheek. She blushed slightly and wobbled on her crutches. 'What was that for?' She asked shyly.

'Just for being you,' he said quietly. She stared up at him, and although she was smiling, he could see the pain in her face and wondered if he had overstepped the mark. 'It's going to be alright,' he said as her eyes filled with tears.

'I know,' she whispered; she shuffled a step closer and leant on him, and then still blushing she stretched up and kissed him gently on the lips. The warmth of her body and the softness of the kiss made his heart pound. He looked down into her grief ridden face and saw something that he knew he wanted to be part of.

Although, he was desperate to kiss her again, he knew that it was neither the time nor the place. 'You'd better go, I know what the nurses are like,' he said ruefully. He gave her head a quick kiss. 'Can we pick up on this when I get out?'

Her eyes sparkled as she nodded. 'You can count on it, Dr Cooper.' He smiled to himself as she made her way slowly to the door again. 'Bye then,' she mouthed.

'Bye, say hi to Monty for me,' he called happily. The next day, he sat in silence as Edward brought him up to date. 'Walker initially denied any involvement in the murders of Rose, Charlie Mason, and Craig MacDonald, or the attack on Heather. He claimed that he had broken into your house to steal and had stabbed you in self-defence. He also said that his van had been stolen a few days before the attack on Heather, but once he was confronted with the forensic evidence, he admitted everything.'

'So why did he kill Charlie mason and Craig MacDonald?' Steven butted in.

'Charlie recognised Heather after Walker had hit her. They thought she was dead, so they wrapped her and the dog in the rug, then carried them up to the top of the quarry and dropped them over the side to make it look like an accident. Then when Charlie heard on the news that she had survived, he panicked and told Walker that he was going to go to the police, so Walker killed him and set fire to the car.

'He lost the phone that he had taken from Heather when he was on the bus going back into York, that's when Richard and Kelly saw him,' Edward explained. 'Craig MacDonald was panicking too, he hired Walker and Mason to kidnap Rowena Montgomery because he thought his wife was having an affair with the boss, but when he realised that they had got the wrong woman, he drove down to the quarry and told Walker to let her go.

'It was him who Heather heard shouting that night. But Walker knew that Rose could identify him, so he decided to kill her, but not before having "a bit of fun", as he put it,' Edward said dryly. Steven listened in silence as he continued. 'We got a cast of his mouth whilst he was in surgery having his jaw fixed and compared it to the bruising on Rose's shoulder.'

'Is it the same?' Steven asked hopefully.

'Yes, no doubt,' Edward confirmed. 'After he had killed Rose, he went back up to Scotland to find Craig MacDonald, but he had disappeared. Walker found him at the ferry port in Stranraer and took him back to Glasgow. He cut his throat with the same knife that he used on you incidentally, and threw him in the Clyde.'

Steven sat back in the chair and sighed. 'Christ! All that death because one man thought his wife was playing away.' Edward nodded. 'So was MacDonald's wife having an affair with James Montgomery?' He enquired.

Edward gave an ironic laugh. 'No! It turns out she was having an affair with Charlie Mason,' he said despairingly.

Standing at the graveside brought back memories of losing a wife and a mother; they listened with tears in their eyes as the vicar committed Rose to heaven. When he had finished, Sheila gave them a tissue each and took Edward's hand. 'I doubt we will ever find out who she was,' Steven said sadly.

The attendants started to fill in the grave and the three of them walked sombrely back through the churchyard. As they neared the gate a maroon car drew up. Steven went over and crouched at the door. Heather gave him a small smile.

'She wanted to come and pay her respects,' Malcolm told them as Steven helped her out.

'I'll bring her home,' he offered. Heather took his arm and they walked slowly over to his own father and Sheila. 'I'll catch you up, Dad; will you ask the restaurant to set another place?' Edward nodded, and then watched as Steven put his arm around Heather and they made their way back down the church path.

More tears fell a week later as they stood together in Steven's back garden looking at the newly dug earth. 'He was a really good dog,' Heather sobbed. Steven put his arm around her and gave her a gentle squeeze.

'He was a good dog, and he died protecting you, but in doing so he provided some of the evidence that will convict Walker.' She looked down as Monty appeared and rubbed himself on her legs. 'Come on, let's go in,' Steven suggested. As they made their way up the garden, Edward and Sheila appeared around the side of the house with Malcolm following closely behind.

Edward nodded discreetly as Steven raised his eyebrows. Steven opened the back door and ushered Heather inside, where she was greeted by a bundle of black fur bounding around the kitchen. Monty jumped onto the draining board with his hair on end. 'Well, I think they will get on ok,' Edward said unconvincingly.

Heather scooped the puppy into her arms and turned to Steven. 'He's beautiful,' she said tearfully.

Steven pulled her close. 'Happy Christmas,' he whispered and bent down to kiss her. Edward stood with his arm around Sheila smiling widely, whilst Malcolm, who was obviously not used to such public shows of affection, tried not to look.

'Hey, come on you two, this is embarrassing; I thought you were cooking lunch,' Edward chided. He gave his son a knowing look as he reluctantly released her.

'Go and sit down then,' Steven ordered. He glanced at the pan as he carried the dishes into the dining room, and smiled to himself as he eyed the dent in the bottom.

Case Two
Close to Home

Chapter 1

Steven opened the curtains; It was only seven o' clock but the June sunshine was already streaming through the window. He leant on the windowsill and could see Heather making her way back across the moors, a small dark dot moving through the blaze of colour. Today was a big day; she had been up since six leaving him to sleep whilst she walked the dog.

Ben, now ten months old was bounding around in front of her. As they neared the cottage, Steven spotted Monty who was walking sedately at her heels. I'm sure that cat thinks he's a dog, he thought, and smiled at the surge of contentment he felt.

Heather had stayed in Sheila's bungalow until the plaster came off; she moved back in with her father until the trial was over, and with Walker sentenced to life imprisonment, she insisted that she was ready to go home. But after calling around one evening, Steven found her in tears, and she had eventually confessed to being terrified of living alone again. Steven calmed her down and told her to pack a bag, and that night he brought her and the dog home with him.

Not yet fit enough to return to work, she had insisted on decorating the house from top to bottom. She seemed to know instinctively that he preferred natural colours and materials, and with a keen eye for detail she had set about turning the somewhat uninviting old farmhouse into a cosy home.

Although, Steven had initially tried to fight his feelings, in the end he couldn't deny that he was in love with her, but having read the transcript from Barry Mason's trial and knowing that intimacy might be an issue, he didn't want her to feel pressured, so he made the spare room up, and left it for her decide if and when she was ready to take the next step.

From the start, they had done a lot of kissing and cuddling. It was obvious from Heather's body language that she wanted to take their relationship further, and of course he did too, but each time he tried to caress her, she froze. 'I'm sorry, it must be so frustrating for you. If you want sex, just carry on I'll not stop you,' she told him after another false start.

Steven stared at her in shock and wondered what kind of a man she thought he was. Then he saw the pain in her eyes, and quickly remembered that in the past she had probably been submissive in order to survive. 'I don't want sex. I want to make love to you, and it'll happen when you're ready,' he told her gently as she started to cry.

It did happen just two days later, when Steven arrived home to find her in the bathroom washing Ben, who having knocked a table over had covered himself in lilac emulsion. 'I'm sorry,' she apologised, and then grimaced as the dog jumped out of the bath to greet him.

'It's ok. It could have been worse, it could have been gloss,' he chuckled. Ben shook himself leaving them both soaked before bounding down the stairs.

'Sorry,' she said again.

'Stop apologising, its only water.' He leant over and gave her a kiss, then went to his room to change. As he took a clean shirt out of the drawer, he glanced in the mirror. Heather was standing in the doorway watching him. 'What's the matter?' He asked as her eyes filled with tears; she came into the room and sat down heavily on the bed.

'Malcolm would have been five today,' she said quietly and then the tears spilled over. Steven knelt down in front of her and pushed the hair off her face.

'You're all salty,' he whispered as he kissed her and tasted her tears. She suddenly gave him a look that he would come to know well, a shiver of anticipation shot up his spine as she ran her slender fingers across his bare chest. She pulled gently at the hair and stared deeply into his eyes before kissing him with a passion that he hadn't felt before.

Then his pulse quickened as she searched longingly for his tongue; he responded, and as they met a surge of desire rushed through his body. 'Are you sure?' He asked when she pulled away.

She stared straight into his eyes. 'Yes,' she whispered and started opening her shirt.

He put his hand over hers to stop her. 'Can I do that?' She hesitated briefly before moving her hands and nodding consent. Still kneeling in front of her, he slowly finished undoing the buttons. As he slid the shirt off her shoulders, she put her arms defensively across her body. 'Do you want me to stop?' He whispered.

'They're ugly,' she muttered and looked down in embarrassment.

Steven gently moved her arms, and thinking that she meant her breasts, unhooked her bra. 'They're not ugly,' he assured her as he discarded it.

She shook her head. 'Not those,' she gestured towards her stomach, 'those.' He looked down and saw that in addition to the caesarean scar, there were several deep stretch marks on her stomach. He was suddenly reminded of a conversation that he'd had with his mother when he was small.

'Life lines aren't ugly,' he leant down to kiss them. Then smiled up at her and kissed them again. 'Life lines are proof that you have lived. They are proof that you have given life. They are something to remember Malcolm by, and they are beautiful,' he whispered.

At that point she relaxed, and stopped him with another long kiss. They spent the night talking quietly and taking time to gently explore each other's bodies. It was the early hours of the morning when she finally whispered, 'Make love to me,' and then cried softly as they became one.

'I'm sorry have I hurt you?' He whispered.

She smiled up at him through her tears and shook her head. 'You've touched my heart; no one's ever touched me there before,' and as he gazed down at her Steven realised that until that moment, his own heart had been untouched. That first night was the start of her emotional recovery.

Gradually, over the months she started to return to her "old self", as her father put it. Steven soon found out to his delight, that her old self was incredibly sexy and tactile, being unable to pass him without touching; she even slept with one hand on him. 'Just to make sure I'm not dreaming,' she explained.

He continued to watch her as she neared the cottage, and gave a sigh of contentment as he realised just how lucky he was. The phone brought him back from his musings. 'Steven Cooper speaking,' he said absentmindedly.

'Are you staring at me again?' Heather demanded; she turned and waved at him.

'I'm sorry, I can't help it,' he laughed as he waved back.

An hour later, he was kissing her goodbye. 'See you at the wedding, don't be late or the bride won't wait,' she chanted.

'She's waited for seventeen years, so I think she would wait a little longer,' he chuckled happily. As he watched her drive away, he found it hard to believe that less than a year ago, she had been on the brink of death. He touched the scar on his neck and realised that both of them were lucky to be alive.

He set off to the railway station in Kimberwick twenty minutes later, Sheila's sister, Dora, and her son, Sam, were due to arrive, having flown into London from Sydney the day before. Steven had offered to pick them up and drop them at Sheila's bungalow on route to his father's house.

He stood on the platform holding up a sign with the name Pickering written on it, and smiled as a small dark-haired woman carrying a huge suitcase approached him. 'Dora?' He enquired.

The woman nodded. 'Sam's in the toilet,' she said before Steven could ask. A few minutes later, a very pale and sweaty looking young man joined them.

'Are you ok?' Steven asked as they shook hands.

Sam nodded. 'It's jet lag. I'll be ok after a good sleep,' he mumbled. Steven picked Dora's case up and led them to the car. Dora chatted constantly as they drove along. Steven listened politely unable to get a word in, whilst Sam sat quietly in the back looking like he was going to vomit.

Steven glanced at him in the mirror. 'Are you sure you're ok?' He asked again when Dora stopped for breath; he glanced in the mirror again and saw Sam nod unconvincingly.

After dropping them at Sheila's door, he made his way down the road to his father's house. Edward was sitting nervously in the kitchen. 'Are you ok, Dad?'

His father nodded and looked at the picture of his last wedding day some thirty-five years earlier. 'You don't think your mum would mind, do you?'

'No, Dad, I don't think she would mind, in fact I know that she would have been more than happy to see you two get together a long time ago, never mind seventeen years later,' Steven said impatiently.

'Do you really think so?' Edward asked anxiously.

'Yes I do, now go and get dressed or are you getting married in your dressing gown?' He enquired exasperatedly.

Steven felt a lump in his throat as he watched his father and Sheila exchanging vows surrounded by family and friends. He took Heather's hand and squeezed it gently, she squeezed back and smiled up at him just as the registrar pronounced them man and wife. Edward turned around. 'I did it,' he mouthed at Steven, and then holding his new wife tightly and smiling broadly, they signed the register before heading to the Firs Hotel for the reception.

Dora walked with Steven as they strolled en-mass to the hotel which was just a few hundred yards from the registry office, and once again she talked nonstop. She told him that she'd married an Australian twenty-three years ago, she had moved to Sydney with him and Sam had been born two years later, and although they had divorced when Sam was five, she loved the country and had stayed on.

'You're more than welcome to come and stay if you want to visit,' she invited. 'I'm sure that Heather would love it.' Steven nodded his thanks; he looked at Heather who was in front of them with Sam.

Her hair which was now long again covered the evidence of the wound that had nearly killed her, it hung loosely down to her shoulders and shone in the sun. He smiled as a slight breeze blew it to one side revealing her slender neck. Having discarded her usual jeans and t. shirt, she was wearing a light blue dress that swayed from her hips as she walked.

Through it he could just make out the shape of her bottom, tanned and toned from working in the garden, she was a picture of health. The only reminder of the attack was a slight limp and the occasional headache. She does look lovely today, he thought, as he mentally undressed her.

He smiled again as he remembered the previous night's exertions. 'You are insatiable woman,' he scolded as she cornered him in the shower with the inevitable outcome.

'I'm making up for lost time,' she explained, and gave him a smile that melted his resolve, not that it ever took much melting. He walked on, still smiling and still watching her whilst reliving the moment. She suddenly turned around. 'You're staring,' she mouthed, and gave him a lecherous look before returning to her chat with Sam.

'She's very pretty,' Dora commented amusedly.

'Yes, she is,' he agreed, and embarrassed at being caught leering quickly looked away. He gave a sigh of relief a few minutes later as they reached the hotel. He stood back to let Dora go in first, and then spotted a familiar face in the foyer. 'Jack, it's good to see you again,' he said genuinely as they shook hands.

'So, he's finally done it,' Jack chuckled.

Steven nodded. 'And it's about time too.' They watched the new Mr and Mrs Cooper greet their guests. 'I've never seen the Guv'nor looking so happy,' Jack commented.

'No, me neither,' Steven agreed. 'Come on I'll buy you a drink,' he offered as he saw Heather heading towards the bar.

Sheila looked radiant as she stood by his father. 'Thank you for meeting Dora and Sam,' she said to Steven.

'You're welcome, and you look lovely,' he complemented. They had just finished the speeches, and as the best man, Steven had given an account of how long it had taken for the two of them to get together. He had seen tears in his father's eyes as he mentioned how happy his mother would be for them.

'Your turn next,' Edward commented with a twinkle in his eye. Steven looked across at Heather, who despite being deep in conversation with his cousin, Bernie, was watching him.

'I don't think so, Dad,' he said as she smiled at him.

'We'll see,' Edward said knowingly. Steven turned back to find them both smiling widely and then jumped as Heather pinched his bottom.

'Come with me,' she said mischievously and pulled him onto the dance floor.

'What was Bernie saying?' He asked as they danced.

She looked up at him. 'Why?'

He shrugged lightly. 'I just wondered.'

She stared at him thoughtfully for a minute. 'He asked if I had managed to tame your foul temper.' Steven frowned, and looked over to where his cousin was still sitting. Heather wrapped her arms around his neck. 'I told him that I didn't know what he was talking about,' she whispered.

He held her close and breathed in deeply; she smelt so good, he loved her scent and the way she moved against him, especially the way she moved against him. In fact, it was true to say that he loved everything about her. He pulled her closer and wondered what she would say if he were to ask her to marry him.

Then he reminded himself that he had known her for less than a year and quickly put the thought out of his head. she looked up at him and smiled as the music stopped. 'God, I love that dimple. I can't wait to get home so I can get you out of that suit,' she whispered suggestively as he smiled back.

Several hours later, most of the guests were leaving. Edward and Sheila had gone home dragging toilet rolls and cans behind the hastily, but now fully restored Morgan. Steven went to collect their coats and found Dora standing in the reception. 'Do you want a lift,' he asked as he tried to stifle a yawn.

Dora nodded thankfully. 'I'm just waiting for Sam; he's been in the loo for ages.' They waited for a few more minutes with Dora looking increasingly worried. 'He's been in and out of the toilet all day. Will you go and see if he's ok?' Steven nodded and headed towards the toilets.

Sam wasn't at the urinals; there were three cubicles all with closed doors. 'Sam?' He called.

'No,' Jack's voice called back over one of the doors. Steven knocked on the other cubicle doors. One swung open being empty but the other one was locked. 'What's up?' Jack asked.

'I'm looking for Sheila's nephew.' Steven knelt down to look under the door of the locked cubicle and saw a pair of feet; he got up and banged on the door with his fist. 'Sam?' He yelled, but there was still no answer. He gave Jack a worried glance, then went into the next cubicle and stood on the toilet seat.

He peered over the partition to see Sam slumped lifelessly on the toilet. 'Christ!' He exclaimed; then hauled himself over the partition and unlocked the door. Jack helped him to move Sam out onto the floor, and unable to find a pulse, Steven started to perform CPR whilst Jack went to call for an ambulance.

Steven worked on Sam for twenty-five minutes until the ambulance arrived; then worn out from his exertions, he watched helplessly as the paramedics battled to restart his heart. He sat in casualty ninety minutes later, and tried to hold back the tears. As the doctor told Dora that they had been unable to save him, barely able to take in the fact that her only child was dead at twenty-one she burst into tears.

'Can I see him?' She sobbed. Steven took her arm as the doctor showed them into a cubicle. Her legs buckled when she saw Sam lying there.

'I'll take you home,' Steven said tearfully and gently led her out. Having been told about the tragedy in a call from Heather, Sheila was waiting for her at home; she led her sister into the house with tears streaming down her face; all thoughts of a honeymoon forgotten.

Steven went to his father's house and found him sitting at the kitchen table drinking tea. 'What do you think?' He asked.

Steven shook his head in despair. 'I don't know, Dad. It was a long flight so it could have been deep vein thrombosis or maybe a heart attack. We will have to wait for the post-mortem.'

Heather came in a few minutes later. 'Sheila's going to stay with Dora so we may as well go home.' Steven took her hand and glanced at his father.

'Will you be alright, Dad?'

Edward nodded. 'There's no point us all being here, I'll call you in the morning,' he sighed wearily.

'Are you sure?' Steven checked, and then reluctantly left his father sitting in the kitchen as he nodded resignedly.

Edward spent his wedding night comforting Dora and Sheila, both of whom cried on and off all night. None of them slept, and when the sun rose, they went into the garden. 'Will Steven do the post-mortem?' Sheila whispered when her sister was out of earshot.

'Well, he is the local pathologist but he may not feel comfortable doing it,' Edward whispered back.

They stopped talking as Dora appeared her eyes red from crying. 'I'm going to see if I can get some sleep.' Sheila got up and hugged her. 'Can I get you anything?'

Dora shook her head. 'Actually, there is one thing you could do,' she said as she turned to go back in. 'Can you ring Graham and tell him what's happened.' Sheila nodded and watched her disappear into the house.

'Isn't it the middle of the night there?' Edward asked as she dialled the number.

Sheila looked at her watch. 'It will only be about eight in the evening.' She stopped talking as someone answered the phone; her voice was shaking as she explained what had happened to Sam's father. Edward could hear his voice on the other end but he couldn't make out what he was saying.

Sheila kept trying to speak but was constantly interrupted; she handed the receiver to Edward. 'Can you speak to him? He's saying that he doesn't want Sam cut up and I can't get a word in,' she said exasperatedly.

Edward took the receiver from her. 'Graham?' The voice went quiet. Edward introduced himself and started to explain that there had to be a post-mortem, and it would be carried out with the greatest dignity.

'I do not want some butcher carving my son up. I will not give permission,' Graham snapped.

'I am afraid it's the law, so permission is not required,' Edward told him calmly.

'I'm catching the next flight over; you better not touch my son,' Graham shouted; then the line went dead before Edward could respond.

'I'm sorry he's hung up, but he says he's coming over on the next flight,' he told Sheila. They turned round as Dora appeared behind them, she burst into tears again when they told her what Graham had said. 'That's the last thing I need, him here throwing his weight about; of course there has to be a post-mortem, I need to know why Sam died.'

She continued to sob hysterically, and unable to pacify her Edward called the doctor who gave her a sedative. Edward put his arm around Sheila as they watched her sleeping. 'I can't imagine how she's feeling,' he whispered.

He felt tears pricking his eyes as he remembered how he had felt less than a year ago when he had nearly lost Steven. 'Let's see if we can get some sleep,' he suggested.

Later that afternoon, Steven and Charlie stood over Sam's body; as his death had been sudden and unexpected, there had to be a police presence, and so Jack was observing. 'Are you sure you want to do this, boss?' Charlie checked quietly. Steven nodded and started to take samples. 'It looks like he's got a couple of broken ribs,' Charlie observed after a few minutes.

Steven glanced at the bruised area. 'That will have been me doing chest compressions,' he sighed inwardly as recalled the struggle to try and restart Sam's heart. He passed the samples to Sue and prepared to open him up. What a waste, he thought, as he remembered chatting to him a little more than twenty-four hours ago.

Charlie suddenly broke into his thoughts 'Are you alright, boss?' Steven nodded but in reality, he was struggling to stay composed. He continued talking his way through the procedure for the tape. Charlie watched as he removed Sam's stomach, then both men exclaimed in shock as he emptied it out.

'You'd better take a look at this,' Steven said to Jack, as a mass of small packages along with several undigested tablets splashed in the bottom of the bowl.

'They're Condoms!' Jack exclaimed; he wrinkled his nose up. 'What's that smell.'

Steven's heart sank. 'Alcohol,' he said quietly. He looked at the condoms. 'We'd better see what's in them,' he sighed, and then dreading what he knew they were almost certainly going to find, he sent them up to the lab and carried on with the post-mortem. All of Sam's organs looked normal; however, he had drunk a large amount of alcohol with very little food intake.

'It's hardly surprising he hadn't eaten anything there wasn't any room left,' Charlie muttered. 'Was he gay?' He asked a few minutes later as he checked his rectum and found fresh lesions.

'I don't know but I'll find out,' Steven said quietly. Charlie swabbed and photographed the area, then as they replaced his organs and started to close him up, Steven suddenly felt tearful. 'Can you finish off for me?' He asked Charlie and quickly retreated to the toilet.

He splashed some cold water on his face and looked at himself in the mirror. The reflection staring back looked completely worn out. 'Sam, you stupid bastard,' he muttered bitterly.

'Pure heroin and the tablets are laxatives,' Sue reported later. She gave Steven the printout and went back upstairs.

'There were nine condoms in Sam's stomach,' Steven told Jack. 'Each one contained two one ml phials of heroin. I found a tenth stuck in his lower bowel, one of the phials had broken and the small shards of glass had torn the condom which allowed the heroin to quickly absorb into his system, and ultimately it killed him,' he finished.

'So that's why he spent most of the day in the toilet, he was trying to get rid of it,' Jack surmised.

Steven rubbed his forehead. 'What a bloody mess,' he groaned.

'You do know that I'm going to have to get your dad in, don't you?' Jack said to Steven's dismay.

'Can't someone else do it?' He asked exasperatedly.

'Well, I could ask Whittle to get someone over from York,' Jack said thoughtfully; he gave an ironic laugh. 'But I doubt the guv would be happy about it.'

Steven had to agree that his father would probably rather deal with it himself. 'Some bloody honeymoon,' he muttered as Jack went to the phone.

Dora stared at Edward in disbelief as he told her the results of the post-mortem 'Heroin! Are you saying that Sam was taking drugs?'

Edward shook his head. 'No, I'm saying that Sam was smuggling drugs inside him, one of the packages had split open and that's what killed him.'

Sheila put her arm around her sister but she shrugged it off angrily. 'It's a mistake, Sam wouldn't do that, he hated drugs,' she sobbed.

'I'm really sorry but there is no mistake. Steven found twenty phials of pure heroin inside him,' Edward said gently. 'I'm going to have to see Sam's personal belongings,' he added.

Dora shook her head in despair. 'Just do what you want,' she choked, and then shaking with grief and anger, she let Sheila lead her along the hallway to the bedroom. Sheila came back twenty minutes later and sat down miserably.

Edward could see that she too had been crying. He sat down and put his arms around her.

'I need ask you something,' he said after few minutes.

She looked up at him. 'What is it?' She asked nervously. He hesitated wondering how to say it. A look of fear crossed her face. 'What?' She repeated.

'Was Sam gay?' He asked quietly.

The look of fear turned to one of shock. 'I don't think so, why?' Her face fell as he told her about the legions around Sam's anus. 'I'm sure he had a girlfriend for a couple of years,' she said and started to cry again.

Sam's belongings arrived at the lab later that afternoon. 'Clothes, toilet bag, passport, wallet, but no mobile phone, that's unusual for a young man,' Sue commented.

Steven tipped the contents of toilet bag out onto the bench; a condom box fell out along with the usual items. 'Only one left; there were ten inside him so that leaves one unaccounted for,' he muttered as he opened it, he inspected the outside of the box and found a price ticket that revealed that he brought them at the airport in Sydney.

'Perhaps he got lucky on the flight and joined the mile high club,' Sue said absentmindedly. 'Anyway, I'll check for alien DNA on everything,' she said quickly as Steven frowned at her.

Chapter 2

Two days later, a heavily tanned man with straggly blond hair walked into the police station. He was dressed entirely in denim; wore a chunky gold chain around his neck and a large gold ring on his middle finger. After announcing very loudly that he was Graham Pickering, and demanding to see whoever was in charge, he sat impatiently in the reception.

Edward and Jack started when they saw him, for apart from being older he was the spitting image of Sam. He looked up and scowled at them. 'Are you going to stand there staring all day?' He snapped in a strong Australian accent.

Edward introduced himself. 'We spoke on the phone,' he reminded him. Graham shook the offered hand in an almost bored manner. It was cold and damp, and although it didn't happen very often, Edward took an immediate dislike to him. 'I am so sorry about Sam, Mr Pickering,' he said genuinely.

Graham stared at him with small bloodshot eyes. 'I want to see my son, where is he?' He gave Jack, who had declined to shake hands, a disdainful glance.

'He's in the mortuary,' Jack told him curtly. Edward sensed the tension between the two men and started to explain what Steven had found.

Graham ignored him and opened the door. 'Are you going to take me to see him or do I have to call a cab?' He asked sarcastically and disappeared through the door.

'Bloody jerk,' Jack snapped angrily.

Edward shot him a stern look. 'He's just lost his son, what do you expect?'

Jack gave a snort of disgust. 'Civility would be a start,' he muttered as they followed him out to the car park. Graham stared out of the window as they drove to the hospital. 'I hope you honoured my wishes,' he said suddenly.

'And what wishes would those be?' Jack enquired.

Edward glanced at him in the mirror. 'As I told you on the phone, Mr Pickering, we have to perform a post-mortem when there is a sudden death, it's the law.' They could almost feel the anger oozing from him as they pulled up in the mortuary car park. 'Try and be a bit more tolerant with him,' Edward told Jack as Graham strode ahead with a determined look on his face. Having been warned that they were on their way, Sam's body had been moved to the small chapel of rest. Steven got up as they came in; he put his hand out but quickly retracted it as Graham narrowed his eyes at him. 'Are you the bastard who cut my son up?' He demanded.

Steven glanced at his father. 'I performed the post-mortem,' he started to say, but was cut short with a punch to the side of the face that floored him. Jack grabbed Graham and held him in an arm lock.

'I said I didn't want some butcher cutting him up,' he yelled. Edward watched tentatively as Charlie helped Steven up. He knew that a few years ago his son would have retaliated with his own fists, and wondered how he was going to deal with the situation.

'Are you ok?' He checked. Steven nodded curtly, but to Edward relief and to his own credit, he didn't say anything. Edward turned to Graham who was still glowering at him. 'There was absolutely no need for that, Mr Pickering. Dr Cooper was only doing his job, and I should inform you that it was him who found Sam, he also spent twenty-five minutes trying to keep him alive.' He waited for a few seconds for an apology but it was unforthcoming.

'Let me see my son,' Graham snapped with no sign of remorse.

'Are you going to behave?' Edward asked. 'Release him,' he told Jack as Graham nodded brusquely.

'Can you take Mr Pickering to see his son please,' Steven asked Charlie.

Judy put a cold compress on Steven's face. 'That's going to bruise. What on earth did you say to him?'

He shook his head. 'I didn't say anything, people react in different ways so don't worry about it.' He was trying to sound calm, but inside he was boiling with anger.

'Well he could at least have taken his ring off first, he's broken the skin.' They looked up as Jack appeared. 'Are you sure you're ok? We can charge him with assault if you want.'

Steven shook his head. 'No it's ok, he's upset, and anyway there's no harm done,' he said quietly.

After he'd seen Sam, Graham sat in the family room flanked by Edward and Jack. 'Heroin?' He questioned. Steven nodded. 'Just heroin?' He repeated.

Steven nodded again. 'Twenty phials of heroin in ten condoms. He had swallowed them, but one of the phials had broken and the contents had absorbed into his blood stream,' he explained.

Graham gave him a disbelieving stare. 'There were ten condoms in his stomach?'

Having managed to control himself for longer than usual, Steven was now starting to lose his temper. 'Yes,' he snapped.

Judy came in and handed Graham a mug of tea, he took it without thanking her and continued to stare at Steven as he took a drink. Then he put the mug down with a bang spilling the contents. 'I'd like to see Dora now,' he got up and went out slamming the door behind him.

Edward and Jack followed him out to the reception but he had already exited the building. Jack scowled at his back as he disappeared across the car park. 'Are you going to let that prick call all the shots?' He asked angrily.

Edward shook his head in frustration, and looked at the blood that was still trickling down Steven's face. 'We'd better catch him up,' he sighed.

Dora was far from pleased to see him. 'You live four roads away and you've only seen him twice in the last six months, and now he's dead, you come half way across the world,' she said sarcastically.

Graham glared at her menacingly. 'Do you expect me to ignore the fact that you let my son swallow drugs.'

Edward intervened before it got nasty. 'Did Sam have a mobile phone?' He asked Dora.

'Yes,' she confirmed tearfully.

'It wasn't amongst his personal things; did he bring it with him?' He checked.

'He never goes anywhere without it; I'll go and have a look for it,' she offered.

'Where are you staying?' Edward asked Graham whilst she was out of the room.

'At the hotel where my son died,' he said curtly.

'It's not here,' Dora told them when she came back.

'Where are Sam's things?' Graham snapped.

'With the forensics department, Mr Pickering, you can have them back when we've finished with them,' Jack answered for her.

Graham scowled at him. 'So not only do you butcher my son against my wishes, but you go through his personal things too.'

160

Edward's patience was starting to run out. 'He was smuggling drugs, Mr Pickering, and we need to know as much as we can so that we can find out who he was working for,' he gave Graham a hard stare. 'You wouldn't happen to know anything about the drugs would you, Mr Pickering?'

'Why would I know anything about them,' he snapped sarcastically. 'As Dora has just pointed out, I've hardly seen Sam for six months.'

Edward wasn't convinced but apologised anyway. 'I'm sorry but I had to ask; now why don't you go with Sergeant Taylor,' he suggested before Graham could say anything else. 'He will take you to the hotel, you can have a good sleep and we'll resume this tomorrow.'

Graham got up and went to the door. 'Come on then, we've had our orders,' he snapped at Jack. Jack was about to say something scathing but Edward shot him a warning, don't lose your rag look.

'I'll see you back at the station, guv,' he said through clenched teeth.

'What a totally obnoxious bastard,' he said when he got back an hour later.

'Who?' Whittle enquired as he came into the office behind him. He frowned as they told him about Graham Pickering. 'Well he has had a nasty shock, perhaps you need to be a bit more sensitive to his feelings,' he suggested sharply.

Jack bit his lip and looked at Edward, who gently shook his head. 'Anyway, I've been on to the police department in Sydney and they are going to look into Sam Pickering's associates,' Whittle continued. He handed Edward a piece of paper. 'Your contact is a Detective Barney Johnston, his number is there too.'

Edward took the note. 'Oh! And congratulations on your marriage,' Whittle said brightly. 'No honeymoon?'

'Postponed, Sir,' Edward answered dryly, and wondered which rock he'd been hiding under.

Whittle beamed at him. 'Right, good, carry on then,' he nodded at Jack and retreated back to his office.

'That's right, crawl back down your hole,' Jack muttered angrily; he sat down and rubbed his eyes. 'God, I'm tired.'

Edward nodded his agreement. 'Come on, let's go home,' he suggested.

'Can you believe that Pickering wanted to see the toilet where Sam died, morbid or what, guv?' Jack said exasperatedly as they walked down to the car park.

'Very morbid,' Edward agreed. 'I think we should keep an eye on Mr Pickering,' he added thoughtfully.

With Sheila staying with Dora at her house, Edward was on his own again. What a start to married life, he thought as he put the kettle on. He leant on the sink and yawned as he waited for it to boil, and then went into the hall as he heard the front door opening. Sheila came in and put her arms around him.

'Dora said she would ring if she needed me.'

He kissed her head; thankful that she was there. 'Have you eaten?' He enquired as they went through to the kitchen.

'No,' she confessed. Edward told her about Graham hitting Steven. 'I can't believe how nasty he is,' he commented, but Sheila didn't seem surprised.

'He always was a bit free and easy with his fist, that's why Dora left him, well one of the reasons,' she said quietly. 'Anyway, can we change the subject for a while,' she leant over and kissed him. 'Dinner won't be ready for half an hour or so and we haven't had a wedding night, have we?' She whispered.

'What happened to you?' Heather exclaimed when Steven got in. She looked at his face and frowned. 'There's a kind of pattern in the bruise.' He sat down and told her about Graham, then closed his eyes as she stood behind him and massaged his shoulders.

'Sam told me that his dad was a bit of a hot head, always shouting the odds and causing trouble. He even hit Dora once and that's why she left him.' He opened his eyes and pulled her down onto his knee.

'And when did he tell you all this?' He enquired.

'At the wedding, he seemed a bit drunk and just came out with it whilst you were doing your speech.' She opened the top buttons of his shirt and kissed the spot on his neck that she knew turned him on. 'Can we talk about something else?' She whispered.

As Steven lay in bed, he went back over the conversation with Pickering; ten condoms, he'd said that twice. 'Almost as though he was making sure,' he muttered. Heathers hand was resting on his thigh as usual; he moved it and spooned around her.

'Who's insatiable now,' she murmured as he gently caressed her breast. They were woken in the early hours by the phone. Steven answered it sleepily.

'Boss,' Charlie's voice said with urgency in his tone. Steven sat up suddenly wide awake. 'You'd better get down here, we've had a break in,' Charlie said to his dismay. He pulled his clothes on and arrived at almost the same time as his father. They went across the car park to the mortuary to find the lab doors had been forced open and the alarms disabled.

'Do we know what happened?' Edward asked the constable on the door.

'Only that a nurse on the night shift saw the mortuary lights on, and when the security guard got here to investigate, someone hit him. He's in intensive care with a suspected fractured skull,' the constable reported.

They went inside. the mortuary labs had been turned upside down. Steven ran up the stairs to the forensics department where it was the same story, drawers and cupboards had been emptied out along with the contents of the fridges. Sue had arrived and was checking to see if anything was missing, and the scene of crime team was busy dusting for finger prints.

He went back downstairs to check on the cold storage area; two of the chiller doors were open, and although it was evident that the stretchers had been pulled out, he was relieved to find the bodies untouched. He closed the doors and started to check the rest of the compartments. He got to the one containing Sam's body and had a feeling that something was wrong before he opened it.

He held his breath and started to pull the drawer out, then swore silently as he saw that the body bag had been opened. He pulled it out further until the body was half exposed. 'You'd better come and look at this,' he called. Edward and Jack went into the chiller room.

They watched in horrified silence as Steven opened the bag fully to expose the gaping hole in Sam's abdomen, and his innards which had been pulled out and were scattered unceremoniously around him.

'Jesus Christ! What's happened here?' Jack exclaimed as he looked at the bloody mess.

The photographer took several shots of Sam's body then Steven pushed him back into the chiller. 'Whoever did this would have needed a knife,' he told Edward. 'So if they left it here we may get prints; that's assuming they didn't think to wear gloves.' He picked the surgical glove box up and inspected it whilst Charlie went to check if any of the mortuary knives were missing.

'They must have been looking for the drugs,' Jack said as they went into the office and sat down.

Sue came in a few minutes later. 'The only things missing from upstairs are Sam's belongings,' she reported.

'And one of the post-mortem knives is defiantly missing,' Charlie confirmed as he followed her in.

'What about the drugs?' Jack asked.

Steven opened the medical safe next to his desk; the nineteen phials of heroin were still on the shelf. 'They didn't think to look in here,' he said wryly.

Jack and Edward were sitting in the canteen at the police station, having been up half the night, they needed breakfast, 'and loads of black coffee!' Jack said as he yawned again. Edward was deep in thought as he ate. It's got to be Graham Pickering, but he knew the drugs had been found, so why?

'How the hell could he do that to his own son?' He asked Jack, who unable to speak with a mouthful of food made do with shrugging. 'We'll see if SOCO come up with anything. In the meantime, don't say anything to Pickering, we'll see if he gives himself away,' Edward mused. They finished their breakfast and went to the incident room to brief the team.

They had just finished when Barney Johnston called from Sydney. The rest of the team watched Edward's expression as listened to what he had to say. 'It would appear that Sam Pickering has no record, just a caution for vandalism when he was fifteen, but his father has been under investigation for the last three months,' he informed them when he had rung off.

'There's a surprise,' Jack interrupted sarcastically.

Edward frowned at the interruption. 'For aggravated theft and handling stolen goods,' he continued before Jack could ask. 'But they have never known him to deal in drugs. The Sydney police department have been building up a case against him.'

'He must be branching out,' Jack interrupted again. Edward shot him a sideways glance. 'Sorry, guv,' he apologised, and then sat in silence until Edward had finished the briefing.

'Right, let's go and see what Mr Pickering has got to say for himself,' he suggested dryly. They made their way over to the Firs. Jack yawned loudly as they got out of the car. 'I hope he's in a better frame of mind today; I don't think I've got the patience for his bolshie attitude,' he grumbled as they went to the reception desk.

'It's room seventeen, but the key is here so Mr Pickering must be out,' the receptionist told them. She stared at Edward. 'Didn't you get married last week?' He gave a brief nod. 'No honeymoon?' She enquired.

'It would appear not,' he said dryly. He took the key and they headed up the stairs to the room. Jack opened the door; the curtains were still drawn leaving the room in semi-darkness. Edward flicked the light on and gasped in dismay as they were met by a scene of devastation.

The bed was lying on its side, the mattress had been ripped open and the filling dragged out. Drawers had been emptied and tossed to one side leaving clothes littering the room, they stood and stared at the mess for a few minutes. 'Get SOCO here,' Edward ordered as he moved carefully through the debris. 'And get Steven here as well,' he said, as he pushed the bathroom door open to reveal Graham Pickering lying face down on the floor in a huge pool of blood.

'It looks like he's had his throat slit.' They turned around as they heard a noise; a chambermaid had come in and was staring in horror at the scene. Edward quickly pulled the door closed and led her out.

Steven arrived within the hour and confirmed that Graham did indeed have a slit throat. 'It looks like he's been beaten up too,' he commented as he inspected the mass of bruising on his face. He called the attendants in to bag him up, and a few hours later for the second time in less than a week, he stood over the body of a Pickering.

Once they had taken his clothes off, it was obvious that Graham had been beaten, and quite severely. There were large weal's and bruises over most of his torso, with the kidney area and genitals being worst affected. There were also bruises on the top of each arm indicating that he had been held whilst the beating took place.

'First impressions?' Edward asked from the observation room.

'Well he has defiantly been beaten, but there are no defence marks on his hands,' Steven reported as he lifted each hand in turn.

Charlie pointed to a graze on Graham's right knuckles. 'What about this one?'

Steven glanced at it. 'That's where he hit me.' He stared at the bare hand. 'Where's the ring, did you take it off?' He asked his father. Edward shook his head. 'The necklace has gone as well,' he observed.

'What did the ring look like?' Charlie asked.

'Like the imprint on my face,' Steven said wryly, he turned towards the light as Charlie took a photograph of the bruise.

'It's an unusual pattern,' he commented.

'What about the weapon that was used to beat him?' Edward asked.

'We'll get some shots of the bruises and put them into the computer for comparisons, but I would say it was a crow bar or similar,' Steven said thoughtfully.

'And the knife?' Edward checked.

He looked away as Steven pulled the wound on Graham's throat apart and peered closely. 'It's a very clean cut so not your usual type of knife. I think it was probably done with the mortuary knife that was taken from here, the same one that was used on Sam's body,' he said despairingly.

They sat in the office ninety minutes later. 'I would estimate that the time of death was between twelve midnight and two am this morning. The cause of death was a slit throat, although with the beating he had taken he was probably barely alive when they did it, and there was arterial spray all over the bathroom, so whoever did cut his throat must have been covered with blood,' Steven reported.

'You said they?' Edward queried. Steven nodded.

'There must have been at least two, one to hold him and one to beat him; Sue's got his clothes upstairs, we may get something from them. Also, there was a large quantity of alcohol in his stomach, so he had been drinking heavily and may have been pretty drunk. We'll have to wait for the blood results to confirm that. But I'm surprised that no one in the hotel heard anything,' he commented.

'Jack's over there now talking to the staff and guests, they may have heard something,' Edward said hopefully.

'You're assuming he was beaten in the hotel then. It could have been done somewhere else and then they finished him off in his room,' Charlie suggested.

'How would they get him through the reception? He would have been barely able to walk with those injuries,' Steven said thoughtfully.

Edward thought for a minute. 'I'll get over to the hotel and see how Jack's doing.'

Steven handed him the preliminary report. 'It'll be a couple of days for the toxicology,' he told him as he went out.

Jack wasn't doing very well. Some of the guests had checked out earlier that morning, which left twenty-five pensioners on a coach tour, a honeymoon couple from Liverpool who couldn't keep their hands off each other, and hadn't seen or heard anything, and two reps from a sweet company who said likewise. The local constables were interviewing the pensioners in the function room.

'It's a mass of whistling hearing aids, loose dentures and walking sticks,' one of them grumbled. When Edward arrived, Jack was talking to a short red-faced man called Cyril Briers, who he introduced as the manager.

'Can we have a staff rota and contact addresses for the guests who checked out this morning,' Edward asked.

Cyril nodded efficiently and scuttled off. 'Mr Pickering wasn't the nicest guest we've had, he upset most of the staff and he was only here for a couple of days,' he commented as he handed the details over.

Jack took the lists and scanned through them. 'A Miss Beverly Penrose from Chester, and Mr and Mrs Smith from London checked out before we got here,' he handed Edward the list. 'Smith? Their real name I wonder,' he mused. 'What time did they leave?' Jack went over to the reception desk. 'Six fifteen, they checked out a few minutes before Beverly Penrose. They told the receptionist that they had an early appointment,' he reported a few minutes later.

'Why bother telling the receptionist their reason for leaving early,' Edward wondered out loud. 'Get on to the local forces and ask them to check them out,' he ordered.

'What about the rest of the guests and the staff?' Jack scanned through the statements. 'The staff that were on duty that morning and the night before have all been interviewed and fingerprinted. The night porter said that Pickering came in at about eight thirty, the barman has confirmed that he sat drinking in the bar until nearly ten, mainly spirits.'

'Was he alone?' Edward interrupted.

'He was sitting alone but apparently Mr and Mrs Smith were in there too. The receptionist gave him his key at about nine fifty, he got into the lift and that's the last anyone saw of him,' Jack finished.

'Except whoever it was that killed him,' Edward muttered.

'Well none of the staff saw or heard anything until the chamber maid walked in behind us,' Jack commented.

'Who was in reception that morning?' Edward enquired. Jack looked down the staff list. 'Chantal Yates, she found Pickering's door key on the reception desk and assumed that he had gone out earlier.'

Mr Briers appeared next to them and cleared his throat. 'Have you finished with the staff?'

Edward nodded. 'Yes, thank you for now at least, but they must stay available, and please don't clean the two rooms that were occupied by the Smith's and Miss Penrose, our forensics team will need to check them out.'

Briers grimaced nervously. 'I'm sorry but both rooms were cleaned as soon as they were vacated, its company policy I'm afraid.' He gave them an apologetic smile.

'Well don't let anyone else into them, and you'll have to let us know who did the cleaning,' Jack ordered a trifle impatiently. Briars looked mortified.

'Just so that we can eliminate them,' Edward quickly assured him.

They went up to the bedrooms where the forensics team were still working, Sue stood up as they entered Pickering's room. 'We've bagged up all his clothes and personal belongings, but there was no suitcase and no sign of a mobile phone.'

'I'll ask the porter,' Jack offered and disappeared down the corridor.

'We've got four sets of prints; I'll check them against the victim and the staff when I get back,' Sue told him. 'And we found this.'

Edward peered at the specimen bag she was holding up. 'What is it?'

'It's a false nail, so he must have had some female company, unless it belongs to one of the staff of course,' she said thoughtfully. 'And the mini bar was empty so he must have been drinking because they replenish them each day,' she concluded as Jack reappeared in the doorway.

'The porter said he had one of those holder type bags and he thinks it was green.'

'Just the one,' Edward checked.

Jack nodded. 'He wasn't very complementary about him either, apparently he was rude to another guest and he'd only been in the building for five minutes.'

'Find out which guest it was and what was said,' Edward instructed.

'It was Mr Smith who Pickering insulted, the porter didn't hear what he said, but apparently there was an angry exchange of words,' Jack reported a few minutes later. 'He seems to have made a habit of rubbing people up the wrong way, doesn't he,' he muttered.

The news from Scotland Yard the next day was as expected; they confirmed that the address Mr and Mrs Smith had given didn't exist. Edward put the phone down and called Jack in. 'Well, that's no surprise,' the sergeant said wryly. 'Smith is a pretty obvious alias to use, plus they paid in cash so there's no record,' he gave a sigh of frustration.

'What about Beverly Penrose?' Edward asked hopefully.

'Nothing yet, guv, Chester are still trying to trace her. Her parents were expecting her back the day after the interview but she didn't return.' They looked up to a knock on the door, a constable came in and handed Edward a sheet of paper.

'It's the list of Graham Pickering's known associates from Australia. We need to put faces to these names and get the receptionist from the firs in to have a look,' Edward said as he scanned through the names. 'I don't recognise any of these,' he said despondently.

Jack looked at the list. 'I do, guv,' he pointed to a name halfway down the page. 'Robin Paige, he owned a pawnbroker shop in London when I was a PC, he's quite a character, but quite a thug as well. I pulled him in a couple times for threatening behaviour,'

Edward looked at the list again 'Do you think he could commit murder?'

Jack shrugged. 'I don't know; maybe if the incentive was big enough.' He took the list and went to arrange photographs to go with the names, whilst Edward started on the mound of paperwork.

Steven was writing a report for the coroner when Sue came in with the results from Graham Pickering's blood sample and clothes. 'The alcohol content in his blood was 0.21, and there was some of Sam's blood on his clothes, so it must have been him who desecrated the body.'

Steven scanned through the results. 'But why when he knew we had found the drugs?'

Sue shrugged as he continued reading. 'There was mucus from an unknown male on the back of his shirt, and the same DNA on the false nail.'

'A man with false nails on?' He asked in surprise.

'That's what it looks like,' Sue confirmed dryly 'We ran the sample through the national database but drew a blank,' she concluded. 'Mucus ,' Edward queried when Steven rang to inform him.

'Yes, whoever it was must have sneezed on him,' Steven explained.

'Charming!' He said in disgust. 'I'll inform Scotland Yard and ask them to get onto Interpol, they may turn something up,' he hung up then looked at the time and yawned. 'I'm going home,' he told Jack.

'How's it going?' Sheila asked when he got home. 'Or aren't you allowed to say?' Edward knew that she was discreet, and so brought her up to date with their progress.

'How's Dora?' He checked.

'She's asleep, the doctor gave her another sedative,' Sheila shook her head sadly. 'I know that they divorced a long time ago but Graham was still Sam's father,' she sat down next to him.

'What do you think she will do?' Edward asked.

169

'I've no idea, go home eventually I suppose. I know she wants to take Sam home to bury him, and she can't do that until this is over, can she?'

Edward shook his head. 'I'm afraid she can't.' He put his arm around her as she snuggled into him and kissed her head. 'I'm glad you're here,' he whispered. A few minutes later, they were interrupted by the phone; Sheila disentangled herself from him and answered it, then handed him the receiver.

'I'm at an incident; the body of a young woman has been found in the Ouse in York,' Steven informed him.

'Why are you there? It's not your patch,' Edward interrupted. 'The local guy's away so I'm covering, anyway she's been identified as Beverly Penrose,' he said to Edward's dismay.

'Are you sure?' He checked.

'Yes, unless the SOS chain she's wearing isn't hers, she's a diabetic,' Steven explained.

'Where are you taking her?' Edward asked despondently.

'I've asked DCI Finch if I can take her back to our place, he said it's fine by him as long as I keep him in the loop, but it may be a good idea if you had a word with him,' Steven suggested.

'Is everything alright?' Sheila asked when Edward rang off from talking to Finch.

'They've found the woman who checked out of the hotel on the morning we found Graham; they've just pulled her out of the Ouse.'

Sheila went white 'Oh my God! What the hell was Graham up to?' She whispered.

'Let's not jump to any conclusions, we don't know if they are connected yet,' Edward said quickly, but deep down he knew that he was trying to convince himself as well as her, and that there was more to the case than met the eye.

'She drowned, but she was probably unconscious when she drowned, and I don't think she drowned in the river,' Steven told him the next day as he examined Beverly Penrose's body.

'Why not?' Finch asked from the observation room.

'Because the water in her stomach and lungs isn't river water. It smells strongly of lavender oil which would suggest that she drowned in a bath, but we'll know for sure if we find chlorine in it, and I would also say that she was dressed after death,' he glanced towards the observation room. 'The buttons on her blouse were done up wrong and her pants were on inside out,' he explained.

'And she was unconscious when this happened,' Finch checked.

Steven nodded. 'It's more than likely, there's a large swelling on the side of her head which was inflicted by a severe blow. It wasn't enough to kill her but it would almost certainly have rendered her unconscious, and there are no marks indicating a struggle,' he added.

'Can you tell the time of death?' Edward enquired hopefully. 'The water damage to the body indicates that she had been in the river for at least forty-eight hours, but you'll have to wait for the tissue results for an exact time.'

'She checked out of the firs at six thirty on Thursday morning, so she must have been killed just after that,' Edward told Finch.

Steven shook his head. 'I think she was dead long before she supposedly checked out, Sue is going over after lunch to take samples so she may find something.'

Edward nodded his thanks. 'By the way, her parents are coming on Wednesday, and I've asked WPC Blackwell to accompany them,' he told him tentatively. Steven glanced at him and frowned. 'Just so you know,' his father added pointedly. 'I think you can deal with the Penrose's,' he told Charlie as he finished stitching.

The rooms that had been occupied by the so-called Smiths and Beverly Penrose were on the landing below Graham Pickering's room, the rest of the rooms were occupied by the members of the coach party. When Edward arrived, forensics were just finishing off. 'Miss Penrose was a naughty girl! The bottles of vodka in the mini bar have been drunk and refilled with tap water, and most of the cans are empty on the shelf, but there are several sets of prints in both rooms. We'll check them against hers and the hotel staff. There were also traces of skin on the footboard of the bed, and these,' Sue handed him a small empty bottle and a specimen bag.

'Lavender bath oil, and several ginger hairs that we found in the bath overflow. I'll get them back to the lab and check them against Beverly.' Edward went into the bathroom and looked around.

'It looks like she was killed in here and then moved, but why?' He sat on the toilet seat and looked at the bath. 'What did she see? And if Steven is right about the time of death, then who checked out as her?' He asked himself.

He went back into the main room and looked across the landing; the forensics team had just finished in the Smith's room. He watched as scene of crime tape was placed over each door before going down to the lobby. The receptionist on duty had been manning the desk when Beverly Penrose checked in.

'Can you describe Miss Penrose?' He asked her.

'She wasn't very tall and I think she had ginger hair,' she said thoughtfully.

'Can you remember what she was wearing?' He asked hopefully.

'Black trousers and a red jacket I think, but to be honest I didn't really take too much notice, the coach party had just arrived and it was really busy,' she said apologetically. Edward thanked her and turned to go. 'Is it true, is she really dead?' She called.

'Yes, on both counts,' he answered without turning around.

Sheila and Dora were waiting for him when he arrived home, and although she was still grieving for Sam, Dora managed to get through dinner without crying. Edward took the opportunity to ask her some questions, and discovered that she had no idea that Graham had been under surveillance in Sydney, and she was genuinely shocked that Edward had even considered that he had used Sam to carry drugs.

'Graham may have been a lot of things but he hated drugs, his mother died from an overdose when he was seven,' she said quietly.

'Do you know any of Graham's associates?' Edward asked her.

'I only met one, but it was a long time ago when we were first married. He came to pick Graham up a couple of times after he lost his license,' she remembered.

'And Graham never brought anyone else home?' He checked. She shook her head. 'Can you remember the friend's name?' He asked hopefully.

Dora thought for a minute. 'I think he was called Bob, but I don't know his surname.' She got up. 'I'll go back to the bungalow and leave you two alone,' she said generously. She turned back as she reached the door. 'He was English.'

Edward pricked his ears up. 'Who was?'

'Bob; and he had a broad cockney accent,' she added.

'Are you sure?' Edward checked, she nodded again, and went out closing the door quietly behind her.

'Bob?' Jack repeated the next morning. 'Do you think it's Robin Paige?'

Edward gave a light shrug. 'Is he a cockney?'

Jack nodded. 'Born and bred in the east end.'

'I'll get Dora to have a look at his mug shot and see if she recognises him,' Edward said thoughtfully, and went to give Whittle an update. He was just leaving Whittle's office when his phone rang.

'Apart from the staff the only fingerprints in the room occupied by the Smiths were Pickering's,' Steven told him.

'That's interesting,' he interrupted.

'The skin sample that Sue found on the bedstead in Beverly Penrose's room was Beverly's, so it's more than likely that she hit her head on it. Some of the hair we got from the bath overflow was hers, but we also found hair prints and DNA from another woman, mainly on the bottles and cans in the mini bar, but also on the bath and toilet. She's not a member of the staff and we're checking them out now,' he finished.

Whittle raised his eyebrows as Edward rang off. Edward updated him the results so far. 'So it looks like Mrs Smith was in the Penrose girl's room,' Whittle surmised. Edward groaned inwardly and wished that he wouldn't jump to conclusions.

'Maybe, but don't you think it's a bit odd that she would take the trouble to remove any trace from their own room, and then not bother in Beverly's room.' He found Whittles unfeeling attitude towards the victim offensive, so he accentuated the name Beverly.

'So you'd better find something to link them,' Whittle continued without acknowledging what he had said.

'Right, Sir,' Edward muttered, and resisting the temptation to slam the door, he left the room before Whittle could jump to anymore conclusions. The results from the alien female DNA came back two days later. 'Trudy Baines, she's a local prostitute. She's been pulled in on a couple of occasions,' Finch told him. Edward looked at her arrest sheet.

'Maybe she was in the room with the previous guest,' Jack suggested.

'Well let's get her in and find out,' Finch said brightly.

Trudy arrived later that afternoon; a twenty-three-year-old red head, who as Paul Finch said, had been arrested several times for prostitution but only cautioned, she was dressed in a pair of tight jeans and an even tighter top that did nothing for her plumpish figure. Edward looked at her sitting in the interview room. 'She looks older than twenty-three,' he mused.

'Nearer thirty-three,' Finch nodded his agreement. 'She's not so cocky now though, she's usually full of lip when we bring her in.' Trudy looked up as they went into the interview room; it was obvious that she was scared.

'They took my fags away, have you got one?' She asked nervously.

Edward shook his head. 'I'm sorry, I don't smoke,' he said apologetically. He asked the constable on the door to fetch her cigarettes and waited until she had lit one, then sat down opposite her. 'How long have you been a prostitute?'

Trudy scowled at him. 'Do I have to answer that?' She asked the duty solicitor.

'I think you should,' he advised; she looked at the ceiling and thought for a while.

'Nine years,' she said eventually.

'So you started when you were fourteen,' Edward exclaimed.

'Well worked out, Mr Policeman,' she said rudely.

'What do your parents think about it?'

She gave a sarcastic laugh. 'Well, I've no idea what my dad thinks, because I've no idea who my dad is, and my mum was the one who got me into it in the first place, so I doubt if she gives a shit.' She lit another cigarette and stared at them.

'Your mother is a prostitute?' Edward checked.

'She was, I've not seen her for years, not since she threw me out for nicking her punters,' she said matter of factly.

Edward gave an unbelieving sigh. 'What can you tell me about last Friday night?'

Trudy stared at him and sniffed. 'Will you do me if I tell you?' She asked sullenly.

'Let's put it like this, if you don't tell us, then I will definitely charge you with withholding evidence as well as prostitution,' Finch butted in 'Well?' He asked sharply.

Trudy gave him a well-rehearsed scowl and started talking. 'Well! It was getting late, about half eleven I think, we were just thinking about packing it in for the night when this car pulled up, officially it was Zoë's pull, but the bloke said he wanted a red head, so she went home.'

'Do clients often ask for a certain hair colour?' Edward interrupted.

'Well, most men have preferences,' she glanced at Finch. 'I bet you like blonds, don't you?' She said smugly.

'Do you and Zoë share a flat?' Edward asked. Trudy nodded.

'Can you speak for the tape please,' Finch requested.

'Yes, we share a flat,' she said impatiently, and lit another cigarette.

'What happened after he'd asked for a red head?' Edward asked.

'I told him it was fifty quid, but he said he had a special job for me and he would give me two hundred, but it would take all night, So I said that an all-nighter was two fifty and he went for it.' She stopped talking to take a drag on her cigarette, then blew the smoke at the listening officers before continuing. 'So I said OK, but no kinky stuff, just straight sex or blow jobs.' She waited for a reaction, but the two officers just stared at her impassively.

'Carry on,' Edward ordered.

'He took me to a hotel in Kimberwick. We went up the fire escape because he said the management were fussy about who they let in, bloody cheek I call it,' she said vehemently. 'Anyway, he took me to a room and told me to stay in there for the night, he said would come back in the morning, and then he just left me there,' she said incredulously.

'Which room was it?' Edward asked.

'Number eleven,' she said confidently.

'And did you stay there all night?' Finch enquired.

'Yep,' she stubbed her cigarette out and waited for the next question.

'What did the man look like?' Edward asked.

'What do you mean?' She counter asked.

'Was he tall or short? What colour hair did he have? Did he have an accent? What was he wearing?' Finch asked impatiently.

'Alright, keep your hair on,' she snapped. 'He was average height with dark hair and he was wearing a long coat thing.' She cocked her head to one side. 'Does that help?' She asked sarcastically.

'Do you want to spend the night in the cells?' Finch threatened.

'So, he took you to the room; what did you do?' Edward asked before she could comment.

'I had a bath, emptied the mini bar and had a good night's sleep,' she said brightly. 'Then about six in the morning the bloke came back. He gave me a case, some money and a jacket to put on. He told me to wait for twenty minutes then go down to the reception and check out, and he would meet me outside the hotel.'

'What colour was the jacket?' Edward interrupted.

'Purple I think,' she said uncertainly.

'And where is it now?' He asked.

'The bloke took it back when he dropped me off.'

'So you put the jacket on and went down to the reception?' Finch checked.

Trudy nodded. 'Yes.'

'Did the receptionist say anything?'

She nodded again. 'She asked for the room number and if my stay was pleasant, so I said room eleven and yes very pleasant, thank you, which it was, you know, getting paid for doing nothing,' she chuckled.

'So, what happened then?' Finch asked.

'Then I paid the bill and went outside.'

'And was he waiting for you?' Edward interrupted again.

'Yes, he was waiting for me in a car,' she confirmed.

'Was he alone?' Finch asked.

'No, he had another bloke and a woman with him,' she turned her nose up. 'At least I think it was a woman; and a bloody ugly one at that.'

'You only think it was a woman?' Edward checked.

'They were in the front, they didn't look at me, they didn't speak, and he didn't introduce them,' she snapped, and then glanced nervously at Finch.

'What did the driver look like?' He asked.

'I don't know, he had a hat on, but I think he had blond hair. I didn't really see his face, but he looked at me in the mirror a couple of times,' she remembered.

'So you saw his eyes?' Finch asked.

'I must have done, but don't ask me what colour they were cos I didn't take any notice,' she said breezily.

'What happened when you got back to York?' Edward asked.

'The bloke paid me and they dropped me back at my pitch.'

'Didn't you think it was a bit odd?' Finch interrupted.

Trudy shrugged dismissively. 'I suppose so, but come on, two hundred and fifty quid for sleeping, would you have asked questions.'

Edward sighed quietly. 'What make was the car,' he tried.

'I dunno, but it was green. Can I go now?' She asked.

'You can go when you've answered the questions,' Finch snapped. 'How many doors did the car have?'

'Four, I think.'

Finch raised his eyebrows. 'You only think?'

She scowled at him again. 'Yes, four; I got in through a back door, so four,' she said semi-sarcastically.

'Did you look in the bag?' Edward asked suddenly.

Trudy looked at her hands. 'Is that what this it's all about?' She mumbled. 'It was only a bit of makeup and some tights,' she glanced up guiltily.

'Did you steal things from the bag?' Edward checked.

'I'll give it back if that's what this is about,' she said defensively.

'No, Trudy, that is not what this is about,' Edward said despairingly. 'Are the things that you took at the flat?' She gave a curt nod. 'I'm going to arrange a car to take you home, and I want you to give everything that you took to the policewoman who will accompany you, do you understand?' He asked sternly.

She nodded again. 'Then what?' She muttered.

'Then we'll decide if we are going to charge you with prostitution and theft,' Finch said sharply. Edward watched as a WPC led her out, she turned round as they got to the door. 'I think he was a Londoner,' she said quietly.

'Cockney?' Edward asked.

'I dunno, he just sounded like that bloke of the telly, you know the one in Eastenders,' she said sullenly.

After realising that he should speak to them himself, and deciding to ignore Tracy Blackwell, Steven was sitting in the reception with Beverly Penrose's parents. They were chatting tearfully about Beverly and both jumped as the phone rang. Judy answered it and offered Steven the receiver. 'It's Heather,' she mouthed.

'Tell her I'll call her back,' he said quietly.

'She sounds upset,' Judy whispered. Steven glanced at the Penrose's.

'It's ok you take it,' Mr Penrose said generously. They watched him as he listened, and his face fell.

'I'll come home now,' he said and replaced the receiver. 'I've got to go we've had a break in at home,' he told Judy; he turned to the Penrose's.

'I'm really sorry about your daughter, you can take her home as soon as the police have finished their enquiries.' He shook Mr Penrose's hand and rushed out to the car park. He reached home twenty-five minutes later and found Heather talking to PC Higgins.

'Are you ok?' He put his arm around her as she nodded confirmation. 'What happened?' He asked anxiously.

'I was out on the moors with Ben and I saw a car coming up our lane. I watched through my binoculars and two men got out. When no one answered the door one of them broke the porch window and opened it,' Heather explained.

'So she rang us but they had gone before I got here,' Higgins finished for her. 'I'm afraid there's quite a mess in there, I've informed your father and he's sending SOCO over,' he added.

'Where were you?' Steven asked Heather.

She pointed to a small ridge about half a mile away. 'I waited there until the police arrived.'

He gave her a hug. 'We'd better go and see if anything's been taken.'

As Higgins had said, the house had been turned upside down, but at first glance there didn't appear to be anything missing; as Steven looked around at the mess, he suddenly realised the cat hadn't greeted him. 'Where's Monty?' He asked.

'He was asleep on the bed when I went out. He didn't want to come with me. I think it was too hot for him, but I've not seen him since I got back,' Heather said worriedly. She went outside and tried calling whilst Steven checked the outhouses, but there was no sign of him.

'He'll be ok,' he said optimistically, but at the same time felt thankful that Heather hadn't been in when they knocked. Edward arrived with Jack a few minutes later and took a statement from Heather.

'What can you tell me about the car?' He asked.

'It was a green saloon, dark green I think,' she remembered.

'And you're sure that there were two men?' She nodded firmly 'Could you make out any facial features?' He asked hopefully.

'No, they were too far away and my binoculars aren't that powerful.'

'But you could tell that they were men?' He double checked.

'Well, they were dressed like men and they walked like men,' she said confidently.

'Hair colour?' She shook her head. 'Are you ok?' He checked lastly, and gave a sigh relief as she nodded confirmation. 'A green saloon,' he said to Jack. 'It could be the same car.' He motioned to Steven to go into the other room. 'I think you should move out, just until we find out if this is connected with Pickering and Beverly Penrose's deaths,' he said quietly.

'Why would it be connected?' Steven asked in surprise.

Edward told him about Trudy and the hotel saga. 'I think Beverly saw whoever it was with Pickering before he was killed, and she was killed before she could say anything. And if they're after the drugs and they think you have them here, then they may come back.'

Steven frowned at him. 'But Graham knew that we had found the drugs, so surely he wouldn't think I'd bring them home, and even if he did think that and told whoever it was, how would they know where I live?' Edward put his hands up.

'I don't know, son, I'm just saying that they could be connected, and it would be safer if you moved out for a while.'

'These two blokes may have just been opportunist burglars,' Steven argued. Edward looked in exasperation at his son's defiant face.

'Except they didn't take anything, did they?' He snapped.

Steven sensed that there was a row brewing and backed down. 'Ok, we'll move out,' he agreed reluctantly. 'You can come and stay with us, we've got loads of room,' Edward said thankfully.

'Monty and Ben will have to come too, assuming Monty turns up that is,' Steven muttered, and then went to find Heather.

Edward went to speak to the SOCO. 'There are a lot of prints; we will have to check them against Dr Cooper and Ms Brooks. There are also several sets of footprints and some tyre marks outside. They're not very clear with the ground being so dry, but we've photographed them and we'll try to get casts,' he reported. Edward nodded his thanks, and then called Sheila to let her know what had happened.

'I've made your old room up,' she told Steven and Heather when they arrived with Ben. She looked at their luggage. 'No Monty?'

Heather shook her head. 'We couldn't find him. I think the intruders frightened him away.'

The two women went into the kitchen whilst Steven took the cases upstairs. The memories came flooding back as he looked around the room. Sheila had replaced his old single bed with a queen size. 'I brought it over from my house, I hope it will be big enough for you,' she told him.

Heather put her arm around Steven's waist. 'I'm sure we'll be very cosy,' she assured her.

'It's nice to have another woman to chat to,' Sheila said later as she and Heather prepared dinner. Steven sat in the kitchen pretending to read the paper, but in reality, he was watching them cook. Heather glanced at him constantly.

'I hope there aren't going to be any Gordon Ramsey type comments or there'll be trouble,' she said with her eyes twinkling suggestively.

Steven knew the look; he tried to keep a straight face but failed miserably. She looked again, and he realised how lucky he was that she was alive and well and had chosen him. He blew her a kiss, then jumped as their silent flirting was interrupted by Edward who had been watching in amusement from the doorway.

'If you two have finished ogling each other maybe we should have dinner,' he said brightly.

'Sorry, Dad, I didn't hear you come in,' Steven mumbled.

Edward rolled his eyes at them 'Let's eat alfresco,' he suggested. Edward brought them up to date over dinner. 'SOCO found a spec of blood on your bed cover, Sue's checking it out.'

Heathers face fell. 'Monty was asleep on the bed when I went out. You don't think they've done something to him, do you?'

'I wouldn't think so, and it was only a tiny spec so let's wait and see what Sue comes up with,' Edward said trying to sound positive. 'I've added the cottage to the patrol route; a police car will check it several times a day,' he told Steven.

'Can you ask them to keep an eye open for Monty?' Heather asked before Steven could suggest it. Edward nodded. 'He'll be ok though, won't he? He's a cat so he'll hunt mice and things.'

'I hope so, although he's not generally a killer, and that's assuming he's not lying injured somewhere,' Steven mused. 'But I'm sure he's fine,' he added hastily as Heather gave him a look of dismay.

Sue came down from the lab as soon as the results came in. 'The blood we found in your house matches the mucus found on Graham Pickering's back.'

Steven stopped what he was doing. 'But there's no match from the national data base?'

Sue shook her head. 'We're still waiting for Interpol to get back to us.'

'What about the fingerprints?' Steven butted in.

'Just your family's prints. They must have worn gloves, we're not having much luck with the footprints or tyre tracks either, the ground was just too dry, but we'll keep trying,' she assured him. Christ! Dad was right, it's a good job

Heather wasn't there when they turned up or God knows what they would have done, he thought 'Are you alright?' Sue checked.

'I was just wondering how they knew where I lived and what they were looking for,' he said thoughtfully.

'Graham Pickering must have told them that the drugs had been found,' she guessed.

'But surely they wouldn't think that I would keep them at home,' he said exasperatedly.

Sue gave a light shrug. 'Who knows what they were thinking. If they're using the heroin then they're probably addicted to it, which means they may be desperate to get it, and we all know that desperate people will think and do anything.'

Steven have her a wry smile 'Thanks for that insight into drug addiction,' he said amusedly.

'You're welcome,' she chuckled and went back upstairs, whilst Steven started on the pile of paperwork.

He thought about the case as he wrote. Sam, Graham Pickering and Beverly Penrose, all killed over drugs. He rested his chin on his hand and stared into space until the phone brought him back from his musings. 'Heather's on line two,' Judy shouted from the reception. He smiled at the thought of hearing her voice and picked the phone up.

'Monty has been seen at home so I'm going to go and get him,' she told him.

'No, I don't want you going anywhere near the house until this is over. I'll pick him up later,' he said firmly.

'You've no basket and PC Higgins is going to wait there until I arrive, so I'll be perfectly safe, and I'll come straight back,' she promised. Steven reluctantly agreed, but rang his father as soon as she had hung up.

'Don't worry, son. I'll make sure Higgins stays with her until she's got the cat,' Edward reassured him. Steven gave a sigh of relief and went into the cutting room where a road casualty had just come in. Two hours later, he had established that the young woman on the slab had been high on drugs when she crashed her car.

'Bloody drugs again, these dealers should be strung up,' he muttered.

'Yep, total bastards eh, boss,' Charlie agreed. He took the body back to the chiller whilst Steven went to write the report for the coroner. When he had

181

finished, he rang Heather's mobile. It rang a couple of times before going to the answering service.

'It's me, did you get Monty? Ring me when you get back.' He blew her a kiss before ringing off.

'How sweet,' Judy called amusedly.

Steven got up and went out to the reception. 'Any chance of a coffee?' He asked hopefully. She put the kettle on and leaned on the table whilst she waited for it to boil.

'Do you think Heather will ever move back to the house in Burney?' She asked casually, the question took him by surprise.

'I hope not, not without me anyway,' he raised his eyebrows. 'Is something of the matter, has Heather said something?' He asked anxiously.

'Don't look so worried,' Judy laughed. 'She loves you, in fact she's crazy about you,' she reassured him.

'So why do you ask about the house then,' he looked round as Charlie came into the reception.

'Well?' He asked nervously.

Steven looked from one to the other. 'Well, what?' He enquired suspiciously.

Charlie took a deep breath. 'Well, as you already know, we are together.' Steven smiled and nodded. 'And as you also know I still live with my mum, and Judy lives in a bed sit, and we've been together for nearly three years now.' Steven nodded again. 'So, we were wondering if you think Heather would rent us her house in Burney.'

Steven laughed at their serious faces. 'Is that all? I'll ask her,' he chuckled.

'Well actually that's not all,' Charlie mumbled, he took hold of Judy's hand and glanced at her guiltily.

'What's happened?' Steven asked.

'Well, the fact is,' Charlie started to say.

'We're pregnant,' Judy finished. They stared at him, looking like a pair of guilty teenagers.

'What both of you?' He tried not to smile at their anxious faces, but quickly gave in and beamed at them. 'How pregnant?' He enquired.

'Nearly five months,' Judy mumbled.

'Five months gone! How the hell did I miss that?' He exclaimed.

'You've been too wrapped up in your own affairs of the heart,' Sue commented, who hearing the laughter had come down from the labs. Steven looked at Judy's stomach, but as usual she was wearing a loose floaty top. He shook Charlie's hand and kissed Judy on the cheek. 'Congratulations,' he said genuinely.

'You see I told you he wouldn't be cross,' Sue said brightly.

'Am I the last to know?' He asked.

'Yes, you are actually,' she called as she went back upstairs. They sat in the reception discussing the impending birth.

'I'm sure Heather will rent you the house. I'll ask her as soon as I get home.' He stopped talking as the phone rang.

Judy handed Steven the receiver 'It's your father.'

There was a slight pause before Edward spoke. 'Have you heard from Heather?'

Steven told him about the answering machine. 'I've not tried since though, why do you ask?' He enquired tentatively.

'I don't want you to panic, son, but her car has been found abandoned on the Kimberwick road,' Edward informed him quietly. Steven's heart started to beat wildly. 'What do you mean abandoned?'

'It looks like she was run off the road, the cat was still in the back,' Edward explained.

Steven felt panic rising in his stomach. 'Where's the policeman who was at the house?' He demanded.

'Higgins stayed with her until she caught the cat and drove away from the cottage. Don't worry, son, we've got a team out looking for her,' Edward told him.

'Don't worry! How can I not worry?' Steven interrupted.

'Just stay by the phone and I'll let you know as soon as we hear anything,' Edward assured him and rang off.

Steven sat down heavily and stared into space. Judy and Charlie looked at him expectantly, and after finding out what had happened, they were ready to go and help look for her. Steven shook his head. 'Dad said to stay here,' he picked his mobile phone up as it rang.

'It's Heather, thank God,' he exclaimed. 'Heather, where are you?' He started to ask; then his blood ran cold as he listened to the voice on the other end.

'You have something that belongs to me, Dr Cooper, and if you want to see this lovely lady of yours again then I suggest you give it back.'

'Let me speak to Heather,' he managed to splutter. There was silence for minute before he heard her terrified voice. 'Steven.'

'It's going to be ok,' he tried to reassure her, but there was no reply.

'Now you've spoken to her,' the voice said.

'What do you want?' Steven asked hoarsely.

'I want my property of course; do you know the roman bridge at the York-Kimberwick junction?'

'Yes,' Steven almost whispered.

'Be there at five o clock with my property and we'll do a swap.'

'If you hurt her,' Steven started to say.

'Don't threaten me, Steven,' the voice snapped sarcastically. 'Just remember that I've got your lady, and if you try and cross me, then we'll see just how much of a lady she is; and one sniff of the cops and she'll be dealt with accordingly. Do you understand?'

Steven swallowed hard. 'Yes,' he choked.

'Good, five o clock and don't be late,' the voice warned menacingly; then the line went dead. Steven stood rooted to the spot staring at the phone.

'Steven?' He looked up with tears pricking his eyes. 'What's the matter? You look like you've seen a ghost,' Judy asked nervously. Steven put the phone on the table and looked away.

'Tell us,' Charlie said urgently. Steven glanced at them with the tears now starting to spill over; he wiped them away and told them what the man had said.

'I assume he means the heroin,' he went to his office and opened the safe.

'You can't give him that,' Charlie exclaimed.

'What else can I do? Christ! She sounded terrified,' he whispered.

Judy put her arm around him. 'I'll ring your dad.'

Steven shook his head 'He said no police.'

'You have to tell him, he'll know what to do,' she insisted.

'No,' he said firmly.

'Be sensible man, what if something happens to you?' Charlie argued. Steven suddenly realised that they were right, and agreed that Judy should ring his father.

Edward arrived less than thirty minutes later. 'What did he sound like? Did he have an accent?'

Steven nodded numbly 'He was foreign, but he spoke English, south African maybe.'

Sue came down and handed him the phials. 'I've replaced the heroin with distilled water,' she told him quietly. Steven put the phials into a bag and got up.

'Let Jack go,' Edward ordered.

Steven shook his head. 'He said to go alone.'

'He doesn't know what you look like; let Jack go in your place,' Edward insisted.

'No, he could have been watching me, so I go alone. I'm not going to risk anything happening to her,' Steven snapped. Edward knew that there was no point arguing; his son was as stubborn as his mother had been, but beneath the stubborn gaze he could see that Steven was scared; not for himself but for Heather. He ran his hand through his hair and sighed in exasperation.

'Alright you can go, but Jack goes too. He can hide in the back of the car; It's none negotiable,' he said firmly as Steven started to object. 'Jack goes with you or you don't go at all.' They stared grim faced at each other for a few seconds, then Edward pulled him close and hugged him tightly.

'You be careful, son, do you hear me? No heroics; just do the swap and get out of there,' he whispered.

Steven's heart was pounding as he approached the bridge. Apart from a few disinterested sheep, the place was deserted, and with nowhere to hide in the open moorland he would be able to see anyone arriving from either direction. 'Nothing yet,' he said to Jack who was lying in the rear footwell. He drove over the bridge and pulled up.

The clock on the dashboard read four fifty-seven, he stared at it willing the seconds away, and with every passing minute the knot in his stomach tightened. The last three minutes until five o' clock seemed like three hours, then as the clock clicked to five o one, he saw a car heading towards him. 'Car coming,' he muttered.

'Be careful,' Jack warned as he pulled the dog blanket over himself.

As the car got closer, Steven saw that it was a dark green rover. It slowed down as it reached the bridge then stopped as it drew level. The driver was wearing a ski mask, and just as Steven was looking into his car, he was checking Steven's car. 'No sign of Heather,' he said through gritted teeth. His heart sank as the car moved off again, it pulled in behind him, and a few seconds later the masked man got out.

Steven took a deep breath. 'Here goes,' he said nervously and opened the door. He stood in the middle of the road. 'Where's Heather?' He demanded.

'Safe! Now where's my property?' The man growled. Steven held up the bag containing the nine phials. 'Put it on the wall,' the man ordered.

'Not until Heather is in my car,' Steven said defiantly.

'You're not going to try and cross me, are you, Steven?' The man asked menacingly 'Because there's a gun pointing straight at you.' Steven looked around; he could see for miles in all directions, but apart from the sheep there wasn't a soul in sight.

'You'll not see anyone, but believe me you are being watched. One signal from me and you, and your lovely lady will be history,' the man said almost gleefully.

Steven's heart felt like it was going to burst through his chest; he gave him a defiant look. 'Where's Heather?' He asked again, the man went to the back of the car and opened the boot.

'She's here,' he leant into the boot, then stumbled back as Heather caught him on the chin with her foot. 'You bitch!' He spat as he dragged her out. Her hands were tied behind her back and there was a scarf over her mouth; she stood in the middle of the road blinking in the light. 'Here she is, now give me the item,' the man demanded.

Steven shook his head. 'I'll put the bag on the wall when she is in my car.' Heather stared at him with terror in her eyes; she had a cut on her forehead and grazing to her knees. Steven's fear suddenly turned to anger. 'Let her get in the car,' he looked down at the fast-flowing water and held the bag over the side of the bridge.

'Let her get in the car or I'll drop it,' he threatened. The two men stared at each other for what seemed like an age. Steven's heart missed a beat as the man suddenly pulled a knife from his pocket, then he cut the ties on Heathers wrists before pushing her roughly towards him. She pulled the gag off and reached him in three or four strides with tears streaming down her face. 'Get in the car,' he said quietly.

'Now my property,' the man demanded. Steven put the bag on the wall and backed towards the car as the man moved in to pick the bag up. 'What the hell is this?' He shouted as he pulled the phials out. 'You bastard!'

Steven leapt into the car and slammed the door before the man had finished speaking; he started the engine and accelerated away, then watched in the rear-view mirror as the man did a u turn in a cloud of dust and started after them.

'He's following,' Steven called over his shoulder. Heather jumped as Jack sat up and looked out of the rear window.

'Put your foot down,' he ordered; then got his radio out and gave the backup cars the order to close in. 'Help's on the way,' he reassured Heather. Minutes later, they heard the sirens and saw the blue lights speeding towards them. The rover spun around to go back the way they had come, but with two police cars closing in behind him, he was blocked in on the narrow road.

Steven pulled over to let the police cars that were heading towards them pass. Jack leapt out as soon as the car was stationary. By now, the rover had skidded to a halt. The man scrambled out and made off across the moors with Jack hot on his heels. He launched into a rugby tackle and floored him, then rolled him onto his back and pulled the ski mask off.

'Hello, Bob, do you remember me?' He asked brightly. Robin Paige glared at him as more officers arrived and hauled him to his feet.

Steven gave a sigh of relief and pulled Heather close. 'I thought I'd lost you,' he pushed her hair back from her face and kissed her. Then she buried her face in his shirt and sobbed.

Jack came over to the car. 'Is she alright?'

Steven nodded. 'I'll take her to the hospital,' he said quietly. They watched as a police car containing the man passed by. 'Do you know who he is?' Steven enquired.

'His name is Robin Paige, he used to run a pawn shop in my old stomping ground, but it looks like he's branched out to kidnapping,' Jack said wryly.

'He's not the man on the phone,' Steven commented. Heather looked up from his chest.

'There was another man,' she said tearfully.

'Did you see his face?' Jack asked hopefully, she shook her head. 'They both wore masks, but the other one had a South African accent.' She pulled a tissue from a box on the dashboard as a tear ran down her cheek.

'You'd better get her to the hospital,' Jack said quietly.

Steven glanced at her as they headed for Kimberwick. She was staring straight ahead; the blood from the wound on her head was bright against her pale face. 'Is Monty alright?' She asked suddenly.

'He's fine,' he reassured her. 'Let's get you checked out and then we'll go home,' he took her hand which was on his knee and squeezed it gently.

She gave a big sigh as they drew up outside the hospital twenty minutes later. 'I hoped that I wouldn't see this place again, not quite so soon anyway,' she tried to smile but couldn't quite manage it. Steven waited outside the treatment room whilst the doctor examined her.

'I've put a couple of stitches in the head wound; the grazes on her legs are superficial but I'll prescribe a course of antibiotics just as a precaution,' he told him when he'd finished. They looked at her through the window. 'I have to say she's in better shape than the last time I treated her,' the doctor commented.

Steven gave a wry smile. 'Can I take her home?'

The doctor nodded. 'Just keep her quiet and calm and watch out for concussion,' he warned.

'There is just one more thing,' Steven said as he turned to go; the doctor looked back expectantly.

Steven hesitated for a second. 'Do you know if she was raped?'

The doctor frowned at him and glanced through the window again. 'Do you think she may have been?'

'The man on the phone made a veiled threat, but she hasn't said anything,' Steven admitted.

'Well, if she was sexually assaulted then I'll need to check her out,' the doctor said seriously. They stood in silence for a minute watching her chatting to a nurse. 'You'd better go and ask her,' the doctor said eventually.

Steven left the doctor outside and went into the treatment room. 'How are you feeling?' he asked.

'Much better now,' she said brightly. He gave her a hug and wondered how she managed to bounce back so quickly.

'This is very déjà vu, don't you think?' He said as he tried to pluck up the courage to ask.

'Very,' she agreed. 'Come on, let's go home,' He took her arm as she went to open the door.

'I have to ask you something first.'

She looked up and saw the fear in his eyes. 'I'm fine, three stitches and a few grazes,' she kissed his cheek. 'Come on, let's go,' she said impatiently.

The words suddenly came out in a rush. 'Did they touch you? The man on the phone threatened to.'

Heather cut him off before he could finish. 'No, they didn't touch me, not like that anyway. I heard them discussing it, but I think they were trying to

188

frighten you into doing what they asked. So can we go home now?' Steven gave a sigh of relief. He took her hand and shook his head at the doctor on the way out before heading home.

He lay on his side that night with what if's spinning through his mind. He had been very tempted to chase Paige himself, but if he had got hold of him, he doubted that he would have been able to control his temper. In fact he knew that he wouldn't.

He watched Heather sleeping, and was amazed that after all she had been through over the last few years, she still managed to smile. He wondered what she was dreaming about as she frowned in her sleep, then as her eyelid twitched, he was reminded of the first time he saw her. He leant across and kissed her gently, making her stir.

She draped her arm across his chest and snuggled into him. 'I love you,' she murmured.

Chapter 3

Robin Paige was sitting in the interview room. 'Get Trudy Baines in for an identity parade, let's see if she recognises him,' Edward told the PC, he looked round as Jack appeared next to him.

'Is he talking, guv?'

Edward shook his head. 'He says he's not going to say anything. We'll wait and see if Trudy identifies him and take it from there.' They looked at him sitting with his arms folded in defiance. 'Shall we have a coffee then?' Jack suggested.

'Was it you who bruised his face?' Edward asked as they headed for the canteen.

'No, guv, that was where Heather kicked him,' he said brightly.

Edward smiled. 'I'm impressed,' he said genuinely.

'Me too,' Jack agreed.

The green rover had been moved to the police garage. A call to the DVLA confirmed the suspicions of all concerned that the number plates were false; a check on the chassis number was the next line of investigation. Heather's red golf stood next to it; the front wheels buckled where she had been forced into the ditch.

'Bastards,' Steven muttered as he inspected it.

Sue took her gloves off. 'There are no prints, but we have got three different coloured hairs from the boot of the rover, along with a packet of cable ties and an old sheet. I'll check the hair samples against Heather and Beverly Penrose. I should be able to get some DNA from them.

'The girls are still working on Paige's and Heather's clothes. We should have some preliminary results this afternoon and that's it for now.' Steven nodded his thanks and went up to see his father.

'You're just in time; will you make the numbers up in an identity parade?' Edward said brightly.

'Do I have a choice?' Steven asked dryly.

'Do you have something to hide?' His father counter asked, and then smiled as his son went into the parade room and joined the line. Trudy was waiting behind the one-way glass. 'Don't worry they can't see you,' Jack assured her. 'Have a good look at them and tell me if you recognise the man who picked you up that night.'

Trudy looked at each man in turn. 'Well actually I recognise three of them, but number five is the man who took me to the Firs,' she said smarmily.

'You're sure?' Jack checked.

'That's him, the one with the bruise on his chin,' she said confidently. Edward thanked her and signalled to the PC to take her home. 'Oh! I nearly forgot,' she rooted in her bag and pulled out a scrap of paper. 'Zoë took the number; we take each other's numbers just in case.'

Jack took the paper. Trudy: green saloon eleven twenty, and a registration number was written on it. 'Why didn't you give this to us earlier?' He asked angrily.

'Because, Mr Policeman, you lot arrested her and she only got out yesterday,' she scowled at him, then turned on her heel and stomped out.

Jack looked at the paper. 'It's a different number, Christ! We may have avoided all this if she'd come forward sooner. I'll get onto the DVLA and see who it's registered to; I doubt its Mr Paige's car,' he said resignedly.

Steven came in a minute later. 'Well?' He enquired.

Edward nodded. 'She's identified him as the man who picked her up, but the receptionist at the Firs and the porter who overheard the argument, both say that he isn't the man who checked in as Mr Smith,' he said ruefully.

A few hours and three post-mortems later, Steven was just thinking about going home when Sue appeared at the office door. 'Of the three hair samples that we found in the boot of the rover, one matched Heather, one matched Beverly Penrose, and the third sample is synthetic,' she looked up from the printout.

'You mean a wig?' Steven said in surprise.

Sue nodded. 'There were no prints in the car, but the cable ties we found in the boot match the ones used to tie Heather's hands.' Steven winced at the memory of her standing in the road. 'We also found Beverly's hair on the back of Heather's clothes, and a trace of lavender oil impregnated in the carpet from the boot, if she was put into there with wet hair after she died, the water would have soaked into the carpet leaving a trace of oil.'

Sue turned the page. 'Heather's hair was on Paige's shirt, but apart from that there was just his DNA, except on the ski mask.' She handed him the sheet.

'DNA on the inside of the mask matches the mucus from Pickering's body, and the blood found at my house,' he exclaimed.

'Paige and the other man must have shared masks,' Sue guessed. Steven picked the phone up. 'I'll just let dad know and then I'm going home.'

'How is Heather?' Sue asked as she turned to go.

'Fine thanks, just a couple of stitches where she hit her head,' he smiled at her trying to look positive.

'And what about you?' She asked.

'What about me?' He counter asked.

'How are you feeling?'

'I'm fine too,' he said brightly; although in truth he was feeling far from it.

'Really?' She gave him an affectionate look as he started to dial out.

'Actually, I feel like thumping someone,' he admitted without looking up.

'It's a natural emotion,' she said gently.

He glanced up at her. 'But that makes me as bad as them, doesn't it?' He said quietly.

'Defending the people you love is never wrong,' she reassured him. 'Go on go home,' she ordered. 'And say hi to Heather for me,' she gave him a motherly smile and went back upstairs leaving him to continue with his call.

Edward was reading through Heather's statement.

"I left the cottage with Monty at about eleven fifteen, at the end of the drive PC Higgins went towards York. I turned onto the Kimberwick road to go back to Edward and Sheila's house. About half a mile along the road, a green rover appeared behind me. I slowed down to let it pass, but when it drew level with me.

"It forced me off the road and into a ditch. Two men in masks dragged me out of the car and put me in the boot of the rover. It was very hot; I think I passed out, because when I woke up, I was in the back of a van with my hands tied behind my back and a gag over my mouth. I could hear people talking, it sounded like two men.

"One had a South African accent and the other one had a London accent. The one with the London accent was saying that the kid had rung Pickering from the train station and he still had it on him, but he had to go because the train was leaving and he would call after the wedding. The other man said that Pickering was sure it must have been found during the post-mortem and the pathologist must have kept it.

"I couldn't hear anything after that just mumbling. After a while, the van door opened; the one with the South African accent took the gag off. He said your boyfriend wants to speak to you. He put my mobile phone to my ear, but I only got the chance to say Steven's name before he took the phone away.

"He put the gag back on and shut the door again. They left me there for ages. I tried kicking the side of the van to attract attention but no one heard. Later, they put me back in the boot of the car and drove off; I didn't know where I was until the one with the London accent opened the boot.

"I kicked him in the face as he leaned in. He dragged me out and I saw Steven standing in the road. They talked for a while, then the man cut the ties and pushed me towards Steven. I got in the car and waited for him."

Edward stopped reading. That girl's really been through the mill, he thought. He put the statement in the folder, then looked at his watch and yawned. It was nearly seven o'clock; no wonder he felt tired. Time to go home, he told himself.

He had only got as far as the stairs when he was stopped by a yell from one of the constables. 'An Inspector Dwight on the phone, Sir,' he called. Edward made his way back up to the squad room. 'Interpol, Sir,' the PC told him. Edward was suddenly wide awake; he listened intently to what the inspector had to say and continued on his way home.

He waited until the next morning to bring Whittle up to date. 'We've got a name; Alex Gorman, he's a South African, age forty-three, he's wanted for smuggling gun running GBH, and suspected involvement in several murders,' he looked up and told him about the conversation with Dwight.

'What the hell is he doing in Yorkshire?' Whittle snapped.

'Hiding probably,' Edward said wryly. 'He's wanted across South Africa, the United States and several other countries as well I expect. Interpol are going to send the file over,' he waited for Whittle to respond, but the Chief Inspector made do with dismissing him with a wave. He went back to his office and called Jack in to update him.

'We'd better brief the team and hope the file gets here soon,' he exclaimed. Edward nodded his agreement; he followed him out, but stopped at the briefing room door.

'Actually, Jack, you brief them, will you? I need to speak to Whittle again.' He left Jack to speak to the other officers and made his way back to the Chief Superintendent's office. Whittle looked up in surprise as he went in.

'Is there a problem?' Edward bit his lip; the Chief Superintendent wasn't the easiest man to deal with, he always did everything by the book even when it was obvious that it wasn't the right thing to do. 'Well?' Whittle raised his eyebrows as Edward sat down.

'Well, Sir. I think that if we are dealing with someone of this calibre, then we should have an armed officer on the team.' Whittle took his glasses off and leaned back in his chair.

'An armed officer?'

Edward nodded. 'Gorman is wanted for gun-running and possible murder, and if he is involved in this case, then he may be armed, and we definitely know that he is dangerous. I don't want my men to be unprepared,' he stared at his boss defying him to disagree.

'I'll think about it,' Whittle said after a minute.

'We know that he was in the room with Graham Pickering,' Edward started to argue.

'I'll think about it,' Whittle repeated firmly.

The next day, there was news from the DVLA. 'The car is registered to a company in London called exotic imports; the owner is a man called Andrew Wells,' Jack reported.

Edward looked up from the paperwork. 'What do they import?'

Jack turned his nose up. 'Cheap mass-produced tacky souvenir type stuff mainly.'

Edward chuckled at his look of disgust. 'Has he reported the car missing?'

Jack shook his head. 'No, he hasn't and I think I know why.' Edward put his pen down.

'Ok, mystic Meg, enlighten me.'

Jack frowned at him. 'I spoke to a mate of mine at the yard, and apparently Mr Wells has been investigated on several occasions on suspicion of importing more than plastic souvenirs.'

'Drugs?' Edward asked hopefully.

'Drugs weren't mentioned but illegal immigrants were,' Jack said dryly.

Edward raised his eyebrows in surprise. 'Really? That's interesting.'

Jack nodded his agreement. 'The word on the street is that he imports women for prostitution, he's been raided twice but nothing was found.'

Edward leaned his chin on his hand. 'I think we should go and see Mr Andrew Wells, don't you?' he said thoughtfully.

The train pulled into Euston station two days later. People crowded onto the platforms, pushing and jostling, their minds set on getting where they were going. 'What did you say your mates name is?' Edward checked as the train stopped.

'Simon Reynolds,' Jack reminded him. 'He's just been promoted to Detective Inspector. I told him I'd give him a ring when we got here, so we should get to Wells' place about the same time, that's assuming we can get a cab,' he muttered as they pushed through the crowds.

There was a long queue at the taxi rank; it took nearly half an hour for them to get to the front, and they pulled up outside a large modern detached house in Hyde Park twenty minutes later. Set behind iron gates and a high wall, it looked out of place amongst the older properties in the area. 'How the other half live eh,' Jack muttered.

'You don't miss working here, do you?' Edward asked.

Jack gave a snort of disgust. 'You must be joking, there's too much corruption.'

The comment shocked Edward. 'In the Met?' He exclaimed.

'Everywhere,' Jack said dryly. Their conversation was cut short as a car pulled in next to them. A stocky man with blond hair got out and grinned at them.

'Jack, it's good to see you, it's been too long.' He gushed as they shook hands warmly. After introductions and congratulations on his promotion, Simon handed Edward the file on Andrew Wells.

'There's not much in it,' Edward commented as he flicked through it.

'That's because we haven't got anything on him,' Simon said a touch disappointedly. There was an intercom built into one of the gate posts. Simon pushed the buzzer and tapped his foot impatiently. 'He knows we're coming. I rang yesterday,' he said angrily.

It was several more minutes before a woman's voice enquired in broken English. 'What do you want?'

Simon gave their names. 'Wait,' the voice said curtly.

'About bloody time,' Jack muttered, as a few seconds later, the gates started to open. When they got to the door it was already open; a small blond-haired woman wearing an apron was waiting in the hallway.

'Come in, wait in study,' she ordered. Edward tried to get a look at her face as she turned and led them through to a lavish but gaudily furnished room. She left as soon as they were seated.

'Nice foreign hospitality,' Jack commented wryly. They got up as the door opened, and a man wearing a track suit that was stained with sweat came in, he spoke with a thick London accent.

'You'll have to excuse Maria she's not been here long and I'm still house training her,' he started to laugh, but stopped as the policemen who were unimpressed by the comment stared at him with obvious distaste. Edward sized him up as Simon showed his warrant card and introduced them.

Middle aged, about five feet eleven tall and thick set, he had short black crew cut hair with flecks of grey appearing at his temples. Two heavy gold chains hung around his neck, there was a matching one around his wrist, and a large gold ring finished the cockney wide boy look.

He ignored Jack and shook Edward's hand. 'Sorry for the delay I was in the gym,' he looked Edward up and down. 'Do you work out, Chief Inspector?' He enquired amusedly.

Edward shook his head. 'No, I don't as it happens, but my sergeant here does.' He gestured towards the chains 'Do you always work out in your jewellery, Sir?'

Wells fingered the chains. 'I never take my gold off, Inspector, there are too many light-fingered people about.' They stared at each other for a few seconds.

'Are you married, Sir?' Edward asked suddenly; Wells gave him a puzzled look. 'It's just that I notice there are no happy family pictures, you know. No lovely wife and kids.' He gave him a sympathetic smile and continued to stare at him.

Simon cleared his throat impatiently. 'Shall we get on then?' He suggested.

Maria came back in with a tea tray a few minutes later; she glanced at them nervously as she set it on the table. Jack smiled at her. 'Thanks,' he said kindly.

Wells slapped her bottom as she passed him on the way out. 'Yes thanks, babe,' he echoed. She gave him a look of pure hate before closing the door with a bang. Wells scowled at the closed door and then forced a smile. 'As I said, untrained,' he muttered.

196

'Where is she from?' Edward enquired.

'Why?' He asked sharply.

'I'm just curious, Sir,' Edward said benignly.

Wells looked heavenward. 'Romania if you must know,' he stared at him, waiting for the next question.

Edward didn't disappoint him. 'Do you know what her last name is?' He asked.

'Of course, I do. It's Catacazi,' Wells said incredulously.

'I take it she has a work permit,' Edward checked.

Wells shifted in his chair, then picked a cup up and sat back. 'Yes, she has. Now what can I do for Britain's finest? I don't imagine you came all the way from Yorkshire to discuss my marital status or my domestic staff,' he said scornfully.

Edward pondered for a second before explaining about the car, but he left out the part about Heather's kidnap and the murders. 'You came all this way just to ask about a stolen car, haven't you got anything better to do?' He chuckled.

Jack glared at him. 'Yes, we did and yes we have; so, if you wouldn't mind answering the question we can get on,' he snapped.

Wells gave a loud exaggerated sigh. 'I have a lot of cars; I'll have to ask my general manager about it. It's not urgent, is it?' He asked casually.

'You must be very well off to have so many cars that you don't know if one is missing,' Edward commented.

Wells shrugged dismissively. 'Business is good,' he explained arrogantly.

'Where is your manager, Sir?' Edward asked.

'Unfortunately, he's on holiday for the next few days,' Wells said apologetically.

'Where on holiday?' Jack asked disbelievingly.

'I've no idea I'm not his keeper,' Wells snapped.

'When is he due back?' Edward enquired.

'He'll be back at the weekend; I'll ask him about the car then,' he said disinterestedly and stood up. 'Is that all?'

Simon got up too, but Jack and Edward didn't move. 'No that's not all, Mr Wells,' Edward informed him dryly; he looked at the file. 'I would like you to arrange for us to have access to your warehouse, the one at Millwall dock.'

Wells sat down again. 'What has my warehouse got to do with a stolen car?' Jack and Simon looked at Edward both wondering the same thing.

'Probably nothing,' Edward admitted. 'But we would like to see it anyway whilst we're here. Today would be good for us unless you've got something to hide of course,' he gave him an insincere smile.

Wells was starting to look uncomfortable. 'Of course I haven't got anything to hide. I'm a legitimate business man,' he said disdainfully.

'Good shall we go then?' Edward suggested 'You can come with us in Inspector Reynolds car.' He started to walk to the door. 'Oh sorry! Do you want to get dressed first, Sir?' He went and sat down again. 'What's your manager's name,' he asked casually.

Wells scowled at him. 'Robin Paige,' he snapped as he left the room.

Wells sat silently next to Jack in the back of the car as they drove to the docks. A man came running over as they pulled up outside a large warehouse 'Oh! Sorry, Mr Wells, I didn't realise it was you,' he apologised as they got out of the car; he glanced at Inspector Reynolds and frowned.

'These policemen want to look around,' Wells told him. The man went pale and started retreating hastily back towards the building.

'Wait a minute,' Jack shouted; the man stopped and turned around. 'Who are you?' Jack asked.

'Jim Masters, my warehouse manager,' Wells snapped.

'He didn't ask you,' Edward told him sharply. He looked at Jim and raised his eyebrows. 'Well?'

'I'm Jim Masters, Mr Wells' warehouse manager,' he said with his voice faltering.

'Like I told you! And he's busy,' Wells said sarcastically.

Edward stared at the nervous looking man for a few seconds. 'Ok you can go.' He rubbed his hands together. 'Right then where shall we start?' He asked brightly. As they approached the building, three vans pulled away. 'What's in those and where are they going?' Edward enquired.

Wells glared at him. 'They're going all over the place; I deal in souvenirs.'

Edward gave a disinterested sniff. 'Yes, I know you do, cheap tacky mass-produced ones I believe.' Jack stared at him in shock; he had never seen him so hostile towards anyone before, it was totally out of character. They went into the main building where a couple of fork lifts were loading more vans with large crates. The drivers eyed the group suspiciously as they passed. Edward glanced around. 'Ok, I think we've seen enough.'

Wells stared at him in disbelief. 'What?' He spluttered.

Edward smiled at him. 'We won't take up any more of your valuable time, Sir.' He started to walk out of the warehouse, then stopped and turned back. 'There is just one more thing,' he called.

'What?' Wells snapped impatiently.

'Do you happen to know a man called Alex Gorman?'

A flicker of anxiety appeared on Wells' face. 'No, I don't,' he said angrily 'Now is there anything else?'

Edward shook his head 'You don't mind making your own way back do you, Sir? My Sergeant and I have a train to catch. Oh! And we'll be in touch about the car,' he added as an afterthought. They made their way back to the car, leaving Wells staring after them in bewilderment. 'Euston station, Sir?' Simon asked as they drove off the docks.

'No, back to Wells' house please,' Edward ordered. He smiled at him as he glanced in the mirror.

'What are you up to, guv?' Jack asked suspiciously. 'I've never seen you like this before.'

Edward sighed quietly 'Did you notice anything about Mr Andrew Wells?'

'Apart from him being a smug bastard who treats his employees like shit you mean?' Jack checked.

Edward nodded. 'Something he was wearing.' He gave as a clue. Simon glanced in the mirror again. 'But of course he didn't shake hands with you two, did he? So you may not have noticed,' Edward mused.

Jack turned around and looked at him. 'A ring?'

Edward nodded. 'Not just any ring though, it looked remarkably like the ring that Graham Pickering was wearing before he was killed,' he said thoughtfully.

'What about the gold chain, do you think that could be Pickering's as well,' Jack asked.

'I don't know but I intend to find out,' he added firmly. They reached the house and Edward jumped out. 'I'll only be a minute,' he pushed the buzzer and was admitted a few minutes later.

'What's he up to?' Simon asked suspiciously.

Jack shrugged. 'He must have one of his feelings.'

Simon lit a cigarette. 'Does he have these feelings very often?' He enquired somewhat sarcastically.

'Actually, his feelings are usually right,' Jack conceded; he started to give him an example but stopped as Edward reappeared.

'Euston Station then thanks,' he said to Simon as he got back in the car. Jack raised his eyebrows. 'I just needed a quick word with Maria, but as it happens, she couldn't help,' he looked out of the window. 'Or was too scared to help,' he said quietly. As they pulled away, a white van came hurtling around the corner with a red-faced Jim Masters at the wheel.

'He's not too busy to give the boss a lift home, is he?' Edward said scornfully; he gave a mock salute as he made brief eye contact with Andrew Wells who was in the passenger seat, and then sat back contentedly.

It was well after midnight when they got back. Edward crept into the house and sat in the kitchen; he knew that he had almost overstepped the mark in London. It wasn't his patch, and Jack was right, he had acted out of character, but there was something niggling at the back of his mind that he just couldn't put his finger on. He looked up as Steven came into the kitchen and sat down opposite him.

'It's nearly one o' clock, don't you think it's about time you went to bed?' He suggested. Edward told him about Andrew Wells and the ring. 'It can't be a coincidence, not with Robin Paige being here and also being Wells' manager.'

'Is there a sample on file for him?' Steven asked.

'I'll check it out,' Edward shrugged. 'I don't know, I'll find out tomorrow.'

Steven glanced at the clock. 'You mean today,' he corrected. 'Did you tell Wells that you've got Paige?'

Edward shook his head. 'No! And apparently he's expecting him back at the weekend. I'll get Jack to ring Simon later, he can ask about the sample and give him the good news about Paige at the same time. Anyway, how's Heather?' He enquired through a yawn.

'She's fine,' Steven confirmed. 'And she's waiting for me, so I'm off.' Edward followed him as he went back upstairs. He went into his bedroom to find Sheila still awake.

'Sorry I'm so late,' he whispered. He sat on the edge of the bed and took his shoes off.

'Well you'd better make it up to me,' she whispered back; the bed creaked as she rolled over to face him. 'Quietly though,' she giggled.

Robin Paige folded his arms defiantly. 'I'm not saying anything until my solicitor gets here,' he announced.

'I didn't expect you would,' Edward said brightly, and went back to the squad room. 'Have you called Simon?' He checked.

Jack nodded. 'He's going to see Wells today, by the way there is no sample on record; yes, it surprised me too, but apparently they've never found anything to justify taking one,' he said to Edward's look of disbelief.

'I find that very hard to believe,' Edward muttered.

Robin Paige's solicitor arrived the next morning; a willowy bottle blond with a thin pinched face and wearing a pinstripe skirt suit. She marched into the reception on sky high heels and introduced herself as Ms Gold. Jack looked her up and down as she waited to be admitted. 'Blimey, guv, that's all we need.'

Ms Gold gave them a look of distain as she was shown into the interview room. 'I wish to speak to my client in private,' she said in a public-school voice, and with an air of authority that Edward took an immediate dislike to.

'Of course you would,' he said semi-sarcastically.

'I've never seen a solicitor like that before,' Jack commented as they waited in Edward's office, he stopped talking as the phone rang.

'You're too late she arrived half an hour ago,' Edward said, as Simon Reynolds warned him to expect Ms Gold. He put the phone down and grimaced. 'Apparently, our Ms Gold is also Andrew Wells solicitor,' he said dryly, and then called, 'Come in,' as someone knocked on the door.

'Mr Paige is ready to speak to you,' PC Higgins informed them.

'Remember that you are still under caution,' Edward reminded Paige. He looked with distaste at the cocky face staring at him across the table. 'You have been identified as the man who picked up a local prostitute.

'You then took her to the Firs Hotel in Kimberwick, where you paid her two hundred and fifty pounds to pretend to be someone else who was later found dead. You were also caught holding a young woman hostage, and DNA from both women has been found in the boot of the car that you were driving.'

Paige stared at him blankly. 'Your point being?'

Edward sighed impatiently. 'How did you know that the heroin had been substituted with water?'

Paige looked bemused. 'What the hell are you talking about?' He looked at Ms Gold. 'What's he talking about?'

Gold looked up from her notes. 'I have no idea, perhaps you could be a little more specific, Inspector.' Jack bit his tongue desperate to say something, but a glance from Edward stopped him. Gold and Paige listened impassively as Edward went through the events of the last few days. 'So, as you can see, we do have evidence to suggest that you are involved in this case.'

'I've never been to the Firs Hotel,' Paige interrupted.

Gold shook her head at him. 'I advise you to say nothing more for the moment.' Jack glared at him as he sat back and folded his arms.

'I've nothing more to say,' he announced, and smiled triumphantly.

'Who are you working with?' Edward persisted. Paige yawned and looked away.

'My client has nothing more to say,' Gold reminded them. 'So shall we talk about bail?' Edward got up and signalled to the PC to take Paige away.

'With the evidence that we have on your client, Ms Gold, bail is out of the question.' She glared at him, then gathered her papers together and stood up.

'I'll speak to you later,' she informed Paige. Edward opened the door for her and watched as she clattered off down the corridor.

Jack could hardly contain his anger. 'What the hell is she up to?' He grumbled.

Edward shrugged. 'She's stalling, she knows we've got him at the scene, and with Trudy's identification and the forensic evidence, she's probably going to go for a deal,' he said in frustration.

Chapter 4

'Heather says there's no problem with you renting the house,' Steven told Charlie that afternoon. Charlie beamed at him and rushed off to tell Judy the good news. Steven looked at the pile of paperwork on his desk and groaned; then smiled to himself as he listened to Judy and Charlie talking excitedly in the reception.

Charlie stuck his head in an hour later. 'Call out, boss; it's the picnic spot between York and Burney. Do you know it?' Steven nodded confirmation and grabbed his bag.

'Let them know I'm on my way,' he said as he hurried out. He knew the spot well having stopped there on several occasions whilst out riding. Something he hadn't done for a while, but since meeting Heather he hadn't felt the need to peddle furiously for hours on end in order to work of stress and anger, or maybe he had just finally grown up enough to control it.

He chuckled to himself as he drove along, then remembered why he had been called out and turned his thoughts to the job in hand. There was a policeman being sick when he arrived; another ashen faced PC came over to meet him whilst he was suiting up.

Steven gestured to his colleague. 'Is he ok?'

The PC nodded. 'We've all been at it. It's pretty grim.' He led Steven over to the car park boundary and pointed. 'It's in there. Chief Inspector Finch is waiting for you.'

Steven pushed his way through the undergrowth and found himself in a small clearing. Finch was sitting on a tree stump smoking. 'Don't say it, I know it's a filthy habit, but sometimes you just need something to get you through,' he stubbed the cigarette out. He then stood up and took a deep breath, before moving a low hanging branch to one side to reveal the naked body of a woman.

Her blond hair was matted with congealed blood. Her face was unrecognisable due to what could only have been a prolonged and savage attack, and her torso was covered in stab wounds and black from being beaten. 'Jesus Christ!' Steven exclaimed.

Finch looked away. 'I'm sorry can I leave you to it for a minute,' he said quietly, then disappeared into the bushes and retched.

Steven was feeling queasy himself, but he managed to control it and took in the scene. 'What a way to end up,' he said to Finch, who had returned as white as a sheet.

'Can you tell if she was killed here?' He asked.

Steven looked around at the immediate area; there was very little blood, the ground was dry and the floor litter was largely undisturbed. He examined the nearest trees and bushes but there was nothing on them. 'I would say that she was killed elsewhere and dumped here.'

He crouched over the body and examined the stab wounds. Apart from one, they were largely superficial, the one that could have done the real damage was just beneath her left breast. 'This one looks deep enough to have killed her.'

Finch took a deep breath and bent over her. 'Can you tell what sort of knife?'

Steven examined one of the wounds closely 'A very thin sharp one; if I had to commit myself, I would say it was a scalpel or something very similar,' he said despondently.

He continued with the examination and found that the end of each finger had been sliced off. 'Someone obviously didn't want her to be identified,' Finch commented. 'Can you tell when she died?'

Steven rolled her over to take her temperature. 'I would say she was killed sometime between ten p.m. last night and two a.m. this morning,' he said as he looked at the thermometer. 'I'll be able to be a bit more precise when I get her back.'

The photographer finished recording the scene, then Steven tied a bag over what was left of her head to preserve any evidence, and they watched in respectful silence as the mortuary assistants loaded her into the van. Charlie's face fell when they unzipped the bag. 'Get anything you want to say out of the way now, and then we can get on,' Steven told him.

'Who in God's name would do such a thing?' Charlie asked.

Steven shook his head sadly. 'Someone who didn't want her to be identified, which means that we make identification a priority; but I think we'll call her Holly for now.' Charlie nodded and started to take samples.

Finch was still feeling nauseous and watched from the observation room. He looked round as Edward came in. 'I don't know how he can deal with this stuff day in day out, or why,' he commented.

Edward looked at his son working. 'He does it to find the truth,' he said without explaining himself. Holly's features had been completely obliterated; her skull was fractured in numerous places leaving shards of bone littering the area.

Steven had never seen such severe head and facial injuries, not even on car crashes victims. He tried to stay focused as he talked his way through the procedure. 'Have you got a cause of death?' Finch asked after ninety minutes.

'Well the good news if that's what you can call it, is that her face was mutilated after she died,' Steven looked across to the observation room. 'She died from a single stab wound to the heart, but she was severely beaten first,' he returned his attention to Holly's body. 'The injuries to her face were caused by being repeatedly beaten with a heavy object; probably a large branch.'

He removed splinters of wood and bark from the bloody mass, and sent them up to Sue for identification. 'And she had green eyes,' he called as he found the remains of one of them. He stood up and motioned to Charlie. 'Come on, let's take a break,' he suggested.

They went to the office with their coffee. Judy came in and squeezed Charlie's shoulder. 'Are you ok, honey?'

He nodded unconvincingly. 'I was just thinking what a shitty world to bring a child into,' he patted her tummy and gave a wry smile.

'Do you want me to finish off?' Steven asked when she had gone.

Charlie shook his head firmly. 'I'm just as keen as you to find out what happened, and make sure the bastard who did this is caught,' he drained his cup and got up. As well the facial injuries Holly had substantial bruising to most of her torso, there were several different shaped bruises around her rib area and one of her shoulders was dislocated.

'They were all done whilst she was still alive, although not necessarily conscious,' Steven told the waiting policemen.

'What about the stab wounds?' Finch asked. After looking at the congealed blood around the wounds, Steven concluded that most of them had been inflicted before death.

'Except for the one that killed her they are all minor, deep enough to hurt but not deep enough to kill. And it looks like our knife again,' he said despairingly. It took a further two hours to finish off.

'There are ligature marks around her wrists, so her hands were tied behind her back at some point; she had sex not long before she died but there's no semen. It'll be Monday at the earliest before we have anything from toxicology and bloods.' He watched as Charlie wheeled Holly back to the cooler. 'You and Judy knock off. I'll finish up here,' he told him.

Charlie gave him a grateful smile. 'Are you sure, boss?' Steven nodded confirmation, and watched them walking across the car park arm in arm. It was obvious that Charlie had been affected by the severity of the attack, and in truth he had struggled to cope himself.

He took a deep breath and stared into space. 'It is a shitty world,' he muttered quietly.

'You've had a bad day,' Heather said when he got in. 'Your dad told me about the body.'

He nodded. 'Bad days come with the job; it's just some days are worse than others. Where are Dad and Sheila?' He asked as he suddenly realised that they were alone.

Heather gave a small smile. 'I think they thought we needed a bit of privacy so they've gone to keep Dora Company.'

Steven sat down and pulled her onto his knee. 'Privacy for what exactly?' He whispered.

'For whatever you like,' she whispered back. 'Come on, Dr Cooper, you need some TLC. But we'd better take the dog out first,' she added, as a whine interrupted their plans. She disentangled herself from him and they set off down the road leaving a very disgruntled Monty watching through the window.

'How much longer will we have to stay here?' She asked. 'Not that I mind,' she added quickly. 'It's just that I miss walking on the moors and Monty likes to come with me,' she ran her hand over his bottom. 'But most of all I miss having you to myself.'

He put his arm around her. 'I'll speak to dad tomorrow,' he promised.

They reached the park and sat on a bench whilst Ben explored. 'I've been thinking that I should go back to work. What do you think?' She asked tentatively.

'You mean go back to the post office?' He asked.

'God, no,' she exclaimed. 'It was ok there but it's not a career. I meant I should go back to what I was doing before I married Barry.'

Steven suddenly realised that he had no idea what she used to do. 'Which was what?'

She gave him an amused look. 'Can't you guess?'

Steven thought for a minute and then shook his head. 'No idea,' he confessed 'It wasn't something racy like pole dancing, was it?'

She dug him in the ribs. 'Sorry to disappoint you, but no, nothing quite so exotic. If you can't guess then I'm obviously no good at it,' she said sadly.

Steven racked his brains again. 'I give up,' he said after a minute.

'Interior design; you know, decorating?' She whispered.

He suddenly remembered her comments when she first visited the house. 'I should have guessed,' he said ruefully. 'But you're wrong, you are good at it, amongst other things of course,' he added mischievously.

'Don't do that,' she ordered semi-seriously.

'Don't do what?'

She leant over and kissed his cheek. 'Don't smile; you know I can't resist your dimple.'

He got up and pulled her up after him. 'Well I'd better get you home then, hadn't I?' He gave her bottom a quick pat, and called Ben to heel.

The door of Sheila's bungalow opened as they passed. 'We're staying here tonight so you've got the house to yourselves,' Edward called. Steven lifted his hand in thanks.

'I told you,' Heather said as soon as they got inside.

'Told me what?' He started to ask, but she cut him off with a kiss mid-sentence. 'So now that you've got me to yourself, what are you going to do with me?' He enquired.

'Absolutely anything you want,' she said suggestively as he started unbuttoning her shirt.

'Anything?' She nodded firmly. 'Well, dad's got a huge bath,' he hinted.

'How very unethical, Dr Cooper,' she giggled as he reached the last button.

Robin Paige was back at the station the following day. 'My client is willing to cooperate with you, in exchange for a full withdrawal of the charges against him and a place on the witness protection program,' Ms Gold informed them curtly; she sat back and looked at them expectantly. Jack scowled at her, then got up and followed Edward out.

'You're not going to go for it, are you, guv?'

Edward shrugged despondently. 'Whittle might, I'll ask him to give us more time before he agrees to anything,' he said without much hope.

Whittle summoned them an hour later and handed over a thick file. 'Alex Gorman's details. I've read through them and I agree with you about the armed officer,' he said to Edward's surprise.

'Blimey, guv, that must have hurt him,' Jack said amusedly.

'What must have hurt?' Edward enquired.

'Agreeing with you,' Jack chuckled. Edward opened the file; a thin faced unshaven man stared out at them. What little hair he had left was going grey, and his small pig like eyes glinted behind wire framed glasses. 'Well, he doesn't look very intimidating,' Jack commented.

'They never do,' Edward said wryly.

'Slightly built, five feet five inches tall, no distinguishing marks. The last definite sighting was three years ago in Cape Town. His current whereabouts is unknown; there are several unconfirmed reports that he was killed by one of his contacts when a deal went sour.

'An informant, who has subsequently been murdered, told them that he disguises himself when he's travelling and he has several false passports,' he put the file down and stared out of the window. The file also told them that Alex Gorman had been questioned in connection with provoking racial violence, and arrested on several occasions for suspected gun running, but nothing was ever proved.

'So, he's not dead, and now he turns up in Yorkshire,' Jack muttered angrily.

Edward gave the sergeant a light slap on the back. 'Don't worry, I'll make sure he doesn't get away with it,' he promised.

'Holly's real name is Zoë Fairfax and she's aged twenty-seven,' Sue told Steven later. He looked up in surprise as she handed him a print out. 'She was arrested a couple of weeks ago for prostitution, so we had her DNA on file,' Sue explained. 'And the wood that was used to disfigure her was Quercus Robur, which is oak,' she added before he could ask.

'Have you informed the police?' He enquired as he scanned through the report.

'DCI Finch is on his way over with your dad,' she confirmed, and then went back upstairs. Steven went into the lab wondering why his father was involved.

'Did you have good weekend?' He asked Charlie.

'Very good, thanks. I felt the baby kicking for the first time.'

Steven leaned on the bench. 'Are you going to get married?' They looked at Judy who was sitting in the reception knitting.

'I hope so but I haven't asked her yet,' Charlie admitted. Judy looked up as she felt their eyes on her.

'What?' She mouthed.

'Nothing,' they mouthed back.

'So why don't you ask her?' Steven enquired.

Charlie gave a small shrug. 'I'm waiting for the right moment, and what if she says no?'

Steven laughed at the look on his face. 'Of course she won't say no, she's besotted.'

Charlie looked puzzled. 'Besotted with what?'

'With you, you idiot,' Steven said exasperatedly.

'What about you then?' Charlie asked.

'I hope she's not besotted with me,' he chuckled.

'Not Judy, you bloody fool, are you going to marry Heather?'

Steven let out a long sigh. 'I don't know, I've only known her for a few months and she had such a terrible time the first time around. I doubt she'll want to rush into it again, if at all,' he said almost wistfully.

Charlie grinned at him knowingly. 'So you have thought about it then?'

Steven gave him a mind your own business look and changed the subject. 'Right, let's get on,' he suggested.

'Ok, you're the boss, boss,' Charlie chuckled, and went to retrieve the next case from the chiller.

'Zoë Fairfax was Trudy Baines flat mate and Trudy has just retracted her statement,' Edward told Jack.

'What!' Jack exclaimed. 'Why?' He asked in dismay.

'She says she was mistaken,' Edward explained wryly.

'And she was scared stiff,' Finch added.

'Does she know about Zoë?' Jack checked.

'Well, let's put it this way, she didn't seem surprised when we told her, so I've put her in protective custody for now,' Edward looked at the time. 'I suppose we should go and see what Mr Paige has got to say for himself,' he said despondently. Robin Paige smirked at them as they went into the interview room.

'I hear that the witness who maintained that my client picked her up has retracted her statement,' Ms Gold said before they had sat down.

Edward gave her a stony stare. 'Yes, that's correct, but it was only retracted this morning so how would you know that?'

Gold gave him a sympathetic look. 'Oh, I have my finger on the pulse, Chief Inspector, I keep my ear to the ground,' she said knowingly.

'No, we don't know, so tell us,' Jack snapped angrily.

Gold ignored him and looked at her papers. 'So now that you only have a trumped-up kidnap charge, and some very dubious forensic evidence, shall we talk bail,' she asked brightly.

'It's hardly trumped up, he was caught at the scene,' Jack said dourly. She ignored him again and raised her drawn on eyebrows at Edward.

'Well, I'm sorry to disappoint you, Ms Gold, but we have just been granted a further forty-eight hours in which to question your client and continue our investigations,' he returned the sympathetic look and started to leave the room. When he reached the door, he turned back. 'Perhaps you had your finger on the wrong pulse,' he said sweetly, and went out closing the door noisily.

'Nice one, guv,' Jack commended. 'But how the hell did she know about Trudy?'

Edward frowned heavily. 'I don't know, but I do know that we have to get something on Paige by Thursday, or he'll be out on bail and then he'll disappear, you can bet your life on it.' He went back to his office and wondered what to do next.

Jack stuck his head round the door a few minutes later. 'Barney Johnston is on the phone, guv.'

Edward stared absentmindedly out of the window as he listened to the Australian Detective. The sun was going down on another day, and they were no closer to finding out what was going on. Maybe I'm getting past it, perhaps I should take early retirement and enjoy Sheila whilst I've still got the energy. He sat down and yawned.

'She hasn't even had her honeymoon yet,' he muttered, then leant back in the chair and closed his eyes.

'Guv?'

He opened them again. 'Jack, what's up?' He asked sleepily; he looked at his watch as he realised that it was dark outside. 'Did I fall asleep?'

Jack nodded. 'You've been out for hours and Sheila's been on the phone.' Edward got up and put his jacket on.

'I'd better go then,' he yawned loudly as he followed him out.

'The Australian police have arrested a man called Henry Fowler,' he told him as they went down the stairs. 'Apparently, he paid Sam to smuggle the drugs, and he's confirmed that there were twenty phials in ten condoms.'

'Did he give the name of the recipient?' Jack asked hopefully.

'No, he refused to name him. He's also denied knowing Graham Pickering, Robin Paige or Alex Gorman,' Edward said in frustration.

'Do they believe him?' Jack enquired.

Edward nodded. 'It would appear so.'

Jack thought for a minute 'What about Andrew Wells?'

'He wasn't mentioned. I'll give Barney a call in the morning,' Edward said thoughtfully.

'I wonder what on earth possessed Sam to do it,' Jack wondered out loud as they reached the car park.

'Well, apparently he wanted to make some fast money.'

'Don't we all,' Jack interrupted.

Edward looked up at the clear sky. 'His girlfriend is pregnant and her family were insisting that they get married, so now I've got to go and tell Dora that as well as losing her only son, she's going to be a grandmother to a child who will never know it's father,' he said despondently as he got into the car.

When he got home he sat outside the house wondering how to tell her, he was so deep in thought that he barely registered the front door opening, and jumped as Steven tapped on the window. 'What are you doing sitting out here?' Edward got out and started to tell him about Sam's girlfriend.

Heather came out of the house a few minutes later. 'Are you two going to stand there all night?' She called.

'I think I'll tell Sheila first,' Edward decided as they went inside.

'Dora's going home, Sheila is taking her to the airport tomorrow morning,' Edward informed Steven later.

'Does she know that she can't take Sam yet?'

Edward nodded. 'She says she's going to sort things out with his girlfriend's family. I wouldn't like to be in their shoes,' he added.

'What about Graham?' Steven asked. 'She said he can burn in hell, so unless he has someone over there to claim him, then I suppose he'll stay here,' Edward sighed.

'Families eh, who'd have them?' Steven said quietly.

'We're ok though, aren't we?' Edward asked.

Steven laughed at his father's worried face. 'Of course we are, I wasn't talking about us,' he assured him. Then he gave him a look, and Edward knew that a, but was on its way. 'But,' Steven continued.

'Oh God! There's always a but,' he muttered.

'But how long are we going to have to stay with you?'

Edward smiled knowingly. 'Missing the privacy are you, son?' He asked mischievously.

Steven felt himself blushing. 'No,' he objected.

'Don't give me that, you can't keep your hands off each other,' Edward teased. Steven started to explain about Heather missing the moors and the cat liking to go on walks. 'Well me and Sheila are going to stay at her house, so you two can have the place to yourselves,' he interrupted.

Steven returned the knowing smile. 'And you two can have her place to yourselves,' he said with a chuckle. 'After all, you are supposed to be on your honeymoon.'

It was Edward's turn to be embarrassed. 'We're a bit past all that,' he said with a resigned sigh.

'Really?' Steven said disbelievingly; Edward nodded ruefully. 'So it wasn't your bed creaking the other night then?' Steven gave his father a quizzical look before losing the battle to keep a straight face.

Edward put his hands up in defeat. 'Ok! It will be nice for all of us to have some privacy, is that better?' Steven nodded. 'But I still think you should stay away from the farm, at least until this Alex Gorman turns up,' Edward insisted. They were still chuckling when Sheila came into the room. 'Man joke,' Edward said quickly to her raised eyebrow.

Sue stuck her head around Steven's door the next morning. 'We have a partial print from the outside of the fire door at the Firs Hotel.'

Steven started to smile. 'Whose is it?'

Sue handed him a printout. 'It's Robin Paige, shall I call your dad or do you want to do it?'

Edward handed Whittle the results a few hours later. 'I think it's enough to keep him.'

Whittle looked at the report and frowned. 'Well, there's no doubt that he was involved in the kidnapping of Ms Brooks, but a partial print from a fire door is hardly conclusive.'

Edward groaned inwardly. 'He denies he was ever there, but Trudy Baines told us that he took her up the fire escape,' he reminded him.

'I understand that she has retracted her statement,' Whittle said knowingly.

Edward clenched his fists behind his back and struggled to keep his temper. 'Yes, Sir she has, but only after her friend was brutally murdered.'

Whittle glared at him. 'I'm well aware of the facts,' he snapped; he looked at the results again; he's going to tell me to let him go Edward thought despairingly. 'Alright, charge him with kidnapping Ms Brooks, but without Trudy Baines statement, I don't think that we have enough evidence to connect him to the murder of Graham Pickering,' Whittle said when he eventually looked up.

Edward gave a sigh of relief. 'Thank you, Sir,' he muttered and turned to go.

'By the way,' Whittle called; Edward looked back. Whittle smiled at him. 'How's married life suiting you?'

Edward tried to smile back, and wondered why he would be remotely interested. 'Well, what I've seen of it is suiting me very well, thank you for asking, Sir.'

Whittle nodded. 'I'm glad to hear it,' he said brightly, and then turned his attention to something on his desk.

'Arsehole,' Edward muttered under his breath. He went to the squad room to collect Jack. 'Let's go and see what Bob has got to say for himself today,' he suggested.

'It'll be a pleasure, guv,' Jack said brightly. 'What did the Chief super say?' He enquired as they made their way to the interview room. 'It must be a bit frustrating for you, Robin, or can I call you Bob?' Edward asked casually.

Robin Paige glared at the two men sitting opposite him. 'What must be frustrating?'

Edward folded his arms. 'You being Andrew Wells lackey.'

'I'm nobody's lackey. I do what I want when I want,' Paige snapped; they glowered at each other for a minute.

213

'Well, Sergeant Taylor informs me that you used to own your own business, a pawn shop I believe.'

Paige nodded. 'What of it?'

'So now you run errands for a scum bag like Wells, it's a bit of a come down,' Edward commented.

Ms Gold cleared her throat. 'Is this questioning leading somewhere Chief Inspector?'

Edward ignored her. 'What were you expecting to get in exchange for Ms Brooks?' He asked.

'My client declines to answer that question,' Gold butted in quickly.

'Do you decline of your own volition, Mr Paige? Or have you been told to decline by Mr Wells?' Edward asked benignly.

Paige glanced at Gold. 'I've already told you that no one tells me what to do.'

Edward gave a small smile. 'Well, I've been told differently, in fact I have it on good authority that you do exactly what Andrew Wells tells you to do, and without question.'

Paige laughed nervously. 'That's a load of bollocks.'

'Oh well she must be mistaken then,' Edward said brightly, and got up to leave.

'Who is she?' Gold intervened.

Edward turned back. 'Maria.' Jack shot him a puzzled look.

'Who the bloody hell is Maria?' Paige demanded.

'Maria Catacazi, she's Andrew Wells' maid,' Edward reminded him.

Paige started laughing. 'She's nothing but a foreign tart, she's only been in the country for five minutes and she barely speaks English.'

Edward sat down again. 'So when exactly did she come into the country?'

Paige suddenly realised that he'd said too much and shrugged. 'What bearing does Mr Wells domestic staff have on this case,' Gold asked.

'Domestic staff; that's the second time I've heard that term used recently,' Edward said thoughtfully; he sat in silence for a minute, then opened a file and changed the subject.

'You knew Graham Pickering, is that correct?' He asked Paige.

'I met him when I was working in Sydney,' Paige confirmed.

'Do you know that he's been murdered?' Jack asked.

Paige nodded curtly. 'I read it in the newspaper,' he said disinterestedly.

'It's a bit of a coincidence, him being here and getting himself murdered, and you being here and under arrest,' Edward commented.

Gold cleared her throat. 'Inspector, I really think...'

'Well don't,' Edward snapped sarcastically. 'Well, Mr Paige, what do you think?'

Paige scowled at him. 'It's pure coincidence, I had no idea that he was in the country,' he said unconvincingly.

'Did you go back to London?' Jack asked.

Paige looked confused. 'When?'

'After Graham Pickering had been killed.'

Paige shook his head. 'No, I didn't go back to London.'

Gold started to say something, but then thought better of it and sat back. Edward gave her a semi-sarcastic smile before resuming the interview. 'Your boss was wearing the exact same ring that Graham Pickering was wearing the day before he was murdered.'

'So?' Paige interrupted.

'So, Graham Pickering wasn't wearing it when his body was found,' Jack said dryly.

Paige shifted in the chair. 'There must hundreds of rings like that,' he said dismissively.

Edward stared at him for a few seconds, and then fired several questions at him in quick succession. 'Like what?'

'Like the one that Graham was wearing,' Paige muttered.

'Do you know what it looks like?'

'No.'

'Do you know what your boss's ring looks like?'

'No.'

'So how do you know that there must be hundreds of them? It could be a one off,' Edward didn't take his eyes off him during the exchange. 'You didn't take it and give it to Andrew Wells then?' He checked.

'No,' Paige said firmly.

'Did Alex Gorman take it?' Edward asked benignly.

'What?' Paige gasped; he gave Gold a horrified glance as she shuffled her papers nervously.

'I really don't see where you are going with this, Chief Inspector.'

Edward continued to ignore her. 'You know him then?' He surmised.

'Know who?' Paige asked innocently.

'Alex Gorman,' Jack reminded him.

'No, I do not,' he insisted.

'But you said what not who? So I assumed that you know him,' Edward commented.

'Well, you assumed wrong,' he snapped.

'So, you deny knowing him then?' Edward checked.

Paige glanced at Gold again. 'My client declines to answer that question, and I would like to speak to him in private,' she said quickly.

Edward gave her a triumphant smile. 'I bet you would,' he muttered.

'Get onto London and tell them to get Maria out of there, say it's an immigration matter,' he told Jack as soon as they were out of the room. He watched Paige and Gold talking as Jack disappeared into the squad room.

'What are you up to, guv?' Jack asked after he had arranged for Maria to be detained. 'What did she say to you when you went back?'

Edward shook his head. 'She didn't say anything, she didn't even open the door, but I'm certain that there was someone in there with her.'

Jack exhaled slowly. 'So all that about Paige running errands was made up?'

Edward nodded. 'But Maria was scared of something, and I know that I've seen her somewhere before. We'll go and talk to her at the detention centre next week,' he said thoughtfully.

Jack nodded his agreement. 'Oh! by the way, Barney Johnston called, and the suspect in Sydney says he doesn't know Andrew Wells, but the way things are going, he's probably lying as well.'

They sat in silence for a while, then looked up but didn't bother to get up, as Ms Gold came into the room. 'Have you finished talking to your client in private?' Edward enquired semi-sarcastically.

'Yes, I have,' she confirmed.

'So you'll be off back to London for the weekends frivolities then,' he said as a statement not a question.

'Are you really interested in my leisure time arrangements, Chief Inspector, or is that your pathetic attempt to politely tell me to go?' She asked amusedly.

'Leisure time,' he repeated, and then got up so suddenly that she jumped. 'Have a nice weekend, Ms Gold,' he said insincerely.

'Are you feeling alright, guv?' Jack asked when she had gone.

'Yes thank you! Why?' Edward asked in surprise.

'Well I've never known you to be so hostile,' Jack admitted.

Edward frowned at him. 'Do you know what I hate more than criminals, Jack?'

'No,' the sergeant confessed.

'I hate bent solicitors.' They went to the window and watched as Ms Gold walked across the car park with her phone clamped to her ear.

'Do you think she's bent then?' Jack enquired.

'Yes I do,' Edward said firmly. Gold suddenly looked up at the window, almost as though she'd heard what he'd said; she stared at them as she continued to talk into her phone. Edward lifted his hand and waved at her. She scowled back at him before turning on her heel and continuing on her way.

Chapter 5

Edward and Jack waited in the visiting room of the detention centre the following week. Maria looked at them fearfully as she was brought in. 'What have I done?' She spoke slowly trying to find the right words.

'You haven't done anything; we just need to ask you a few questions,' Edward reassured her.

'I have work permit, Mr Wells arrange for me,' she said nervously. Edward looked into her terrified face; she looked so familiar that it was beginning to prey on his mind.

'Do you like working for Mr Wells?' Jack asked.

'No,' she said firmly. 'I need job. I'm lucky, some didn't get job,' she said earnestly.

'When did you arrive in Britain?' Edward asked.

She counted on her fingers as she thought. 'Four months.'

Edward nodded. 'Where do you come from?'

'Bicaz,' she said tearfully.

'Where is that?' Jack asked.

'Romania, I come to find my sister, Jenica.'

Jack handed her a tissue from the box on the table as she started to cry. 'When did Jenica come to Britain?' He asked gently.

'Two years ago, she comes for work,' Maria explained.

'Is Jenica older than you?' He checked.

'Five years older,' she said quietly.

'So how old are you?'

She wiped her eyes and blew her nose noisily. 'Twenty-two, can I go now?' she whispered.

Edward sat back and folded his arms. 'Did Mr Wells arrange for you to come here?'

Maria looked confused. 'He brought me,' she pointed to the PC by the door.

218

'Not to the detention centre, did Mr Wells arrange for you to come to England?' Jack asked.

'No, it was the other man,' she said tearfully.

Edward sat forward expectantly. 'Which other man? Do you know his name?'

She shook her head. 'No name, but he shout at us,' she said bitterly.

'You said us, who was with you?' Edward asked.

Maria gave a small smile. 'The other girls who were waiting for jobs. The man scared us but Ronnie tell him to shut up,' she chuckled.

'Who is Ronnie can you describe him?' Jack asked.

'Not him, she is woman; she brought clothes for us,' Maria said to their surprise.

Jack glanced at Edward. 'How do you know her name?' He asked suspiciously.

'We ask for our bags, but the man says Ronnie will bring clothes,' she explained.

'Can you remember what she looked like?'

Maria shook her head again. 'I only see her from the back.'

Jack sighed despondently. 'Can you remember what colour her hair was?'

'It was blond, but I see the dark coming through,' she said confidently.

'What about the man?' Jack asked hopefully; she gave a small shrug.

'Maybe I remember,' she said unconvincingly.

'We'll send an artist here tomorrow, you can tell him what the man looked like and he will draw him, is that ok?' Edward said slowly. Maria nodded; she looked down as he put a photograph of Robin Paige in front of her. 'Do you know this man?'

'Yes!' She exclaimed. 'He took picture of us.'

Edward shot Jack a triumphant smile. 'Did he take pictures of you at Mr Wells' house?' He asked with his hopes rising. She shook her head. 'Have you ever seen him at Mr Wells' house?' Edward tried.

'No,' she said firmly.

Edward gave a silent sigh of frustration. 'Where did you stay when you first arrived in the UK?'

She gave a small shrug. 'In a house.'

'All of you?' He checked.

'Yes.'

'Did Mr Wells come to the house and ask you to work for him?'

She gestured to the photograph of Paige. 'That man took picture of us, he say Mr Wells look at them and he pick me.'

Edward looked at her thoughtfully. 'How much did you have to pay to come here?' Maria looked confused. 'Money. Did you give money to come to the UK?'

She shook her head. 'No money, we have to work to pay,' she said despondently.

Jack sat forward. 'Did you come on a boat?'

'No, we came in truck.'

'How long were you in the truck?' He asked gently.

'Three days,' she said miserably.

'How many travelled with you?'

They watched as she counted again, nodding her head for each person she remembered. 'Eleven,' she said eventually.

'All women?' Edward asked.

'Yes,' she said quietly.

'Were they all young women?' Jack checked.

'No some aged thirty I think,' she said seriously.

Edward tried not to smile as Jack continued. 'Do you know where the other women are?'

She shook her head. 'Mr Wells pick me to work and the rest,' she shrugged despondently.

'How long will you have to work?' Edward asked.

'Mr Wells say a year, then when I work enough, I can go,' she said with hope in her voice.

'So where will you go when you've worked enough?' Edward asked.

'Wherever I want, I need to find Jenica,' she said in desperation.

Edward nodded at the warder. 'Ok thank you, Maria.'

'I can go?' She asked hopefully.

'I'm afraid you will have to stay here for a while, but we will do everything we can to help you,' Edward promised.

'So we've got Paige but not Wells,' Jack said bitterly when she had gone. 'Well he may not be the big fish, but I know he's involved somewhere along the line,' Edward took an evidence bag from his pocket and retrieved Maria's discarded tissue from the table. 'Just curious,' he said before Jack could ask.

They got on the train an hour later. 'Three days in a truck,' Jack said in disgust. 'I wonder what happened to the other ten.'

'They're probably working their tickets off somewhere, and I dread to think how,' Edward muttered. They walked through the carriages trying to find a seat. 'I'm going to get someone to question Maria in more depth,' Edward said when they finally sat down. 'If we can get a statement from her saying that Wells is sexually assaulting her, then we may have more leverage to dig deeper.'

'Do you think he is?' Jack asked in surprise.

'Well, why else would he have to see pictures of prospective members of his domestic staff?' Edward asked dryly. 'Anyway, get onto your mate, Simon, and ask him to check out the work permit, will you?' He sat back and yawned. 'I hate trains,' he grumbled.

'Well, I did offer to drive,' Jack reminded him.

'I really wanted to get there in one piece,' he muttered before falling asleep.

Steven looked at the middle aged smartly dressed couple who were waiting in the reception. 'Do they know what happened to her?'

Judy gave a small shrug. 'I don't know, but they are adamant that they want to see her.'

He looked at them again; they were sitting with their heads bowed and their hands clasped together. 'Give them a coffee and tell them I'll be with them in a minute.' He went into his office and pulled Zoë Fairfax's file out. 'Mother, special needs teacher; Father, accountant. No siblings. 'Christ,' he muttered.

Charlie stuck his head around the door. 'The Fairfax's are waiting,' he came all the way in. 'Are you ok, boss, you look very pale.'

'They want to see Zoë,' Steven said quietly.

'Do you want me to speak to them first?' Charlie offered.

Tempting though it was, Steven shook his head. 'No, it's ok. I'll do it.' He took several deep breaths and then stood up as the Fairfax's were ushered in; they looked at him with trepidation as they sat down. 'I understand that you wish to see your daughter,' Steven said gently.

Mrs Fairfax nodded. 'Yes, where is she?' She whispered.

Steven looked at their hands which were still clasped together. 'Zoë is in the cold storage area; you are aware that the attack was particularly brutal.' He said as a statement rather than a question.

Mr Fairfax stared at him with pain in his eyes. 'She wasn't raped, was she?' His face was almost begging Steven to say no.

'She had intercourse not long before death, but there's no evidence to suggest it was against her will,' he told them to their obvious relief. 'But whoever killed her tried to stop us from identifying her. Have you been told the extent of her injuries?' He asked tentatively.

Mrs Fairfax started to cry. 'They said her face was battered and she had been stabbed.'

Steven nodded. 'Yes, that's right,' he confirmed.

'So how did you identify her?' Her father enquired.

Steven glanced at the file and wondered if they knew that she had been arrested for prostitution. 'Medical records,' he said quickly, and with relief as they appeared to accept his explanation. 'But I do strongly advise you against seeing her,' he added.

Her father took his wife's hand and blinked back his own tears. 'Please, Dr Cooper, we just want to say goodbye to our girl,' he begged.

Steven looked at the two distraught faces and knew that he didn't have the right to refuse. 'If you would like to give me a few minutes, I'll move her into the chapel of rest,' he said resignedly. He got up and went into the reception. 'Can you be ready to deal with them?' He asked Judy.

'I should warn you, that you may not recognise your daughter,' he told them as he led them to the chapel. 'I suggest that you leave Zoë covered, so that you can remember her as she was.' Her parents were visibly shaking as they approached their daughter's body.

They stared at her for a minute before her father reached out and placed his hand on the sheet. Steven held his breath willing him not to do it. Mr Fairfax hesitated briefly, then clenched his fist and withdrew his hand. 'I'm so sorry but I think the doctor is right, we should remember her as she was,' he whispered to his sobbing wife.

Steven gave a silent sigh of relief and led them back to the family room where Judy was waiting. He sat with them whilst they composed themselves. 'When she died, was it quick or did she suffer?' Mrs Fairfax asked suddenly.

'The wound that killed Zoë penetrated her heart; death would have been almost instantaneous,' Steven said quietly.

Mrs Fairfax closed her eyes and mouthed, 'Thank God.' She gave her husband a tearful nod.

'We've taken up enough if your time,' Mr Fairfax said as they got up, he put his hand out. 'Thank you for being so honest with us, Doctor.' Steven shook the offered hand and found the grip firm and genuine. He watched as Judy showed them out and then sank back onto the couch.

'I just lied to them,' he said when she came back in.

'No, you didn't; they asked if she suffered when she died not before she died.'

He put his hands over his face and took a deep breath. 'Why the hell do I do this job?' He muttered tearfully.

Judy pushed a hankie through his fingers. 'You do it because you care.' He looked up at her; she looked radiant.

'You suit being pregnant,' he said, and then quickly wiped his eyes as Charlie came in.

'Are you ok, boss?' He checked.

'Absolutely,' Steven said brightly. 'What's next?'

Charlie handed him an evidence bag. 'Sergeant Taylor dropped this in, Andrew Wells maid blew her nose on it; your dad thinks he knows her and wants her DNA checking out,' he explained.

Whilst Steven was dealing with the Fairfax's, Edward and Jack were standing in front of the evidence board trying to make sense of what they had. 'So what, if anything, was in the missing condom? And where is Sam's mobile phone?' Jack muttered. They had tried ringing the number given to them by Dora but it was switched off, and although a nationwide alert had been put out for Alex Gorman, they weren't holding their breath.

'He's probably out of the country by now,' Jack said gloomily. 'Anyway, I'd better go, I'll see you tomorrow, guv.' Edward looked at the clock and raised his eyebrows. 'You wanted an armed officer; apparently that's me, and Whittle says I've got to go on a refresher,' he said dryly.

'We've located Trudy Baines' mother, she lives in Newcastle; the local boys have been to see her,' PC Higgins reported later.

Edward smiled with relief. 'Good, Trudy could do with a friendly face. Are they bringing her over?'

Higgins shook his head. 'No, Sir! She said and I quote, "If that little trollop has got herself into trouble, then that's her hard luck".'

Edward gave a sigh of disbelief. 'Has the duty solicitor been called?' He enquired exasperatedly.

'Yes, Sir, he's on his way,' Higgins confirmed.

The duty solicitor arrived after lunch. He sat next to Trudy in the interview room. 'Why did you retract your statement?' Edward asked her.

She glanced at him nervously. 'I told you I was mistaken,' she was trying to sound her normal cocky self but not quite managing it. 'Have you let him go?' She asked anxiously.

'Have we let who go?' Edward asked.

'That bloke, you know the one with the bruise,' she said almost desperately.

Edward shook his head. 'No we haven't. Why would we?'

Trudy paled a shade and looked at her hands. 'Because I told you it wasn't him,' she whispered.

'Why did you say it was him if it wasn't?' Edward asked; she shrugged without looking up. Edward glanced at the solicitor. 'Do you know what happened to Zoë?' He asked gently. Trudy's hands started to shake; she put them under her legs and shrugged again. 'Do you care what happened to her?'

She looked up sharply, her eyes betraying her fear. 'Of course I bloody well care. Zoë was my best friend,' she snapped.

'So do you know what happened to her?' Edward asked again.

She blinked furiously to try and stop the tears. 'She was killed by a punter, it's an occupational hazard,' she said quietly.

'Are you sure it was a punter?' Edward checked.

'Yes,' she mumbled.

'Did you see her go off with him?' She nodded. 'Did you see what he looked like?'

'No, it was dark,' she said unconvincingly.

'But you would have taken the cars registration number, wouldn't you?' Trudy stared at him, wide eyed with fear. 'You told us that you take the numbers just in case, do you remember telling us that?' She gave a small nod. 'So where is the number of the car that Zoë got into?'

'If you know anything then you should tell them,' the solicitor advised.

Trudy thought for a minute. 'I forgot my pen that night,' she said sullenly.

'Really?' Edward muttered disbelievingly.

'Yes,' she said firmly.

'What colour was the car?' He tried.

'I can't remember,' she mumbled.

'Can you remember what time Zoë got into the car?'

She glanced up at him nervously 'About eight o' clock.'

'Eight in the evening?' She gave a light nod. Edward looked at her seriously. 'Do you know what today's date is Trudy?'

She leant back and rolled her eyes at him. 'Of course I do; it's the twenty third of July. I'm not stupid,' she said sarcastically.

'I know you're not stupid, but I do know that you are frightened,' he said gently.

'Frightened of what?' She said nervously.

Edward leant on the table as she avoided eye contact. 'Frightened of the man who killed Zoë.'

'I don't know who killed her,' she insisted.

'But you must have seen him when she got into the car,' Edward questioned.

'I already told you it was dark,' she said impatiently.

'And you're sure that this was at eight in the evening?' He checked again.

'Yes,' she snapped impatiently.

Edward sat back and studied her intently. 'It's the middle of summer, Trudy, and at eight o' clock in the evening, it's still light.' Trudy went white and looked at the table. 'Did he kill Zoë to make you retract your statement? If you know who killed her then you must tell us,' he insisted.

A tear ran down Trudy's face. 'I need to go to the toilet,' she whispered without looking up. Edward motioned to the WPC by the door and then watched as she was led away.

'I assume you will be keeping her here,' the solicitor checked.

'Well, if I don't, then I think she'll end up in the same state as her friend,' he said wryly.

A PC stuck his head around the door a few minutes later. 'Sorry to disturb you, Sir, but DC Nash says that Miss Baines has been taken ill in the toilet, I've called the duty doctor.' Edward nodded his thanks.

'I'll call you when she's better,' he told the solicitor.

'It's fear; she's so terrified that it brought on stomach spasms, and that's what caused the vomiting,' the doctor told him an hour later. They looked at her through the window of the custody suite.

'Will she be alright?' Edward checked.

The doctor nodded. 'I'll give her a sedative for tonight; she should have calmed down by tomorrow, but you'll have to tread carefully,' he warned.

Sue burst into Steven's office the next day. 'You are not going to believe this,' she exclaimed.

'You're not pregnant as well, are you?' He joked; she turned her nose up and sat down.

'Not bloody likely, two's enough,' she said firmly.

'I've always thought that three would be a good number,' Steven said thoughtfully. 'Well you wouldn't think that if you had to give birth,' Sue chuckled. She gave him a motherly look. 'I assume that you want kids then?'

'Eventually, I suppose,' he conceded.

'You suppose? Well, don't leave it to long or you'll be too old to enjoy them,' she warned.

Having said enough, and unwilling to go any deeper, he changed the subject. 'So, what is it that I'm not going to believe?' She waved a sheet of paper at him; he took it from her and started reading. 'Bloody hell! Are you sure?'

She nodded enthusiastically. 'I ran it through twice.'

'Ran what through twice?' Charlie asked as he came into the office.

'Doesn't anyone think to knock anymore?' Steven asked in mock anger.

'Sorry, boss,' Charlie went out again and knocked, then stuck his head around the door and grinned at them.

'Very funny,' Steven chuckled.

'So what did you run through twice?' Charlie asked again. Steven handed him the report. 'Bloody hell!' He exclaimed.

'That's exactly what Steven said,' Sue commented; she looked round as Judy came in.

'What did Steven say?' She enquired.

'You forgot to knock,' Charlie scolded.

'Oh sorry!' She turned to go out again.

'For God's sake, it's like Piccadilly circus in here, just come in will you,' Steven said in exasperation.

Judy looked at them expectantly. 'What's going on?' She asked Steven. 'Do you remember the tissue that my dad got from Andrew Wells' maid?' Judy nodded. 'Sue got a match,' he said triumphantly.

Judy looked at each of their grinning faces in turn. 'Well?' She said impatiently.

'It's Rose; the sample from the tissue has the same mitochondrial DNA as Rose.'

Judy looked bemused. 'And that means what exactly?'

'It means that they are sisters, or at least they share the same mother,' Steven told her.

'Bloody hell!' She exclaimed.

'Are you feeling better today?' Edward asked Trudy. She gave a light nod. 'Do you feel up to talking?'

'Yes,' she confirmed.

'Do you still want to retract your earlier statement?' he checked. She hesitated for a second before shaking her head. Edward gave a sigh of relief. 'So will you tell me what happened that made you so scared?'

Trudy gestured to the solicitor. 'He says you'll protect me, is that right?'

Edward nodded. 'You're safe here, but we really need to catch whoever killed Zoë. Will you help us?' He asked gently.

'Can I have a fag?' She asked nervously. Edward nodded. She lit a cigarette and blew the smoke out slowly. 'Yes, I will help you.'

Edward switched the tape recorder on. 'In your own time.'

Trudy glanced at the solicitor who nodded encouragingly; she took a deep breath and started talking. 'I was at the pitch when Zoë rang; she said that the punter she was with wanted another girl and did I want to join them?'

'Did you see her go with the punter?' Edward interrupted; she shook her head.

'No, I'd been to the loo, and when I came back she had gone.'

'And what time was that?' She twisted her fingers nervously.

'About eight o' clock.' Edward nodded for her to continue. 'I don't usually go in for threesomes, but it had been quiet and Zoë said he was paying good money, so I said ok. I told her that he should come and get me, but she gave me an address in Nubbin, and said to get on the bus and get there as quickly as I could.'

'Can you remember the address?' Edward interrupted again.

'It's the old station house at the end of pool-hey lane,' she said quietly. 'I got there just after nine. I knocked on the door and it swung open; I called out and Zoë shouted to come upstairs, but when I got onto the landing, someone grabbed me from behind and pushed me into the bedroom.' She stopped talking and took drag on the cigarette.

Edward waited until she had exhaled. 'Was there anyone in the bedroom?'

She nodded miserably. 'Zoë was in there; she was tied to a chair in the middle of the room. She didn't have any clothes on, there was a scarf tied around her mouth and her face was all bruised.' Trudy's eyes filled with tears 'The person who had pushed me into the room tied me to another chair and put a scarf around my mouth.'

Edward put his hand up to stop her. 'Did you recognise either of them?'

'No, they were both dressed in blue overalls with the hoods up, and they had mask things on, like ski masks with just their eyes showing, and pink rubber gloves like you use to do the washing up,' she stubbed the cigarette out and took another deep breath. 'The person behind me held my head so that I was looking at Zoë,' she continued.

'You say the person, was it a man or woman?' Edward asked.

'I think it was a man because he smelt of aftershave,' she remembered.

'Do you want to take a break?' The solicitor asked.

She shook her head and continued talking. 'Then the other man started to stick a knife in Zoë, just little cuts like this,' she demonstrated with a jabbing movement.

'Could you see what sort of knife it was?' Edward asked gently.

She frowned as she tried to remember. 'It was a little silver thing I think. Zoë tried to scream but the scarf was in her mouth. The man said that if I didn't tell the police that I had made a mistake, then he would do the same to me,' she looked up at Edward.

'A mistake about the man who picked you up and took you to the hotel?' He checked.

'Yes,' she said quietly.

'So you agreed?'

'Of course I bloody well agreed. I wanted him to stop hurting Zoë, but he didn't stop. He just kept on stabbing her and hitting her, and all the time she was staring at me,' she wiped her nose on her sleeve. 'Zoë managed to get one of her hands free and tried to hit him, but he twisted her arm back. I think he broke it because there was a crack,' Trudy started crying.

'Can I have another fag?' She sobbed. Edward nodded; she lit it with shaking hands. 'He called her a bitch and stuck the knife in her chest and she stopped moving, then he went away and came back in with a log. He kicked Zoë in the chest and the chair fell over.' She took a deep drag on her cigarette.

'Then he started to hit her in the face with the log. I closed my eyes, but the person behind me forced them open, so I had to watch. The other man kept hitting her until her face and head were all gone. It was like he was going mad; there were bits of her all over the place.

'He had blood and bits all over him, and all the time he was hitting her, he was shouting that he would do the same to me, only he wouldn't kill me first.' By now, Trudy's voice was high pitched with terror. 'When he had finished, he asked me if I understood what I had to do, so I just nodded, then the other person untied me and pushed me out of the door.

'I threw up on the stairs and ran to the bus stop,' she started sobbing uncontrollably. 'I should have helped her; I should have tried to stop him.'

The solicitor looked at Edward in horror. 'It's ok. I won't ask her anything else,' he said quietly.

Paul Finch was very interested in Trudy's statement. 'I really hate to be the bearer of bad news,' he said when Edward had finished. 'But the old station house burnt down in the early hours of the day that Zoë was found.'

Edward cursed inwardly and stared out of the window. 'We thought it was an insurance thing until we found the body, well I say body, it's more like a pile of bones, there's not much left,' Finch reported.

'Do you know who it is?' Edward asked with his interest restored.

'We don't even know what sex it is. York mortuary is snowed under; they still haven't replaced Murdoch and the pathologist hasn't had time to start on it.' Edward's brain went into overdrive. 'I'll send it over to your son, shall I?'

Finch offered before he could suggest it. 'Yes, thanks,' Edward said gratefully; then looked up in surprise as Steven came in.

'Rose!' Edward exclaimed. He looked at the still from the hospital in Scotland, and compared it the mortuary pictures, even in death he could see the family resemblance. His mind wandered back to the image of her body lying in the sheep shed. 'Are you certain?'

Steven nodded. 'How did you make the connection, Dad?'

Edward shrugged. 'She just looked familiar.' He stared at the picture for a few more minutes. 'I suppose I'd better go and tell Whittle,' he sighed.

Whittle rubbed his hands together gleefully. 'The girl with red hair, eh.' Well, let's get the sister here and have a look at her then.'

Edward stared at him in disbelief. 'Why should we bring her here?'

Whittle puffed his chest out proudly. 'Publicity of course, the unknown red head identified,' he gushed.

'Except she wasn't really a red head,' Edward corrected dryly.

Whittle ignored the comment and looked out of the window. 'It's a good bit of police work, what did you say her name was?' He checked.

'Which one?' Edward asked, trying to hide his rapidly growing anger.

'The dead one,' Whittle said without compassion.

'Jenica Catacazi,' Edward said through gritted teeth.

'That'll baffle the press, you'd better make sure you give them the right spelling,' Whittle chuckled.

Edward dug his nails into the palm of his hand to try and contain himself. 'I hardly think she'll be bothered about the correct spelling when she finds out what happened to her sister.'

Whittle gave him a stern look. 'I'm well aware of your feelings towards the press, and I want you to be civil, do you understand?' The two men glared at each other for a few seconds, and then not trusting himself to be even remotely civil to the Chief Superintendent, Edward turned on his heel and left the office without bothering to answer him.

'Total bloody arsehole,' he muttered, and slammed his own office door so hard that it bounced open again.

Jack stuck his head in. 'It went well with Whittle then, did it?' He enquired brightly.

'Don't ask,' Edward took a deep breath and put Whittle out of his mind. 'So how did the refresher go?'

Jack came all the way in and sat down. 'Well I'm refreshed and ready to go if needed.'

Edward spent the next half hour bringing him up to date with developments. Jack shook his head in disbelief when he told him about Trudy. 'Poor kid; where is she?'

'I'm keeping her in the family suite for now. DC Nash is going to arrange a safe house.'

Jack nodded his approval. 'Well, at least we've got enough to keep Paige here. I saw Ms Gold in the reception so we'd go and tell them the good news,' he said gleefully.

'What do you mean she's retracted her retraction?' Ms Gold exclaimed.

'Just that,' Edward said benignly.

'Why?' Paige asked suspiciously.

'Maybe she saw it as her civic duty to tell the truth,' Jack muttered.

'I doubt that a little tart like that would know her civic duty, even if it bit her in the arse,' Paige said sarcastically.

Edward looked up sharply. 'So you do know her then?'

Paige looked uncomfortable. 'No, I don't.'

'But you called her a tart,' Paige shrugged and looked away. Edward nodded at Jack to continue. 'Miss Catacazi has identified you as the man who took photographs of her and ten other young women when she first arrived in the country.'

'Well, she's lying,' Paige snapped.

'She also said that Andrew Wells looked at the photographs and choose her to work for him.'

Paige glanced at Gold. 'She's lying,' he repeated.

'Are you going to charge my client or just play games?' Ms Gold chipped in.

'Your client is going to be being charged with kidnap. He may also be charged with photographing illegal immigrants for the purpose of supplying prostitutes, and he will be kept in custody at a remand centre to await trial until we have finished our enquiries. Is that clear enough for you, Ms Gold?' Edward enquired.

'What about bail?' Paige snapped.

'Unless you start to cooperate, I won't even think about it,' Edward snapped back.

'I'll go back to the office and start proceedings to get you out,' Gold told Paige.

Jack jumped up and opened the door for her. 'Give Andrew Wells my regards when you see him,' Edward called after her.

When Gold had gone Jack went to the bus depot to check out Trudy's story; the bus driver remembered her vividly. 'She was wearing a tiny skirt and a big belt, showing off her black knickers she was. If I had my way, we wouldn't allow tarts on the buses, they upset the other passengers,' he said sarcastically.

Jack stared at him, and wondered how earth such a horrible little man managed to hold down a job that required customer relations. 'She was full of lip on the way there. Can you believe she wanted me to change a twenty for a four quid fare,' the driver continued.

'And did you?' Jack interrupted.

'Did I what?' The driver asked.

'Change a twenty,' Jack said exasperatedly. 'Of course I did, I wasn't going to let her on for nothing, was I? Not with the amount of money that they make,' he scoffed.

'And how would you know what they make?' Jack asked suspiciously.

The driver went red. 'I don't,' he mumbled.

Jack decided not to pursue the matter 'How many other passengers were there?'

The driver shrugged disinterestedly. 'Just two I think, on the way there.'

Jack frowned at him. 'And on the way back?'

'She was the only one,' he said confidently. 'It was the last run and she only just caught me, she came running down the road in those bloody stupid shoes, if I'd known the state she was going to be in I wouldn't have waited.'

'What sort of state?' Jack interrupted again.

'Crying and sniffing, looking around as if someone was following her,' he said amusedly.

'Did you ask her if she was alright?' Jack asked.

'Why the hell should I? If she'd got herself into trouble then that's her own stupid fault,' he said scornfully.

'But you still had a good look at the black knickers, didn't you?' Jack snapped.

The driver's mouth fell open. 'What are you implying?' He demanded.

'Nothing at all,' Jack said dryly. 'Thanks for your time, you bloody arsehole,' he muttered.

Charlie looked at the charred twisted remains in front of them. 'Where did it come from?' He enquired.

'From the house where Zoë Fairfax was allegedly killed,' Steven told him.

'There's not much left, how do we identify it?' Charlie asked as they prepared to make a start.

Steven shook his head. 'I don't know, we'll take an x-ray and see if we can determine sex; then we can name it.' The x-ray revealed a narrow pelvic opening and a fairly heavy mandible, which led them to believe that the victim was probably a male. 'He's got short long bones though, hasn't he,' Charlie commented.

Steven nodded. 'We'll call him Max for now,' he decided. Apart from gender, the x-ray also revealed a metal object wedged between two of Max's ribs. Steven gently cut through what was left of this chest and extracted a thin piece of steel. He held it up so Charlie could see. 'What do you think?'

'I think it looks like the end of our missing knife,' Charlie said in dismay.

Steven compared it to the one in his hand. 'I think you're probably right.' They worked on in silence, trying to find a means of identifying him. Steven handed Charlie a molar. 'Try drilling into this, there may be enough pulp left to get a sample.'

Charlie took the tooth over to the bench, leaving Steven examining the head. The hair had been burnt away, as had the gristly parts of the face and head. As he examined it closely he noticed something stuck to the side of the head.

He picked up a pair of tweezers and retrieved a thin piece of melted blackened wire from the area where the ear had once been. He slid it under the microscope and photographed it for the records, then returned to the x-rays. There were multiple fractures to both legs and the pelvis. Steven deliberated for a while and then called Charlie over.

'I don't think these are heat fractures.'

Charlie peered at the x-ray. 'Do you think they were broken before the fire?'

Steven shook his head. 'I'm not sure.' He went out to the reception. 'Can you get onto the fire brigade and find out which unit attended the old station house?' He asked Judy.

'They're out on a call, the Chief is going to get back to you,' she shouted after the call. Charlie was still working on the tooth, a few minutes later he held a swab aloft complete with a tiny amount of pulp.

'Let's hope it's enough,' Steven said wryly. Charlie took the sample up to Sue, leaving Steven checking Max's body cavity. Most of the organs had been destroyed; the lungs and liver were identifiable but badly burned. He took a sample from the liver without feeling hopeful of it yielding anything useful.

Edward tapped on the window half an hour later. 'Without sounding stupid, can you say what the cause of death was?' He asked hopefully.

'Well, we think it's a he, we've called him Max for now, and I'm afraid the short answer is no,' Steven said to his disappointment. 'But we did find part of what we think is our missing knife embedded in his ribs,' Steven showed him the piece of metal. 'It didn't kill him, it had snapped off before it reached any vital organs, but we compared it to the wounds on Zoë and Pickering and it's probably the same knife.'

233

The fire station officer called back a couple of hours later. 'Was it just a fire or was there an explosion?' Steven asked him.

'The propane cylinders went up just as we got there, that's why we had to let it burn until we knew there weren't going to be any more explosions; but we've not released the report yet so how did you know?' The officer asked. Steven explained about the broken bones, and asked where the body was in relation to the cylinders.

'It was in the lounge; we think it fell through from the bedroom when the first floor collapsed. Two of the cylinders were in the lounge, one in the hallway, and the fourth one flew into the garden when it exploded,' the fire officer reported.

Steven was puzzled, he used propane himself and the cylinders were kept outside. 'Why were the cylinders kept in the house?' He queried.

'They weren't, they'd been disconnected from outside and the valves had been left open,' the officer explained.

'But the fire itself, started in the bedroom?' Steven checked.

'Yes, we found traces of accelerant in the collapsed floor of the room above the lounge.' A bell suddenly rang in the background.

'Is it safe for us to go in? I'd like my team to have a look at it,' Steven asked.

'Sorry I've got to go,' the officer told him. 'We'll let you know when the structure is safe,' he rang off, leaving Steven staring into space still holding the phone.

Meanwhile, Edward was pondering on the identity of the body; thinking that it may be Andrew Wells, he rang Simon Reynolds. 'It can't be him. He's got a surveillance team on him and he hasn't left London,' Simon informed him. Edward outlined the case to him. 'Was the fire accidental?' Simon asked when he had finished.

'The fire investigators said it was one hundred per cent deliberate. There was petrol all over the place and the propane cylinders had been left open, the house is completely gutted.'

'Does the pathologist think he can identify the body?' Simon interrupted.

'He's having a go, we know it's a male but I think the odds of identifying him are a zillion to one,' Edward said ruefully.

'Well, good luck on that one,' Simon muttered. 'By the way, I checked out Maria Catacazi's work permit and it's genuine.'

Edward swore silently. 'Well it was just a thought,' he said disappointedly.

'Your Chief super has asked us to send her to you, is that right?' Simon enquired.

'Yes, it turns out that she is the sister of an unidentified body that we found last year,' Edward explained; the line went silent for a minute.

'Well, that is a coincidence, how did you make the connection?' Simon said eventually. Edward explained about Maria looking familiar and the sample he got from the tissue. 'Well done,' Simon congratulated, albeit with a hint of sarcasm in his tone. 'Anyway, I've got to go. Give us a call if we can help anymore,' he said, and then hung up before Edward could thank him.

Jack came in a few minutes later with the letting agent's description of the old station house. "As described, the house was attached to Nubbin station before the line was closed; Situated at the end of Pool Hey Lane. It is secluded but not remote.

"This one bed roomed cottage has been completely restored and renovated to a high standard. It has the added advantage of backing onto the old rail path which runs between Nubbin and Kimberwick, excellent for those who enjoy a good walk".

Edward stopped reading. 'Excellent for hiding out,' he muttered. 'What else have you got?'

Jack handed him the agent's statement. 'It's not particularly helpful,' he remarked as Edward started to read.

"The old station house is used as a holiday cottage. I let it to a couple called Mr and Mrs Brown for one week starting the thirtieth of June. They said they were touring and came in on spec, they asked for somewhere private as they were honeymooning, and they paid cash for the week. I didn't see what Mrs Brown looked like as she waited outside, but I think she had blond hair.

"Mr Brown was fairly short and unremarkable looking. He had an accent, but I can't place it. I think he was wearing glasses. I told him that the house would be available in the afternoon, as the previous visitors had only just vacated and the cleaner needed to go in.

"He appeared agitated that he had to wait, but he came back after lunch to collect the keys and sign the papers. I gave him directions and wished him a good holiday. He came back the following Saturday.

"I assumed he was going to return the keys, but he asked to extend his stay, and enquired as to how long the cottage was available for. As there were no bookings until the first week of August, I agreed to extend the arrangement, and

235

once again he paid in cash. I haven't heard from him since, and the first I knew of the fire was when the police contacted me. I have informed the owners of the cottage who live abroad."

Edward looked at the two signed agreements. 'Mr B Brown; well it makes a change from Smith I suppose,' he said dryly. 'I don't expect the home address he's given exists, but check it out anyway,' he told Jack.

'Maybe the body is Mr Brown's, whoever he is,' Jack said thoughtfully.

'It's a bit odd a holiday cottage not booked for the whole of July,' Edward commented.

'Well, July and August are the most expensive months and there's only one bedroom, so it's not much good for families,' Jack observed.

Edward looked at the price list in the brochure. 'Four hundred pounds for a week! That's over two grand,' he exclaimed. 'The agent didn't seem very worried about security, did he?'

'Well it's not his house, is it?' Jack said sarcastically. 'He would only be interested in making sure that he got his cut of the takings,' he got up to leave. 'I'll show him the picture of Alex Gorman, and I'm going to speak to the people who live up the road this afternoon,' he said as he went out.

The nearest neighbours to the station house were an elderly couple; they lived half a mile away and had seen the Browns when they first arrived. 'They stopped and asked us for directions, but it was the woman who asked,' the old man told him.

'Were there just two of them?' Jack checked.

'We only saw two,' the man confirmed.

'We thought it was odd that they were in a van though,' the old lady chipped in.

'Why did you think it was odd?' Jack asked.

'Because the woman was smartly dressed and very well spoken. She didn't look the type to travel in a van.'

'Can you remember what they looked like?' Jack asked hopefully. 'The woman had blond hair and wore big sunglasses, but the man didn't get out of the van, so we didn't get a look at him.'

Jack sighed despondently. 'Was there any writing on the van, a logo or anything?' He asked almost in desperation.

The old man shook his head. 'I don't think so, but I didn't have my glasses on.' Jack groaned inwardly; there's no point asking if he if he remembers the registration number then he thought despondently.

Once the fire department had finished at the station house, they gave the ok for the forensic team to go in. 'Trudy said she was sick on the stairs, and she said that Zoë was killed in the bedroom,' Steven told Sue as they stood in what was left of the hallway.

Sue looked around at the devastation; the first floor had collapsed and the roof was completely destroyed, leaving the shell open to the sky. The charred remains of the stairway, now virtually freestanding and leading nowhere, stood alone amongst the debris. 'I doubt we'll get anything from this, but I'll give it a go,' she said ruefully.

They went into the lounge where the three blackened propane cylinders lay. Steven stood them upright and examined each one carefully, then called Sue over. 'Does that look like tissue to you?' He pointed to a minute piece of what looked like lard stuck in the valve of one of the cylinders.

She extracted it with a pair of tweezers and examined it. 'It could be.' She put it into in a specimen pot and went back to the stairs.

Steven went into the garden and inspected the remains of the last cylinder, which having been blasted clear of the house was severely dented but less fire damaged than the other three. As he inspected it he spotted a smear of blood on the valve handle. He took a swab, then rolled the cylinder over to examine the sides.

He found what he was looking for fairly quickly; then he sealed the sample and went back inside. Sue had turned her attention to the remains of the bedroom which lay in a charred heap in the middle of the building. 'It must have been one hell of an explosion,' she commented as she started sifting through the pile of debris.

Whilst Steven was at the station house Edward was doing paperwork; he looked up as Jack stuck his head around the door. 'Whittle wants to see us, guv.'

Edward put his pen down. 'Us?'

Jack nodded. 'I don't know what he wants, but he sounded pissed off and he said now.' They went down to Whittle's office and knocked on the door.

'Come,' Whittle called sharply. The Chief Superintendent was looking out of the window. 'Sit down,' he ordered without turning around. Jack pulled a face as he sat. 'I hear you've been treading on toes in London.'

'In what way?' Edward objected.

'I haven't finished,' Whittle snapped, and turned around so sharply that his glasses fell off. 'Did you or did you not obtain a saliva sample from a witness without permission?'

Edward frowned at him. 'Who told you that?'

'It doesn't matter who told me, the fact is that you took it without asking,' he replaced the glasses and glared at them.

Edward glared back. 'This has nothing to do with Sergeant Taylor,' he said firmly.

'Really?' Whittle scoffed disbelievingly.

'Yes, really,' he insisted.

'Well, I understand that it was Sergeant Taylor who provided the tissue that the sample was taken from,' Whittle said knowingly. Jack glanced at Edward.

'The tissue came from a box that was on the table in the detention centre, and if you really want to split hairs then it was a sample of mucus not saliva,' Edward informed him sourly.

Whittle sat down and stared at them. 'Mucus?'

Edward nodded curtly. 'Or if you want it in layman's terms, snot.'

Whittle's face twitched angrily. 'You can go, Sergeant Taylor,' he said without looking at him. Jack got up and left the room closing the door quietly behind him. Edward and Whittle stared at each other with distaste.

'I know you don't have any respect for me, Edward, but if you ever speak to me like that in front of another officer again, then I won't hesitate to suspend you, do you understand?' Whittle snapped.

Edward nodded curtly. 'Yes, Sir, I'll make sure that we are alone in future.' Whittle glared at him, and then unable to think of a suitable retort, he turned his attention to a file on the desk. 'For your information, it was my counterpart in London, Chief Superintendent Knox, who informed me of your actions, and he wasn't very happy about your conduct. You could at least have had the decency to inform them of your intentions.'

Edward stood up unable to contain his anger any longer. 'My intentions were thoroughly discussed with Inspector Reynolds. He was fully aware that I was going to speak to Miss Catacazi. The sample I took wasn't planned, it was a spur of the moment action, and it was based on the fact that I recognised her.

'She isn't a suspect or a witness, she is a victim who will arrive here next week, and who I hope will be able to tell us who brought her and ten other young women into the country, probably illegally and probably for the vice trade,' Whittle opened his mouth to say something, but Edward carried on, cutting over him.

'I will then no doubt have the dubious pleasure of telling her that her sister was brutally murdered last year, only weeks after giving birth,' he looked around the office. 'I assume that you still want the press informed of the good police work, Sir?'

Whittle had gone crimson. 'Have you quite finished?' He spluttered.

'Yes,' Edward confirmed curtly.

Whittle drummed his fingers on the desk and stared into space 'Right! That will be all,' he snapped.

Edward opened the door. 'I wonder if you would mind calling your counterpart, Chief Superintendent Knox, and ask him to arrange for a saliva sample to be taken from Andrew Wells. Just so that we can eliminate him from our enquires,' he said over his shoulder, then he closed the door with a bang before Whittle could respond. 'Don't ask,' he mouthed at the sea of expectant faces staring at him.

The forensics from the station house were not very conclusive. The fire damage was so great that they could find no trace of Trudy's vomit, and no evidence that Zoë had even been there. 'The blob of tissue is likely to have come from the body, but it's not definite, and the blood from the tap on the cylinder in the garden is male, but he's not on the data base,' Sue told Steven.

'Try the firm that supplied the gas, it could have come from one of their guy's,' he suggested, then leant back and stared into space. 'Check it against all the samples connected with the case,' he called after her.

'The girls are working on it now,' she yelled from the top of the stairs.

'Good old Sue always one step ahead,' he chuckled to himself, and then looked up as his father came in, closely followed by Detective Inspector Finch. 'I think that whoever Max is, he was right on top of the propane cylinders when they went up,' he told them. The two men inspected the x-ray that Steven was holding up.

He turned to the body and pointed out the corresponding breaks. 'These breaks are consistent with blast damage, not falling,' he explained.

'Was he dead when they went up?' Finch asked.

Steven shook his head. 'I don't know, but he is defiantly a male. We got enough pulp from the tooth to determine sex, but not enough for an identity.'

Edward scratched his head. 'What about the teeth?'

'Not unless we have dental records to compare with. Do you have any idea who it could be?' Finch shook his head despondently.

'Can you tell us anything about him?' Edward asked hopefully.

'I can tell you that he was a small man, only standing about five feet four, he was slightly built and probably wore glasses,' he showed them the photograph of the piece of melted wire. 'I think this is the remains of a pair of glasses,' he pointed to the area where he found it. 'It's the bit that goes round the ear.'

'Where are the samples from the site?' Finch asked.

'Upstairs. Sue's still working on them.'

'Was there something else?' Edward checked as Steven bit his lip.

'I found some burnt material stuck on the gas cylinder in the garden, and it's consistent with overall material,' he paused for a second. 'It's the same material that the police scenes of crime overalls are made of,' he looked at Edward. 'Trudy Baines said they wore blue overalls, didn't she?' Edward was shocked at the implication and made do with nodding.

'Where are his hands?' Finch asked.

Steven showed him the splintered bone at the end of the right arm. 'This one was blown off in the blast and was probably incinerated in the fire,' he picked the other arm up. 'But there's no fracture to this bone. The heat was intense and the bones are so small, that rather than being blown off it probably just burned away.'

Edward stared at the body. 'A small man who probably wore glasses,' he muttered quietly.

'You're thinking of Alex Gorman,' Finch guessed.

'Well it would make sense, we know he was in the area, we know he was in Steven's house, and that he was involved with Graham Pickering's death.'

'I suppose dental records are out of the question,' Steven butted in.

'I'll get onto Interpol again, but don't hold your breath,' Edward advised.

'Well, Sue's checking the samples from the station house against all the samples from the case, so we may get lucky,' Steven said hopefully.

Sure enough, two days later, Sue had the news they had been waiting for. 'The blob of fatty tissue matches the mucus found on Graham Pickering and the blood from your house,' she reported.

'It is Alex Gorman then?' Steven checked. She nodded confirmation.

'So at least he won't be killing anyone else,' she said thankfully.

Chapter 6

'Robin Paige is asking to see you,' the voice on the end of the phone told Edward the next morning. He put his hand over the mouthpiece. 'When is Maria due?'

Jack glanced at his watch. 'Anytime now, guv.'

Edward returned to the call, and told the remand warden that he would speak to Paige the following day. 'Let's see what Maria has to say first, has her statement arrived?' Jack nodded and went to get it.

Thinking that it would be easier for Maria to remember and explain in her own language, Edward had asked for an interpreter to help with a more thorough interview the previous week. Jack returned and handed him a file. 'I hope we can get something on Wells from this,' he muttered, and then he sat back to read.

"I went to Bucharest to meet the man who arranged my travel. I was told to go to a bar in the town and wait, there were ten other women waiting in the bar. The man took our passports from us and then he took us to a warehouse. He told us to get into a truck and not make any noise.

"The truck was full of boxes; he made us sit in the middle of them. There was not much room and we were very frightened, but looking forward to our new life in England. There was no privacy in the truck, we had to go to the toilet in a bucket and it got very smelly.

"When the driver opened the door, we asked if he would empty the bucket, but he threw some food over the boxes and told us to be quiet. I think we were in the truck for three days. On the third day he opened the back and told us that we were going on a train, and had to be extra quiet. He emptied the bucket this time.

"We could hear men shouting before we were on the train, then the van door opened and someone said something. I didn't understand the language, then the door closed again. I don't think we were on the train for very long. We stopped for a long time before the doors opened.

"A different man told us to get out, we were pleased to get out but it was dark and raining, and we were cold. The man took our bags from us and said we would get them back when we got to the house. He told us to get into a different truck. We were only in it for a while, and then we were at a house.

"It was small and there were not enough beds, and only a bit of food. We asked for our bags, but the man shouted at us, he said Ronnie would bring us clothes. Later, the man in the photograph came and took a picture of us. We asked why he needed it, but he didn't answer us.

"After two days, some of the girls were taken to their new jobs and the day after that the man took me to the house of Mr Wells. I was given some more clothes, and told that I would work for him until I had paid for my ticket, then I would be free to go. Mr Wells was nice to start with and told me I was doing well. He let me watch the television, but he said I must not leave the house.

"After a few days, he said that if I wanted to pay my ticket off quicker, I would have to be nice to him. I didn't know what he meant until he came to my room one night and got into my bed. I was frightened, I had never been with a man before and he hurt me, but he said if I told anyone then he would send me back to Romania.

"He came to my room lots of times after that, and I just let him because I wanted to get out as quick as I could, so that I could go and find my sister, Jenica. I think he knew my sister, because once when he was on me, he said her name. I asked him if he had seen her, but he said I was a silly girl, and kept on me.

Edward looked up in shock 'Have you read this?' Jack nodded. 'We might not get him for bringing them in, but we must have enough for false imprisonment and rape, and definitely enough to request a sample.' They looked at the artist's impression of the man that Maria had remembered.

'Not particularly helpful, he could be just about anybody,' Jack said ruefully.

Edward stared at it for a while. 'Ask a PC to show it the letting agent, you never know he may be our mystery Mr Brown.' Jack left him thinking and went to find a constable. Edward stared out into the car park for a while, then got up and went to see Whittle. 'Did you request a swab from Andrew Wells?'

Whittle gave him a hard stare. 'No, I didn't, there are no grounds to request one.'

Edward stared back. 'Well, you may change your mind after reading this.'

He handed him the statement, and went out before Whittle could object. He came into Edward's office half an hour later, closely followed by Jack. 'As soon as this girl arrives, I want her examined by the police doctor,' he ordered, and then marched out without waiting for a response.

Jack raised his eyebrows. 'I think you've put his nose put out of joint, guv.'

Edward gave a contented sigh and stretched. 'Well, whatever it takes to get the job done,' he said brightly. 'Anyway, you'd better get onto Simon Reynolds and let him know what's happened. I think he was a bit put out himself, the other day,' he added.

Maria arrived later that day, and as requested the doctor gave her a thorough examination. He reported that although it was obvious that she had been having intercourse. There were no signs that she had been raped. Edward had her taken to the family suite; he collected a female family liaison officer and prepared himself to tell her about Jenica.

Maria looked at them suspiciously as they entered the room. 'Before we start, can you tell me if this is the man who took you to the house when you arrived in the UK?' He put a picture of Alex Gorman in front of her.

She stared at it for a while and then looked at him. 'Why am I here? Why did doctor look at me?'

Edward pointed to the picture. 'Have you seen him before?'

Maria looked at it again and frowned. 'He had more hair and it was dark, but I think it's his eyes.'

Edward put the picture away and opened her statement. 'You say that Mr Wells came to your room a lot of times?' Maria stared at him with embarrassment on her face. 'You've done nothing wrong,' he assured her. 'We just need to be clear about things.'

She looked at her hands and nodded. 'Yes, lots of times,' she said quietly.

'And always for sex?' He checked.

She went a deeper shade of red. 'Yes,' she whispered.

'Did he use protection when he had sex with you?' He asked gently. She looked confused.

'Did he use a condom?' The liaison officer explained. She shook her head.

'When was the last time he came to your room?'

She swallowed nervously and thought for a minute. 'I think three days before you come to house.'

Edward gave her a concerned smile. 'And not again before you were taken away?'

She shook her head again. 'No, I cycle.'

Edward looked at the liaison officer for clarification. 'Period,' she mouthed.

Edward glanced at the statement. 'You say that he said your sister's name when he was on you.'

Maria picked an invisible piece of fluff from the arm of the couch. 'Yes,' she whispered.

'Was this whilst he was having sex with you?'

She nodded, and then looked at him sharply. 'You know where Jenica is?' She demanded.

Edward handed her the still from the hospital security tape. 'Is this your sister?'

She stared at it for a minute. 'Yes, this is at hospital?' She looked up at him.

'Yes, this picture was taken last year.'

Her hands started to shake. 'Why is she at hospital?' She whispered. Edward took a deep breath, and then told her of the events the previous year, when he had finished, she shook her head in disbelief.

'No, it can't be,' she cried, then her face crumpled and she burst into tears.

'I'm so sorry,' he said quietly, and went out leaving the liaison officer to do her job.

Having heard from forensics that the burnt body was that of Alex Gorman, and Maria had to some extent identified him as the man in London, Edward went to update Whittle. 'I was just going to send for you,' he said when Edward went in.

'Really?' Edward said dryly, and wondered what else he could have said or done to cause offence.

Whittle ignored the sarcasm in his voice and looked at him seriously. 'I believe that you were going to make a deal with Robin Paige in exchange for information.'

Edward shook his head. 'He asked to speak to me regarding information, but I have in no way agreed to a deal. I'm going to see him this afternoon,' he stopped talking, and scrutinised his senior officer. There was frustration etched on his face. 'You said were going to make a deal, has something happened?' He asked tentatively.

Whittle nodded. 'Yes, I'm afraid something has happened,' he cleared his throat and shuffled the papers on his desk. 'Firstly, we received a message from the remand centre last night, stating that Paige had changed his mind and wouldn't speak to you, and secondly, Robin Paige was found dead in his cell this morning.'

'What?' Edward gasped.

'I think you heard me,' Whittle retorted.

Edward's heart sank. 'How did he die?'

'That's for Dr Cooper to find out,' Whittle said matter of factly. 'I've told them to send the body over to him. I don't need to tell you how serious a death in custody is, so tell your son that I want this given top priority. That will be all,' he said pompously.

'Oh! Actually there is one more thing,' he said as Edward opened the door. 'The swab that you requested from Andrew Wells should arrive today,' he said to Edward's surprise. 'Check with your son and let me know if it needs chasing up.' Edward nodded his appreciation, and in a sharp contrast to his earlier exits, he went out and closed the door quietly behind him.

'He must be having a good day,' Jack said brightly. 'It's a bugger about Bob Paige though; I don't suppose we'll ever find out now.'

Edward stared out of the window. 'Paige dead, Pickering dead, and Gorman dead, there are still two people unaccounted for. Or maybe only one,' he added thoughtfully.

'What do you mean?' Jack asked.

'The woman who Trudy saw in the car, who I assume booked into the hotel as Mrs Smith, and the man with the London accent who killed Zoë, unless they are one and the same person.'

Jack suddenly realised what he was getting at. 'There were fibres from a wig in the boot of the rover.'

Edward nodded. 'Did you get hold of Simon?'

Jack shook his head. 'He's gone off on emergency leave, some family crises or another. I left a message for him to ring when he gets back,' he looked thoughtful for a minute. 'Steve said that the material he found on the gas cylinder was the same as police scene of crime suits.'

'Yes,' Edward said slowly.

'You don't think that Simon could be involved, do you?' Jack said tentatively.

Edward stared at his Sergeant thoughtfully. 'I don't know, you know him. Do you think he could be involved?'

245

Jack rubbed his head. 'I don't know, but I do know that he doesn't have any close family, and with him going off so suddenly it got me thinking.'

Edward got up. 'Well, let's hope that you're wrong,' he said dryly. 'And by the way, Steven doesn't like being called Steve!'

'Why's that then, guv?' Jack enquired with a grin.

'I have no idea,' Edward admitted. 'Anyway, do you want the post-mortem or the remand centre?'

Jack turned his nose up. 'Neither really.'

Edward got a coin out of his pocket. 'I'll toss you for it.' Jack nodded his agreement, and then watched as the coin fell to the floor.

Steven was attending a road traffic accident when Edward arrived at the mortuary. Charlie had just taken delivery of Paige's body, and was preparing him for the post-mortem. Edward went up to the labs to check if the sample from Wells had arrived, and being told that it hadn't, he rang Whittle from the reception.

'When the results from Paige's post-mortem are in, I want a verbal report from the pathologist, so that we can avoid any smug comments over technical terms,' Whittle said sharply before hanging up.

'Pratt,' Edward muttered; he accepted the offered coffee from Judy and sat down to wait for Steven. He looked at Judy's tummy as she went about her business and smiled to himself. Steven had always expressed a wish to be a father. Edward was looking forward to being a granddad, but often wondered how long he would have to wait.

'I don't just want one though,' Steven had divulged in a moment of lucidity. 'It's not nice being an only child.' Edward had almost told him of his own desire to have more, but Elizabeth had been adamant that one was enough. He chuckled quietly to himself.

It was the only thing that they had ever really argued about, but in the end, he had conceded that it was she who had to give birth, and if she didn't want to go through it again then that was her decision, but at least they had Steven. He smiled again as he remembered the elation when he had been born, and the pride he had felt when he held him for the first time. A cough brought him back from his thoughts; he looked up to see three pairs of eyes watching him.

'Back from cloud cuckoo land, are you? Should we ask or is it a private joke?' Steven asked amusedly.

Edward took a deep breath and got up. 'I have no idea what you are talking about, son,' he said haughtily.

Charlie broke into their father-son moment. 'Mr Paige is ready for our attention,' he announced.

'Are you coming in or watching from the observation room?' Steven asked his father. After deliberating for a minute, Edward decided to brave the cutting room and followed them through to gown up.

'It must be serious for your dad to come in,' Charlie whispered as Steven took blood samples.

He nodded his agreement and handed the samples to the waiting technician. 'Ask Sue to look for the obvious first,' he told him.

'The obvious being what?' Edward enquired.

'Drugs,' Steven said simply and continued to examine the body.

There were several healed scars on Paige's torso. 'It looks like he's been in the wars,' he commented to no one in particular. 'This one would have definitely hospitalised him,' he pointed to a particularly large one, then called Charlie to help turn him over.

'It looks normal,' Edward commented as they examined his back.

'Except for this,' Steven pointed out a small red swelling on one side of Paige's buttocks; he pulled the magnifier over and peered closely. 'What do you think?' He asked Charlie.

'Injection site maybe?' He suggested.

Steven picked up a pair tweezers. 'Well, whoever injected him left this behind,' he gently pulled part of a broken syringe needle from the site and held it up. 'That must have been incredibly painful,' he looked at his father. 'I'm going to open him up now, will you be ok?' Edward nodded and then closed his eyes as Steven started cutting.

They finished two hours later. 'If you want to wait, I'll print a preliminary report for you to take to Whittle,' Steven said as he washed his hands. He glanced in the mirror as Edward shook his head. 'I thought he said it was urgent,' Steven muttered.

'It is,' Edward assured him. 'But Whittle wants the report straight from the horse's mouth, and I'm afraid the horse in question is you, son.'

Steven scowled as he dried his hands. 'Why can't you tell him?' He asked in exasperation. 'I've got crash fatalities to deal with.'

'I confused him with mucus, he thinks you'll be gentle with him,' Edward chuckled. With three bodies waiting, Steven wasn't happy. 'Well we'd better not keep Mien Fuehrer Whittle waiting then, had we?' He said bitterly.

'Mien Fuehrer Whittle! I like that,' Charlie laughed.

'You make a start on the first RTA victim,' Steven instructed. 'I'll not be long.' Charlie smiled as he followed Edward out grumbling to himself.

Steven sighed impatiently as they waited for Whittle to finish writing. He glared at the top of his head, and smiled inwardly as he noticed the beginnings of a bald patch. Whittle eventually put the pen down. 'Sorry to keep you waiting, Dr Cooper, I know that you're very busy,' he gestured towards the desk and grimaced. 'Paperwork you know,' he said wryly.

'Yes, I do know,' Steven muttered.

Whittle leant back and pushed his glasses up his nose. 'So, what can you tell me about the death of Robin Paige?' He asked importantly.

Steven glanced at his father. 'He died between nine p.m. last night and two a.m. this morning. First indications suggest that cause of death was due to a huge dose of morphine being introduced by hypodermic syringe into the left gluteus Medius, which once absorbed into the system, caused depressed breathing, and as there was no medical intervention, it eventually stopped. This induced cardiac arrest which obviously killed him.'

Whittle looked baffled whilst Edward battled to keep a straight face. 'What stopped exactly?' Whittle enquired.

Steven stared at him deadpan. 'His breathing and then his heart.'

'Oh right, is that it then?' Whittle checked.

Steven nodded. 'That's what killed him.'

Whittle sat back and thought for a minute. 'Could it have been self-inflicted?'

Steven gave a small shrug. 'It's possible but I doubt it,' he said dismissively.

'Why do you doubt it?' Whittle demanded to know.

'Well, I understand that Mr Paige was right-handed,' Steven said seriously. Whittle nodded knowingly, even though he had no idea which hand Paige used 'Well, it would have been easier for him to inject himself in the right gluteus Medius or one of his quadriceps,' Steven explained.

Whittle scratched his head. 'So where did you say the morphine was injected?'

Speaking slowly and deliberately so that there was no confusion, Steven repeated. 'The left gluteus Medius.'

Whittle's face twitched angrily. 'Perhaps you would be good enough to give me the information in layman's terms, Dr Cooper?' He glanced at Edward daring him to comment.

'Oh, I'm sorry,' Steven said innocently. 'A large dose of morphine was given by injection into the left buttock, which in layman's terms stopped him breathing. This caused his heart to stop and so killed him. If it had been self-inflicted, then I would have expected the injection to have been given in the right buttock or in the thigh.'

Whittle stared at the two men standing in front of him and wondered what they were thinking. They stared back until Steven broke the silence. 'Well, if there's nothing else, I had to postpone three other rather urgent post-mortems to fit Mr Paige in,' he gave Whittle a benign smile and turned to leave.

'Of course, thank you, Dr Cooper,' Whittle said insincerely and forced a smile as they left the office.

'What a plonker,' Steven muttered once they were outside.

'Is there a technical term for that as well?' Edward chuckled.

Charlie was halfway through the first of the postponed post-mortems when Steven got back, he watched from the observation room for a while. 'Are you coming in to verify, boss?' Charlie enquired without looking up.

Steven gowned up and went in. 'You finish that one and I'll make a start on the boy.'

Charlie looked up in surprise. 'Finish it, boss?'

'Yes, why not? You're more than capable,' Steven said generously. He started to examine the second body, that of a six-year-old child. He always dreaded doing children and clearly remembered the first time he had seen a dead one. She was an eleven-year-old girl who had been missing for two days before being found in the river.

He stood around the post-mortem table with his fellow students. The pathologist pulled back the sheet to reveal the most horrific abdominal injuries. 'If you can deal with children then the rest are easy,' he said, and then waited for the mass exodus. Seven students had dropped out that day.

Steven was nearly the eighth, but as he debated with himself if this was really what he wanted to spend his time doing. He remembered Sally and a quote he had been told on his first day of training. 'The deceased must be protected and given a voice,' his tutor said to them. So Steven gritted his teeth and stayed.

'You know I'd hate to lose you,' he said to Charlie a while later.

'You're not going to lose me I'm not going anywhere,' Charlie said firmly.

'Exactly,' he muttered. Charlie glanced up at him. Steven stopped what he was doing and leant on the table. 'You're too good to be a technician, why don't you train to be a pathologist?'

Charlie looked at the two bodies; a mother and her son, both killed when a lorry ploughed into their car; and in the chiller the lorry driver, who they would find out later had died from an undiagnosed heart defect. 'Are their families coming in tomorrow?' He asked.

'I expect so.' Steven sighed unenthusiastically.

'And you'll have to tell them how they died,' Charlie checked. Steven nodded. 'Well there's your answer then, boss. By the way the swab from that Wells bloke arrived so I sent it up to Sue.' He turned back to the table and resumed sewing.

Jack put copies of the relevant pages from the remand centre visitor's books on Edward's desk; one book for official visits and one for family and friends. There were two entries for Robin Paige. Ms Gold had a meeting with him the day before he died. She stayed for two hours, she visited again the afternoon prior to his death.

She arrived at four forty-five and stayed for less than thirty minutes. The guard who was watching the monitor reported that it looked like they were arguing; he went in to check and Ms Gold had told him everything was fine. Edward turned to the statements; one from the guard on morning duty and one from the prisoner who was sharing Paige's cell.

The guard had been alerted by the cell mate at six fifteen, Paige was already dead and rigour had started to set in. The cell mate stated that he had not seen or heard anything and no syringe was found in the cell. 'I wonder if V stands for Veronica,' Edward mused.

'I'll get onto her practice chambers and find out,' Jack offered, and disappeared into the squad room. 'You're right, guv, how did you know?' He asked a few minutes later.

'Well apart from there not being many girls' names beginning with V, I think that Ms Veronica Gold's nickname could be Ronnie,' Edward said thoughtfully. 'Anyway, the observation tapes from the remand centre meeting room should be here in the morning, so we may get something from them,' he leant back and yawned. 'I need to go home,' he muttered.

Sheila was in the garden when he got home; she smiled with delight as he drew up. 'You're early,' she exclaimed.

'I'm tired,' he admitted; he put his arm around her as they went into the house. 'I'm thinking that maybe I should pack it in,' he said as she dished the dinner up.

She gave him a puzzled look. 'What's brought this on?'

He yawned again. 'I'm tired,' he repeated.

'You've got a big case on, you've been busy,' she sat down and looked at him earnestly. 'What's really brought it on?'

How does she know me so well, he thought. 'You have, you've brought it on,' he said quietly.

A look of dismay crossed her face. 'I don't want you to pack it in, I know how much you love your job.'

He nodded thoughtfully. 'I do love my job, but not as much as I love you. I've wasted so much time. I should have married you years ago. We could have had children; you would have made a great mum,' he continued wistfully.

Sheila got up and kissed him. 'I couldn't have children,' she whispered.

He looked at her in shock, and could see the pain of the memory in her eyes. 'Why not?'

'Because when I was seven, I was raped by a neighbour, and there was too much internal damage,' she said tearfully. 'And when Elizabeth told me how much you wanted more children, I thought you would find someone who could give you some.'

He stared at her in disbelief. 'What happened to the man who raped you?'

She shrugged dismissively. 'He killed himself, which was just as well because otherwise my father would have killed him,' she said matter of factly.

'So all that time, you were waiting in the background thinking I would fall for someone else,' he checked.

'Yes, but when you didn't, I thought you were still grieving,' she smiled tearfully. 'I would have waited for you forever.'

He stared into her tear-filled eyes. 'I know you would, and that's why I think I should pack it in, so that we can have the rest of forever to enjoy each other.'

He smiled as she sat on his knee. 'Shall we start enjoying each other now then?' She suggested, and then kissed him with all thoughts of dinner forgotten.

The smell of sweet and sour sauce hit Steven as he opened the front door. Monty and Ben came bounding down the stairs to meet him; he picked the cat up and went through to the kitchen. 'No cooking tonight,' Heather said mysteriously. She removed the cat from his arms, then took his hand and led him up the stairs into the bathroom.

'Is everything ok?' He checked.

She gave him a seductive smile and nodded. 'I thought that we could have a bath before dinner.' He watched as she poured oil into the warm water. 'Shall I help you off with these?' She whispered as she unbuckled his belt.

'Are you sure you're ok?' He checked again.

'Perfectly ok, thank you,' she pulled the T shirt over his head and kissed him longingly.

'Feeling frisky, are you?' He murmured when she finally pulled away; she looked him in the eye and nodded again as she finished undoing his jeans.

He watched her through half closed eyes an hour later and his mind wandered back to what Charlie had said. She gazed at him as she sponged herself, unaware that he was looking at her. He had never felt like this about anyone, certainly not Amy, and although he found it hard to admit, Sally neither.

He did want to marry her; he'd known it from the first time he kissed her. It seemed so long ago, but in truth it was less than a year. As he had pointed out to Charlie, her first marriage had been so awful he would be surprised if she wanted to go there again. They were lying top to toe in the huge bath, with her feet resting against his stomach.

She curled her toes and gave a contented sigh as he ran his hands up her legs. God, she's beautiful, he thought; he smiled as he relived the last hour. Heather stroked his tummy suggestively with her foot. 'Do you know that your dimple really turns me on?'

Steven opened his eyes and looked down. 'Yes I do; but I also know that the water is nearly cold and the dinner will be dried up.'

She put her lip out in disappointment then pulled herself up. 'I'll nip down and turn the oven off, and you top the bath up,' she ordered.

Chapter 7

The observation tapes from the remand centre were waiting on Edward's desk when he arrived the next morning. He slid the first one into the player, and sat back to watch two hours of Gold sitting at the opposite end of the table to Paige. He yawned as Jack came in. 'Any joy?'

Edward shook his head. 'They're just sitting there,' he ejected the tape and started to load the second one.

'Shall I get coffee?' Jack enquired.

'You'd better bring a pot,' he chuckled, then pressed play, and prepared to be bored stiff. Gold entered the room, she was wearing a tight skirt, low cut top, high heels, and carrying a thick file. Paige was already sitting at the table. She sat down opposite him with her back to the observation camera, then leant forward on the table and opened the file.

Edward stopped the tape as Jack came back in with the coffee. 'Well that's odd for a start, she was wearing the pinstripes for the first interview and now she looks like a common tart,' Jack chuckled at his description and restarted the tape. There was no sound, but from the expression on Paige's face and his agitated body language, they deduced that they were arguing.

Every so often Gold pointed to the file. Paige suddenly stood up and jabbed his finger at her, his face twisted in anger. He backed off slightly as the door opened and the guard entered the room. Gold looked round and said something; the guard went out again and closed the door.

Gold went back to looking at the file whilst Paige paced up and down behind her. He stopped pacing as she turned and said something; he was standing between her and the camera so she was partially obscured.

He suddenly spun around and looked up directly into the camera lens, then a look of pain crossed his face. He turned back to face her and nodded as she spoke. Gold picked the file up and went to the door. She gave his bottom a light tap as she passed and said something else before disappearing out of the camera range.

The guard came a few seconds later and escorted Paige out. 'Back to his cell to die,' Edward muttered. They rewound the tape and played it again. Gold had positioned herself in just the right spot so they couldn't see her face or what she was doing.

'Not daft, is she?' Jack commented.

'She didn't have a bag with her, just the file,' Edward observed; he stopped the tape at the point where she opened it.

'Look at his expression,' Jack pointed to Paige's face as he looked at the file. 'Is that fear or anger?' He wondered out loud.

'Both from the look of it,' Edward said dryly. They watched the tape through to the end again. 'Do you know what we need?' Edward asked.

'A stiff drink?' Jack suggested hopefully.

'Well, that as too,' he agreed. 'But I was thinking more along the lines of a lip reader.'

Jack grinned at him. 'I'll get onto it, guv.'

Edward ran the tape on again; he stopped it as Gold left the room and tapped the screen determinedly. 'I'll get you,' he muttered.

The lip reader arrived that afternoon and introduced himself as Norman; he watched the tape through twice before commenting. 'Well I obviously can't see everything that the lady says, but they are arguing.'

Jack turned the tape recorder on. 'Just tell us whatever you can please.'

Norman looked at the screen again and studied Paige's face as he spoke. 'About bloody time! Are you going to get me out of here?' Norman looked up. 'Am I going too fast?'

Edward shook his head. Norman looked at the screen and continued. 'Then the lady said something and he said, "I'm not going to carry the can for this, Ronnie, I'm going to do a deal with that copper". Then the lady said something else, and he said, "He's coming tomorrow and I'm going to tell him".'

When they reached the moment where Gold pointed to the file, Norman looked embarrassed. 'It's alright, we need to know exactly what was said,' Jack reassured him.

'He says "What the fuck is that?", then the lady speaks and he said, "You wouldn't dare".' At that point, the guard came in and Gold's face was visible as she turned and spoke.

'What did she say?' Jack asked.

'She said "Its ok, sweetie, everything's fine".' Edward and Jack looked at each other in dismay. 'Shall I continue?' Norman asked. Edward nodded. 'He said "What the fuck is he up to? He's supposed to be protecting us". The lady said something and he says, "No they bloody well can't".'

Paige was now staring into the lens. 'He said "You fucking bitch".' Norman looked at them and raised his eyebrows. 'Very colourful language,' he commented dryly. By now, Paige's back was to the camera. 'She said "Do you understand?" and he nods.'

Gold had got up and was heading for the door. 'Can you tell what she said as she went out?' Edward asked.

Norman ran the clip through several times studying it intently. 'It looks like "Next time it won't be water".'

Got you! Edward said to himself. 'Send someone to the remand centre and bring the guard in,' he told Jack when Norman had gone but the word came back that the guard was on holiday and wasn't due back for another week. 'I want him here as soon as he gets back,' Edward said impatiently.

'What on earth are you wearing?' Sue asked Steven as he went into the lab; he looked down at his ensemble and frowned.

'Clothes?'

Sue shook her head. 'Not the clothes,' she leant closer and sniffed a couple of times. 'What is it, some new-fangled aftershave?'

Realisation suddenly hit him; he stuck his nose down the top of his shirt and breathed in the sweet aroma of bath oil. 'It's bath oil.'

'Bath oil,' she repeated amusedly.

'Yes, it helps me to relax,' he said indignantly.

'I thought you rode your bike to relax,' she smirked at him as he gave her a look of distain.

'Did you call me up here to discuss my relaxation techniques, Mrs Cole, or did you have something to tell me?' He said in his most superior voice.

Sue handed him a print out. 'It's the result from Andrew Wells' swab, the blood on the gas cylinder isn't his but look at this,' she tapped a result a few lines down.

'Oh well done!' He exclaimed. 'Dad will be pleased.' He stared at the result for a couple of seconds. 'Can you run it through again just to be doubly sure?' Sue gave another sniff and nodded as Steven went back downstairs.

There was a policeman standing in the reception looking decidedly queasy. 'Are you alright?' Steven asked.

The PC took the glass of water that Judy offered and gulped a mouthful down. 'Yes, thanks,' he said unconvincingly. 'Inspector Finch sent me over with this,' he handed Steven an evidence bag. 'It's a hand, Sir, we found it on the old railway path at Nubbin and it's wearing a rubber glove,' the PC told him, then he made his excuses and left.

'Is that him who smells like a tarts handbag or is it you?' Judy chuckled.

Steven went into the cutting room and gave Charlie the evidence bag. 'Present for you,' he said brightly.

'Is this whose I think it is?' Charlie asked as he opened it.

'Well, I bloody well hope so,' Steven muttered. They took the hand out and examined it; still encased in the remains of a pink rubber glove, it was blast damaged but not destroyed. 'It must have been blown off in the blast,' Steven pointed to small punctures in the rubber. 'Maybe a fox or a dog picked it up and carried it off.'

After gently peeling away the remains of the glove, they were delighted to find the hand virtually intact. Steven examined it closely; there was a thin scratch across the back of the hand. 'That looks like a Monty type scratch,' he said as he remembered the drop of blood which was found on his bed.

As well as the scratch, three of the finger nails had residue of some kind stuck to them. After taking samples they took the hand to the chiller unit where the burnt body lay. Steven held the hand against the end of the arm; although the bone had been badly damaged by the fire, they both agreed that the two ends matched.

'We'd better wait for the results from upstairs before we make it official,' Steven said thoughtfully.

'I've arranged for Andrew Wells to come here,' Whittle told Edward as he was about to go home. 'I think that he should be given the opportunity to explain himself, and I don't want you trailing all the way down to London again.'

Edward raised his eyebrows in surprise 'That was very industrious of you, Sir.'

Whittle frowned at him. 'Well, apparently he's bringing his solicitor with him, so you can question her about Robin Paige whilst she's here.' Edward nodded his thanks and went to the squad room.

'He'll have to have a lie down for a while; all that thinking will have worn him out,' Jack joked.

'Well at least he's on our side this time,' Edward commented dryly. 'So let's hope he stays there,' he muttered.

Veronica Gold arrived at the police station first thing the next morning. 'She got here sharpish, didn't she,' Jack commented. A WPC showed her into an interview room and explained that Mr Wells hadn't arrived; she declined the offer of a cup of tea and sat staring into space. Edward and Whittle watched her through the observation glass.

'You'd better be right about this, Edward,' Whittle threatened, then straitened his jacket and went in. Gold looked up in surprise as he entered. 'I'm sorry to bother you, but we've come up short for an identity parade, and as you have blond hair, I wonder if you would mind making the numbers up?' He asked humbly.

Gold looked at him in disbelief as he gave her his most apologetic smile. 'It's a local bag snatcher and she swears blind that it wasn't her,' he glanced towards the observation room.

'And it's somebody local?' Gold checked.

'Yes, she's well known to us,' Whittle lied. Gold sighed loudly.

'Well I suppose so, as my client hasn't arrived yet, but I'm surprised that you have to deal with such mundane matters,' she commented as he led her to the parade room.

Maria looked along the line and shook her head. 'I don't know.' Whittle frowned impatiently. 'I only see her from the back,' she reminded him. Whittle called the PC in and told him to ask the women to turn around. Edward watched Gold's face closely as they were given the order.

'Well?' Whittle asked.

Maria stared at the women, all of whom had blond hair, either natural or dyed, and who with the exception of Gold were all police women in civvies. 'Her hair was like that,' she pointed to a WPC halfway along the line whose dark roots were showing through. 'But she was taller.' Edward glanced at Whittle who was looking increasingly agitated.

'I will know if she speaks,' Maria said earnestly. 'She say "shut up will you" to the man.' Edward called the PC in again and gave him the instruction; he switched the speaker on and they waited for the first woman to speak. 'Shut up will you.' Maria shook her head as each woman said the words in turn; when it was Gold's turn, it went quiet.

'Number nine please say the words,' the PC instructed.

'Shut up will you,' she said quietly in her public-school voice.

Maria frowned. 'Can I hear again?'

'Number nine; please repeat the words,' the PC ordered.

A smile crossed Maria's face as Gold snapped the words out. 'She is Ronnie,' she said confidently. Just to be sure the last two in the line-up were asked to speak. Maria shook her head and pointed to Gold. 'Not them, her,' she said firmly.

Edward and Jack went into the interview room twenty minutes later. 'Has my client arrived yet?' Gold asked. 'Who is this?' She demanded as the duty solicitor came in and sat down next to her.

'This is Mr Rusden,' Edward said blandly and turned the tape recorder on. 'Read Ms Gold her rights please, Sergeant Taylor,' he instructed. Gold's mouth fell open as Jack cautioned her. 'Right down to business,' Edward said brightly and opened a file. 'Your first name is Veronica, is that correct?'

Gold glared at him. 'No, Inspector, that is not correct.'

Edward looked at the file again. 'You sign your name as V. Gold, so what does the V stand for if not Veronica?' She stared at him nervously but didn't answer. 'So the V stands for what exactly?' He asked again a little more forcefully.

'Veronica is my middle name,' she snapped.

'So what is your first name?' Jack asked impatiently.

'Gloria,' she glared at him as he started to smile.

'Gloria Veronica Gold?' She nodded curtly. 'Your chambers told us that you are registered with them as Veronica,' Edward commented.

'I am,' she stuck her chin out defiantly. 'I don't use my first name, Inspector, you asked if Veronica is my first name, which it is not.'

Edward tried not to react to the self-satisfied look she was wearing. 'You have been identified as the woman who was referred to as Ronnie, by a man who we now know was Alex Gorman,' he looked up.

'I understand that Ronnie is short for Veronica?'

She shook her head dismissively. 'Who identified me?'

He smiled sadly. 'I'm afraid that's confidential; you of all people should know that.' Gold gave an indifferent sniff and looked away. 'You visited Robin Paige at the remand centre shortly before he died,' Edward continued.

'He's my client; I'm entitled to visit clients, and you of all people should know that, Chief Inspector,' she put her head on one side and smiled.

Edward smiled back. 'What did you talk about?'

'I'm afraid that's confidential,' she said sweetly.

Edward looked at Jack and gestured to him to continue. 'He called you Ronnie whilst you were in the meeting room,' Jack said casually.

Gold gave a barely audible gasp. 'There is no audio surveillance in the meeting rooms, so how you can possibly know that is beyond me,' she said superiorly.

'Nevertheless, he did call you Ronnie just minutes before you injected him with a lethal dose of morphine,' Edward interrupted.

Gold gave a nervous laugh and sat back. 'Do you have any evidence to back up that ludicrous claim, Inspector?'

Edward ignored the question and looked at the transcript from the lip reader. 'Who was he referring to when he said and I quote, "What the fuck is he up to? He's supposed to be protecting us".' Gold pursed her lips together suddenly deflated. 'It is your right to remain silent, but of course you know that already, don't you? And in answer to your earlier question, Ms Gold, yes, we do have evidence that you murdered Robin Paige,' Edward said dryly.

'Would you like to speak to me alone?' Mr Rusden asked.

Gold gave him a scornful look and watched as Edward and Jack left the room. WPC Blackwell handed Edward a memo as they went into the squad room. 'A message from Dr Cooper, Sir,' she gave him a fearful glance before scuttling off.

'Blimey, guv, what have you done to her?' Jack enquired.

'I have no idea,' he muttered, and looked at the memo. 'There was a wound on the hand which is consistent with being scratched by a cat, and there was glue resin on the nails that matched the resin on the false nail in Graham Pickering's room. So Gorman was wearing false nails?' He muttered.

'Trudy said the woman in the car was ugly, I bet that was him,' Jack chuckled.

Edward nodded contentedly. 'Well that's one piece of the puzzle solved, and we'll see where Andrew Wells fits in when he gets here,' he looked at the time. 'Let's go and get something to eat,' he suggested.

A gold bedecked Andrew Wells arrived after lunch looking decidedly angry. 'Smug bastard, isn't he?' Jack commented as he was led into an interview room.

'Yes, he is,' Edward agreed. 'But hopefully not for much longer,' he looked at Wells sitting with his arms folded in defiance. 'Let's get to it then.' He opened the interview room door but was stopped by a shout from the squad room.

A PC waved the phone at him. 'Dr Cooper for you, Sir.'

'Tell him I'll call back,' he instructed.

'He says its urgent, Sir,' the PC called. Edward entered the interview room two minutes later.

'Am I under arrest?' Wells demanded before he had even sat down.

'No, Sir, you are helping us with our enquiries,' Edward said brightly.

Wells scowled at him. 'Why can't I help with your bloody enquiries from London?' He looked round as Whittle came into the interview room. What the hell is he doing here? Edward thought as the Chief Superintendent sat down quietly in the corner. 'Where's my solicitor?' Wells demanded.

Edward glanced at the duty solicitor. 'He's sitting right next to you.'

Wells gave a sarcastic snort. 'Not him, where's Ms Gold?'

Edward opened the file in front of him. 'Ms Gold is unavailable,' he said dryly. 'But Mr Rusden is a very good and honest solicitor,' he gave him a satisfied smile. 'Shall we start? I'll take that as a yes then,' he said brightly as Wells glared at him.

He looked at the file then sat forward and leant on the table. 'You chose Miss Catacazi to come and work for you after seeing a photograph of her, is that correct?'

'I suppose so,' Wells admitted, and then yawned loudly. 'Is this going to take long I've got a business to run.'

Edward ignored him. 'Miss Catacazi has identified Mr Robin Paige as the man who took the pictures of her and ten other young women.'

Wells shrugged disinterestedly. 'What he did in his spare time was up to him.'

Edward glanced at Jack who he knew had spotted the mistake. 'Why did you choose Miss Catacazi?'

'I didn't choose her; I just picked the first one from the pile. It could have been anyone,' he said dismissively.

'You don't mind what your domestic staff look like then?' Edward checked.

'No, I don't,' Wells said amusedly.

'So why go to the trouble of arranging work permits for foreigners, when you could have employed someone local or from an agency?'

Wells gave a sly smile. 'Because they're cheaper, Inspector.'

Edward raised his eyebrows. 'How cheap? How much did you pay for her?'

'I didn't pay for her,' Wells snapped.

'Oh! I'm sorry; I meant how much did you pay her?' Edward asked.

For the first time, Wells looked uncomfortable. 'The going rate,' he muttered.

'Which is what?' Wells shrugged dismissively. 'Which is what?' Edward persisted.

'I don't know; my manager deals with the wages. I'll have to ask him,' he snapped.

'Did you withhold her wages until she had paid off her ticket into the country?' Edward asked matter of factly.

Wells looked at the solicitor. 'Aren't you supposed to advise me not to answer these questions?' He enquired sarcastically.

'If you've nothing to hide then you should answer,' Mr Rusden advised. 'Do you want to speak to me alone?' He asked.

Wells gave him a look of distain. 'No,' he sneered, as if it was the most ridiculous thing he'd ever heard. 'I'll wait for Ms Gold to be available, and until she is, I'm not saying anything else,' he folded his arms and gave them a triumphant look.

'Well, I'm afraid you may have a long wait Sir, because Ms Gold has been arrested and may well be charged with murder,' Edward informed him. 'Now shall I go on? Or are you going to stop wasting our time?'

Wells looked at him impassively 'Murdering who?' He asked innocently.

'I think you already know the answer to that, Mr Wells,' Edward said sharply.

'I've no idea,' he snapped. Jack stopped the tape and rewound it. Edward watched Wells closely as his voice echoed from the speaker. 'What he did in his spare time was up to him.' Jack turned the tape off.

'You were using the past tense, did and was, you then tried to correct yourself by saying that you would have to ask him about Maria's wages.' They waited for a comment, but Wells didn't speak. 'I think you knew that Robin Paige was dead before you even set foot in here, and as we haven't released details to the press yet, the only way you could possibly know that is if you know who killed him,' Edward accused.

'I had nothing to do with his death,' Wells insisted.

'That is yet to be established,' Edward muttered. 'But we've digressed, haven't we?' He said brightly. 'Miss Catacazi has stated that you regularly sexually assaulted her for nearly four months.'

'Well, she's lying,' Wells interrupted.

'Really?' Edward said disbelievingly.

Wells nodded curtly and looked at the solicitor. 'Tell them to charge me or let me go,' he instructed.

'When did your wife leave you?' Edward asked suddenly. Whittle gave him a puzzled look.

'What the hell has that got to do with you?' Wells asked incredulously.

'Just answer the question please,' Edward snapped.

'About two years ago,' he sniffed. 'Why did she leave you?'

Wells looked at his hands. 'I decline to answer that,' he said quietly.

'Was it because you were sleeping with the domestic staff?' Wells looked up sharply. 'Did you choose Maria Catacazi because she looked like her sister?' Edward persisted.

Wells rolled his eyes. 'What the hell are you talking about?' Edward sighed impatiently.

'It's a simple enough question, Mr Wells; did you choose Maria Catacazi because she looked like her sister?'

Wells shook his head. 'I told you I just took the first one off the pile,' he said firmly.

'So you don't know Maria's sister?' Edward checked.

'No, I do not,' he insisted.

Edward watched him carefully. 'She was called Jenica Catacazi,' he said pointedly.

The muscles in Well's face twitched. 'I've never heard of her,' he said disinterestedly.

'Well Maria said that you called her name one night whilst you were in bed with her,' Jack told him.

'I've never been in bed with her, where's your evidence?' He asked arrogantly.

'We have only got her word that you assaulted her,' Edward conceded.

'So what the hell am I doing here then?' Wells asked incredulously; he got up and looked at Whittle. 'You're the big cheese around here, are you going to order him to release me?'

'Did you rape Jenica Catacazi, Mr Wells?' Edward asked him.

'I told you I don't know her,' he said impatiently.

Edward looked him straight in the eye. 'Did your wife leave you because she caught you in bed with her?'

Wells' face twisted into a sneer. 'You've no evidence that I slept with either of these girls, so you'd better let me go or I'll sue you for harassment.'

Edward glanced at Whittle who had also got up. 'I'm afraid that's where you're wrong, Sir,' he said semi-triumphantly; he looked at the file. 'When Jenica Catacazi ran away from you, and she did run away from you,' he said firmly, to the denial that started to fall from Wells' lips.

'When she ran away from you, she was pregnant with your child, so although Jenica is dead and can't give us a statement, her child,' he looked up. 'That's your daughter, Mr Wells,' he told the now ashen faced man. 'Your daughter is living proof that you not only knew Jenica, but did sleep with her on at least one occasion, whether it was against her will or not,' he drummed his fingers on the table.

'Now sit down please, Sir.' He waited until Wells had sat down. 'Do you wish to speak to the solicitor in private now?' He checked.

Wells shook his head. 'So, I got some tart pregnant, there's no law against it,' he said defiantly.

Edward ignored the comment and changed the subject. 'Where did you get your ring from?'

Wells looked bemused. 'What ring?'

'The lovely big gold ring that you were wearing on your little finger the day we met at your house,' Edward sat back and waited for him to answer.

'I can't remember where I got it from, it was probably a gift,' Wells said dismissively.

'So where is it now, Sir?' Edward enquired. Wells looked at his bare hands. 'Only I seem to remember you saying that you never take your gold off,' Edward reminded him. 'And I see you are still wearing the two necklaces and the bracelet, but not the ring,' he said thoughtfully.

'I must have lost it,' Wells mumbled.

'That was very careless of you, Sir,' Edward quipped. 'Would you mind if we had a quick look around your house?'

Wells face twitched nervously. 'Not without a warrant,' he hissed.

Edward looked at Whittle. 'Right, I'll arrange that then,' he said as the Chief Superintendent nodded his approval. 'Perhaps you would like to stay here for a while, just until we've got it sorted out,' he got up and leant over the table. 'Maybe we can find your ring for you, Sir,' he whispered.

Whilst Edward was interviewing Andrew Wells, a team of officers were searching the remand centre car park and surrounding area. Forensics were going over Gold's car in the police garage; as expected they found prints all over the interior of the car, but there was also a set on the top of the driver's door window. 'It looks like someone tried to stop it closing,' Sue commented.

She opened the door and checked inside. 'Has someone taken a hair sample from Ms Gold?' She enquired as she retrieved several strands from head rest of the passenger seat.

'It's already at the lab,' someone called. Sue started searching the car, but there was no sign of the syringe or morphine, however underneath the driver's seat, she found the file that Gold had taken into the remand centre. A few minutes later, she hit the jackpot, as she opened the boot and removed the spare wheel, to reveal a bloodied jack handle lying in the well.

The team at the remand centre didn't have such luck; the bins had been emptied the day after Gold's visit, and the contents taken to the nearest landfill site which was twenty miles away. A fingertip search of the whole car park and service area came up blank. 'Don't tell me we're going to have to sift through tones of rubbish,' Jack groaned.

'Let's wait for the forensics from the car first,' Edward said thoughtfully.

Jack knew the look and wondered what he was thinking, but he also knew that it was better not to ask and changed the subject. 'Are you going to get a honeymoon then?'

Edward shrugged. 'I may just take a permanent one when this case is closed, but that's between you and me for now,' he said firmly.

The guard from the remand centre arrived two hours later, at just twenty-five he had been in the service for less than a year. 'Justin Lewis?' Jack checked; the young man nodded. 'We need to take a swab and fingerprints for elimination purposes,' Jack explained.

Edward came in as the doctor was taking the swab; he sat down in the corner and observed. 'Ms Gold referred to you as sweetie when she was with Mr Paige,' Jack said when the doctor had gone.

'Yes,' Justin confirmed.

'Do you know Ms Gold personally?' A red tinge appeared around Justin's ears. Jack raised his eyebrows enquiringly.

'I met her when she came to the centre,' Justin admitted.

'So how do you explain the sweetie comment?' Jack enquired.

Justin shrugged. 'I can't,' he mumbled.

'Did Ms Gold leave the centre as soon as the interviews were over?' Jack tried.

'Yes,' he confirmed and looked at the table.

'Ok you can go,' Edward said suddenly.

Justin looked up. 'Really.'

'Yes, for now, but we may need speak to you again, so don't leave the area.' Justin got up and nearly tripped over himself in his haste to get out.

'What do you think?' Jack asked.

Edward rubbed his hands together. 'I think he's a naïve new boy who was taken advantage of, but we'll know soon enough when we get the forensic results,' he said contentedly. The results didn't take long; the first batch was back within two days, and unsurprisingly most of the hair found in Gold's car was hers. 'But there were also three alien samples; One from an unknown female, one from a male that matched the blood sample found on the gas cylinder, and one matching Justin Lewis. He also left fingerprints on the door handle. The second set of prints on the window don't match anyone on file,' Sue reported.

Edward called Justin back in. 'I'll get straight to the point. You maintain that you only met Ms Gold when she came to the centre to speak to Mr Paige.' Justin nodded. 'Well, we found your fingerprints and samples of your hair in her car; can you explain how they got there?'

Justin swallowed nervously and stared at him. 'I sat in her car when I finished my shift,' he admitted.

'Which shift?' Edward enquired.

'The shift on the day of her first visit,' he said quietly.

'So you lied when you said you didn't know her?' Edward accused.

'No, I didn't lie,' he insisted.

'So why were you in her car then?' Jack asked.

'You don't have to answer that,' the solicitor advised.

'But it would be better for you if you did,' Edward said firmly. The red tinge started to appear on Justin's neck again. They waited patiently whilst he tried to decide what to do.

'She was waiting for me when I finished my shift,' he said eventually.

Edward sat back and folded his arms. 'Why was she waiting for you?'

The tinge crept up Justin's face. 'She said she fancied me,' he said embarrassedly.

'So you got into her car?' Jack checked. 'Yes,' Justin confirmed.

'How long were you in there for?' Edward asked.

'About fifteen minutes,' he mumbled.

'What did you do?' Justin stared at his hands but didn't answer. Edward reworded the question. 'Did you have sex?'

Justin shook his head. 'No, not really,' he glanced up at the two policemen; his face was now bright red.

'What do you mean not really?' Edward asked.

'She gave me a,' he looked down again.

'She gave you oral sex, is that what you are trying to say?' Jack finished for him.

He nodded miserably. 'She said she couldn't have sex because she had a monthly.'

Jack gave a small sigh 'So then what happened?'

Justin gave them a puzzled look. 'When?'

'What happened after she had given you the blow job?' Jack asked impatiently. Edward frowned at him.

'I, well you know,' he mumbled.

'What happened after she had finished and you had, well you know?' Jack asked sarcastically.

'I went home,' he said quietly.

'Did you arrange to see her again?'

'No,' he said firmly.

'Why not if she fancied you enough to wait for you?'

Justin looked at his hands again. 'Because I've got a girlfriend,' he said quietly.

'So it was a spur of the moment thing, like a one-night stand?' Edward checked.

'Yes, you won't tell her, will you?' Justin begged.

'Tell who?' Edward asked.

'My girlfriend,' he said anxiously.

'No, I'm not going to tell her, but maybe you should,' Edward suggested, he got up and opened the door. 'You can go, but you will be needed again,' he warned.

'I'm sorry, guv,' Jack apologised, as they watched him scurrying across the car park. 'I just hate sex being used as an excuse.'

'So do I,' Edward admitted. 'But it happens and we have to deal with it apathetically,' he gave wry smile. 'Come on, let's go for a pint,' he suggested.

'I think he's holding something back,' Jack commented as they made their way to the pub.

'So do I,' Edward agreed. 'We'll give him a day or two to stew and then get him back in,' he said contentedly.

'So, is it your round then, guv?' Jack enquired as they reached the pub.

They called Justin back in two days later. 'Did Ms Gold give you anything else?' Jack asked the still embarrassed young man.

'What do you mean?' Justin enquired nervously.

'I mean apart from performing a sex act on you, did she give you anything else?'

'No,' he said confidently.

'Did she ask you to do anything for her?'

A flicker of guilt crossed his face. 'Like what?'

Edward eyed him suspiciously. 'Did you know that she had a syringe hidden in the file she was carrying?'

Justin looked at the solicitor and then put his head in his hands. 'She had it in her bag on the first visit. She said it was insulin for her diabetes, and she had to carry it with her at all times,' he said despairingly.

'For Christ's sake! Insulin doesn't come in bloody great big syringes,' Jack snapped.

'Well how was I to know that,' Justin snapped back. 'Anyway, I told her she couldn't take it in, but she was waiting for me in the car park after my shift,' he stopped talking.

'Go on,' Edward instructed.

'She asked if I was on the same shift the next day, and when I said I was, she asked me if I wanted to have some fun, but after we had,' he stopped talking again and nodded. 'Well, you know?'

'Yes, we know,' Jack said dryly.

Justin glanced at Edward. 'She asked me to take the syringe in for her when she came back the next day, so of course I said no,' he said earnestly.

'Of course you did,' Jack butted in.

'Yes, I did,' Justin insisted. 'But she said if I didn't take it in then she would tell the warden what we had done, and I would lose my job, so I hid it in my sandwich box and slipped it between the rings of the file when she arrived,' he looked up. 'I swear I didn't know what she was going to do; she said it was hers,' he said almost desperately.

'So you handled the syringe?' Edward checked.

Justin nodded. 'Oh my God! the bitch is going to say it was me,' he stared in horror at the policemen.

'What happened to the syringe?' Jack asked.

'I don't know, but she asked to use the toilets on the way out. I let her use the staff ladies. I bet she threw it in the bin in there,' he suggested helpfully.

'And was this after speaking to Paige for the second time?' Edward checked.

'Yes,' he confirmed.

'And I assume that you will be willing to testify to all of this in court?' Justin nodded eagerly. 'Ok you can go, but don't discuss this with anyone,' Edward warned. 'Like I said; naive,' he muttered as they watched him go. 'Get someone over to the remand centre to check the toilets, and the sanitary bins will need to go to forensics,' he added thoughtfully.

Sue stuck her head around Steven's door the next morning. 'There were two blood samples on the jack handle, one came from the security guard who was hit when we were broken into, and the other one is Graham Pickering's,' she gave a triumphant smile, quickly followed by a grimace. 'And now I've got four sanitary waste bins from the remand centre to go through, I hope your father is right,' she muttered unenthusiastically.

'Only about twenty per cent of the time,' Steven teased. 'Do you want me to do it?' He asked.

'Do you want to do it?' She counter asked incredulously; he gave a light shrug.

'I don't mind.' They looked up as Judy knocked on the door.

'The lorry driver's wife and children have arrived,' she said quietly.

'Phew! Saved by the bell,' he chuckled. 'Good call, Dad, we've got the syringe. It was all wrapped up in a sanitary towel ready to go to the incinerator,' he told Edward later the same day.

'Fingerprints?' Edward enquired hopefully.

'Sue's working on it now; by the way that was one nasty job you sent in, so a personal thanks to Sue wouldn't go amiss,' he added. 'I'll see what I can do,' Edward promised. Sure enough, a bouquet arrived at the pathology unit the next day. 'From an admirer?' Charlie enquired mischievously. Sue went red and gave him the card to read. 'Thanks for all your hard work during this busy period! Don't worry; it won't be a regular occurrence. With thanks from all on the Pickering case.' Sue looked at Steven and raised her eyebrows; he put his hands up defensively.

'Nothing to do with me,' he chuckled.

'Really,' she said disbelievingly, and went back upstairs still blushing.

She was back down an hour later with news on the syringe. 'I've never been thanked in all the years I've been here, and I've dealt with a lot worse than that,' she told Steven when she got him alone. He gave her an affectionate smile; he had a genuine respect for the hard-working scientist.

'Well that was before I got here. This place would grind to a halt if it wasn't for people like you,' he smiled again as she went red. 'Anyway, what have you got there?'

'The sanitary towel that the syringe was wrapped in was unused, so no blood for testing, and it was the same brand as the vending machine dispenses.' Steven's heart sank. 'But I lifted Ms Gold's print from the lid of the bin,' Sue continued.

'And the syringe?' He asked tentatively.

'The guards prints were on the barrel as expected, but there was also a partial print on the plunger.'

'And?' Steven interrupted impatiently.

'And it is Veronica Gold's.'

Steven sighed triumphantly. 'Great result,' he congratulated. 'I'll let you call dad with the good news.' Sue smiled, but instead of getting up, she just sat there looking at him. 'Is there something else?' he enquired. She gave a light nod. 'Go on then?' He encouraged and sat back expectantly.

'You've got something on your mind,' she told him.

'Have I?' He said in surprise.

She gave him one of her motherly looks. 'Come on, you can tell me.'

He stared at her, feeling like a schoolboy who'd been asked to grass on his mates. 'Tell you what?' She returned his gaze, then raised her eyebrows and got up. 'Do you think it's too soon to ask Heather to marry me?' He suddenly blurted out, much to his own surprise.

Sue sat down again. 'Do you love her?'

Just the thought of her made him smile. 'Oh God! Yes.' He found himself spilling his heart out; telling her everything; from the moment he realised that she was alive, to the visits in hospital. Sue chuckled as he recalled the misunderstanding over the Westlife CD and the cat.

'Have you told her all of this?' She enquired.

'Not all of it. I don't want to scare her off,' he admitted.

Sue smiled at him. 'I don't think there's any chance of that happening.'

'So you don't think it's too soon then?' He asked anxiously.

'Well, when did you first realise that you were in love with her?' She asked seriously.

He told her about the kiss in his hospital room. 'It felt like I'd been kicked. I couldn't breathe,' he bit his lip suddenly embarrassed. 'Sorry, you don't need to hear all this mush,' he mumbled.

Sue chuckled at his embarrassment. 'I'll let you into a secret, shall I?' Steven nodded enthusiastically. 'Freddie asked me to marry him after three weeks,' she confessed.

'Three weeks! That's quick.'

She smiled at the memory. 'It was quick, and he said he would have asked me after the first date, but he didn't think I would say yes. But if he had asked me earlier, then I would still have said yes, because I knew that he was the one,' she said happily.

'Well you've probably got better judgment then me,' he said ruefully. 'I mean look at Amy,' he stared into space for a minute. 'Mind you, I should have realised what she was like when she refused to wear mum's engagement ring.'

Sue tutted in disgust. 'But you were with her for five years?' Steven nodded. 'And it's my understanding that she proposed to you.' Sue checked.

'If that's what you can call it,' he said dryly.

'So if you had really wanted to marry her, surely you would have asked her,' she said matter of factly.

He suddenly saw the logic and smiled. 'Yes, I suppose I would,' he conceded.

'Ask her,' Sue advised. 'She's as crazy about you as you are about her.' She looked at the time and got up. 'I'll go and give your dad the good news.'

'Sue,' Steven said as she reached the door; she turned back.

'Don't worry I'll not say anything,' she promised.

'I've arranged for Mr Wells' house to be searched tomorrow and I would like one of you to be present,' Whittle told Edward and Jack that afternoon. Edward was just about to ask why when Whittle answered his unasked question. 'It has come to my attention that his premises have been searched on several previous occasions.'

Edward nodded. 'And as they failed to find anything, and in light of your feelings about the man,' he looked directly at Edward. 'I think a fresh pair of eyes would be useful,' he stood up and opened the door. 'Decide between yourselves who goes, and let London know what time you will be arriving,' he ordered.

They watched as he strutted off down the corridor, reminding them of a cockerel in the hen house. 'Toss you for it then, guv,' Jack suggested brightly.

Jack lost the toss, and after a dash down the motorway the next morning, he sat outside Andrew Well's house and waited for his colleagues from the Met to arrive. He got out of the car as two police cars drew up, and expecting Simon Reynolds to be there, was surprised to see his old boss, DCI Jackson. He enquired after Simon as they shook hands.

Jackson was obviously not impressed by his absence. 'He's still on emergency leave; shall we get on?' He suggested curtly. Jack handed over Wells' house keys, that he had ungraciously relinquished the day before, and they went inside. It was nearly five o' clock before he got back. He put a package on Edward's desk.

'I can't understand how London missed these before,' he said exasperatedly. 'They were in the safe along with a load of counterfeit documents, but I only brought the stuff that's connected to our case, and the Met want him after us.'

'So where was the safe?' Edward asked.

'Hidden in the floor of a walk-in wardrobe. I found it as soon as I went in.'

Edward nodded thoughtfully. 'And what did Simon say when you found it?'

Jack shrugged. 'He wasn't there; he's still on emergency leave. It was DCI Jackson who led the search.'

Edward looked at the contents of the bag and smiled. 'Let's get this stuff over to forensics and see if they come up with anything,' he glanced at his watch. 'I don't suppose they'll be able to do anything until tomorrow though, so Wells will have to stew for another night,' he said contentedly.

It was late afternoon the next day before forensics had a result for him. Jack looked at the report and gave a satisfied smile as they went into the interview room. Wells was sitting at the table with a face like thunder. 'I hope you realise that you are going to be sued for false imprisonment.'

Edward sat down and smiled at him. 'I think I got it wrong with you,' he said thoughtfully. 'You didn't choose Maria Catacazi because she looked like her sister, did you?'

Wells gave him triumphant look. 'At last, the country copper has seen sense,' he said scornfully. 'Does that mean I can get back to running my legitimate business?' he enquired.

'Sit down please, Mr Wells,' Edward instructed as he stood up. 'I got it wrong, because you choose both the Catacazi sisters because they resembled your ex-wife.'

Wells sat down heavily. 'You don't know what you're talking about,' he said, and although he was trying to sound blasé there was a hint of nervousness in his voice.

Edward opened the folder, and took out three pictures. 'Do you recognise this lady?' He put one of the pictures in front of him.

Wells glanced at it and nodded. 'Of course I do, it's Rosanne, my ex-wife.' Edward put the other pictures on the table and watched his expression closely. Wells swallowed nervously and stared at the pictures of Maria and Jenica Catacazi. 'Where did you get those from?' He almost choked on the words.

'My sergeant found them in your house, in your safe to be precise, you know the one built into the floor of your lovely walk-in wardrobe, the one that you didn't think would be found,' he nodded sadly. 'I'm afraid they had to dismantle it, but I doubt that you'll be needing a safe in the near future.' Wells stared at him but didn't speak. 'I believe they found some other items as well,' Edward continued.

'Passports, false work permits, things like that, but I'm only interested in these pictures, and this of course,' he produced the ring from his pocket and put it on the table in front of him. Wells glanced at it and then looked away. 'Did you know that Graham Pickering hit our pathologist, leaving the imprint of a ring on his face?' Edward asked.

Wells shook his head. 'I don't know Graham Pickering.'

Edward put a picture of Pickering in front of him. 'Do you know him now?' He checked.

'No, I don't,' Wells said firmly.

Edward put a picture of the bruise on Steven's face in front of him. 'Can you see the grazing in the middle of the bruise?'

Wells glanced at it. 'Yes,' he said curtly.

'Well, the grazing was made by this ring; can you see the shape of the graze?'

Wells looked up. 'What are you getting at?'

Edward picked the ring up and studied it closely. 'This ring was found in your gym; do you recognise it?'

'Well, if you found it in my gym then it must be mine, so obviously I do recognise it,' he snapped sarcastically.

'It's quite unusual,' Edward said absentmindedly as he continued to examine it. 'How long have you owned it?'

'A couple of years I suppose,' Wells sighed.

'Are you sure about that?' Edward checked.

'Yes,' he said firmly.

'But you can't remember where you got it from?'

Wells scowled at him. 'I told you it was a gift; I get a lot of gifts.'

Edward raised his eyebrows. 'Well, this particular gift would have cost over two thousand dollars. That's over a thousand pounds, and that is a very generous gift.' Wells shrugged indifferently.

'It's an eighteen-carat gold nugget ring, and the gold is of the highest purity,' Edward continued; he looked up. 'Do you know where it was made?' Wells stared at him with a disinterested smirk. 'The gold comes from Ballarat in Australia,' Edward told him.

'And each ring is unique, due to the differences in the size and shape of the nuggets. Do you know what else makes this particular ring unique?' He waited for a reply, but Wells remained silent. 'I'll tell you then, shall I?' Edward asked brightly.

'After the ring was found in your gym, we sent it over to our forensics department, and we have an excellent forensics department here, they're very thorough,' he said proudly. Seemingly unable to think of anything smug to say, Wells made do with staring at him. 'Can you guess what they found between the nuggets?' Edward asked; but there was still no answer.

Edward tilted his head and stared back at him enquiringly. 'No? You can't guess? I'll tell you that as well then, shall I? They found traces of our pathologist's skin; can you explain that?' And then without giving Wells time to answer, he recapped.

'So, an Australian man, that's Graham Pickering by the way, arrives in this country less than two months ago. He's wearing a gold nugget ring which also comes from Australia. He then hits someone in Yorkshire, taking the skin off with said ring,' he stopped talking and smiled.

'Are you following this?' He checked. 'Anyway, Pickering is then found murdered but the ring is missing. Now we know that your manager, the late Mr Paige, was involved in his death, and yet you maintain that you've had an exact replica of this ring, complete with the skin of a pathologist from Yorkshire for a couple of years. Now that is a huge coincidence, don't you think?

'Do you happen to know our pathologist, Sir? And if so, have you hit him recently?' He asked benignly.

'I would like to speak to the solicitor now,' Wells said quietly.

Chapter 8

Steven watched Heather get into bed and wondered if he had the nerve to ask her. Having decided that she was the one he wanted to spend the rest of his life with, it was just a case of choosing the right moment. He lay on his back with his hands behind his head looking at the ceiling.

'What are you thinking about?' She whispered.

He gave a small laugh. 'Everything and nothing.'

She leant on her elbow and looked down at him. 'Are you ok?'

'Yes,' he confirmed.

'Can I ask you a favour then?' He squinted at her in the half light. 'Will it cost me money or cause me pain?'

Heather manoeuvred herself on top of him and kissed his nose. 'It'll only cause you pain if you say no,' she whispered wickedly, and then moved her knee so that it was resting between his legs.

Steven ran his hands slowly down her back. 'Well in that case what can I do for you?' He enquired.

'Can I borrow your car tomorrow to go and see dad please?' She asked coyly.

'Oh, I don't know about that,' he teased, and gave her buttocks a gentle squeeze.

'I'll do that thing you like,' she promised.

He suddenly caught her off guard and rolled her onto her back. 'And what particular thing that would be?'

'You choose,' she giggled.

'Well as you do so many things I like, I can't really say no, can I?' He kissed her neck. 'Of course you can use the car, you can drop me at work with my bike and I'll cycle home,' he continued to kiss her as he moved down her body. 'These are very sexy,' he murmured as he reached her stomach and ran his tongue along the life lines.

275

She slid down the bed and joined him under the duvet. 'It's supposed to be me doing the thing you like,' she scolded.

Judy looked up in surprise as Steven pushed his bike into the reception the next morning. 'Heather's borrowed the car to go and see her dad,' he explained to her quizzical look.

'Aren't you worried about her driving on her own?' She asked.

He had been worried, but Heather was determined to go. 'I'll keep to the main roads and I'll ring you when I get there,' she promised. 'I'm more worried about her threat to clean the car out,' he muttered, but Judy had returned to her knitting so he went to get changed.

'Don't forget we're going for a scan later,' she called after him.

He stuck his head out of the locker room. 'Brain scan?' He enquired, and then hastily retreated before she could find anything to throw at him.

'Come and look at this, boss,' Charlie called a couple of hours later. Steven went into the reception where they were inspecting a print out of the latest scan. 'Look, you can see his little willie,' Charlie said excitedly.

Steven peered closely. 'Isn't that an arm?' He teased.

They were so engrossed in the scan that they didn't hear the reception door opening. 'Hello, Stevie,' a familiar voice said quietly.

Steven turned around with his stomach lurching. 'My name is Steven, and what the hell do you want?' He said through gritted teeth.

The slim and immaculately dressed brunette woman standing behind him smiled nervously. 'Well, that's no way to greet an old friend,' she took a step closer, and glanced at Judy and Charlie who were watching with interest. 'Aren't you going to introduce me to your new friends?' She asked, almost as if she was talking to a child.

Steven shook his head. 'What do you want?' He repeated.

The woman looked around and spotted his bike leaning on the wall. 'Still riding the silly old bike then,' she chuckled nervously.

'Hardly at all actually since you have been out of my life,' he snapped. 'Now what do you want?'

She gave a little shrug. 'I just want to talk, ok?'

Steven gave an incredulous laugh. 'No, not ok. I've got absolutely nothing to say to you and no interest in anything you have to say, so you might as well just crawl back to Martin,' he went to the door and held it open. What the hell did I ever see in her, he thought, as she stood in the middle of the reception, looking like a pathetic over made up Barbie doll.

'Actually, I'm not with Martin, we split up a couple of months ago,' she said quietly.

Steven gave a sniff of distain. 'Well like I said, I'm not interested, now if you don't mind, I'm busy.' His head started to pound as she took a tissue out of her bag.

'Please, Steven,' she begged with her lips quivering under the bright red lipstick. 'I just need to talk to someone,' she dabbed her eyes and sat down.

'Well you should have found someone closer to home to talk to and saved the petrol,' Steven said sarcastically. He turned to Charlie. 'Get her out of here please, and if she won't leave, then call security,' He pushed his bike through the doors, then peddled furiously out of the hospital grounds and headed towards the moors road without looking back.

'I assume you're Amy?' Charlie said dryly; she nodded and offered him her hand. Charlie ignored it and opened the door. 'I think you had better leave,' he said firmly.

'Will you tell Stevie that I'll call back another day?' She said brightly, her tears mysteriously gone.

Judy, who had been silent up to now suddenly found her voice. 'You must be bloody joking. I'm surprised you can even show your face after what you did to him,' she said vehemently.

Charlie stared at her in amazement. Was this his mild tempered Judy who always saw the best in everyone? 'You've got a nerve,' she continued. 'Now get out and don't bother coming back because you're not welcome.'

Amy stared at Judy's stomach. 'Are you seeing Stevie then?'

Judy took a step towards her. 'His name is Steven, now get out,' she hissed. They stood at the door and watched as she drove away.

'Remind me to never make you angry,' Charlie said in wonder. 'By the way will you marry me?' He added, but Judy didn't hear him.

'Bloody cow,' she muttered as she stared after the car. 'I hope Steven's alright,' she said concernedly. 'Sorry honey, what did you say?'

Charlie rolled his eyes at her. 'I said will you marry me?'

Her face broke into a beaming smile. 'At last, I thought you'd never ask,' she exclaimed.

'Is that a yes then?' He asked hopefully. She nodded happily and went back to looking at the scan.

Twenty minutes later, still peddling furiously and with his head feeling like it was going to explode, Steven had reached the moors road. Seeing Amy again had brought back memories of the humiliation and anger he had felt when she abandoned him at the altar. 'Bitch,' he said bitterly; he stopped peddling and freewheeled, then realised that he was still wearing his mortuary overalls and behaving like an idiot.

'You bloody fool,' he muttered; then turned around and started to make his way back. He thought about Heather as he rode along. 'She's worth more than a thousand Amy's,' he told himself, and wondering if she would be home. He bypassed the hospital road and headed towards his father's house.

His car wasn't outside when he got there, and having left work so suddenly he had nothing with him. 'Shit! No house keys,' he said to himself. He stood in the road for a moment contemplating whether or not to go back to work.

'Steven,' a voice behind him said nervously. He turned around and saw Sheila, who having spotted him had come out of her house. 'Has something happened to Edward?' She asked anxiously.

He shook his head and explained about Amy, and after declining her offer of a cup of tea and a chat, he borrowed her key and made his way next door but one. Monty came to great him as he opened the door, then purred loudly as he bent down to stroke him. 'You'll never guess who turned up today,' Steven said to the cat.

He was suddenly aware of someone walking up the path behind him, the cat disappeared up the stairs as he stood up and turned around. 'Dr Steven Cooper?' The man who was approaching the door enquired.

'Yes,' he confirmed.

The man stared at him for a second; then produced a gun from his pocket and pushed it into Steven's chest. 'Get inside,' he ordered.

Edward leaned on the desk and stared at the full evidence board. 'If it's not Wells, then who the hell is it?' He said exasperatedly.

'I don't know,' Jack admitted. 'Right, let's start from the beginning again,' he said, and then groaned impatiently as they were interrupted by the phone. Jack picked it up and handed it to him.

'Well bring her up then,' he said to the voice on the other end. 'Heather's down in reception,' he answered to Jack's enquiry.

There was worry etched on Heather's face when she was shown in two minutes later. 'Is everything alright?' Edward asked. She shook her head, then delved into her bag and took two items out.

'I found these in the back of Steven's car.' She put a mobile phone and a package on Edward's desk. Jack unrolled the package, and a large pink diamond fell out.

'Bloody hell,' he exclaimed.

'I found them in the storage pocket behind Steven's seat,' Heather explained before they could ask. 'Sam must have put them in there when he picked them up from the station.'

Jack held the diamond up and watched the reflections on the wall as the light caught it. 'Christ! It's enormous.'

Edward picked the phone up. 'Which one do I press to turn it on?'

Jack put the diamond down and took it from him. He switched it on and waited for it to beep into life. 'Right! Let's see what we've got,' he muttered as he scrolled down through the phonebook. 'Well there's no Alex or Gorman,' he quietly read the names out.

'Oh my God,' he said suddenly. 'He's got a Simon R in here,' he glanced at Edward nervously, and then got his own phone out. 'It's not the same number as I have though.' He picked Sam's phone up again and looked in the call log. There were a dozen missed calls and several text messages.

Most of them were from his father, but there were a couple from Simon R, all made on the day, or the day after the wedding. He looked at Edward again, his horrified expression asking the question that he couldn't bear to ask verbally. 'It would explain an awful lot,' Edward said seriously.

They stared at each other both hoping that they were wrong. 'Well there's only one way to find out,' Edward said eventually.

'Shall I do it?' Jack shook his head.

'No, it's ok,' he pressed the number and waited. It rang several times before a familiar voice told him to leave a message. He went white and sat down. 'It is him,' he said quietly. 'For God's sake,' Edward muttered angrily as the internal phone rang again; he picked it up. 'What?' He snapped.

'Sorry to disturb you Sir but your wife is on line three and she says it's urgent,' the duty officer told him.

Edward took a deep breath and pressed the button. Jack and Heather watched his expression change as he listened to what Sheila had to say. 'Are you certain?' He checked. 'Lock yourself in until we get there,' he ordered.

'What is it, guv?' Jack asked as he put the phone down.

'Apparently, Steven has just been forced into the house by a man with a gun,' he told them.

Heather sat down heavily. 'What?' She whispered in horror.

'You stay here,' Edward ordered as he and Jack ran out of the door.

Steven was standing in his father's hall, staring into the face of Inspector Simon Reynolds. 'Do you know who I am?' Reynolds asked. Steven shook his head and tried to stay calm. 'But you know what I want, don't you?' Reynolds checked.

He shook his head again. 'Come on, Steven,' Reynolds said disbelievingly. 'You surely can't think that I'm that stupid,' he produced a pair of handcuffs. 'Hands behind your back,' he ordered. 'Just in case you decide to be a hero,' he growled sarcastically as he snapped the cuffs on. 'Now where is it?'

Steven stared at the gun. 'Where's what?'

Reynolds face twisted into a sneer. 'I'm not a patient man,' he warned menacingly. 'Now where is it?'

Steven couldn't take his eyes off the gun. 'I don't know what you are talking about,' he said nervously.

'I'm talking about the diamond of course,' Reynolds snapped. Steven looked up in shock.

'What diamond?'

Reynolds narrowed his eyes. 'The bloody diamond that Sam Pickering brought into the country up his arse of course.' He moved closer, his eyes were now blazing with anger. 'You picked him up from the station, you found him in the toilet and you did the post-mortem, so you must have found it,' he snapped.

'I don't know anything about a diamond,' Steven said quietly, trying desperately to stop his voice from shaking. Reynolds gestured towards the lounge. 'Get in there.'

A knot started forming in Steven stomach as Reynolds paced around the room muttering to himself; he sat down still keeping his eyes firmly on the gun. 'Get up,' Reynolds snapped; he gave him a look of contempt. 'Your family has caused me an awful lot of grief,' he said bitterly as Steven got unsteadily to his feet.

'That bloody father of yours just couldn't leave well alone, could he? We could have been thousands of miles away by now,' he suddenly stopped pacing. 'That it isn't it? He's in on it too.'

Steven desperately tried to imagine what was going on in Reynolds mind. 'In on what?' He asked.

'You're going to wait until the fuss dies down and then sell it?'

Steven's throat suddenly felt constricted. 'I told you I don't know what you are talking about.' It suddenly occurred to him that this was probably the man who had already killed at least four people, and he wouldn't think twice about killing him. Christ! I'm going to die, and I haven't told Heather that I love her. His legs turned to jelly, and he could feel his pulse beating wildly in the scar on his neck.

'Where the fuck is it?' Reynolds repeated menacingly; he jabbed the gun into his side. 'Well?' Steven looked into his enraged face and wondered what he could say to convince him. He glanced at the gun, barely able to speak for fear.

'Heroin, all I found was heroin, ten phials, nine intact one broken,' he gasped. Reynolds was starting to sweat. He pushed the barrel hard into Steven's neck.

'Don't play fucking games with me. The kid still had it on him at the station when you picked him up,' he said through gritted teeth.

Steven stayed quiet, unable to think of anything else to say that might persuade him, but his heart was pounding so hard that he could hear the blood rushing around in his head. He caught sight of a picture of his parents on the sideboard and stared at it.

Reynolds cocked the gun and put his mouth close to his ear. 'Are you really going to die for it?' He hissed. Steven shook his head; then closed his eyes and tried to concentrate on his legs, which were now on the verge of giving way. 'Scared, are you?' Reynolds chuckled. Steven opened his eyes and looked at him. 'Last chance doc,' but he didn't get to finish the sentence, as a single shot rang out.

Steven watched in horror, as the bullet smashed through the window and into Reynolds forehead. His head snapped back with the velocity of the hit, then the bullet passed through his brain and blew a hole in his skull as it exited, spraying Steven, who was just inches away, with blood and tissue, before embedding itself in the wall. The gun dropped to the floor as Reynolds fell back. He landed on the coffee table with his eyes fixed in shock at the suddenness of death.

Steven's pulse continued to race as he stared at him. Then the police announced their arrival with a loud crash as they broke the door down; shouting and footsteps followed, and seconds later his father's arms were around him, as his legs finally gave way.

He sat in the casualty department two hours later. 'I'm alright. I just want to go home.' He looked up as he heard Heather's voice, she pushed her way into the cubicle and threw her arms around him.

He buried his face in her hair. 'I love you,' he whispered.

The doctor and Edward retreated to the next cubicle. 'Can he go home?' Edward asked quietly.

'I think that would be the best place for him,' the doctor agreed. They moved to a respectable distance as they heard tearful whispering coming from next door. 'What about the officer who shot the gunman, do you want me to arrange counselling?' The doctor asked.

Edward shook his head. 'He'll be seeing the police psychologist. Of course, it's not going to help that the man he shot used to be one of his best friends,' he added. Four days later, Edward was ready to give Whittle his report. 'Sit down,' the Chief Superintendent invited. 'I need to speak to you when you've finished.' Edward was totally exhausted and keen to get home, but he sat down with a sigh, and hoping that Whittle wouldn't notice, he started giving a condensed report.

'Three years ago, a rare pink diamond was stolen from a diamond house in Cape Town. Alex Gorman was the main suspect, but he disappeared soon after it was stolen, it was later discovered that he had fled to Australia. The police assumed that he intended to lie low until the fuss had died down and then sell it on.

'Whilst he was in Australia, he met Graham Pickering, he told him about Robin Paige, who he knew had been in the pawn trade, and having also dealt in stolen goods. He had the connections to sell the diamond on for him. Graham also knew that his son, Sam, was flying over for the wedding and would be less likely to be suspected of smuggling, so he recruited him to bring diamond into the country.

'What he didn't know was that Sam had already agreed to carry the heroin. He agreed to carry the diamond as well, but as it was too big to swallow, he inserted it into his rectum instead; this caused the legions around his anus which were found during the post-mortem. Steven thinks that it was the diamond that caused of one of the phials break,' he paused for breath before continuing.

'Robin Paige was also working for Andrew Wells, who was bringing in illegal immigrants for the vice trade. Paige was his general manager, and they used his business as a front.'

Whittle put his hand up to stop him. 'Where does Inspector Reynolds fit in?'

Edward turned the page. 'During the course of one of the investigations into his company, Simon Reynolds discovered what Wells was doing, and for a cut of the profits he kept the police off his back, we also think that as Sam Pickering had his mobile number in his list that he was the contact for the heroin. We are still waiting for the Sydney police department to get back to us on that. Perhaps you could chase them up?' He suggested.

Whittle nodded, and indicated for him to continue. 'Robin Paige told Reynolds about the diamond, and after Sam died, he decided that as he had lost the heroin, he would take a cut of the profits from the sale of the diamond instead. When I informed Graham Pickering of his son's death, he flew over to the UK, bringing Alex Gorman with him. They met up with Reynolds and booked into the Firs hotel under the name of Smith.'

'What about the wig and false nail?' Whittle interrupted.

'Alex Gorman disguised himself as a woman,' Edward reminded him. 'When Graham Pickering told Gorman and Reynolds that he hadn't found the diamond in the toilet where Sam had died, and he was unable to search his belongings, they thought he was lying and going to keep it. They had an argument in the hotel which was witnessed by the porter, and then they ransacked Pickering's room looking for it. But obviously they didn't find it and so they beat him up.'

Whittle put his hand up again. 'Where did they do this?'

Edward frowned at him. 'We can't be sure but we think it was in their room at the Firs. We also think that Beverly Penrose either heard or saw them doing it, so they killed her by drowning her in the bath, having first rendered her unconscious. Then they drove to the mortuary in Gold's car and forced Pickering to cut his own son open to see if the diamond was still inside him.'

He looked up as Whittle cleared his throat. 'How do you know it was Gold's car?'

'Because we found both Graham Pickering's and the security guard's blood on the jack handle,' Edward explained.

'And how was Gold involved?' Whittle checked.

'She was Reynolds girlfriend; she dealt with the legal side of things, and with the connections she had through her work as a solicitor, she provided false work permits, passports, and any other legal documents that they needed.' He waited for Whittle to comment but he made do with nodding. 'Whilst they were at the mortuary, Paige was dumping Beverly Penrose in the Ouse and picking Trudy Baines up.

'He then took her back to the hotel to pose as Beverly,' Edward took a deep breath and turned the page.

'When they didn't find the diamond inside Sam or amongst his belongings, Gorman and Reynolds assumed that the pathologist had found it during the post-mortem. They took Pickering back to the hotel; they went in through the fire door that Paige had left open. Once they got Pickering back to his room, they slit his throat with the knife they had taken from the mortuary.

'They knew that the body would be found fairly quickly, so Gorman and Reynolds checked out early the next morning, leaving Pickering's key at the reception. Trudy Baines checked out as Beverly Penrose minutes after them, and was dropped off at her pitch. Her statement is supplement one.

'They then went back to London to decide what to do, but stupidly they had removed Pickering's ring and gold chain which they gave to Wells. He was wearing the ring when I questioned him about the car that had been used in the kidnap of Ms Brooks. Gorman came back from London with Gold and they rented the station house, this time using the name Brown.

'In the meantime, Reynolds had looked Steven up on the police computer; he sent Paige and Gorman to search his house, but when they didn't find anything, they kept watch until Ms Brooks returned to collect the cat. Then they then ran her off the road and kidnapped her. The report on her kidnapping and her statement is supplement two.

'Trudy Baines identified Paige when he was caught, so Gorman, probably posing as a punter, picked Zoë Fairfax up. He took her to the station house where Reynolds was waiting and got her to call Trudy and entice her to the house with the promise of good money, but when she arrived, she was forced to witness Zoë's murder, with the threat that the same thing would happen to her if she didn't retract her statement.

'Trudy's statement and the pathologists report is supplement three. Gorman took Zoë's body and dumped her at the picnic spot; then he went back to the station house, where as we now know from Veronica Gold's statement, he made a pass at Reynolds.'

'So, Gorman was gay!' Whittle exclaimed.

Edward nodded. 'Which we can only assume led to a fight, resulting in Gorman being stabbed. The wound didn't kill him but it would have disabled him. Reynolds brought the propane cylinders into the house and laid the probably unconscious Gorman over the top of them, but he must have cut his hand because his blood was found on one of the tanks.

'After starting a fire in the bedroom where Zoë had been killed, he opened the valves on the cylinders and drove back to London leaving the house to burn. Gorman was blown up along with the cylinders when the fire ignited the gas, which would explain the massive damage to his body. The fire officer's report, pathology and forensics are supplement four.

'With Paige on remand and threatening to talk, Reynolds dispatched Gold to deal with him. Reynolds hair and fingerprints were found in Gold's car, along with those of the remand centre guard. His statement, forensics from Gold's car and the transcript from the observation tape are supplement five.

'By now, Reynolds was on emergency leave having invented a family crisis. He came back to Yorkshire and was watching Steven. He followed him back to my house where he confronted him. Reports and statements are supplement six,' Edward took a deep breath. 'And that's about it,' he stood up, desperate to get home.

'Very thorough,' Whittle commended.

Edward was unmoved by his senior officer's uncommon praise. 'Is there anything else, Sir?'

'Actually there is,' Whittle said brightly. Edward sat down again as he pulled a sheet of paper from his drawer. 'According to the diamond house that it was stolen from, the diamond that Ms Brooks found in your son's car is worth an awful lot of money,' he looked at the sheet. 'In fact, it was valued at two million south African Rand.'

He raised his eyebrows and waited for a reaction, but Edward was trying to stifle a yawn, and hardly registered what he had said. 'A reward was offered for its return,' Whittle continued.

'Right. Sir,' Edward responded, as unable to stop it the yawn broke through.

Whittle handed him the paper. 'I'm not quite sure who should have the reward,' he said exasperatedly.

Edward looked at the paper. 'That's a lot of Rand, how much is it in sterling?'

Whittle gave a triumphant smile, and produced a currency converter from his desk. 'I've been dying to try this out,' he said as he tapped the numbers in. 'It was a birthday present from my wife,' he added unnecessarily. He nodded approvingly as the conversion was revealed. 'Just under ninety thousand pounds.'

Edward raised his eyebrows in shock. 'I think the money should go to Maria Catacazi,' he said after a minute.

'Why?' Whittle enquired dryly.

Edward scowled at him, wondering if he had a compassionate bone in his body. 'Because in her country, it would set her up for life, and she is going to try and get custody of her murdered sister's baby, which if she succeeds, will need money.'

'What about Ms Brooks, she found the diamond so surely she should get the reward,' Whittle said quite rightly.

Edward gave a light shrug. 'Ask her if she wants it,' he suggested.

'And if she doesn't then ask her if she thinks the Catacazi family should have it, or did you have another charitable case in mind?' He enquired semi sarcastically.

'Now if you don't mind, I really do need to get home to my wife,' he got up again and went out, leaving Whittle staring at the report.

'You'll be happy to know that Andrew Wells has been charged with bringing illegal immigrants into the country with the intention of supplying the vice trade, and also with aiding and abetting a murderer,' Whittle told him a couple of days later. 'There were traces of Zoë Fairfax's blood found in one of his vans,' he explained to Edward's quizzical look.

'Obviously, he couldn't be charged with false imprisonment or rape, as we only had the Catacazi girl's word, and although he fathered her baby, there's no proof that he raped the sister either.' He stared into space for a while. 'Anyway, as you suggested I spoke to Ms Brooks, and she agreed that the reward money should go to the Catacazi family, so I have put the wheels in motion,' he gave a satisfied smile and nodded. 'I'm not completely heartless you know,' he said brightly.

'It never crossed my mind that you were,' Edward lied, and smiled to himself as he went out.

Chapter 9

A few weeks later, Steven gripped Heather's hand tightly and watched as Jack took the stand. After being sworn in, he sat down, and the coroner asked him to relate the events that led to the shooting of Inspector Reynolds. The courtroom was silent as Jack looked straight ahead and started talking.

'After the call from Inspector Cooper's wife, we alerted the armoury and arranged to be met at the location with the necessary equipment.'

'The necessary equipment being what?' The coroner interrupted.

Jack looked over to him. 'An HK33SG1 sniper rifle, Sir.' The coroner nodded and told him to continue. 'It took us less than ten minutes to reach the location; we didn't sound the sirens as we didn't want to panic the gunman into doing anything rash. When we arrived, the road had been sealed off and the weapon was on site.

'After taking instructions from Detective Chief Inspector Cooper, I positioned myself in the bedroom of the house opposite. From this position I could see into the property using the scope that was attached to the rifle,' he stopped talking and took a drink of water.

'What did you see?' The coroner asked.

'I looked through all the front windows of the house. When I got to the bay window on the ground floor, I saw that the gunman was Inspector Simon Reynolds, and Dr Cooper was with him.' Jack glanced at Steven. 'Dr Cooper had his back to the window; I could see that his arms were handcuffed behind him. Inspector Reynolds was facing him and he had a pistol pushed into his neck.'

Heather tightened her grip on Steven's hand as Jack continued. 'Inspector Reynolds was saying something, obviously I don't know what, but from his expression and body language I could tell that he was very angry.'

The coroner put his hand up to stop him. 'Was negotiation an option at that point?'

Jack shook his head. 'No, Sir, as I watched, I saw him cock the gun, and I knew that I had to act quickly.'

The coroner looked at his notes. 'Did Detective Chief Inspector Cooper give you the order to fire?'

'No, Sir, I made an independent decision to fire based on the fact that I was the only one who could see what was happening, and I believe that if I had waited then he would have shot Dr Cooper.'

Steven put his arm around Heather as she started to shake. 'It's ok,' he whispered.

'So you took aim and fired?' The coroner enquired.

'Yes, Sir,' Jack confirmed.

'Just one shot?'

'Yes, Sir.'

'Where about on his body did you shoot him?'

'In the forehead.'

The coroner wrote something down. 'How long after reaching the scene did you actually pull the trigger?'

Jack glanced at Steven again. 'Three minutes and twenty-seven seconds,' he said precisely. Steven closed his eyes as the memory of being only minutes away from death flooded back.

'What did you do after you had fired the weapon?' The coroner asked.

'I said target down. I waited until I saw the officers enter the house. A colleague then confirmed verbally that the target was dead. I put the safety catch on the weapon, and handed it over to be returned to the armoury,' Jack let out a long breath.

'Do you have anything to add?' The coroner asked him.

'No, Sir,' he said firmly. The coroner raised his eyebrows. 'I'm informed that Inspector Reynolds was a friend of yours, Sergeant Taylor.'

Steven looked up in shock as Jack nodded. 'We were colleagues in London.'

The coroner looked at his notes and frowned. 'You were more than colleagues, weren't you? I believe that you were good friends,' he gave him a serious look. 'Wasn't he the best man at your wedding?'

Jack looked at Edward before answering. 'Yes, Sir, he was.' A small gasp echoed around the hushed room. 'But that doesn't alter the fact that he had already killed four people and was going to kill another one,' Jack continued. He looked at the bench, and addressed the coroner directly. 'I don't condone killing,

288

Sir, but when innocent people are being threatened, they have a right to be protected.'

The coroner nodded. 'Thank you, Sergeant Taylor, you may step down.' Steven was stunned by what he had just heard; he watched as Jack made his way back to his seat, and then got up to give his own evidence as his name was called.

'Jack, have you got a minute?' He called an hour later.

Jack turned around and smiled as he sprinted over to him. 'Hi, how are things?'

Steven nodded. 'Fine, thanks,' he hesitated as he tried to find the right words. 'I just wanted to say thanks again for what you did,' he said humbly. 'I don't really know what else to say.'

Jack put his hand up. 'I was just doing my job,' he insisted.

'I know but he was your friend.'

'Was my friend,' Jack interrupted. 'Was as in the past tense, he stopped being my friend when he started killing people.' Steven nodded and the two men shook hands. 'You can buy me a pint sometime,' Jack chuckled; he smiled warmly and then pulled him into a hug. 'Go on, Steve, someone's waiting for you,' he whispered.

Steven turned around and saw his father and Heather watching them. 'A pint it is then,' he promised.

Jack watched as he went over them. 'I'll hold you too it,' he called before joining his own wife who was waiting in the car.

Chapter 10

Steven looked out of the kitchen window thinking how lucky he was. Having first installed alarms, they had moved back to the cottage and he was happy to be home. Heather came in and patted his bottom. 'Penny for them.'

He sighed contentedly and kissed her. 'I'm just happy to be here,' he admitted.

'Yes, me too,' she agreed. 'Come on, let's take Ben out, then we can celebrate,' she wrapped her arms around his neck and gave him a long lingering kiss.

'Oh right,' he smiled when she pulled away.

The sun was starting to go down leaving the sky a mass of colour. 'It is beautiful up here, I must try and get up more often,' he said as they set out across the moors.

She put her arm around him. 'You should,' she agreed. Twenty minutes later, they stopped at the top of a rise to look at the view. Steven glanced down at her; wondering if now would be a good time to propose. He fingered his mother's engagement ring which was in his pocket, and which he had been carrying around with him, waiting for the right moment.

Ben bounded around chasing nothing in particular, until he saw Monty picking his way through the gorse. He ran over to play then swerved as the cat hissed at him. 'You coward,' Heather chided; her face lit up as she laughed at them. Steven stared down at her thinking how much he wanted her. 'You're staring,' she scolded and gave him a light dig in the ribs.

'I was just thinking that the dog isn't the only coward,' he said quietly.

'What do you mean?' She asked.

'I mean that I'm a coward too,' he said nervously.

'You're not a coward. You're the bravest person I know,' she exclaimed.

'Well, you can't know that many people then,' he muttered.

She pulled him around to face her; a look of fear appeared in her eyes as she stared at him. 'What are you talking about?' He stared back unable to answer. 'Are you trying to tell me something?' She demanded.

His stomach flipped as he looked into her worried face. 'For God's sake, Steven, if you've got something to tell me then just say it, I'm a big girl I can take it.'

He gave a nervous laugh. 'I don't have anything to tell you, but I do have something to ask you.'

'Spit it out then,' she ordered. Steven's mouth suddenly felt very dry; he licked his lips and smiled nervously. 'Well?' She demanded.

'I love you,' he whispered.

Heather frowned at him. 'I know you do, but that's a statement not a question.'

Pull yourself together man; just ask her, he told himself. 'Do you love me?'

A smile played on her lips. 'You know I do,' she waited for a minute. 'Is that it then?' He hesitated and then nodded. 'Right, so now we've established that we love each other,' she started to walk away but he grabbed her hand and pulled her back.

'Actually, that's not it,' he took a deep breath. 'What I really wanted to ask is if you will marry me?' He swallowed hard even though his mouth was bone dry. Heather gave him a look of disbelief. 'You don't have to decide right now, just have a think about it when you've got time,' he said quickly.

'Why do you want to marry me?' She asked incredulously.

'Because I love you,' he spluttered. His heart sank. Shit! I knew it was too soon, she's going to say no he thought miserably.

'Is that the only reason?'

It was his turn to be puzzled. 'What other reason would there be?'

She started to smile. 'Well, I thought that you being, and I quote "a sort of doctor" you might have guessed that I'm pregnant.'

Steven's jaw dropped. 'What?'

'I'm pregnant,' she repeated.

'Pregnant? When? How?' He spluttered.

'Well, if you don't know at your age,' she teased.

He laughed nervously. 'I didn't mean how did it happen, I thought you were on the pill.'

Her face fell. 'I am, it must have been the antibiotics they gave me for the gash on my head,' she said tearfully.

He suddenly realised that she thought he was cross. He put his arms around her and kissed her head. 'Don't cry, it's fantastic news.'

She looked up at him through her tears. 'You're not angry then?'

'Are you kidding. It's the best news I've had since,' he stopped talking and kissed her again.

'Since what?' She asked.

'Since they told me that you were going to pull through last year.'

She smiled up at him impishly. 'So you didn't ask me to marry you because you've got me up the duff then?'

He shook his head and tried not to laugh, but failed miserably. 'Absolutely not,' he assured her.

'In that case, I would love to marry you, Dr Cooper.'

He scooped her up and hugged her. 'Wow! More good news,' he exclaimed. He suddenly remembered the ring, he put her down and dug it out of his pocket,' 'I hope you don't mind,' he said as he slipped it on her finger. 'It was mums.'

She looked at it with tears in her eyes. 'It's beautiful, a bit big, but beautiful.'

He leant over and kissed her gently. 'Well that can soon be fixed, so now the dogs been out, what about that celebration?' He reminded her.

A week later, they drove Edward and Sheila to the airport to start their delayed honeymoon. 'Are you sure you've got everything?' Steven checked.

Edward squeezed Sheila's hand. 'I've got the most important thing.' Heather smiled at their beaming faces as Sheila blushed. Having decided to tell them about the baby as they went to the plane, they could barely contain themselves.

They sat in the café trying not to smile too widely. 'Are you two alright?' Sheila asked; they nodded in unison both wearing silly grins. She looked at them suspiciously, then got up as their flight was called.

'Have a great time,' Heather said as she kissed them goodbye.

Steven shook his father's hand and gave Sheila a kiss. 'Look after him for me,' he whispered.

They watched as they made their way towards the departure lounge. 'Now or it'll be too late,' Heather said urgently. Steven put his arm around her.

'Dad, Sheila,' he called as they reached the security gate. They turned around and waved happily. 'You're going to be grandparents,' he yelled as they were ushered out of sight.

Case Three
Two Months Later
For the Love of Heather

Chapter 1

Are you excited, boss?' Charlie asked. Steven nodded and looked at the clock for the umpteenth time. Just another hour to go. Heather was calling to collect him before her first scan and he couldn't wait. The hour ticked by incredibly slowly as he tried to concentrate on the pair of lungs in front of him.

'Go on then,' Charlie nodded towards the observation room. Steven looked across and saw Heather watching him, and although he had only seen her a few hours earlier, his heart leapt.

'Come on,' she shouted through the glass.

'Will you finish this?' He asked Charlie.

The younger man nodded; with Judy on maternity leave and only a few weeks away from giving birth herself, he knew the anticipation that Steven was feeling. 'See you later,' he called as they rushed out.

Steven held Heather's hand tightly and watched as the radiologist, a ruddy face woman called Sandra, ran the probe across her stomach. She pointed to a small pulse beating away. 'That's a good strong heartbeat.' She moved the probe to the other side and frowned as she studied the monitor, then she moved back to the heartbeat again.

'What's the matter,' Heather asked anxiously.

'Try not to move but don't worry,' Sandra ordered. She moved the probe again then looked up at Steven and smiled.

'Well, Dr Cooper, what do you make of that?'

Steven stared at the image on the monitor, then gave a small gasp, as the realisation of what the she had seen hit him. 'Bloody hell!' He exclaimed. He looked down at Heather's worried face. 'There are two,' he whispered.

'Is there a history of twins in either of your families?' Sandra enquired.

Steven shook his head. 'I'll ask dad,' Heather said excitedly. They looked in wonder at the two heartbeats pulsating on the screen.

Sandra smiled at their beaming faces. 'I assume you'll want a photo,' she commented.

Steven could hardly contain his joy as he made his way back to the mortuary. As Heather's father was out of the country, she was going to ring him when she got home, but they had decided to tell his father and Sheila in person that evening. Charlie looked up as he went in. 'How was it then?'

Steven put the photograph in front of him; he picked it up and studied it. 'Very nice,' he commented, then looked harder.

'What?' Steven asked innocently, Charlie frowned at him. 'It looks like…'

'Yes, it is,' Steven butted in.

'What is what?' Sue asked as she came in.

Steven showed her the scan. 'Twins,' he said ecstatically.

He gazed at the picture again until Sue dampened the mood. 'Here are the results from the nasty pancreas,' she said brightly. Steven tore his eyes away from the scan and took the report.

'Killjoy,' he muttered, and reluctantly put the picture down. 'Right, what's next?' He asked Charlie.

'Where's Marjorie?' He enquired as the phone rang an hour later. The Marjorie in question was a prim sixty something lady who had been sent from an agency, and who had been described as an exceptional receptionist.

Charlie shrugged. 'She went out for lunch I think.'

Steven glanced at the clock and groaned. 'Bloody temps,' he muttered. The phone stopped but rang again almost immediately. Steven put the scalpel down and swore to himself.

'I'll get it, boss,' Charlie offered; he took his gloves off and went into the reception.

'Was it important?' Steven asked when he came back a few minutes later.

'You could say that,' he said almost in despair. 'It was Marjorie; she's not coming back,' he put a new pair of gloves on and returned to the bench. 'Apparently, she couldn't bear the thought of being in the same building as dead bodies,' he muttered. 'Anyway, I've switched the phone through to here,' he told Steven wryly.

Across town, Edward was ploughing his way through a mountain of paperwork, and wondering if he would ever reach the bottom. He gave a sigh of relief as Jack stuck his head around door. 'There's someone here to see you, guv.' He opened the door wide, to reveal Maria Catacazi standing in the squad room with a small dark-haired child in her arms.

'I just came to thank you and to introduce my niece,' she said in much improved English. The child looked at him suspiciously with big brown eyes before burying her face in Maria's neck. 'Don't be shy, Jenica,' she murmured.

Edward raised his eyebrows. 'Her names Jenica?'

Maria nodded. 'Jenica Rose after her mother; you called her Rose before you knew her name, and it's such a nice name,' she explained tearfully. She glanced at the clock. 'We can't stay for long as we have a plane to catch, and as I said, I just came to thank you and Mr Wattle for what you did for my sister and me.'

Edward looked around at the officers working in the squad room, who with the exception of WPC Blackwell were all trying to stifle sniggers. 'Not a word,' he ordered amusedly.

'I'll fetch the Chief Super,' Jack offered, and disappeared down the corridor without even attempting to keep a straight face. He returned a few minutes later with Whittle, who was looking more than annoyed.

'Miss Catacazi wanted to thank you, Sir,' Edward explained before he could complain about being disturbed.

Maria put her hand out. 'Thank you, Mr Wattle. I have been told that you put in words for me.' Whittle looked at her over his glasses.

'Miss Catacazi is Jenica's sister,' Jack reminded him; recognition suddenly flooded his face.

'Of course! The girl with red,' he stopped himself and shook her hand. 'You're welcome,' he said with a rare smile playing on his lips. 'And it's Whittle actually.'

Maria nodded at him. 'Of course, but now we must go, and thank you again,' she said sincerely. They watched as she made her way out with the child looking over her shoulder at them.

'You can tell who the daddy is,' Jack commented.

'She's Wells' daughter alright,' Whittle nodded resignedly. 'Well, a happy ending anyway,' he glanced around the room. 'For her at least,' they heard him mutter as he disappeared back into his office.

Later that evening, Edward sat on the couch next to Sheila and looked at the picture of the scan. He had put his house on the market and they had moved into Sheila's bungalow. 'I love the house and have some wonderful memories, but Sheila couldn't bear to live there after what happened,' he told Steven.

And after what had happened, he wasn't expecting a lot of interest, and prepared himself for a long wait. But he had underestimated the morbid fascination of the general public, and a steady stream of people had arrived to view it. Many paying particular attention to the lounge where Simon Reynolds had been shot just a few months earlier.

'I wish they'd been able to do this before you were born,' he said as they studied the scan. Sheila beamed as she looked at it.

'It's wonderful, I can't believe that I'm going to be a step-grandma,' she said excitedly.

'You'll be their true grandma,' Steven told her, then sat back and waited for them to notice.

They both looked up at the same time. 'Their?' They said in unison. 'Twins,' Sheila checked, and then burst into tears as Steven nodded. Edward gave her a tissue and looked at them seriously.

'What's the matter?' Steven asked.

'I suppose I should have told you this a long time ago,' Edward said tentatively.

Steven frowned at his father's obvious discomfort. 'What?' He asked again.

Edward looked at his hands. 'There is a history of twins in our family,' he said quietly.

'I was going to ask you about that,' Steven said, and wondered why he was looking so worried. 'Come on, Dad spit it out.'

Edward took Sheila's hand and watched Steven closely. 'Well the fact is that you were one of twins.' The words came out in a rush; he flinched as he waited for the backlash.

'What?' Steven said hoarsely.

'Your mum miscarried early on in pregnancy,' Edward said quietly. 'I'm sorry, son. We always intended to tell you, but then when your mum died, I couldn't find the words.'

Heather squeezed Steven's knee. 'Did you know?' He asked Sheila.

'Elizabeth told me,' She confessed.

All sorts of emotions hit him as he tried to take it in. He looked into the guilty faces of the two people sitting opposite him, and knew that they were waiting for him to explode with anger. He glanced at Heather and gave a wry smile. 'Well, that explains it then, doesn't it,' he said eventually.

'I suppose I should go for a long bike ride just about now,' he let out a long breath and smiled at them. 'But I really can't be bothered,' he said brightly.

'You're so beautiful,' he whispered to Heather as they lay in bed that night.

'You won't think that when I'm the size of a house,' she leant closer and kissed him. 'I never thought I would find anyone who I could love and trust,' she whispered.

Steven slid down the bed and kissed her slightly swollen tummy. 'Well, I'm glad it's me,' he smiled happily and snuggled up next to her. 'Can I ask you something?' He enquired a few minutes later.

'Anything you like,' she whispered. He leant on his elbow and looked at her seriously. 'What did you mean when you said that you trust my hands?'

'Who told you that?' She asked suspiciously.

'Dad said that's what you told Sheila,' He confessed.

'And there's me thinking that anything you tell your hairdresser is confidential,' she said in mock disgust. She took his hand and traced the lines on his palm. 'It was your hands that found my pulse, so if they're strong but gentle enough to find that, then they're strong enough to find my soul but gentle enough to look after it,' she said quietly.

'That's very profound, Ms Brooks,' he said gently.

'Anyway, guess what?' She whispered a few minutes later; she stroked his chest and kissed him longingly. Then ran her hand down to his stomach and pulled lightly at the fine hair.

'I'm not sure that a woman in your condition should even be thinking such things,' he murmured.

'Well, you'll just have to gentle with me, won't you?' She whispered. 'You won't go off me when I've got more stretch marks, will you?' She asked anxiously.

He pushed the covers back and scrutinised her body. 'I told you before they are life lines, and they are very, very sexy,' he kissed her again. 'Now what was that about being gentle?' He whispered.

Edward sat in his office the following morning, thinking how proud Elizabeth would have been of the way that Steven had reacted the night before. He glanced out of the window and smiled. Not even the freezing weather could dampen his mood.

He was still smiling as he started on the paperwork. Jack stuck his head in a few minutes later. 'Have you swallowed a coat hanger, guv?' He enquired.

Edward invited him in and told him the news. Jack smiled broadly. 'Congrats, granddad, you'll have your hands full then.'

Edward nodded happily. 'Yep, and I can't wait.'

Their baby talk was interrupted by Chief Superintendent Whittle. 'I'm sorry to disturb you, Edward,' he said in a rare moment of humanity. He closed the door and sat down with a grave look on his face. The two men stared at him suspiciously.

It was highly unusual for him to come out of his own office to speak to them. They would normally be summoned to the "inner sanctum", as it was known around the station. Edward sensed that his boss was about to deliver a bomb shell. 'What's the matter?' He asked tentatively.

Whittle glanced at Jack. 'Do you want me to leave, Sir?' He enquired.

'No! Stay please,' Edward said firmly.

Whittle cleared his throat. 'Well, I don't want to cause any undue stress to your son and his fiancé, especially now there's a baby on the way.'

'Babies,' Edward interrupted. 'Twins,' he explained to Whittle's blank look.

'Oh right, well I'd better just spit it out then,' he shifted uncomfortably in his chair. 'I'm afraid I have to inform you that Barry Mason, who as you know is Ms Brooks ex-husband, has absconded from the mental institution where he was being held.' He stopped talking and looked at Edward's horrified face.

'When?' Jack enquired.

'Last week actually,' Whittle admitted ruefully. 'And I think that Dr Cooper and Ms Brooks should be made aware of the situation.'

'It's supposed to be high security, how the hell did he get out?' Jack demanded, to his credit, Whittle managed looked embarrassed.

'Well, it appears that he was out on a shopping trip with several other inmates,' he stopped talking again as anger appeared on both men's faces. 'It's part of a rehabilitation program,' he explained.

'Rehabilitation,' Edward repeated. 'He killed his baby son less than six years ago, he shouldn't be due for anything for at least another five years,' he said bitterly.

'Didn't he have a guard with him?' Jack checked.

'Of course he did,' Whittle said sharply. 'Apparently, Mason went into a shop to use the lavatory and overpowered the guard who went with him. He then strangled him with his bare hands, and killed a member of public in order to steal his coat, hat and wallet.'

'So why have they left it until now to tell us?' Edward asked despairingly.

'They didn't consider him a danger to the general public,' Whittle started to explain.

'You just said that he killed two men,' Jack interrupted sarcastically.

'So they didn't want to alarm them, but they now have reason to believe that he was in York three days ago,' the Chief Superintendent finished, and then glared at Jack.

Edward stared at him in disbelief. 'York?'

Whittle nodded. 'Someone tried to use the stolen bank card; anyway, I'll leave you to tell your son,' he said curtly.

'Thank you, Sir,' Edward muttered; he waited for him leave and looked at Jack. 'Jesus Christ! How the hell do I tell them?' He asked.

Chapter 2

'Two bunches of flowers!' Charlie exclaimed as Steven went into the mortuary.

'Yes! And this time one of them is for a certain lady not too far away,' Steven said happily. He left Charlie manning the mortuary and drove over to York. He stopped at home en route, and found Heather in the kitchen eating cocktail cherries straight from the jar; she looked up guiltily as he came in.

'Sorry, I just fancied them,' she mumbled.

Steven picked one out and popped it in his mouth. 'Well it could be worse. It could have been gherkins or something equally smelly.'

'I suppose so,' she chuckled, and then smiled as he gave her a bunch flowers. 'When I was pregnant with Malcolm, I couldn't get enough piccalilli. I used to eat it with everything, but now I can't even stand the thought of it,' she told him.

Steven watched her closely as she spoke, and realised that it was the first time she had talked about Malcolm without crying. 'You're staring,' she accused suddenly.

'Yes I am,' he agreed happily.

'Do you want me to come with you?' She offered when he explained where he was going, and although he was tempted to say yes so that he that could spend more time with her, he shook his head.

'No, I'd better go alone,' he said ruefully. What he didn't tell her, was that he had decided to make this his last trip to Sally's grave.

When he got to the small cemetery on the outskirts of York, he was surprised to find a fresh plant on Sally's grave; he looked around and wondered who had put it there. As far as he knew, he was the only person who ever visited. He replaced the old flowers with new, and started to tell Sally about Heather and the babies.

'I'm sorry, Sal, but I'll not be visiting again. I've got to move on,' he whispered; then stood up as he felt the usual tears pricking his eyes.

'Hello, Coop, we thought we'd find you here today,' a male voice said from behind him.

Steven took a sharp intake of breath. Coop had been his nickname at catering college, and he hadn't been called it for years. In fact, Coop had been the last word uttered by the person lying in front of him six feet under. 'I don't feel well, Coop,' she said before collapsing in his arms. He could remember it vividly and it had haunted him.

He slowly turned around and was confronted by an elderly couple and a man of his own age; the man stared at him for a minute. 'My God, you've not changed a bit,' he exclaimed.

Steven started to walk away unable to think of anything to say. 'Steven!' It was the woman who called his name this time. He turned back and saw that she was crying. He took a deep breath and looked at her enquiringly. 'We had a letter and we want to talk to you,' she said tearfully.

Steven glanced at the man; he could still see the pain in his eyes. 'What are you doing here, Mick?'

The man gave a wry smile 'Looking for you, we want to talk.'

Steven put his head on one side. 'I believe we exhausted anything we had to say to each other fourteen years ago,' he glanced at the old couple. 'If you'll excuse me, I have to get back to work,' he clenched his fists and started to walk away again.

'Please, Steven we really need to speak to you,' the woman begged. 'We know it wasn't your fault that Sally died and we want to say we're sorry,' there was a desperation in her voice that he couldn't ignore. He stopped again, but unwilling to let them see the tears that were now running down his face, didn't turn around, he rooted through his pockets for a tissue; then wiped his eyes on his sleeve as Sally's father put a hand on his arm.

'We had a letter about the pathologist who did the post-mortem. They said that they were investigating his old cases, and they asked if we wanted them to re-examine Sally's case,' he told him gently.

Steven looked back at the grave. 'They didn't exhume her, did they?'

Her father shook his head 'They still had blood and tissue.' Steven swallowed his pride, and listened as Sally's parents told him what he already knew; that there was no evidence of drug abuse and it was an allergic reaction to the ecstasy tablet that had killed their daughter.

'We've been trying to find you for ages,' Mick told him.

'Why?' He asked semi-sarcastically.

'To say we're sorry that we didn't believe you, and to thank you for what you've done for Sally,' he said quietly.

Steven stared at the sombre faced trio in front of him for several minutes; then he nodded slowly and put his hand out. 'Let's just forget about it then, shall we?' He suggested.

Mick looked at him in wonder. 'I was wrong, you have changed,' he said as he shook the offered hand.

Steven suddenly felt like a huge weight had been lifted from his shoulders. 'I've not changed, I've just grown up,' he whispered.

Judy was sitting in the reception when he got back. 'What are you doing here? You should be at home resting,' he scolded.

'I'm just answering the phone,' she assured him. 'Congratulations by the way, double trouble for you.'

He nodded happily. 'Don't overdo it. will you?' He ordered.

Almost on cue, the phone rang. 'Just answering the phone,' she said to the caller; after a few pleasantries she handed the receiver to Steven. 'Your dad,' she mouthed.

'Don't go anywhere,' Edward ordered and hung up before he could ask why.

He arrived less than half an hour later bringing Jack with him. 'What's so serious that you couldn't discuss it on the phone?' Steven started to ask, but the grave look on his father's face stopped him. He listened in horrified silence as Edward told him about Barry Mason.

'Shopping? What the hell were they playing at?' He exclaimed. And more to the point how the hell do I tell Heather, he thought.

'We think you should move to a safe house until he's caught,' Edward told him.

'If only for the safety of the babies,' Steven scowled at him. 'I don't see why we should move, we've only just got back after the last crisis,' he grumbled.

Edward's patience was wearing thin. 'For God's sake, use your head,' he snapped, and then desperate to avoid falling out with him suggested having a police officer in the house.

Steven shrugged. 'I'll see what Heather says, and anyway I've got to tell her about Mason first,' he muttered angrily.

'Well go and tell her now,' Edward ordered. 'And I'll go and see Whittle about protection.' Steven put his jacket on and disappeared across the car park.

'He's not very happy is he, guv?' Jack commented as they watched him drive away.

'Well would you be?' Edward enquired dryly.

Heather was out with Ben when Steven got home; frustratingly he didn't know which way she had gone. He didn't want to ring her mobile and tell her over the phone, so he watched anxiously through the kitchen window until he spotted her coming back across the moors, and then hurried to meet her.

Her face lit up when she saw him. 'Can't you keep away, daddyoh,' she laughed, and then saw the tension in his face. 'What's the matter?'

Struggling to find the right words, Steven told her as much as he knew. Her face drained of colour. She looked frantically around, almost as though she was expecting Mason to appear from behind a gorse bush. 'The chances of him trying to find you are so remote,' Steven started to say, and then realised that he was trying to convince himself as well as her.

'You don't know him,' she said quietly.

'You'll be fine,' he reassured her, then put his arm around her and walked back to the house in silence.

Heather was adamant that she wasn't going to move out again, but agreed that a police officer could move in to protect her. 'Wait with her until Jack arrives,' Edward ordered when Steven rang him.

'Jacks married. Why does he have to do it?' Steven asked angrily.

'You know why; now do as you're bloody well told, will you?' Edward ordered. Steven knew by his father's tone that it was pointless arguing anymore, so he agreed to wait and put the phone down.

'What did he say?' Heather asked; she was just about to make the same objection as Steven but he stopped her.

'There's no point arguing, I've already tried it,' he told her exasperatedly. 'Hopefully it won't be for too long and they'll catch the bastard before he kills anyone else,' he muttered.

'I'm really sorry about this Jack,' Steven apologised when the Sergeant arrived.

'Don't be, it couldn't have worked out better. The wife's mother is coming to stay,' he explained to Steven's raised eyebrow. 'Anyway, I'll try to keep out of your way.'

Heather knew that if it hadn't been for Jack then Steven would be dead. 'You don't need to keep out of the way, treat the house as your home,' she told him as she showed him up to the spare room.

'All night poker with the lads tonight then,' he said gleefully.

With Jack installed at the farm, Steven went back to work and put Charlie in the picture. 'Bloody hell! Do you think he'll try and find her?'

'Well if he does find her, then he'll have to get passed Jack,' Steven said brightly; he was trying to sound confident, but in reality, feeling far from it. They went into the mortuary where the body of a young man lay. 'This is Peter Kenmuir, aged nineteen,' Charlie told him.

'Another waste of a young life,' Steven said quietly as he looked at Peter's battered face. There was a black oily substance on one of his cheeks, and the same substance was also present on his clothes. Steven leant over and sniffed; it smelt like oil.

He took a sample and they turned him over; there was a wound on the back of Peter's head, indicating that he had been hit with something heavy. Steven parted his hair and found orange coloured dust adjacent to the wound. He took a swab then left Charlie to carry on and ran up to the labs with the samples.

By the time he got back downstairs, Charlie had undressed Peter and was busy taking photographs. 'This is very odd,' he called. Steven looked at the bar shaped bruises presenting at different angles on both sides of Peter's torso.

'It looks like something with a fairly flat edge. I'll download the photographs and see what the computer comes up with, as well as the bruising on his torso.' There were numerous smaller bruises over the rest of Peter's body; both of his arms and one of his legs were broken along with most of his ribs. 'He's taken quite a beating,' Charlie commented.

'I'm not sure that he was beaten,' Steven said thoughtfully. 'Where was he found?'

Charlie looked at the admission notes. 'Outside the casualty department. They think he managed to stagger there, but he collapsed and died before they got to him.'

Steven shook his head. 'Not with wounds like this, and definitely not with a broken leg. I would say he was dumped there, but he was already dead, and these bruises were made at different times,' he pointed out the slight difference in colouration. 'But all within the space of an hour or so,' he added thoughtfully.

On closer inspection, they discovered that the broken ribs had punctured one of Peter's lungs. 'Ruptured spleen, split liver, and a substantial tear to his diaphragm.' Steven looked up from the table. 'He died from massive internal bleeding.'

'Maybe he was run over?' Charlie suggested.

'It's a possibility, but there are no tyre marks; with the breaks and bruising it looks to me like he fell from a substantial height, but more than once though.' They were still puzzling over the severity of the injuries when Sue appeared and handed Steven the preliminary results from the black oily substance.

'Diesel oil,' Steven exclaimed. 'It looks like you were right, he may have been run over.'

'Actually, its train diesel,' Sue butted in.

'So the bruises could be from train tracks,' Charlie suggested. They went upstairs and Sue loaded the pictures into the computer, after a few minutes the familiar bleep of a match sounded.

'Standard gauge rail track,' Sue confirmed.

'So he fell onto the track and then someone took him to casualty,' Charlie surmised.

'He had bruising to both sides of his body, so he fell or was pushed more than once, either way there was someone else involved so I'll have to report it,' Steven sighed.

Edward arrived with Peter's mother the next afternoon; she identified her son and then sat in the family room. 'When did you last see Peter?' Edward asked her.

'Two days ago, he had arranged to meet a man who was interested in buying his car,' she said tearfully.

'Do you know where he was meeting the man?'

She blew her nose and nodded. 'He came to the house and Pete went with him for a test drive. Then when he hadn't come back after a couple of hours, I tried to ring him but his phone was switched off. I tried all his friends but none of them had seen him, so I waited until the next day and reported him missing.'

'Did you see the man?' Edward asked gently.

'Only from the window,' she whispered; she wiped her eyes and looked at Steven.

'Did he suffer?' She asked anxiously.

'He received a blow to the head which would have caused him to lose consciousness fairly quickly,' he answered truthfully, and then waited for the question that most parents asked.

'Was he,' she stopped, unable to finish the question; then took a deep breath before starting again.

'Was it a homosexual attack?' Steven shook his head. 'There was no sign of sexual interference.'

She gave a barely audible sigh of relief, then looked at Edward and gave a small smile. 'You can tell that you are father and son, Chief Inspector, you must be very proud of him.'

Edward nodded. 'I am proud, but don't tell him or he'll get big headed,' he whispered.

'I pray that you don't outlive your children,' she chuckled sadly. After agreeing a time to go to the station the next day, she got up and made her apologies. 'I have to go and tell his sister that he's dead,' she explained.

'Where is she? Can I arrange someone to drive you,' Edward offered; she shook her head.

'She's at Bristol University. Peter was selling the car to help her with her student fees,' her eyes filled with tears again. 'They are very close, were very close,' she corrected herself.

'Is she older or younger?' Edward asked.

'Peter was older by three minutes,' she managed to say before the tears spilled over. Steven watched as she made her way out; she stopped briefly in the reception and spoke to Judy before disappearing across the car park.

'That poor woman; after all she's been through, she still wished me good luck with the baby,' Judy said sadly.

Steven put his head in his hands. 'I hate this job,' he muttered. Peter Kenmuir's car was found burnt out on the moor's road the next day, and with forensics unable to get anything from it, Edward hoped that Mrs Kenmuir would be able to give them an accurate description of the man.

She arrived late afternoon along with her daughter, Susan, who was as expected distraught at losing her twin. Edward took them down to graphics and waited patiently as she tried to remember what the man looked like. When she had finished, he took them into the family suite.

'Would you mind answering a few questions?' He asked as they sat down.

Mrs Kenmuir blinked to try and stop the returning tears. 'Will it help to catch whoever killed him?' Edward nodded and passed her a box of tissues. She blew her nose and took her daughter's hand. 'Ask away,' she said quietly.

'Where did Peter advertise his car?' Edward started.

'In the local paper and a couple of shops.'

'Do you know which shops?'

She thought for a minute. 'The newsagents on Kimberwick high street and the post office in Burney I think.' Edward wrote it down.

'Did the man ring the house?'

She shook her head. 'He rang Peter's mobile phone, have you found it?'

'No, we haven't, but we did find his car early this morning.'

Susan started to cry. 'He loved that car, he was selling it for me; it's my fault that he's dead,' she sobbed.

Her mother put a protective arm around her. 'It's not your fault,' she said firmly. 'Is it, Inspector?' She looked at Edward for confirmation.

'No, it's the fault of the man who did this terrible thing,' he assured her.

Susan looked up at him through her tears. 'You will catch the bastard, won't you?'

Edward nodded. 'I'll do my very best but we need your mum's help.' Mrs Kenmuir gave him a small smile. 'Can you give me the number of Peter's mobile phone before you go?' He asked her.

'When can we bury him?' She whispered.

'I'll let you know as soon as forensics have finished,' he promised.

'I've spoken to my counterpart in Chipping Norton,' Whittle told him later that day. 'And I think it would be a good idea if you interviewed Mason's sister. Just to get a different aspect on the case, you never know you may find something they've overlooked,' he explained to Edward's puzzled look.

'I'll get onto the local station and arrange it,' Edward agreed.

'It's already done; you are meeting a Sergeant Ansell tomorrow morning,' Whittle informed him. 'And they tell me that the sister can be awkward, so I've taken the liberty of arranging a warrant.' Edward's opinion of the Chief Superintendent suddenly went up a notch as he handed him the paperwork.

Chapter 3

'What did you say she does?' He asked Sergeant Ansell as he knocked on the door of the smart detached house the following morning.

'Officially, she works in the local pub,' Ansell said dryly.

Edward raised his eyebrows. 'And unofficially?'

The door opened before the Sergeant could answer. 'What the hell do you want now?' The heavily made up forty something brunette who was standing in the doorway demanded. Edward sized her up as she scowled at them.

He was just over six feet tall, and she stood a good inch or two over him. He looked down and saw that she was wearing sky high heels, even so she must have been at least six two. A pair of fishnet clad legs stuck out from beneath a micro mini skirt. He noted with amusement that she had the knobbiest knees that he had ever seen on a woman.

The look was finished with an almost sheer blouse, with a plunging neckline that left little to the imagination. He grimaced at her long nails which were painted black, and realised that he didn't need to ask what it was she did unofficially. She shot him an acidic look.

'Who's your friend?' She asked Ansell sarcastically. Sergeant Ansell introduced Edward and explained why they were there. 'I've already told you lot what I know, so why don't you tell him?' She snapped sarcastically.

'Because I would like to hear it from you,' Edward told her dryly.

'Oh, it speaks,' she snapped rudely.

Edward ignored her rudeness. 'Can we come in and have a chat?' He asked.

'Have you got a warrant?' She counter asked.

'Actually I have,' he said brightly.

Her face fell as he produced it from his pocket. She snatched it from him and scowled as she read it. 'Well you'll have to wait because I've got company,' she said sullenly and started to close the door.

Ansell put his foot in the way to stop her. 'Just tell whoever it is to get his trousers on, and we'll need his name on the way out, if it's not too much trouble,' he said sweetly.

As it was there were two men in the house, both emerged red faced and mumbled their names to the constable at the gate, before disappearing in opposite directions. 'I hope you've not lost too much money,' Edward said with mock concern.

'I enjoy sex, Chief Inspector, and I don't charge for it because that would be prostitution and that's illegal,' she gave him a scornful look. 'Right, what do you want?' She asked impatiently.

'When did you last see your brother?' Edward asked.

'Which one?' She asked innocently.

Edward gave her a pitiful look. 'The one that isn't dead obviously.'

Diane's nostrils twitched slightly. 'That was rather cruel, Inspector,' she commented.

'So answer the question and stop trying to be clever,' he suggested sharply.

'I haven't seen Barry for over six weeks. He hasn't contacted me and I don't know where he is,' she snapped.

'Has he contacted your mother?' Edward asked.

'I would hardly think so,' she said incredulously.

'Why not?' He enquired; she sniffed indifferently and lit a cigarette.

'Because she disowned us five years ago and we have no idea where she is,' she said disinterestedly.

'I was led to believe that she was in a nursing home in Chipping Norton,' Edward commented.

Diane took a long drag and then blew the smoke out slowly. 'And who led you to believe that?' She smirked at him and took another drag. 'Was it that bitch Heather?' She asked amusedly.

'It doesn't matter who it was,' Edward said firmly.

'Really?' She scoffed. 'Well that woman ruined our lives.'

He raised his eyebrows. 'In what way?' He enquired dryly.

'You'll have to ask her that, won't you?' She sneered.

'Do you think that Barry will try and find her?' He persisted.

'I hope so, and if he does ask if I know where she is then I'll tell him,' she said snapped.

The vitriolic outburst shocked the two men. 'Do you know where Ms Brooks is?' Edward asked suspiciously.

'No, I don't. but you do, and I know that you've come from Yorkshire, so it doesn't take a genius to work out that she's still in that area,' she said confidently.

'That comment could be construed as a threat,' Ansell butted in sternly.

She sat back and shrugged dismissively. 'Construe it however you want; so, is that all then?' She asked impatiently.

'If you could just give me the name of the nursing home that your mother used to live in,' Edward asked.

'It won't do you any good, she's completely senile and can't remember her own name most days,' she said sulkily.

'Well, I'd still like the address,' Edward said firmly.

Diane gave an exaggerated sigh and scribbled an address down on a piece of paper. 'Now get out,' she ordered.

'What a hateful woman,' Edward said as they reached the car.

'Look here,' Ansell said quietly; he nodded towards a man who was walking up her drive. Edward looked up and saw Diane standing in the window gesturing for him to go away. The man turned around; he saw them watching and hurried off with his head down.

Ansell gave Diane a wave as she scowled at them through the window. 'Oh dear! Another lost sale,' he laughed.

'Did you find out anything useful?' Whittle asked the next day.

'Diane Meriwether; that's her married name,' Edward chuckled.

'So she's married, is she?' Whittle butted in.

Edward shook his head. 'Unsurprisingly, she's now divorced,' he said dryly. 'Anyway, she says she hasn't seen Barry Mason for over six weeks and he hasn't contacted her.'

'Do you believe her?' Whittle interrupted again.

'No, I don't, but I'll find out if she's telling the truth when I go to the hospital,' he stopped talking and waited for a comment.

'Go on,' Whittle ordered.

'I asked her about Heather, Ms Brooks that is, and she was most vitriolic about her. She's blaming her for destroying their lives but she wouldn't elaborate, she told me to ask Ms Brooks, but I don't really want her to know that I've been to see her,' he admitted.

Whittle nodded. 'It's probably best that she doesn't know,' he agreed. His mouth fell open in shock as Edward reported the rest of the conversation 'What a bitch!' He said to Edward's surprise.

'I agree, Sir, I've asked Chipping to put surveillance on her just in case Mason turns up, and they're waiting for the go ahead for a phone tap, but my gut feeling is that he'll keep away.' Whittle had obviously done his homework. 'What about the mother?'

'She's in a nursing home, we're trying to find out which one and arrange to go and see her. Although, I don't know how much help she'll be, because according to Ms Meriwether, she's senile; but I'll keep you up to date,' he went out to the squad room wondering why the Chief Superintendent was taking such an interest.

Whilst Edward was discussing Diane Meriwether, Steven was preparing to start on the day's list. 'Who have we got here?' He asked as Charlie brought the body of a woman out.

Charlie looked at the admission sheet. 'Victoria Morris, aged fifty-six.'

Steven stared at the woman. 'Vicky Morris?'

Charlie looked at the notes again. 'Yes, do you know her?'

Steven nodded slowly. 'If it's the same woman then she worked with Heather at the post office in Burney.' He read through the admission sheet and discovered that Vicky had been found by the post master who had gone to see why she hadn't turned up for work. When she didn't reply to his knocking, he went around the back of the house to look through the window and saw her lying on the kitchen floor.

PC Higgins appeared in the observation room. 'DCI Cooper sent me to observe,' he explained.

'Aren't you going to come in?' Charlie asked.

'I'd rather not if it's all the same to you,' he said quickly. He was already looking nauseous even though Vicky was still wearing the pink floral dressing gown that she had been found in. Steven opened the buttons and they started to undress her; as more of her body was exposed it became obvious that she hadn't died of natural causes.

'What are those marks?' Higgins enquired.

'Burns,' was the short reply that he got from a shocked Steven. 'You'd better get my dad over here,' he added. They covered Vicky up and went into the reception to wait for Edward.

'What's up?' Judy asked.

'Nothing for you to worry about,' Charlie told her, he looked at her tummy, then got up and went out to the porch.

Steven went after him. 'Are you alright?'

Charlie nodded, then changed his mind and shook his head. 'We're supposed to be a civilised race. I don't understand how someone could do that to another human being, especially a defenceless woman,' he said quietly. Steven nodded his agreement; his mind wandered back to Zoë Fairfax and the horrific injuries that she had received.

They stood in silence staring at the rain which was almost horizontal. 'I hope to God I don't breed a monster,' Charlie muttered suddenly.

'With parents like you and Judy, I would say that's a definite impossibility,' Steven said genuinely. Charlie gave a resigned smile and nodded towards the car park as Edward arrived.

'We'd better get to it then I suppose,' he said glumly. Edward followed them into the cutting room.

'She has ligature marks around her wrists, so she was tied up at some point, there's bruising and traces of blood around her inner thighs so it's possible that she was raped, and she was tortured,' Steven told his father. He uncovered Vicky to reveal a mass of burns that stretched across her breasts and down her torso to her groin.

'Christ!' Edward exclaimed. Charlie photographed the wounds which were in regular sets of five with each individual burn an inch apart. Some were no more than blisters and others were deep enough to have destroyed the tissue. 'Can you tell what made them?' Edward asked.

'It looks like the prongs of a large fork,' Steven said thoughtfully. They turned Vicky over which revealed the same burns across her buttocks. 'Bastard,' Steven said silently.

After examining Vicky's organs, they discovered that the cause of death was a massive heart attack. 'Hardly surprising,' Steven commented, and then spotted something wedged in her oesophagus. He picked up a pair of tweezers and gently pulled out a strip of paper.

'What is it?' Edward enquired from the observation room.

'It's a piece of paper,' Steven called. 'What do you make of that?' He asked Charlie as he carefully unrolled it. 'It says "hard luck she told me!".' He gave his father a puzzled glance. Do you think she told him the combination of the safe?'

Edward shook his head. 'I don't know. I'll go over to her house and see what I can find, let me know if you find anything else?' He ordered and hurried out.

As Steven continued with the post-mortem, he discovered that Vicky had indeed been raped and quite viciously. 'She was a virgin,' he said angrily as he examined the damage. 'But whoever he was, he wasn't very careful because he didn't use protection, so hopefully it's someone on record,' he muttered as he took a swab.

'There are fingerprints all over the place,' the scene of crime officer told Edward when he arrived at Vicky Morris's neat terraced house. Edward went inside and looked around the kitchen; there were four caddies on the counter all neatly in line with the labels facing the front, the kettle shone. Six mugs hung on the hooks along the cupboard, everything had its place and everything was neat and tidy.

It was the same story in the lounge, even the ornaments were arranged symmetrically. A PC came down the stairs and handed Edward a bag of jewellery. 'Nothing appears to have been taken, so it doesn't look like burglary was the motive.' Edward glanced around the room again, there was something not quite right but he was unable to decide what.

Then as he went into the hall he noticed two horse brasses, one hanging on either side of the front door and he suddenly realised what it was. He went back into the lounge; there was a pair of coal tongs hanging on one side of the fireplace but the hook on the other side was empty. 'There's something missing from here, search for any fire related tool,' he instructed.

He took one last look around the kitchen and spotted a notepad with the start of a shopping list written on it. He tore off the top sheet and headed back to the station. He called at the post office on route to find it closed; Jim Abbot the post master, who was still in shock at finding her had been sedated. 'You'll not be able to talk to him until at least tomorrow,' the doctor informed him.

'Can you get me the security tape from the observation camera?' Edward asked Jim's wife.

'I've no idea where it is. I never go in there,' she admitted.

Well can you at least let me in so that I can look for it?' He asked hopefully.

'I'm sorry. I don't know the code for the alarm,' she said apologetically.

315

Edward swore inwardly. 'So are Jim and Vicky the only people who know the code?' He asked exasperatedly.

'Ms Brooks might know, or you could ring the head office,' she suggested.

'Stay here and as soon as Mr Abbot wakes up, ask him for the code,' he told the constable.

Heather answered the phone an hour later and handed the receiver to Jack, he watched her as Edward put him in the picture. 'What?' She asked nervously as he hung up. Jack told her about Vicky's heart attack, but left out the details of the rape and torture.

'Can you remember the alarm code?'

Heather was obviously upset; she tried to remember but shook her head after a few minutes. 'It's too long ago,' she said tearfully and went into the kitchen to prepare dinner. 'Tell them to try 1564,' she called ten minutes later.

Jack stuck his head around the door. 'Jim's a Shakespeare nut, it's the year he was born,' she explained. Jack went to call Edward and then went back to the kitchen. 'What can you tell me about Vicky?'

Heather stopped what she was doing. 'She was just a normal woman. I met her for lunch in Kimberwick a couple of weeks ago. She was going to knit the baby a jacket; we didn't know it was twins then,' she added, anticipating the question.

Jack wondered how far he could push her before she got suspicious. 'Has she got any family?' He asked casually.

Heather shook her head. 'Not that she ever talked about.'

'And she never married?' He ventured.

Heather suddenly turned the tables on him. 'She had a heart attack, you say?' Jack nodded. 'Well she never mentioned a heart condition to me, so I wonder what brought it on,' she looked at him enquiringly. 'Is this something to do with Barry?'

'Not as far as we know,' he said not untruthfully, and then keen to avoid any more questions went upstairs.

'Don't disappear. The dog needs to go out,' she shouted after him. Jack wasn't keen on walking.

'Where do you go?' He asked as they set off across the moors an hour later.

Heather pointed towards a rise about a mile away. 'Usually up to the top and back around past Bob's place.'

Jacks heart sank. 'That's miles.'

Heather gave him a dig in the ribs 'It's only a couple of miles and at least it's not raining,' she chided.

They walked on in silence for a while, with the cat at Heather's heels, and Ben bounding about in front; every so often she stopped to look through her binoculars. 'Do you ever see anything unusual?' Jack asked trying to sound interested.

'There were a pair of buzzards the other day but no sign today,' she offered the binoculars over.

'It's ok, thanks,' he grumbled. The moors were bleak and cold and there were miles of it. Jack had never understood the lure of walking, especially not in the winter, and especially if there wasn't a pub at the end of it. He looked around feeling completely bored; but his boredom was short lived as he saw a reflective flash in the distance.

'Can I have a look?' Heather handed him the binoculars; he focused on the area where he saw the flash and scanned around. 'What does Bob look like?' He asked as caught sight of a figure moving quickly through the dead bracken.

'He's not very tall and he's got black hair, if it is him then he'll have Sandy with him,' Heather said apprehensively. The figure disappeared down a dip a few seconds later; Jack gave the binoculars back.

'Who's Sandy?' He asked.

'His dog, it's a golden retriever,' she looked panic stricken.

'Well it must have been him then, I thought it was a sheep but obviously it was the dog.' A look of relief swept over her face. 'Shall we get back then?' He asked hopefully.

Whilst Jack was trudging across the moors, Edward was with Whittle. 'Whoever it was, forced Vicky to swallow the paper,' Edward told him.

'Why?' Whittle asked.

'I have absolutely no idea,' Edward said dryly, and wondered why on earth he thought he would know.

'And there's been no break in at the post office?' Whittle checked.

'No, we're trying to get hold of the security tapes for the last few days, but apparently they only keep them for a week and then they tape over them.'

Whittle sighed heavily before asking him the very question that had been niggling at the back of Edward's own mind. 'Do you think it could have something to do with Barry Mason?'

Edward sat down. 'Well, given the message on the note and the fact that Heather used to work with Ms Morris, I think it's very possible.'

They sat in silence for a couple of seconds. 'I'll get onto the division dealing with Mason's case and ask them to send us everything they've got,' Whittle told him, he got up and looked out of the window. 'In the meantime, make sure Ms Brooks has an armed officer with her at all times,' he ordered.

'It's already in place, Sir,' Edward assured him. 'Is everything alright, Sir?' He asked sensing that something was troubling him.

Whittle nodded again. 'Fine thank you, Edward,' he turned around and forced a smile. 'Thank you for asking.'

Edward knew that his superior officer was lying, but he smiled back and returned to his office, hoping that he wasn't withholding something connected to the case.

Higgins knocked on his door a while later. 'We may have discovered what was missing from the fireplace, Sir.' He put a pair of coal tongs and a fire rake on his desk. 'I got them from the ironmongers in Burney. I showed him the tongs from Ms Morris' house and he sells the exact same make as a set along with the rake.'

Edward counted the fingers of the rake; there were five. 'You'd better get them over to forensics, and give them this too,' he gave him the shopping list. 'I'm assuming this is Ms Morris' handwriting, ask their graphologists to compare it against the handwriting that was on the note, and well-done constable,' he praised.

'Well, it's the same shape,' Steven observed when Higgins arrived; they retrieved Vicky from the chiller and compared the fingers of the coal rake against the burns.

'Perfect match,' Charlie said in dismay. 'But that's not the actual rake, is it?' Higgins shook his head. 'We've not found it yet.'

'Well, let's hope the bastard isn't planning to use it on anyone else,' Steven said angrily. They returned Vicky to the chiller and went up to the labs where Sue and the graphologist were looking at the note.

'First impressions say that it is her handwriting,' the graphologist pointed to the note. 'But this one was probably written under duress. I'll go into them in more depth and let you know for sure.' Higgins nodded his thanks, and waited whilst Charlie wrote a preliminary report before heading back to the station.

'Well done,' Jack said to Heather a while later; she looked up in surprise 'The code,' he explained.

'Oh good. Well, I hope it helps,' she smiled as Steven came in; he gave her a kiss and patted her tummy. Her eyes lit up as he produced a jar of cocktail cherries from his pocket.

'You're a saviour,' she gave a sigh of contentment and started eating them with a fork.

'Yuk,' Jack said in disgust. They watched in amusement until she was sated. 'Right, dinner time,' she said brightly.

Steven thought about Vicky Morris as he stood under the shower later. 'I'm sure Heather thinks it's something to do with Barry Mason,' Jack had told him earlier.

'She may be right,' he mused.

Jack also told him about the figure on the moors, who didn't have a dog in tow and who he was sure had been watching them through binoculars. 'It could have been a bird watcher,' he said unconvincingly.

'Well I'm glad you're protecting her,' Steven said gratefully, and then quickly changed the subject as Heather appeared. He finished in the shower, and instead of wandering across the landing naked as he usually did, he remembered that they had company, and wrapped a towel around his waist. Then having decided to tell Heather the truth but only if she asked.

He went into the bedroom and braced himself for the questions. Heather was sitting on the bed staring into space. 'Are you ok?'

She nodded slowly. 'Don't worry I'm not going to ask,' she said quietly.

'You can ask me anything,' he said truthfully; she gave him a small smile.

'I know I can, but I also know that you're not allowed to discuss your work.' She suddenly got up and pulled the towel from around his waist; before pushing him backwards onto the bed. 'But I don't want to talk, I want you to make love to me like you did the first time.'

She knelt across him, then leant down and kissed him longingly. 'We'll have to be quiet though,' she whispered as they heard Jack coming up the stairs.

'Well, it's you who makes all the noise,' he whispered back, then grabbed her hand to avoid a playful slap. 'Maybe we should abstain whilst Jacks here,' he suggested amusedly. Jack's voice suddenly floated down the landing. 'I sleep like a log, so you two carry on as normal, I won't hear a thing,' he assured them.

319

'That's not very comforting considering that you're supposed to be protecting Heather,' Steven called back.

'Oh I'm sure that you're more than capable of looking after her,' came the amused reply.

Heather smiled triumphantly. 'Well what are you waiting for, Dr Cooper,' she asked as she shed her dressing gown.

Steven woke hours later with a feeling that something was wrong. He gently moved Heather's arm that was draped over him, then pulled a pair of boxer shorts and a T shirt on and went onto the landing. Jacks' door was slightly ajar. 'Jack,' he whispered, but there was no reply, he pushed the door open to reveal an empty bed.

'Shit,' he said silently, then crept down the stairs with his stomach lurching. Ben was lying in his basket in the hall; he gave a low growl as a shadow appeared at the porch door, quickly followed by the sound of a key being tried in the lock. Steven looked around for something to use as a weapon, he jumped as Jack appeared at the lounge door with a gun in his hand.

Having been unable to open the door, the shadow had moved away. Jack opened the front door and looked through the porch window; then he unlocked the door and disappeared into the night, just as the blue lights of a police car came speeding down the lane. Muffled shouting and the sound of a scuffle quickly followed.

Steven ran outside as the police car arrived in the yard, and saw Jack coming around the side of the house with a figure in an arm lock. 'Can you put the light on?' Jack called.

Steven turned the outside light on and gave a sigh of relief when he saw who Jack had got. 'It's Bob from up the road,' he told the policemen.

Bob was obviously drunk and could hardly stand up. 'Wrong house, mate,' Jack scolded as he bundled him into the police car. 'Take him home, lads,' he instructed then looked at Steven. 'How about a quick brew,' he said hopefully.

'Are you ok?' Heather asked drowsily when Steven snuggled back down next to her twenty minutes later. 'Fine,' he assured her; then he laid his hand on her tummy and fell asleep to the rise and fall of her breathing.

Chapter 4

The information from the psychiatric unit arrived on Edward desk the next day. 'Where's Heather?' He asked as Jack appeared in his office.

'She's in the squad room, we're going shopping,' he explained a little less than enthusiastically. 'So what's happening with Mason?'

Edward handed him the report. Jack looked at the picture of hard-faced man staring at the camera. 'He looks nothing like the picture on his arrest sheet from five years ago,' he commented as he read the report.

'Apparently, he used to fight all the time and had to be excluded from the communal areas, then about a year ago he asked to see the clergyman, and in their words "he found God", which turned him into a model patient. As a reward for his good behaviour, they arranged for him to use the gym to help work off his aggression,' he stopped reading and looked up at Edward.

'The down side being that it transformed him into a six-foot-one muscle bound thug,' he said angrily. 'A year ago,' Edward repeated. 'About the same time as Heather was attacked by Warren Walker,' he looked up and saw Heather watching him through the open door. 'Anyway, you'd better go shopping,' he chuckled at Jack's look of despair.

'I'm going to the psychiatric unit to find out what triggered the miraculous transformation, but don't mention any of this to Heather,' he said quietly. He waved at Heather then waited until they were out of sight before going to see Whittle.

Higgins was waiting with the security tape from the post office when he came out. They slotted it into the machine and sat back to watch. 'This looks likely,' Higgins said, as a thick set man entered the shop.

'He's too short, Mason is six foot one,' Edward reminded him. 'And too old,' he muttered as the man turned around. They watched for a while longer. 'This one looks a more likely candidate,' he tapped the screen where a tall man with a crew cut, and wearing an anorak that was obviously too small for him was waiting.

'See if you can get a description of the coat that he stole, and get the local PC to look at the tape, he may recognise some of the other customers,' Edward told Higgins. The man kept his back to the camera as he moved up the queue, when he reached the counter, he leant forward. Edward could just make out Vicky Morris saying something, and then still keeping his face turned away from the camera the man left.

Higgins came back in with a file a few minutes later. 'It was a blue anorak and a navy tartan hat.' They rewound the tape and looked at the man, the coat was definitely too small for him but he wasn't wearing a hat, and the coat could have been any colour.

'Mason has a crew cut as well,' Edward handed him the photograph from the psychiatric unit and took the tape out. 'Let's see if we can get this enhanced. Mrs Kenmuir said that he was quite tall. His nose was a funny shape and he had short hair.

She also said that Peter had put an advert in the post office window, so if the man on the tape is Mason, then he may have seen it,' he sat back in the chair and yawned. 'Give Mrs Kenmuir a call, ask her if she noticed if the jacket looked too small?' He told Higgins; then he yawned again and decided to go home.

'There have been three viewings today,' Sheila told him.

'Any likely looking buyers?' He asked hopefully.

'A young couple,' she raised her eyebrows. 'Both male! A Chinese couple with their seven children, and a very odd man who said he was looking for an investment property.' Edward stared into space; he probably wants to knock it down and build twenty-seven luxury flats with no gardens and no privacy, he thought.

'Oh well, none of them sound very promising,' he said despondently. 'Still, it's early days,' he put his hands over his face and yawned loudly. 'I feel completely drained,'

'Have an early night then,' Sheila suggested.

Edward looked heavenwards. 'It's probably the early nights that are wearing me out.' He pulled her onto his knee, 'and I wouldn't have it any other way,' he whispered.

Despite his fatigue and Sheila's relaxing massage, Edward found it hard to wind down. When he did eventually fall asleep it was littered with images of

Vicky Morris lying in the mortuary, but she wasn't dead, she was talking incoherently in a high-pitched terrified voice whilst Steven cut into her. Edward stood in the observation room watching in horror.

He banged on the window as his son started to remove her organs. 'Steven, stop,' he yelled. Steven did stop, but as he turned around Edward saw that it wasn't his son, it was Barry Mason. He stood in front of the observation room window smiling manically. 'Look what I found,' he said gleefully; he held out his hand.

Edward looked down and saw Vicky's heart still beating in his bloody palm. Edward tried to open the door but it refused to move. Mason smiled at him with a glazed expression. 'Hard luck,' he chuckled. 'But don't worry, you'll soon be joining your bastard son.'

Edward picked a chair up and hurled it through the window. 'Where's Steven, you bastard,' he yelled, and started to climb through the broken glass.

He suddenly felt someone pulling him back. 'Edward?' A familiar but frightened voice said. He opened his eyes and saw Sheila's terrified face looking down at him. He stared at her for a few seconds, shaking uncontrollably and drenched in sweat.

Then he sat up breathing heavily. 'Are you alright?'

He looked around the bedroom in relief and nodded slowly. 'It was just a bad dream,' he reassured her.

He was still trying to put the dream out of his mind as he sat in his office the next morning. It had been so vivid that he could remember every detail. He shuddered at the memory and turned his attention to the reports on his desk.

PC Higgins came in a few minutes later and put a pile of statements in front of him; he pushed the reports to one side and read through them. The resident police constable in Burney had watched the security tape, and after identifying the customers in the post office had subsequently spoken to them. One of them remembered the man as he had been behind him in the queue. He asked for a dog license which is why he stuck in his mind.

'So he asked for something that he knew no longer existed?' Edward commented. Higgins nodded. 'Did Vicky Morris wear a name badge?' Edward asked thoughtfully.

'They put their name plates in the serving hatch window when they're on duty. So that's what he was doing, getting near enough to the counter to see her name, but he had to ask for something when he got there so as not to arouse suspicion,' Higgins exclaimed.

'So he knew exactly who to follow,' Edward said bitterly. He picked the phone up to call Steven, and gave a sigh of relief when he heard his voice. 'Have you got anything for me?' He enquired.

'It's going to tomorrow at the earliest,' Steven told him. 'Are you alright, Dad?' For Christ's sake, pull yourself together man it was only a dream, Edward told himself sternly. 'Dad?' Steven repeated.

'Yes, thanks, son. Are you?' After assuring him that he was fine, Steven promised to call as soon as he had anything and then hung up. Edward sat and stared at the phone, then looked up at Higgins who had come back in.

'Are you alright, Sir?'

Edward put the receiver down. 'Yes thanks, so what have you got?'

'Mrs Kenmuir didn't notice if the jacket looked too small, and she thinks it was green.'

Edward groaned inwardly. 'Well let's hope that forensics come up with something,' he said despondently.

'It's Mason,' Sue told Steven the next day. 'His fingerprints were in the house; the semen is a match and the handwriting on the note was defiantly Vicky Morris'.'

Steven was horrified. 'So Mason made her write the note and then swallow it.'

Sue nodded. 'That's what it looks like.'

A sudden feeling of panic hit Steven, and after speaking to his father, he conceded that Heather should be moved to a safe house. 'I'll call Jack and tell him to get her out of there,' Edward started to say.

'You're going to have to tell her why,' Steven butted in.

'Well, perhaps you'd better go and tell her then,' Edward suggested. 'How did she take it?' He asked Jack when he rang.

'She's terrified,' Jack whispered. 'But I think we should stay here, guv. It's open moorland, I'll see anyone coming from a mile off and the dog will let me know if anyone is about.'

Edward pondered for a minute, then agreed that it was as safe there as anywhere and it would make sense for them to stay put. 'I'll have to run it past Whittle though,' he said without much hope of him agreeing.

But to his amazement, Whittle did agree. 'Make sure that Sergeant Taylor has direct communication to the station,' the Chief Superintendent ordered.

'He's got his radio and the regular patrol will be in the area,' Edward reminded him.

Whittle nodded his approval. 'Give your son and his fiancé my regards when you see them,' he said to Edward's surprise.

'Thank you, Sir, I will,' he assured him, and then left the room as Whittle dismissed him with a nod.

'Has he been drinking?' Steven asked when Edward rang him.

'I've no idea, but let's take advantage of his good mood while it lasts,' his father suggested, and then changed the subject.

Steven gave a sigh of relief when he told him that they could stay at home. 'In that case, why don't you come over to dinner tomorrow night. I'm sure Heather will be glad to see Sheila, but not too much shop talk with Jack, I don't want her upset, ok?' he ordered.

Edward hung up and turned his attention to a recent break in. The front door had been forced and the house ransacked. Nothing was taken apart from a pair of binoculars, but all the photographs had been ripped up and the intruder had urinated on the carpets.

Edward looked at the address and went out to the squad room. 'Where is this house?'

Higgins pointed out the location on the map. 'On the moors road, Sir, it's only just in our patch about a mile away from Dr Cooper's house.'

Edward stared at the map. 'Kids do you think?' He enquired.

'Probably not, it's right out in the sticks. Mr Jackson, the homeowner, thinks it's down to his ex-wife's boyfriend,' Higgins told him.

'Does he say why he thinks that?' Edward asked suspiciously.

Higgins pulled the case up on the computer. 'She has recently lost a court case to increase her divorce settlement. Apparently, Jackson is quite well off and she thought she deserved more. They live on the other side of York. Inspector Finch is dealing with them,' he added before Edward could ask.

Edward went back to his office and called York, only to be told that Inspector Finch was out. After leaving a message for him call back he sat and stared out of the window. 'I suppose it could be a coincidence,' he muttered before reluctantly going back to the paperwork.

Finch rang back several hours later. 'The ex-wife and boyfriend are in the Caribbean, so they're out of the frame.'

A gut feeling told Edward that the break in wasn't a coincidence. 'There were several sets of prints in the house, one set belongs to Mr Jackson and the rest aren't on file, so can you fingerprint them when they get back?' He requested, and hung up just as Whittle came in.

'They've found Alice Poole; she's in a nursing home in Southport. I'm going to see her on Friday,' he told Jack quietly that evening.

'That's a long way from Chipping, expensive as well she must have a few bob,' Jack commented, he stopped talking as Heather came in.

'Who must?' She asked.

'Just some old woman who had her bag snatched,' Edward lied.

'Really?' She said disbelievingly.

'I said not too much shop talk,' Steven shouted from the kitchen.

Edward changed the subject and gave a sniff. 'What's for dinner then?'

'Steven's cooked so you'd better ask him, because I can't even pronounce it,' Heather said as Steven came through from the kitchen.

'What is it, son?' Edward enquired.

'Sole meuniere.' They all looked at him blankly. 'Fish in butter sauce, you heathens,' he chuckled.

'Well, I think it looks lovely,' Sheila said generously.

'Will there be pudding?' Jack asked as he eyed the steaming dish. 'And more importantly will we be able to pronounce it?'

'You may mock, but once you've tasted it, you'll eat your words,' Steven scolded as he went back into the kitchen.

'I thought we were going to eat the fish,' Edward whispered.

'I heard that, Dad,' he shouted, and then reappeared with the vegetables and a jar of cocktail cherries.

'What do you think?' He asked as he looked at the empty plates twenty minutes later.

'I think you are in the wrong job. You should come and work in the police canteen,' Jack complemented.

Ben followed Steven through to the kitchen, and then ran into the hall barking loudly as the doorbell rang. 'Are you expecting anyone?' Edward asked.

'I'm not,' Steven said.

Heather shook her head. 'No, me neither.' Jack got up and stood behind the dining room door as Steven went into the hall. He switched the porch light on and saw Bob Jackson standing on the step.

'I just wanted to apologise for the other night. I'm sorry if I gave you a fright,' Bob muttered embarrassedly.

Steven shook his head. 'It's alright these things happen. Do you want to come in?'

Bob looked tempted, but declined when he heard voices coming from the dining room. 'No, it's ok. You've got company, and I've got a taxi waiting,' he started to walk down the drive. 'Oh, by the way, did your friend find you?' He called.

'No! Did he give a name?' Steven asked thinking it may have been Mick.

'He didn't say his name but he asked about Heather,' Bob called. Jack had been listening to the conversation and came out. Bob stared at him warily. 'You're not going to flatten me again, are you?'

Jack shook his head. 'What day was this?'

Bob frowned thoughtfully. 'A couple of days ago I think.'

Edward appeared at the door as well. 'What did the man look like?'

Bob shrugged. 'I didn't take much notice of him. I was busy cleaning up the mess after the break in,' he said bitterly.

'Well try and remember,' Jack snapped, and then softened his tone. 'Anything you can tell us please.'

Bob exhaled loudly as he tried to remember. 'He was fairly tall with a crew cut and a few days stubble.'

Edward's heart sank. 'Can you remember what he was wearing?'

'A green jacket I think. I didn't really look. He said he was an old pal of Steven's from the Territorial Army and hadn't seen him for years.'

Jack glanced at Edward. 'Did you tell him where the house is?'

Bob nodded. 'Shouldn't I have?' He asked worriedly.

'If you see him again then call the police straight away, and don't let him in,' Edward instructed.

Bob looked at the three men in dismay. 'Isn't he a friend then?'

Steven shook his head. 'I was never in the territorial army.' Bob went pale; he spluttered his apologies and made his way back to the waiting taxi.

'Don't say anything to the girls,' Edward said quietly as they went back inside.

'Who was it?' Heather enquired. 'Bob from up the road,' Steven said without elaborating.

'Right, what's for pudding then,' Jack asked resuming the previous conversation.

'Pears belle Helene,' Steven said with a flourish.

'Oh good, my favourite,' Jack mouthed.

Chapter 5

The next morning, Edward showed his warrant card to the guard on the gate of the psychiatric unit and waited for the barrier to be lifted. As he drove up the long winding drive, he wondered if the inmates were responsible for the neat lawns and full flower beds. He rounded a bend a few seconds later and the hospital came into view.

An imposing Victorian affair; it had served as a military hospital during the Second World War, and after lying empty for two decades, it had then been turned into a psychiatric unit, with the secure wing being added five years later. There was a smartly dressed man waiting in the car park; he hurried over as Edward pulled up and introduced himself as Phillip Ball, the governor.

'I thought this was a high security unit,' Edward commented as they went to his office.

'Meaning what?' Ball asked defensively.

'Meaning, how is it that a man who killed his baby son was allowed to go out shopping?' Edward retorted.

Ball gave an exaggerated sigh. 'Mason was moved from the high security wing three months before he absconded. Small groups are taken out into the community as part of the rehabilitation program, and I should point out that he had been out a dozen times or more before he absconded,' he added icily.

Edward stared at his defensive expression, and wondered if it had even crossed his mind that Mason had gained their trust in order to escape. 'So why was he moved?'

Ball gestured for him to sit down. 'I have already given this information to the Detective involved, maybe you should speak to him.' He pulled a file from a drawer and flicked through it. 'His name is Detective.'

'I am well aware of who is investigating Mr Mason's disappearance, I am investigating the death of a woman who knew his ex-wife, who also happens to be under my protection,' Edward interrupted.

Ball closed the file and raised his eyebrows quizzically. 'Did Mason kill this woman?'

'She died of a heart attack after being severely tortured and raped,' Edward replied without blinking. 'Would you like details of her injuries or are you going to answer the question?' Ball was obviously used to having the last word and started to argue.

'I could make it formal and take you back to the station to answer the questions,' Edward threatened.

Ball realised that he meant business and gave in. 'Mason was moved to the minimum-security unit because he was no longer deemed to be a threat.'

'And how was that deemed?' Edward interrupted sarcastically.

'I'm not sure that I like your tone, Inspector,' Ball complained.

'I don't really care if you like my tone or not, now please answer the question,' Edward snapped.

Ball glared at him. 'He started going to church and reading the bible. He had numerous sessions with the psychiatrist, who reported him to be sociable and compliant. He integrated with the other patients and he even started a football team,' he said almost proudly.

And these so-called professionals didn't see through the charade, Edward thought despairingly. 'Did he ever have visitors?' He asked.

'Only his sister over the last year, but I believe his younger brother visited not long before he himself was murdered,' Ball replied dourly.

Edward did a quick calculation. 'That would be about the time he found God then?'

Ball nodded. 'The psychiatrist believes that the death of his brother helped him to come to terms with what he had done,' he said curtly.

'When did his sister last visit him?' Edward checked.

'I don't know,' Ball said unhelpfully. 'I'll have to look in the visitor's book,' he stared at Edward but didn't move.

'You go and look then and I'll wait here,' Edward said benignly. Ball scowled at him, then got up and left the room. He came back two minutes later and dropped a ledger on the table. Edward flicked through it; as Diane had said it was nearly seven weeks since she'd visited. He closed the ledger with a snap. 'Can I see his cell now please?'

Ball glanced at the clock impatiently. 'I have a meeting shortly so we'll have to be quick, and we don't call them cells they are rooms,' he said firmly. Mason's room was small but comfortably furnished; there was a divan bed against one wall, with a wash basin and combination wardrobe opposite, a small television sat in the corner.

'How long does he spend in here?' Edward asked as he looked around.

'He only sleeps in here, the rest of his time is taken up with therapy sessions, exercising in the gym or garden, reading in the library, and as I've already told you he played football,' Ball informed him impatiently.

Edward opened the wardrobe which was full of carefully folded clothes; he looked with disgust at the designer labels. 'Do they wear their own clothes?' He enquired.

'Yes. Once they are out of high security, we like to make life a bit more comfortable for them,' Ball explained.

'And who buys their clothes?' Edward asked dryly. Ball glanced at his watch. 'The sooner you answer the question the sooner I'll be out of your way,' Edward told him sharply. 'So, who buys their clothes?' He repeated.

Ball sighed loudly. 'They earn money for working and for good behaviour, then they order what they want from the internet,' he snapped.

'They have access to the internet?' Edward asked incredulously.

'Yes,' Ball confirmed.

'Unrestricted access?'

Ball gave a sarcastic sniff. 'Of course it's not unrestricted. They have a warden with them; now I really do need to get to my meeting.'

Edward nodded and started to close the wardrobe door, then opened it again as he noticed a newspaper sticking out from under a pile of clothes. 'Where did he get this from?'

Ball shrugged. 'From the magazine trolley I expect, and yes they do have access to newspapers and magazines in minimum security,' he snapped before Edward could ask.

Edward looked at the paper and then passed it over. 'Well, if you look closely at the date, Sir, you will see that this paper is over a year old.' Ball peered at it and went white. 'Would you like to read it out, Sir?' Edward asked the nervous looking governor.

He put the paper on Whittle's desk the next morning. 'I found it in Mason's wardrobe.' Whittle picked it up and started reading.

'The woman found badly injured at the disused quarry in Burney on Thursday morning, has been named as Heather Brooks aged twenty-nine. Her dog, Harry, was found dead a few feet from where she had lain all night. She is currently in a critical but stable condition at Kimberwick hospital.

'Ms Brooks works at the local post office in Burney, her colleague Vicky Morris said "Everyone is deeply shocked by what has happened, and we wish Heather a speedy recovery." The police are treating the case as attempted murder.' Whittle stopped reading and looked up. 'How the hell did Mason get hold of this?' He demanded angrily.

'I can only assume that Charlie Mason gave it to him on his last visit before Walker killed him,' Edward said despairingly. 'It was published the day before Heather got the sympathy card, and also just before Mason turned into a model prisoner.'

Whittle stared at the paper. 'So Mason has been planning this for a year,' he said thoughtfully.

'It would seem so,' Edward agreed. 'That's how he knew how to find Vicky Morris.'

'And why he tortured her to find out where Ms Brooks is,' Whittle finished for him.

Edward nodded. 'I'm going to see his mother tomorrow, so hopefully she can shed some light on what's going on in his head,' he said optimistically.

'Have you thought any more about what I said?' Steven asked Charlie the following day.

'About what, boss?'

'Training to be a pathologist,' he reminded him.

Charlie frowned at him. 'I told you I'm not interested, you're not trying to get rid of me, are you?'

Steven looked up from the body he was working on and watched as the younger man dissected a spleen. 'Absolutely not, I just thought with a baby imminent, you may need more money.'

Charlie stopped what he was doing and stared into space. 'We could always use more money.' Steven smiled at him knowingly. 'What?' He asked suspiciously.

'Well, if you're not interested then there's no point telling you is there?'

Charlie was intrigued. 'Spit it out then, boss,' he ordered.

'Let's finish up here and we'll have a chat,' Steven said mysteriously.

They sat in his office an hour later. 'So?' He said impatiently. Steven handed him a letter and watched as he read it. 'Another pathologist here?'

'To take some of the load off York,' Steven explained.

Charlie looked at the letter again. 'They want someone who's already qualified,' he pointed out.

'Actually, you're probably more qualified than I am, the only difference between us is a scrap of paper; or your lack of it,' Steven sighed heavily. 'I would rather train you here for a couple of years, than have some newly qualified geek who is full of himself.'

Charlie smiled at him. 'You were a newly qualified geek once,' he reminded him.

'Which is exactly why I would rather have someone who I know and trust, and who knows me and the way I do things,' Steven said brightly. 'And just for the record, I was never a geek, so what do you say?' He asked, but before Charlie could answer there was a knock on the door. 'Just a minute,' Steven called.

Judy stuck her head in. 'I haven't got a minute, my waters have just broken,' she informed them calmly. 'So can you finish your chat sharpish?' Charlie looked panic stricken.

'Go on then,' Steven urged. 'Good luck,' he called as they rushed out.

Chapter 6

Edward drove slowly down the road looking at the house names. Nearly everyone was followed by rest home nursing home or retirement home. He spotted the one he was looking for and pulled up. "The Grange rest home" was written in gothic style writing on the nameplate.

It was a large grey stone building with a mass of small leaded windows, how awkward they must be to clean, he thought as he made his way up the drive. A ramp to one side of the steps indicated that at least some of the residents were infirm. When he got to the top, he found himself standing outside a huge porch that was littered with wheelchairs, walking sticks and raincoats.

The door opened before he had time to ring the bell, and a woman wearing a green nurse's dress gave him a welcoming smile. 'Chief Inspector Cooper?' Edward nodded, and showed her his warrant card. She chatted pleasantly as she showed him into a small lounge. 'Mrs Poole is just having her dressing changed, she'll not be long,' she said brightly.

'Will she be up to talking today?' He asked hopefully.

'Alice is always up to talking,' the nurse laughed, then excused herself and left the room.

Edward sat down and wondered why it was, that regardless of how clean they were kept, all nursing homes smelt like mothballs. He looked around and hoped that he never ended up in such a place, and then stood up as an elderly lady wearing a nightdress and bed jacket was wheeled in. He tried not to stare at the heavily bandaged stump halfway up her right leg.

'Don't get up on my account,' she chuckled with her eyes twinkling. She looked around at the nurse who had pushed her in. 'Thank you, Millie, I have a feeling that the Inspector would like to speak to me alone. I'll call if I need you,' she smiled at Millie as she went out, and then looked at Edward.

'Chief Inspector Cooper?' She looked closely at his warrant card. 'Yorkshire?' She said in surprise.

'Yes, you were told I was coming?' He checked.

'Yes, I was, but coming from Yorkshire it's obviously not about what I thought.'

Edward studied her as she spoke; she was well spoken and articulate, certainly not the senile old woman that he had been expecting. 'What was it you thought I was here for, Mrs Poole?'

She tutted mischievously. 'Well, that would be telling, wouldn't it, Chief Inspector, and please call me Alice,' as she rearranged the blanket over her leg Edward noticed that her hands were disfigured with arthritis. 'Now what can I do for you?' She asked.

'I would like to ask you about your son,' he started to say.

'My son is dead, Inspector,' she butted in sharply.

Edward shook his head. 'Not Charlie.'

'I don't have another son,' she butted in again.

He sighed heavily and looked into her defiant face. 'I know that you have disowned Barry and Diane, but I really do need to ask you about them,' he said firmly. Alice set her lips in a straight line and nodded curtly. 'Why did you disown them?'

Alice gave an ironic laugh. 'I assume you know what they did to my grandson?'

'Yes, I do,' he confirmed.

'Well wouldn't you disown someone who could do that to an innocent baby?' She enquired.

'Yes, I would,' he admitted.

'So you know why,' she said wryly.

'You said they?' He queried.

Alice stared out of the window for a minute. 'Barry Mason may have done the deed, Inspector, but it was his sister who told him to do it. Maybe not the particular method used, but all the same.

'It was her who put the idea into his head. It's just a shame that the police didn't realise and lock her up too,' she said to Edward surprise. She looked at him with tears in her eyes. 'They killed my grandson and ruined the life of the nicest girl I've ever known,' she said with her voice faltering.

'Do you mean Ms Brooks?' He checked. Alice nodded. 'Your daughter said that it was she who had ruined their lives, can you explain that?'

Alice shook her head. 'No, I can't I'm afraid, you'll have to ask the tart what she meant,' she said with her composure restored.

'Do you mean Diane?' He asked.

'Well, I certainly don't mean Heather,' she said ironically. 'Have you met Heather, Inspector?'

'Yes, I have,' he confirmed.

'And how is she?' She asked concernedly.

'She's very well,' he assured her. He shifted in the chair. 'Has your son contacted you, Alice?' She gave him a stony look. 'Has Barry Mason contacted you?' He corrected.

'No why would he?' She asked disinterestedly.

'You do know that he's escaped from the psychiatric unit, don't you?'

She gave an exasperated sigh. 'No, I do not. I don't watch the news or read the papers, Inspector, and even if he wanted to contact me, then he doesn't know where I am, and that's the way I want it to stay,' she said firmly.

Edward looked into the wrinkled but perfectly composed face and wondered what she was thinking. 'You want to know if he'll try and find Heather?' She surmised.

'We know that he is. He's already killed at least one person who knew her.'

Alice closed her eyes and started to mouth something. Edward watched closely and saw that she was praying. She suddenly opened her eyes. 'I'll tell you a story, shall I?'

Edward nodded. 'If you think it will help us to catch him.'

Alice gave him a small smile. 'Well, you can be the judge of that when I've finished,' she rearranged the blanket again, then took a deep breath and started talking. 'I married John Mason in nineteen sixty. It was an exciting time, he was attentive and loving, but he changed after we married.

'He became violent and accusatory. He stopped me seeing my family and friends, eventually I plucked up the courage to leave him. I took the children and we moved to Chipping Norton to start a new life,' she smiled as she remembered.

'It was a good life for a few years. I met a lovely man called James and we had a son.'

'Charlie,' Edward interrupted. 'But his surname was Mason as well?' He questioned.

'We thought that it would be easier for him to have the same surname as Diane and Barry, and I never married James,' she explained. 'But we were very happy. James treated the older children as his own and they seemed to love him. Then when Charlie was three, John found us,' she pulled a tissue from her pocket and wiped her eyes.

'It was terrible, Inspector. He turned up one night, and when James opened the door, he forced his way in. He beat him unconscious with the coal bucket,' she stopped talking and looked at him with the pain of the memory evident in her face.

'And then he killed him, Inspector. He strangled him with the flex from the iron.'

Edward could see that although the memories were difficult to bear, she was trying to stay composed. 'Did you call the police?'

She shook her head. 'I was very scared, the children were asleep upstairs and I thought he was going to turn on them,' she said quietly. She took another deep breath. 'So whilst he was leaning over James's body and gloating about how he had ruined my life, I took the poker to him. I beat his brains out, Inspector, what few he had,' she said defiantly.

Edward was shocked by the confession. 'And you thought I was here because of that?' He asked.

'I thought you must have dug them up. I buried them in the garden, together unfortunately. The next morning, I told the children that Daddy had left,' she explained.

'And they accepted it?' He asked.

'Children are very gullible, Inspector, do you have any?' she enquired.

'I have a son,' he confirmed.

'Then you will know what I mean.' Edward nodded slowly, and tried to remember Steven ever being gullible.

'But the seed was set,' Alice continued.

'And as Barry grew up, he turned out like his father, and with Diane egging him on, I didn't have any control over them, even Charlie started to get into trouble. I did think that when Barry married Heather, he would change his ways, especially when she got pregnant. I was so excited to be a grandmother, but of course he didn't change and I saw history repeating itself,' she said resignedly.

'Was Malcolm your first grandchild?' He asked.

She nodded sadly. 'My only grandchild, Inspector. Charlie wouldn't settle down. He had a different woman every week, and Diane couldn't have children, so she was very jealous when Heather got pregnant. I think she thought that I loved her more than them.

'It was Diane who put the idea that Heather was being unfaithful into Barry's head.' She suddenly lost her composure again. 'Maybe I did love her more. I used to wish that my children had turned out like her. She was so loving and kind, and she doted on baby Malcolm, what little time she had with him,' she spluttered.

She stopped talking as the door opened and Millie stuck her head in. 'Do you want some tea?'

Alice wiped her eyes. 'I think tea would be lovely.'

Edward put his hands over his face and groaned inwardly. As much as he didn't want to, he knew that the disclosure that Alice had just made would have to be investigated. 'You're going to have to give me the address of the house in Chipping Norton,' he told her.

She nodded brightly. 'I'm not worried about that.' She patted what was left of her leg. 'I'll not be around for much longer anyway. Bone cancer,' she added, anticipating the question.

'They thought they'd got it all but sadly it's not to be. I would have liked to see Heather happy and settled before I die, but given what happened, I doubt she would want to see me anyway,' she added wistfully.

Millie came in with a tea tray a few minutes later. 'Is everything alright?'

Alice smiled at her. 'Perfectly fine, thank you. I wonder if you could do me a small favour and fetch the box from the bottom of my wardrobe please.' Millie nodded and went out.

Alice watched as Edward poured the tea. 'I'm sorry about the plastic cup but I do find it easier to hold.' She took the offered cup and gave him a resigned smile as Millie returned with the box. When she had gone out Alice asked Edward to open it. There was a small pile of photographs on the top.

'Give those to Heather for me, would you. I know that Barry destroyed all of hers.' Edward took them out and had a quick look through them. They were all of Heather and the baby. The most poignant one being of her just after delivery, she was still hooked up to machines after the emergency caesarean, but looked a picture of happiness.

He felt tears pricking his eyes as he looked at it. 'Christ,' he whispered.

Alice handed him a tissue. 'You know her well then?' She guessed.

Edward nodded. 'Why didn't Barry destroy these?'

She smiled sadly. 'Because he didn't know they existed.' Edward took a deep breath and stood up.

'I'll make sure that she gets them, and don't worry we'll look after her,' he promised.

Alice put her hand out. 'And the other matter?'

He smiled warmly as he shook it. 'I'll deal with it at a later date,' he told her kindly.

'Is Heather with someone and happy?' She called as he opened the door.

'Yes, on both counts,' he assured her.

'Well it's probably not Heather you should worry about then,' she said without turning around. 'I would keep a close eye on her new man if I were you.'

Edward went cold. 'What do you mean?' He almost whispered.

'Well if Barry is as much like his father as I think he is, then he'll hurt Heather by hurting the people she loves. Does she love her new man?' She turned the wheelchair around. 'Are you alright, Inspector, you've gone quite white,' she said concernedly.

'Yes, on both counts again,' he said quietly. 'I'm sorry but I've got to go.' He gave her a small nod before quickly leaving the room.

He called the mortuary as he ran down the drive. Sue answered the phone. 'He's not here. He's gone over to the maternity unit to see Judy. What's happened?' She asked hearing the panic in his voice.

'Lock the doors and stay put,' he ordered; then rang off and tried Steven's mobile. He cursed as the monotone voice told him that it was switched off.

He rang off again and called the hospital. 'He's just left,' the sister on the maternity unit informed him.

'For God sake.' He slammed the car into gear, and knowing that it was going to take at least two hours to get back, he pushed Jack's number. 'If he turns up, keep hold of him and get some cars out looking,' he ordered. He tried not to panic as he sped towards the motorway, then as fatherly instinct took over, he turned the blue light on and put his foot down.

Chapter 7

Steven was in high spirits as he drove towards the moor's road and home. Judy had delivered a healthy 7 lb. 13oz boy, and they were both doing well. Charlie had been overcome with emotion and burst into tears. He smiled to himself and wondered if he would follow suit when his babies were born.

He glanced in the rear view mirror a minute later and slowed down as he noticed a car approaching at top speed. 'Bloody idiot,' he muttered, as it flashed by and disappeared around the bend heading towards the moor's road. A few minutes later, he turned into the moor's road himself.

It was a fairly straight run and in the distance he could see a car parked at an angle across the road. As he got closer, he realised that it was the same car; as he passed, he saw someone slumped over the steering wheel. He pulled over and retrieved his phone from the dashboard, he switched it on and dialled 999 as he ran over to the car. 'Ambulance for the moors road,' he said to the operator, then opened the car door and leaned in.

'Steven?' A voice behind him enquired, he looked up just in time to see the missing coal rake hurtling towards his head.

Edward managed to reach Kimberwick in just over an hour and a half. Whittle met him at the top of the station steps. 'There was an emergency call made for an ambulance an hour ago,' he told him.

'Where?' Edward asked nervously. 'On the moor's road, we think the call was made by your son but he was cut off, and when the ambulance arrived, they found a woman stabbed to death in her car. There was no sign of your son or his car, just his mobile phone in the road.'

Edward's stomach started to churn. 'Have you tried his house?'

Whittle nodded. 'Sergeant Taylor is aware of the situation.' Edward tried to keep his voice from trembling as he relayed the conversation that he'd had with Alice just hours earlier. 'Well, we didn't see that coming,' Whittle commented.

'But I should have, even the note inside Vicky Morris gave us a clue. "Hard luck she told me". It was meant for Steven not Heather,' Edward said angrily.

'I think you should wait here,' Whittle advised as he started to walk back to the car park. 'I have six cars out looking.'

Edward shook his head. 'I can't just sit around I need to go and look,' he said firmly.

'You'll be better off waiting here for any news,' Whittle insisted, his tone was firm but kind, and Edward knew that for once his superior was right.

Steven opened his eyes and tried to focus. His head was throbbing, and unable to move his arms and legs, his first thought was that he was paralysed. Then as his vision returned, he fixed on a bare bulb hanging directly above him.

'Good! You're awake,' a voice commented. Steven turned his head and saw a man sitting at a table. Unshaven and unwashed, he had the appearance of a wrestler. His biceps bulged against the filthy T shirt he was wearing, and he had a distinct lump on the bridge of his nose, which was bent slightly to one side, indicating that it must have been broken on more than one occasion.

He got up and dragged a chair over to where Steven was lying. 'I bet you wish you'd stayed at home today,' he chuckled. Steven groaned as he pulled him to his feet, and he realised that his inability to move was due to being bound hand and foot.

He looked around the room; it was small and windowless. A flight of wooden stairs led up to a heavy door. He guessed it was a cellar, and apart from two chairs and the table, which was strewn with food wrappers and beer cans, the room was empty. The man sat Steven on a chair, then sat down next to him and gave him a sympathetic look.

'You don't know me, but I know all about you,' he said brightly.

Steven stared at him, 'You're Barry Mason.'

The man smiled again 'Yes I am, and you are the bastard who has been screwing my wife,' he said vehemently, then got up and slapped him hard across the face. 'That's just for starters.' Steven gritted his teeth against the sting and tried to look defiant.

'I don't suppose I can blame you though because she's very sexy,' Mason said thoughtfully. The smell of stale beer and unwashed skin hit Steven's nose as he leant closer. 'I knew I had to have her the first time I saw her, and then you came along and ruined it.'

341

The fear that Steven had felt seconds earlier was replaced with anger. 'She's not your wife anymore, and it was you who ruined it when you murdered your child.'

Mason suddenly pulled a knife from his pocket and plunged it into Steven's thigh making him gasp with pain. 'And in future you'd better think before you speak.' Steven tried to loosen the rope from around his wrists, then he gasped again as Mason pulled the knife out. He ran his finger down the blade and looked at the blood.

'Where is she?' He asked casually. Steven shook his head and continued to work on the rope. Mason sat down again. 'I don't actually care where she is,' he said dismissively. 'I've spent a long time thinking about it, and I've come to the conclusion that I can hurt her more by killing the things she loves. I'm surprised that she loves you though, you don't look her type,' he said scornfully.

He put his head on one side and looked at him thoughtfully. 'She likes real men, and you look like a wimp to me.' Steven resisted rising to the bait and looked away, but Mason was undeterred. 'Do you enjoy her as much as I did?' he goaded.

Steven glanced at him and gave a small smile, but kept his lips firmly together. 'She said she'd been faithful. She must have thought I was stupid. You only had to look at that bastard baby to see that he wasn't mine,' Mason scoffed.

He moved the chair closer and stared hard into Steven's face. 'In fact, I would say he looked more like you, it was you who falsified the DNA test, wasn't it?' Steven returned the stare and tried to wriggle his hands free as he felt the rope slacken. Mason suddenly got up and brandished the knife at him.

'But what do I do about it?' he dug the point of the knife into Steven's crotch. 'Do I take the humane option and stop you from breeding again?' He moved the knife up to his throat. 'Or do I send you to join your bastard son,' he sat down again, 'Decisions, decisions,' he sighed.

Steven was unable to keep quiet any longer. 'You're fucking mad,' he muttered.

'I know, and that's the beauty of it, because if they do catch me, all they'll do is send me back to the hospital, whatever I do,' Mason added menacingly, and started to chuckle at what he obviously saw as his own good fortune. Steven suddenly spotted the coal rake lying on the floor. Mason saw him looking; he picked it up and caressed it in his palm. 'Useful little thing this. I only had to burn the silly cow once and she told me everything.'

Steven gave him an icy stare. 'You are a sadistic bastard.'

Mason nodded his agreement. 'I am I admit it. I really enjoyed experimenting on her, and as for the sex thing, well she was a bit old for me, but a shag is a shag. As I hadn't had the pleasure of a woman's company for quite a while, I just couldn't help myself.

'It's just a shame that she keeled over before I'd finished with her,' he was still caressing the rake as he spoke. 'Did you get my note by the way? A nice touch, don't you think?' he chuckled. A sudden rumbling made him look up; he glanced at his watch and smiled. 'That's the three fifteen to York. Whoops! You've missed it,' he said sadly as the noise faded away.

'Never mind there's always the next one,' he gave a sly smile. 'I was planning to drop you over the edge like I did with your bastard son, but I tried it with the kid and it took three trips to finish him off, so you'll have to catch the train I'm afraid,' he said ruefully.

He suddenly grabbed Steven's hair and pulled him forward. 'Don't try that again or I'll make sure that she gets little bits of you every birthday for the next ten years,' he growled as he retightened the rope. Steven started to work on the rope again; he looked up and saw Mason glaring at him.

'I need to go to the toilet,' he said hoping that he would untie his rapidly numbing legs. Mason shrugged dismissively. 'Tough! You'll just have to wet yourself. You'll be doing that soon enough anyway when you see what I've got planned.'

Steven wiggled his toes to try and keep the feeling in his feet. The blood from the stab wound was soaking through his jeans. he could feel it running down his leg as he stared unblinking at the maniac sitting in front of him.

'Have a good look whilst you still can,' Mason sneered, and then seemingly unnerved by his unwavering stare he looked away.

Edward was sitting anxiously in his office. He looked up hopefully as Higgins came in. 'The driver of the three fifteen York train reported an abandoned car matching Dr Coopers. It's by the track at lower Nubbin,' he reported.

Edward jumped up. 'Get onto Sergeant Taylor and tell him to get over there,' he ordered, knowing that Jack was nearer and would get there quickly. He ran out to the car park where was surprised to be joined by Whittle, but his concern for Steven stopped him from even asking why he was there. They got into a rapid response car and sped towards Nubbin with the sirens wailing.

343

Edward took deep breaths and tried to stay calm as they navigated the traffic, but inside the terror was starting to build. He looked out of the window as the countryside flashed past, then glanced at the speedometer, and although they were going a hundred miles an hour, he closed his eyes and prayed that the driver would go faster.

'So! Do you think you can walk with that nasty wound?' Mason asked a while later. Steven ignored him and continued to work on the rope. Mason got up and pulled the knife out again. Pain shot into Steven feet as he cut the rope from around his calf's, allowing the blood to flow back.

Then he cut the laces and took his shoes and socks off. 'Just in case you try anything silly, now get up,' he ordered.

Steven scowled at him. 'Why don't you make me.'

Mason grabbed the front of his shirt and tried to haul him to his feet, but the pain in his thigh and the numbness in his feet made it impossible for him to stay upright, and he sank to the floor. 'Get up,' Mason ordered again.

'I can't,' he muttered through gritted teeth.

Mason picked up a length of discarded rope and threaded it under his arms. 'I'll just have to drag you then, won't I?' He tied the rope across Steven chest and started pulling him across the floor. When they got to the steps he stopped. 'Are you going to walk or shall I cut you up here and take you out in pieces?'

With the feeling starting to return to his feet, Steven managed to get to his knees. Mason pulled him to his feet and he unsteadily navigated the stairs. It was going dark, but once they got outside, Steven saw that they were at a railway station.

What he thought was a cellar, was in fact a disused storage room housed in one of the supports of the narrow cattle bridge which stood above them. 'Have you wet yourself yet?' Mason asked as he dragged Steven towards the bank. He looked back and smiled. 'We're nearly at my favourite bit,' he sniggered, then started clambering up the gravel bank pulling Steven behind him.

Steven's bare feet slipped on the freezing gravel, and unable to steady himself with his arms still tied behind his back, he fell over and slid back to the bottom taking Mason with him. Mason tugged on the rope. 'Get up, we're going to miss it,' he shouted angrily.

Steven lay face down by the track with his head pounding. 'If you're going to kill me just fucking well do it here,' he gasped.

'You must be joking, you're going the same way as your bastard son,' Mason scoffed.

Steven looked up at him and started to laugh almost hysterically. 'I didn't even know Heather then, you stupid prick.'

Mason grabbed the rope again and started hauling him backwards up the slope. 'Of course you fucking well did,' he muttered. By now, Steven was oblivious to the pain. He dug his feet into the loose gravel and jolted him to a halt. 'We'll have none of that,' Mason spat, he landed a well-aimed kick in his kidneys and resumed pulling; only to stop again as a mobile phone rang.

He pulled a phone out of his pocket and stood with one foot on Steven's neck. 'What?' He snapped angrily. 'I'm on my way up there now; I'll call you when it's done.' He put the phone away and continued up the bank, by the time they reached the top he was panting heavily.

He rolled Steven over with his foot and put the knife to his groin. 'Now get up, or I'll castrate you and send them to her.' Steven glared at him as he managed to get to his knees. 'All the way,' Mason growled; then grabbed his arm and pulled him roughly to his feet. Steven made his way to the middle of the bridge, limping heavily and with his head spinning.

Mason walked behind him with the knife pushed into his back. The walls of the bridge stood about four feet high. Steven could see the tracks stretching into the distance. 'Stop here,' Mason ordered. He pushed him towards the wall as he heard the train approaching. 'Just in time,' he said menacingly.

Steven's heart was pounding so hard it felt like it would burst through his chest. 'You know I thought even a wimp like you would have put up more of a fight,' Mason commented almost disappointedly.

'You're not worth the fucking effort,' Steven sniffed.

'Well, let's hope the next one has more guts than you,' Mason said sarcastically.

Steven glanced back at him. 'What do you mean the next one?' he asked suspiciously.

'Well as I told you before, the best way to hurt her is to destroy the things that she loves,' Mason chuckled. 'So, when you've gone and she finds someone new to love, I'll kill them as well, etcetera, etcetera,' he gave a small laugh. 'All this time they've been protecting the wrong person.'

Steven looked at him again. 'I'm not afraid to die,' he said defiantly.

Mason pushed him closer to the wall. 'Maybe not, but you'll die wondering if your unborn child is going to be next.' An image of the scan flashed across Steven's mind, it felt like someone had plunged a knife into his heart. 'The Morris woman told me, what do you think about that?' Mason whispered in his ear.

Suddenly, Steven was nineteen again; an uncontrollable rage that he hadn't felt for a long time surged through his veins. 'I think you're going to regret saying that,' he muttered.

'Really,' Mason sneered disbelievingly.

Steven glanced back again 'Yes, really,' he gritted his teeth and leant forward as if to climb onto the wall.

'Well, I don't give a fuck what you think,' Mason started to say, but he was cut off mid-sentence, as using all his energy and with an almighty yell, Steven threw himself backwards and head butted him. Pain shot through Steven's entire body, as the back of his head smashed into Mason's face, but the adrenalin was now flowing freely and quickly blotted out the agony.

He spun around and launched himself at Mason, who having dropped the knife had staggered back, dazed and clutching his bloodied nose. Steven hit him squarely in the chest with his shoulder before he could recover, and propelled him backwards until he was lying across the wall. Mason let go of his nose; he grabbed Steven's shirt and pulled him so close that their faces were only inches apart.

'If I go over then you go with me,' he spat.

'That suits me fine,' Steven spat back. He stared him in the eye with the hate he felt erupting inside, then threw his head back and butted him again. A fireball of pain swept over him as their heads connected with a sickening crack. He closed his eyes and jammed his knees against the wall as Mason overbalanced.

He hung in mid-air for a second, then lost his grip and fell backwards into the path of the oncoming train, leaving Steven balanced like a pendulum, with just his knees stopping him from following him down. There was a squeal of brakes followed by a thud as the driver failed to stop in time, then deathly silence for a few seconds before the shouting started.

Steven was suddenly aware of footsteps on the bridge. He opened his eyes, but closed them again immediately as nausea swept over him. Then he felt a firm grip on his shoulders as someone dragged him off the wall, and he sank to the ground breathing heavily.

The police cars skidded to a halt by the track. Edward and Whittle jumped out and looked towards the bridge, just as a figure silhouetted against the darkening sky fell into the path of the braking train. Edward put his hand over his mouth in horror. 'Oh my God! Steven,' he gasped, and with his legs barely able to support him, he started to stumble towards the now stationary train.

Whittle grabbed his arm. 'Let go,' Edward sobbed; he tried to pull away but Whittle kept a firm hand on him.

'Stay here,' he ordered and beckoned for a constable to hold him back. Edward watched weak with fear, as the Chief Superintendent disappeared around the front of the train. He reappeared white faced minutes later.

Edward sank to his knees and stared at him in terror. Whittle leant down to him. 'It wasn't Steven,' he whispered as he helped him up.

'Can you hear me, Steve?'

Steven opened his eyes and looked up hazily at Jack who was bending over him. 'Is Heather alright?' He asked hoarsely.

'She's in the car,' Jack said gently, he picked up the dropped knife and cut the rope. Steven groaned with pain as his arms fell free.

'I'm going to throw up,' he warned, then leant over and retched before passing out. Heather appeared at the end of the bridge. She stopped, not daring to go any closer.

'It's ok, he's just passed out,' Jack called as he put him into the recovery position. He looked down onto the track and saw Edward and Whittle looking up. 'He's alright, guv,' he shouted.

Heather knelt down next to Steven and wiped the blood out of his eyes. 'Where's Barry?'

Jack looked over the wall and grimaced at the bloody mass illuminated by the lights from the train. 'He's down there,' he put his arm around her as she burst into tears.

The air ambulance arrived a few minutes later, and having landed in the adjacent field, the paramedics accompanied by a doctor were quickly on the scene. Edward had scrambled up the bank onto the bridge, and was trying not to cry at the sight of his unconscious son. He gently moved Heather to one side so that the doctor could treat him.

Then they strapped him onto a stretcher before loading him into the waiting helicopter, and although Edward was desperate to go with his son, he pushed Heather in after them. He waited until they had taken off, then slumped to the ground with his hands over his face. 'I can't take much more of this, that's three times I've nearly lost him,' he said with his voice choking.

Jack crouched down beside him and pulled his hands away from his face. Edward looked at the Sergeant through his tears. 'But you didn't lose him, because he's got too much to live for,' Jack said gently.

Edward wiped his eyes. 'I know he has,' he whispered.

Jack stood up and put his hand out. Edward looked towards the train as he pulled him up. 'Let Whittle finish up here. It's about time he did some field work,' Jack chuckled. He gave his boss a light slap on the back. 'Come on, guv. I'll drive you to the hospital.'

Steven came round several hours later. He blinked a couple of times and tried to focus on Heather, who was sitting next to him holding his hand. 'Are you ok?' He asked anxiously as a tear ran down her cheek. She nodded and tried to smile, but couldn't quite manage it.

'I love you,' he mouthed, then closed his eyes and drifted back to sleep. Edward came in a few minutes later.

'I can't believe he did it,' Heather whispered, and started to cry again.

Edward put his arm around her. 'I don't think he had a choice; it was him or Mason.'

She shook her head. 'I can't believe that he did it for me,' she sobbed.

'He did it for all of you,' he said gently.

They looked up as the doctor came in. 'You should go home and rest,' he told Heather concernedly.

'I'm not leaving him,' she said firmly. The doctor shot Edward a help me look. 'I'll make sure she doesn't overdo it,' he assured him.

They watched as the doctor checked him over. 'How is he?' Edward asked anxiously.

'Badly concussed, he's taken several hard hits to his head. One needed stitching along with a wound on his leg. He also had a dislocated shoulder, but we put that back in the chopper whilst he was unconscious. There's a lot of bruising and superficial grazing, but physically he'll be fine,' the doctor said brightly.

'What do you mean physically? Is he going to be brain damaged?' Heather demanded.

The doctor shook his head. 'No, not at all, we've given him a scan and he'll be ok. I meant I don't know how he's going to cope with the knowledge that he killed a man.'

'He wasn't a man, he was a monster,' Heather butted in. The doctor looked at her tear-stained face and then glanced at Edward.

'Well as he has already killed her son, and he tried to kill mine as well, then I'm afraid I would have to agree with her,' he said dryly.

Steven's head was still pounding when he woke up the next day. He turned towards the monitor as the events of the day before slowly came back. Christ! He'd killed a man. A tear ran down his face, as the enormity of what he had done hit him.

He jumped as someone wiped the tear away, and looked up at Heather who was still sitting next to him. 'This could be a full-time job for me,' the relief in her eyes was obvious as she smiled at him.

'I'm so sorry,' he whispered.

'For what?' She asked in surprise.

Steven frowned at her. 'You know? And for crying.'

She leant over and kissed him. 'I wouldn't love you if you didn't cry. If you didn't cry that would make you as bad as him,' she wiped his eyes again. then looked up as the door opened and Edward came in with Jack. Edward tried not to look too shocked at the state of his son's face, which now the bruising had come out was black and blue.

'Do you feel up to talking?' Steven pushed himself into a sitting position and nodded. He flinched as the movement sent a searing pain through his head. Edward sat down next to Heather. 'It may be better if you didn't hear this.'

She took Steven's hand. 'I'm not leaving him,' she said firmly.

'I could insist that you leave,' Edward reminded her. She tilted her head to one side and raised her eyebrow. 'Go on then, but you'll have to carry me out,' she said defiantly.

Steven squeezed her hand gently. 'Maybe you should go and get a cup of tea,' he suggested. 'Is Sheila here?' He asked his father.

Edward nodded. 'She's outside.'

Steven smiled at Heather. 'Go on, I'll still be here when you get back.'

She gave a resigned sigh then leant over and kissed him. 'I love you,' she whispered.

'I love you too,' he whispered back.

When she had gone Jack got his notebook out. 'Ok, son, just tell us in your own time whatever you can remember,' Edward said gently. Steven closed his eyes and breathed deeply a couple of times before recalling every detail. Edward listened in shocked silence whilst Jack scribbled notes.

When he got to the phone call Edward stopped him. 'Did he say a name?'

Steven shook his head; he flinched again as lightning streaked across the back of his eyes. 'Shit! That hurt,' he muttered.

Jack glanced at Edward. 'Perhaps we should leave it for now, guv,' he said quietly.

'No, let's just get it over with,' Steven insisted. 'I'm ok as long as I don't move to suddenly,' and although he was desperately worried and wanted him to rest, Edward knew that he had to get the statement whilst it was fresh in his mind.

'Go on then,' he encouraged.

When Steven had finished, Edward stared at him in wonder. He tried to imagine what he had been through and wondered if he would ever recover, but at the same time he felt incredibly proud of him. 'Are you alright, Dad?' Steven checked.

Edward nodded. 'I was just thinking that it's only taken you thirty-three years to take my advice.'

'Which particular piece of advice would that be?' Steven enquired.

Edward got up and leant over him. 'To use your bloody head,' he whispered. 'Anyway, we'd better get back, Whittle is waiting for an update.'

Jack grinned at Steven. 'Fathers eh!' he chuckled, and then stood aside as Heather rushed back in.

'Are you decent, boss?' A familiar voice enquired a few minutes later. Steven smiled as Charlie came in, closely followed by Judy who was carrying the baby. 'How are you feeling?' Charlie asked concernedly.

'I'm ok,' he looked at the baby. 'How's he doing?'

Charlie beamed at him. 'Fine thanks, do you want a hold?'

As Judy laid the baby in Steven's arms, the relief that he was alive and would soon be holding his own babies overwhelmed him. He bit his lip to try and keep the tears away. 'Have you named him yet?'

Judy nodded. 'We are going to name him after the person who we hope will agree to be his godfather.'

Steven looked up from cooing over the baby. 'Who's that then?'

Charlie looked at Heather and rolled his eyes. 'You of course, you bloody fool,' he chuckled. 'And by the way, I've decided to take you up on your offer,' he added.

'Great,' Steven said genuinely; he looked down at the sleeping baby again. 'Hello, Steven,' he whispered.

Edward's letter of resignation was sitting on the kitchen table. 'You really don't have to do it,' Sheila said as he picked it up.

'I know I don't but I want to,' he reassured her.

When he got to the station, he found Jack waiting in his office. 'Whittle wants to see you, guv,' he said as soon as he went in.

Edward turned on his heel and made his way to the Chief Superintendent's office. He passed WPC Blackwell in the corridor. She put her head down to avoid eye contact and hurried away. Christ! She's not still sulking, is she?

He thought as he watched her go. He fingered the letter in his pocket and knocked on the door. Whittle's face was grim as he invited him to sit down. Edward settled into one of the large chairs and looked at him expectantly. 'You wanted to see me, Sir?' He enquired.

'Firstly, how is your son?' Whittle asked.

Edward nodded. 'He's going to be ok. Thank you, Sir.'

Whittle smiled. 'Good; and you will be pleased to hear that Diane Meriwether is in custody. Chipping Norton arrested her last night.'

Edward was very pleased. 'I assume that it was her who rang Mason?'

Whittle nodded confirmation. 'The technical boys managed to salvage the phone that we recovered from the tracks. They found several text messages from her on it. She's not a very nice woman, is she?' He said despondently.

'No, she's not,' Edward agreed.

Whittle got up and looked out of the window. 'I know that we haven't always seen eye to eye,' he said suddenly.

Well, he's right there Edward thought, and then noticed that Whittle's hands were shaking. 'Are you alright Sir?'

Whittle gave a sigh and turned around. 'Actually, I'm not,' he forced a nervous smile. 'Do you think that I'm a self-centred egotistical bastard? And I want you to be honest with me.'

Edward stared at him, too stunned by the question to answer. Whittle sat down and returned the stare. 'Come on, Edward, you've never been lost for words before,' he said impatiently.

351

Edward searched his bosses face for a clue. 'Can I ask what this is about, Sir?' He asked after a minute.

Whittle cleared his throat. 'Well as you probably know my wife has left me,' he looked up for confirmation that he did know.

'I had no idea,' Edward confessed to Whittle's obvious surprise.

'Well everyone else in the station seems to know,' he muttered.

Edward shrugged and wondered where the conversation was going. 'I don't listen to idle gossip, Sir.'

Whittle nodded. 'No, of course not. Nevertheless, Christine did leave me, and the reason she gave was that I was a self-centred egotistical bastard,' he stared into space. 'And maybe I am,' he said quietly.

'I wouldn't say so,' Edward heard himself say.

'What would you say then?' Whittle snapped and then gave him a wry smile. 'I'm sorry,' he apologised.

'I think you could be a bit more sensitive to the feelings of others sometimes,' Edward said thoughtfully. 'But on saying that so could we all,' he added generously.

Whittle gave him a grateful smile. 'Thank you, Edward, now I believe that you wanted to see me,' he said brightly.

Edward took the letter out of his pocket. 'My resignation, Sir.' Whittle looked shell-shocked. 'I want to spend more time with my wife and soon to be born grandchildren whilst I've still got the energy,' Edward explained. Whittle sat back in his chair and stared at him thoughtfully. He's going to tell me something, Edward thought, and he wasn't wrong.

'You're not the only one who will be leaving,' Whittle confessed.

It was Edward's turn to be shocked. 'Are you resigning as well?' Whittle nodded. 'But why?' He asked incredulously.

A pink tinge appeared on the Superintendent's face. 'I'm afraid I've committed an indiscretion.'

Edward stared at him and wondered if he'd been fiddling the finances or not filling in the report sheets properly. 'What sort of indiscretion?'

Whittle rearranged the papers on his desk and cleared his throat nervously. 'Apparently, I had an improper encounter with one of the police constables, one of the female police constables,' he added hastily. He looked up with the embarrassment now plain to see. 'I'm telling you this, because regardless of your feelings towards me, I respect you as an officer, and I wanted you to hear it from my lips without all the embellishment that it will undoubtedly attract,' he said quietly.

Edward's mind went into overdrive. 'You said apparently?'

Whittle nodded and went a shade redder. 'I don't actually remember the incident,' he admitted. 'However, I was very drunk at the time, and I did wake up in the young ladies' bed,' he took a long deep breath. 'And I was stark naked.'

Edward suddenly felt very sorry for the embarrassed man in front of him and slipped into interrogation mode. 'Was she in bed with you when you woke up?'

Whittle shook his head. 'No, I was alone.'

'So you only have this woman's word that you actually had sex with her?' He checked.

'Yes, but something must have happened, because I was all sticky,' he took his glasses off and put his head in his hands. 'And apparently there is a video tape as well,' he muttered.

'Have you seen the tape?' Edward asked suspiciously.

Whittle shook his head and anticipated the next question. 'Would you want to see a film of yourself in a compromising situation?' He enquired semi-sarcastically.

'No, I don't suppose I would,' Edward agreed. He rubbed his chin thoughtfully. 'Has she asked for anything in return for the tape?'

'No, and it wouldn't matter if she did because I won't be blackmailed,' Whittle said firmly.

Edward gave him a look of regard. 'Who is it. Sir?'

Whittle shook his head. 'It wouldn't be fair of me to divulge her name,' he said quietly, although from his tone Edward could tell that he was desperate to do just that.

'It wouldn't happen to be WPC Blackwell, would it?' He asked dryly. Whittle's mouth fell open. 'For God's sake, John, can't you see what she's doing? I mean apart from getting you into bed, what the hell was she doing filming it?'

He stopped talking as he realised that he had addressed a senior officer by his first name. 'I'm sorry, Sir, but the woman is a bloody menace,' he said angrily.

'It was at a party in her flat, she said that someone else took the film and she didn't know that we were being filmed,' Whittle muttered.

'Did she say who it was?' Edward butted in.

'No, she wouldn't tell me,' Whittle said despondently.

'And you don't remember anything about it?' Edward checked.

He shook his head. 'The last thing I remember was sitting on the couch, then I woke up in her bed the next morning naked and with a massive hangover,' he said miserably.

Edward blew out silently. 'When exactly was this?'

'A couple of weeks ago,' Whittle mumbled. The two men stared at each other for a few minutes.

'Don't do anything yet, I'll speak to her,' Edward said eventually.

'No! I don't want her to know that I've told you, she's embarrassed enough as it is,' Whittle exclaimed.

I'll bet she is, Edward thought. 'So you're going to throw your career away because a tart like Tracy Blackwell says that you had sex with her?' He said angrily.

'That's hardly fair,' Whittle snapped 'It takes two to make love.'

'Make love?' Edward almost choked the words out. 'If you were so drunk that you can't remember anything about it, then it sounds more like rape to me, and that's assuming that anything actually happened.'

Whittle stared at him in horror. 'But there's a tape,' he started to say. 'You're assuming that it exists even though you haven't seen it?' Edward interrupted.

Whittle looked like he was going to burst into tears. 'Why would she say it exists if it doesn't?'

Edward shook his head in disbelief at his superior's naivety. 'You obviously don't listen to idle gossip either,' he observed. 'Don't do anything rash, let me deal with it,' he told the distraught man. 'I'll be very discreet,' he promised as Whittle started to object. He sat in his own office with the door ajar, and watched WPC Blackwell working in the squad room. She glanced up and saw him looking and quickly looked away again. 'What do you think about WPC Blackwell?' Edward asked Jack when he came in a few minutes later.

'As an officer or a person?' Jack enquired.

'Both,' the Sergeant shrugged disinterestedly.

'Mediocre officer and a tart. Why do you ask?'

Edward pondered for a moment. 'Did you know that Whittle's wife had left him?'

Jack nodded. 'I heard a rumour in the canteen; what's going on, guv?' Edward knew that Jack would be more likely than him to find anything out, so he told him what had happened to Whittle. 'Poor bastard,' he exclaimed. 'So what are you going to do?'

Edward shook his head. 'Not me; you are going to try and find out what really happened. Find out if there is in fact a tape, and if so what's on it and who has seen it.'

Jack got up. 'Right, guv.'

'Discreetly though,' Edward warned as the sergeant disappeared into the squad room.

It didn't take Jack long to get the gossip. 'Well, Whittle was definitely at the party, and apparently, he was pretty hammered before he even got there. Tracy picked him up in a pub and invited him back to her flat. He hadn't been there for long before he fell asleep on the couch. Tracy told a couple of the lads to put him on her bed out of the way,' he reported.

Edward gave him a quizzical look. 'And?'

Jack shrugged. 'And nothing. The blokes I spoke to said he was still there when they left, and they were the last to leave.'

'Did they say if he was naked,' Edward asked.

'They put him on top of the bed fully clothed, so either she undressed him or he undressed himself,' Jack surmised. 'But if he was so drunk that he can't remember anything, then he probably wouldn't have been able to get it up anyway. I know I can't when I've had a few,' he said thoughtfully.

'That really is too much information Sergeant,' Edward scolded.

Jack grinned at him. 'Sorry, guv,' he chuckled.

'Did you find out who took the film?' Edward checked.

'According to the gossip, she did. She was filming everybody, including a couple of the new recruits. Apparently, she stripped them naked and covered their genitals with cream, she told them it was an initiation test,' Edward listened open mouthed in disbelief, and wondered if that would explain Whittle's sticky bits. 'Then she disappeared into the bathroom with the pair of them for over an hour,' Jack continued.

'And Whittle was asleep on her bed whilst all this was going on?' Jack nodded.

Edward sat back and sighed. 'So did anyone see her filming him?'

'No, guv. She's told everyone that she filmed him snoring on her bed but bonking wasn't mentioned.'

Edward frowned at him. 'Bonking! What sort of a word is that?' He asked exasperatedly.

'It's a nicer word than shagging,' Jack chuckled. 'Anyway, DC Nash told me that Whittle gave Tracy a dressing down a while back for fraternising with the public in reception, and she wasn't very happy about it.'

'Fraternising?' Edward repeated.

'Yes, but DC Nash said that she was flirting; so, what now, guv?' he enquired.

'Now you are going to nip out and buy a can of cream, and then we are going to fraternise with WPC Tracy Blackwell,' he said with a satisfied smile.

She knocked on his door a couple of hours later. 'You wanted to see me, Sir?' She said nervously.

Edward nodded 'Come in and sit down,' he invited, then picked the phone up and dialled his home number. He tapped his nail on the phone. 'She always takes ages to answer,' he said, knowing full well that Sheila was out.

'Where were you, darling?' He asked the answering machine. 'You were in the bath, well that sounds nice.' He watched Tracy's face closely whilst Sheila was supposedly speaking. 'Yes, she's with me now, are you absolutely sure that you want me to ask her?'

He put his hand over the mouthpiece. 'She's determined,' he told Tracey. 'I'll see what she says and call you back,' he said to the answering machine. 'Sorry about that,' he said as he put the receiver down. 'It's just that now we know there is someone willing to do it, she's getting impatient.'

Tracy looked bemused. 'Willing to do what?'

Edward sat up straight and gave her a look of surprise. 'Willing to film my wife and I making love of course,' he said innocently, as if it was the most natural thing in the world. 'What did you think I meant?'

Tracy's mouth fell open 'What?' She spluttered.

'Chief Superintendent Whittle told me that you have a friend who does that sort of thing,' Edward explained. 'He's really looking forward to seeing the film of you and him by the way,' he added. 'Anyway, I thought it would be nice for my wife and I to have something to look back on. You know in the cold dark evenings when there's nothing on the television.

'I'd rather you didn't say anything to anyone though,' he tapped the side of his nose. 'Not for squad room gossip if you get my meaning,' he smiled benignly. 'So can we come to an arrangement then?'

But Jack burst in before she could comment. 'Oh! Sorry, guv. I thought you'd be finished,' he gushed.

Edward beckoned him in. 'It's ok, we're nearly done,' he said brightly.

'Have you asked her?' Jack enquired excitedly.

'Well, I've asked her about me, you can sort yourself out,' Edward said amusedly.

Jack got a diary out of his pocket. 'When your friend has finished with the Inspector and his wife, I'd like to book him.'

'I hope it is a, him. I'm not sure that I could perform in front of a woman,' Edward interrupted.

Jack shook his head. 'No, me neither, guv.'

Tracy had gone white. 'Look, I've no idea what you've heard.' She stopped talking as she saw the look on both men's faces.

'I want the tape and any copies you have made on my desk first thing in the morning,' Edward told her sternly. 'Along with a written explanation, an apology to Chief Superintendent Whittle, and your letter of resignation. You will take official sick leave until your notice has been worked. Now get out of my sight,' he ordered.

They waited until she was safely out of ear shot before creasing up. 'That went well,' Jack spluttered as tears of laughter streamed down his face.

Tracy arrived first thing the next day, minus her uniform and tarted up to the eyeballs. She threw three tapes and two letters on Edward's desk and started to leave without a word. 'Just a minute,' Edward called. He picked the tapes up.

'Are you sure that these are all of them?' She nodded sullenly. 'Who has seen them?' He asked.

'No one has seen them. Now if you don't mind, I have an appointment at the job centre,' she snapped.

'One last thing,' Edward called as she opened the door.

'What now?' She said impatiently.

He produced the can of cream from a drawer and put it on his desk. Tracy stared at it in horror. 'If you ever speak about this, if I find out that there are any more copies of the tape, or if I hear that you have done anything like this again, I will tell everybody that you propositioned me last year,' he fingered the can. 'Do you understand?'

Tracy gave him a look of contempt and went out slamming the door behind her. Edward sat back and gave a satisfied sigh. 'I think we've seen the last of her,' he said contentedly.

Jack picked the can up and tried to stifle a giggle. 'She propositioned you, guv?'

'Don't sound so surprised,' Edward chided and then laughed himself. 'She thought she was speaking to Steven,' he admitted.

Jack eyed the tapes. 'What do you think? A quick look or shall we just give them straight to Whittle?' He asked.

The look of relief on Whittle's face was priceless. He opened the letters and chuckled to himself. 'Silly girl,' he muttered and handed them to Edward.

'So she's ruined her career because she thought you humiliated her. What did you say to her? If you don't mind me asking, Sir,' he enquired.

'I simply told her that she shouldn't fraternise with members of the public in the police station, and she should save her flirtatious behaviour for when she was out of uniform and off duty,' he looked at the tapes and smiled. 'What did you say to her to her to get these?'

Edward took a sharp intake of breath. 'I couldn't possibly say, Sir.'

Whittle got up and put his hand out. 'Well, thanks. I owe you,' he said generously as they shook hands.

Six Months Later

Steven did cry when Heather pushed his perfect twin girls into the world. 'God! You're so beautiful,' he whispered. 'Just like your mum,' he looked into Heathers tired but ecstatic face. 'I love you so much,' he whispered, and then unable to contain his joy he started crying again.

Edward and Sheila were waiting nervously outside along with Heather's father. Once Heather and the babies were cleaned up, Steven called them in, as the proud grandparents took photographs, Heather suddenly burst into tears. 'I'm sorry. It's just so different from the last time.'

Edward looked at her tearstained face and wondered if she would ever recover from the loss of her first born. He put his hand in his pocket where he still had the photographs that Alice had given him, but unable to find the right moment he had put off giving them to her. 'Are you ok, Dad?' Steven checked.

'Can I have a quick word outside, son?' He asked.

Steven gave Heather a kiss. 'I'll back in a minute,' he whispered. 'What's up?' He asked once they were outside.

Edward handed him the photographs. 'Alice asked me to give these to Heather.' Steven looked through them, and then glanced back through the window. Heather was watching them.

'What?' She mouthed.

Steven put the photographs in his pocket. 'I'll give them to her,' he promised and turned to go back in.

Edward put his hand on his arm to stop him. 'Hang on, son. I need to ask you a huge favour,' he said nervously.

Six Week Later

'You can go in now,' the nurse told Edward. 'But she's very frail so please don't stay for long.'

Edward went into Alice's bedroom. She was lying in bed with her eyes closed. 'Hello, Alice,' he said quietly. She opened her eyes and raised her eyebrows. 'Hello, Chief Inspector. I didn't think I would be seeing you again,' she said in surprise.

'Oh! I've been keeping tabs on you,' he said seriously.

'I'm really not planning on beating anyone else to death,' she whispered mischievously.

Edward smiled at her. 'I know that.'

She gave him a quizzical look. 'So why are you here?'

Edward took a deep breath. 'Have you been informed of Barry Mason's death?'

She gave a light nod. 'I read about it,' she said casually.

'You said you didn't read the newspapers,' he reminded her.

'I changed my habits after your last visit; it's a prerogative of old age,' she informed him amusedly.

'So, are you aware of how he died and who was responsible for his death?' He checked.

Alice gave a light nod. 'They didn't give names, but I assume that it was Heather's fiancé.'

Edward frowned at her. 'And how do you feel about it?'

'Indifferent, Chief Inspector, and from what I read it was self-defence. So I hope that he's not been charged with anything other than caring,' she said sternly.

Edward gave a silent sigh of relief. 'Well, obviously there was an inquest, but no charges were made against him.'

She smiled brightly. 'I'm glad to hear it, so have you come to arrest me now?'

He shook his head. 'The other matter can wait a little longer; but I have brought someone to see you if you're up to it.'

Alice looked surprised and then nodded. 'Prop me up a little first,' she told him. After helping her to sit up, he went to the door.

Her face crumpled as Heather came in. 'Hello, Alice,' she said apprehensively.

Alice took her face in her hands as she sat down on the edge of the bed. 'I'm sorry,' she managed to splutter before hugging her tightly.

'It wasn't your fault,' Heather whispered, and started to cry.

Alice pulled away and looked at her. 'You look well.'

Heather wiped her eyes. 'I am well.'

Alice smiled at her with her eyes twinkling. 'It must be the love of a good man,' she glanced briefly at Edward. 'Is he here too?'

Heather nodded. 'He's called Steven. He's outside.'

'Well bring him in,' Alice exclaimed. 'Wait,' she said as Heather got up. 'Do I look alright?'

'Perfect,' Edward assured her.

'Right wheel him in then,' she looked towards the door as Heather went to get him. Her face crumpled again as Steven came in carrying the twins. 'Oh my goodness,' she sobbed. Heather took one of the babies from him, and looked on as he gently placed the other one across Alice's lap.

'She's called Patricia, Alice,' he told her quietly.

'And the other one?' She spluttered, barely able to speak for tears.

'Elizabeth Heather,' Steven whispered.

Alice looked up into his concerned face and smiled. 'Well, it's no wonder that you left in such a hurry the last time, Chief Inspector,' she gave Edward a stern look. 'You didn't tell me that it was your son that she had fallen in love with.'

She frowned as Steven started to apologise for killing her son. 'I don't want apologies. I want to know that you will look after them all,' she butted in.

'I will,' he promised.

She looked down at the baby. 'You've got a beautiful mummy and a brave daddy,' she told her as the tears started to fall again.

One Month Later

Heather put the phone down and snuggled into Steven. 'They're fine,' she whispered.

'I told you they would be,' he said sleepily as she snuggled closer.

'Thank you.'

He opened his eyes and yawned. 'For what?' She manoeuvred herself on top of him and gave him a long deep kiss.

'For loving me, and for giving me a happy ending,' she said when she pulled away.

Steven wrapped his legs around her and rolled her onto her back. 'Who says it's the end,' he enquired, and then slid down the bed. 'Now then, Mrs Cooper, I do believe that there are some new lifelines down here that need exploring,' he murmured.

Ingram Content Group UK Ltd.
Milton Keynes UK
UKHW021928220623
423799UK00003B/26